Mind'

(Mindfire:

L D Houghton

Table of Contents

Prologue 4

1..6

2..15

3..19

4..25

5..31

6..42

7..50

8..59

9..67

10..73

11..80

12..89

13..94

14..102

15..110

16..119

17..125

Interlude 133

18..134

19..137

20..142

21..149

22..155

23..161

24..170

25..180

26 186

27 194

Interlude 204

29 213

30 224

31 235

32 244

33 251

35 261

36 276

37 285

38 294

Interlude 302

39 303

40 308

41 316

42 324

43 325

44 331

Epilogue..334

ABOUT THE AUTHOR...343

Prologue

He ran.

As he always did, he ran, and there was nothing they could do to stop him.

And as always, the blood was on his hands.

He'd managed to hold it in for what felt like months this time, caging and crushing the fear and anger and *hate* into a ball deep inside until he could hold it no more.

Until it took control, as it always did.

There was no way to stop him, once the pressure burst outwards like a dying star in its final, vengeful act. There was no armour thick enough, no *Lock* strong enough.

They couldn't stop him, and he couldn't stop himself.

The worst part was, he could see in the minds of those who held him that they understood little of what he was, or the danger he posed. To them he was just another enemy of the state, a terrorist whose ability to use Aether was merely a point of note. They weren't *permitted* to know anything else.

They were only following orders.

So he tried to keep it caged, even when they kicked and spat at him, but it would always, eventually, become too much. The cold stares, the barked commands, the ruthless treatment if he stepped out of line. The pressure would build, and build and build and build until...

He stared out at the Waste, its poisoned, lethal emptiness stretching out around him in all directions. The wind whipped at his cheeks and brought the acrid smell of chemical desolation with it. The facility he had just escaped from stood only a short distance behind him, as devoid of life now as the hundreds of kilometers of dead earth surrounding it.

Dust and jackals, carcinogens and dross; the promise of a thousand deaths was all that lay before him.

He'd survived worse.

In the back of his mind, though, he knew it was fruitless. Wherever he ran, whatever direction he chose, they would find him.

They would watch him through drone and satellite, chase him by land and air, pursue him relentlessly as they had every time before, until exhaustion overcame him and he collapsed, unable to run anymore.

Then they would bring him back, back to a facility already scraped of the char and ash that was all that remained of its previous occupants, ready to accept yet another contingent of unsuspecting staff.

And what if he did somehow manage to escape? What if, beyond all possibility, he shook off their unblinking gaze, threw off their invisible chains?

Even if he escaped them, *it* would always find him.

He was tired. Tired of it all. Tired of *fighting*.

So this time he did not run, but walked. This time he stepped calmly into the Waste, willing it to take him.

This time, he would not resist.

1

The Agency is founded upon secrecy. The Far Academy remains at the forefront of Aether research and its usage, and dissemination of these findings must be kept strictly limited. This is a question of public safety; should Aether usage become widespread, our ability to control it would be lost. And if secrecy is the foundation of the Agency, control is the bedrock.

Agency Principles and Practice: Section 2, 3.7

It was night, and nothing was moving. Nothing, that is, except that which had authorisation to do so.

The guards gathered around the screens of the security room in the main watchtower, for instance, had the requisite permissions. They sat at desks or leaned against counters, chatting and idly watching over security cameras operating with such effective anomaly-identification algorithms as to make their watching essentially obsolete. Spotlights drew bright spears through the thick darkness, passing slowly across the wide courtyard below or out into the desolate Waste beyond the perimeter walls.

The solitary sentry standing on an observation platform at one far corner of those perimeter walls, also, had the right credentials, though the crafty cigarette he was surreptitiously smoking in the rain and gloom would have earned him a disciplinary hearing if anyone else were around to see.

The few tired-looking, faceless bureaucratic drones shuffling between offices and record-rooms, too, had permission to be there, carrying a seemingly endless supply of documents, e-disks, and data-pads too sensitive to be allowed on any network.

Nothing else was permitted to be there, so nothing was. Except...

There was one shadow where no shadow had any right to be. Within this complex of shadows layered on shadows, this one patch of darkness was somehow unnatural, out of place even in the gloom. It seemed to move, too, though that could have just been the shifting of the moon behind the clouds.

But there was no reason to think it was anything other than a strange effect of the dull light, some curious optical illusion caused by too long in the darkness. After all, this strange patch of void caused no sudden screech of alarm from the search algorithms; nothing showed up in infrared to indicate anything other than a patch of empty air, the same temperature as the space around it.

The shadow stole across the open courtyard as the guard above swore and cursed at his lighter, refusing to spark up enough to relight his now damp, extinguished smoke. It moved silently to merge with another patch of shadow beneath the main building, the slender shape pressing up against the wall and carefully making its way towards a featureless, gunmetal grey doorway a small way further down.

The door was lit fitfully by a single gently glowing touchpad requesting both passcode and iris-scan confirmation, and just as there was no way someone could be moving through the facility without the right credentials, there was no way this door could be opened by someone without the corresponding access rights.

Hence, no one was even thinking to watch that area as the door slid quietly open, the gentle hiss of its mechanism and the brief golden glow of lights inside swallowed by the rain for the brief few seconds it remained ajar. The shadow stepped in with one quick, smooth motion before the door closed behind it.

Now the shadow merged with the white walls of the facility interior, somehow blending into the featureless surfaces without apparently changing colour. It simply… changed with the light, taking on the colours around it and reflecting them back; not a mirror, but a million infinitesimal facets, each refracting and echoing the shades and tones of the light around them.

When the shadow, now a shadow of light, moved, it was as if the air shimmered with heat haze. When it was still, it simply… wasn't there.

Only the most carefully trained eye would have made out the faintest outline betraying the shadow's presence, and, apparently, not even the most carefully programmed security cameras. These, and there were several of them, continued their steady, relentless watch over the hallways, never reacting to the wraith that moved beneath their unblinking stares.

The shadow moved onwards, making its way slowly down first one, then another, of the long white hallways. It moved steadily, seemingly knowing its path, never quite rushing yet with the feeling of growing impatience… or fear.

And if an observer had been standing *very* close, they may have heard the slight, soft sigh of released tension as the shadow came to a stop before a set of large, white double doors. Above these doors, in large, red lettering, were stamped the words:

Grupo Disidentes y Actividades Sediciosas

The shadow paused and stood unmoving for a few seconds. Then, as if it had somehow *reached* through the doors and sensed the emptiness on the other side, it gently pushed the doors apart.

If the shadow really had Reached through, though, its abilities were clearly not sufficient to encompass the entire room. The space beyond the doors was vast, row upon row of tall black databanks running fifteen metres or more down from the doors and to both sides. And, right at the far end but looking directly in the direction of the doors with mouth agape, a suited man carrying a box of files under his arms.

"He... hello?"

The figure's first mistake was stopping to call out, instead of immediately raising the alarm. The second was to continue to stare dumbfounded as the shadow suddenly sprinted towards him, covering the distance between itself and the man in seconds.

Though the shadow merely came close and did not actually touch him, the files fell from the man's arms as he curled up into himself, eyes rolling upwards until only the whites were visible. Then he lay there, gently twitching.

But the speed the shadow moved at had destroyed the illusion. No longer was it a shadow, but a figure, form covered from head to toe in a kind of glittering, shining fabric like the sequins of some mad fashion designer with a molecular fabrication device. Even as the man fell, the suit began to twinkle and fade, merging once more into the background light, but the cameras had seen her.

Alarms blared out across the facility all at once, doors slamming shut behind security locks that guaranteed those inside would not be getting out.

"Damn," said the figure.

Moving quickly now, faster than the suit's effect could keep up with, the woman moved down past the fallen man and made her way directly to a single databank towards the back. It stood high and wide, looming over her, but there was nothing to distinguish it from any of the other identical banks lined up in rows throughout this room.

Nevertheless, she stepped determinedly up to it and held a slim, featureless metal device to its front.

Nothing happened.

"Come on, come on..." said the voice, youth still clear in her tones.

With a loud clanking sound, as if something moved within the databank - though of course, this was impossible with the solid state memory drives held within - the machine lit up, small screens and light all over its face flickering then brightening into a fierce, green glow.

"Yes," hissed the figure, triumph in her voice.

There was another clanking sound, and the room went dark.

"O... kaaaaay," said the voice, now formless in the darkness. "Power went down, just like he said. Now I just have to get out and..."

The disembodied voice was cut off by the sound of the doors at the front of the room being forced open. Which meant guards, trying to get in.

She knew the layout of this place; she'd spent days memorizing the floor plan. The only way out was through them.

The shadow dived behind the closest row of databanks, crouching down and moving swiftly through the cover afforded by the high metal blocks. Status lights on each of the machines flickered a dull red, indicating that they were running on backup power, as expected. Each bank had an individual emergency source of power, in the event of a catastrophic full-facility shutdown such as had just occurred.

The sound of the doors giving way to the insistent pressure of those forcing their way in reverberated across the room, followed by the sounds of booted footsteps rushing in and spreading out. The beams of rifle-mounted flashlights cut through the darkness, casting long, thin shadows as they swept by.

"Comms are down, too," came a strangely toneless electronic voice.

"How the hell'd they do this?" came another voice, virtually identical to the previous one in its cold, emotionless words. "They got both main power and the security grid. Shouldn't be possible."

"Some kind of EMP?"

This could have been the first speaker or another.

"Voice filters still work, weapon targ-software's still good. No way this was an EMP."

"Quiet, all of you!"

This last was delivered with a force that carried its irritation even through the electronic filtering software of the masks they wore. It came from right in front of the doors.

"You see anything?" the voice demanded.

"Negative, sir."

There was a long, silent pause. The shadow slunk back, alerted to the presence of one of the rifle-bearing guards nearby only because they had responded with that last comment. Their dark black uniforms were almost as good at concealment in this gloom as her own.

"The alarm came from here, right?" asked the voice closest to the doors. It was by now apparent that this was the person in charge.

"I... I think so, sir. The shutdown happened only a few seconds after, but I'm fairly sure it was here."

"*Fairly* sure, Ramirez?" asked the first voice again. "Remind me to have a discussion with you about situational awareness once this is over."

"Sir."

Groaning came from the far end of the room, where the unwelcome visitor had left the bureaucrat twitching.

"There's someone over here!" called one of the filtered voices. Footsteps and the light of their weapon indicated they were heading towards the sound. "Think I've got a man down here. Yep, he's out."

From where the shadow hid she could see the guard roll the fallen man over and shine the flashlight in his face.

"Looks like he's having some kind of fit. Sir? Should we send for a medic?"

Footsteps, heavy ones leading away from the main doors.

"Show me," said the leader.

There was a short silence, in which the shadow made its cautious way from one aisle to the next, edging ever closer to the exit.

"Shit. Everyone, weapons ready. Stay alert, stay focused. We've got one of those Aether freaks in here."

The leader's words were followed by the sounds of postures shifting and weapon safeties clicking off. The air in the room became heavier, thick with a tension that hadn't been there a moment before.

The guards began moving in formation in the silence that

followed, no longer communicating verbally but moving through the rows of databanks in some kind of pre-arranged pattern. The shadow was forced to shrink back as one of the figures made its way towards where she had been crouching, making her way slowly and quietly back down the narrow aisle. She had to be as quiet as possible; the guards would have implants connected to their auditory nerves able to pick up the slightest sound.

Suddenly the shadow jumped, stretching out her hands above her head as if trying to reach the top of the databank beside her. It was a small jump, one that took her no higher than a few feet, and certainly not sufficient to reach a handhold on the top of the databank.

But then she jumped *again* and *again*, as if there were a series of steps below her feet somehow invisible to the naked eye. One, two, three, each jump taking her slightly higher until, stretching as far as she could, her fingers found purchase on the lip of the tall machine. She pulled herself up, hissing through gritted teeth at the strain of this exertion as quietly as she could.

"What was that?" came an electronic voice.

Not quietly enough, then.

She moved along the top of the databank as quickly as the low ceiling allowed, forced to bend almost completely at the waist. Below, lights moved quickly towards where she had just been, one from either end of the aisle.

The nearest of the two rushed past below her, coming to a stop no more than a metre or two away. She dropped quietly to her chest and flattened herself against the metal surface beneath as torch light flicked across the ceiling nearby. Head flat against the top of the databank, she was now unable to see the figures hunting her... but that didn't mean she couldn't *sense* them.

"Anything?" came a voice from somewhere nearby.

"Nothing. Uh...."

The hesitation in the guard's voice was rendered strange and flat by the vocal filters.

"What is it?" asked what the shadow could only assume was the one in charge.

"You... uh... you hear something?"

"Hear something? What? What can you hear?"

Below her, two flashlight beams swung rapidly from left to right, floor to ceiling. Their movements quickly became erratic, and heavy

11

panting came through the vocal filters.

"There! There's something there!"

The filters failed at hiding the panic in the speaker's voice, the lights of their weapon waving frantically down towards the end of the aisle they stood in.

"Where? Where?" The second voice came almost as fast as the first, the light of their rifle joining the first.

"Open fire!"

The room lit up with muzzle flare as the screaming guard beneath unleashed a burst of rapid fire towards some unseen target.

"CEASE FIRE!"

Whoever was shouting now, the force of their voice completely overrode the vocal filters. This voice was deep, almost certainly male, and filled with the absolute certainty of authority. The commander, the shadow thought.

"Who the *hell* was that?" the commander demanded.

"Uh, sir. Me, sir. Sawyer. I, uh… I don't know what happened…"

This voice, too, was no longer rendered toneless by vocal filters. Whether this 'Sawyer' had turned it off because of some protocol or had turned it off in panic, the shadow didn't know. His voice was trembling, and surprisingly young.

"Get it together, Sawyer. The freak's in your *head*," said the commander. "They can do that; make you lose your cool; make you feel like a kid afraid of the monsters under the bed."

There was a pause, only the heavy breathing of Sawyer to be heard, gradually slowing.

"Good, Sawyer. Good," the commander said. "Now, now you've stopped being a *maldito cobarde* you need to search your area. They can't be far; the effect only works when they're close."

Sawyer's rifle swung upwards as he stepped back, flashlight illuminating the top of the databank with bright, clear light.

But whatever had been there was already gone.

The shadow let out a long sigh as the doors swung shut behind her, the distraction caused by the terrified Sawyer affording her the chance to hit the guard closest to the door with Slowtime and slip into the darkened hallway beyond.

That had been too close; she was just lucky one of them came close enough for her to hit him with *Fear*, without being visible herself. Then, all she had to do was wait a few seconds for the man's overstimulated amygdala to stimulate the flooding of adrenocorticotropics and adrenaline into his bloodstream, and make sure she was well away when the effects kicked in.

Still, it wouldn't be long before they realised she was gone, and they'd be ready for a similar attack next time. Though *Fear* was one of those techniques that worked well on victims experiencing stress, an awareness that it was happening could render it useless.

So she moved as fast as she could back down the hallways using the same route she had entered by, her speed neutralising the blending effect of her suit and turning it into a quite visible mass of glittering stars in the ill-lit corridors.

Those stars went supernova as the facility lights abruptly returned, each microscopic reflective surface catching the light and bouncing it back with increased intensity for one brief second before returning to their soft, sparkling state. The woman in the suit wasted no time marvelling at the effect, however, but increased her sprint as she approached the security door by which she had entered. It stood at the end of the hallway, closed and solid white, a small red light blinking above it indicating total security lockdown.

The woman's pace didn't falter as she sped towards the door, though perhaps an observer would have heard a whispered prayer, and just when it seemed she was certain to smash into unforgiving metal the light above the door blinked green, the door sliding open and shut in a fraction of a second; just enough for her to get through. The light returned immediately to a baleful red as if challenging any observer to say differently.

The courtyard outside was in chaos. Up on the perimeter walls, guards were wrestling with spotlights gone suddenly rogue, lights blinking on and off in strange patterns as their automated tracking routines swung them around to chase phantoms through the air.

Security wasn't totally distracted, though. The moment she dashed through the door into the courtyard beyond bullets spattered against the ground where the brief flash of light from inside had betrayed her. Slightly slower, and they would have hit her too.

Her dash carried her to the base of a section of the perimeter wall that surrounded the entire facility, tall, slick, and impenetrable. Thankfully, it was also entirely a dull, metallic grey turned black in the night's darkness, and the instant she stopped moving she was once more simply a shadow amongst shadows. Rifle-mounted flashlights shone their beams down from the walkways above but were too weak to penetrate the gloom to any distance. The spotlights were meant to do that.

Whispering thanks to the endless grey clouds that blocked out the light of the stars and the moon from the ruined skies, the woman sidled her way slowly along the wall, pausing often to strain her ears for the sounds of footsteps from overhead. None came, though yelling rang out all around, sentries attempting to maintain cohesion without the comms and networks they usually relied on.

She made her way slowly towards the huge gate in the centre of the north wall, a gate made up of two sections of chain link fence topped with barbed wire. Unfortunately, she knew, this was purely mechanical in nature, an unsophisticated thing of manual locks and heavy bolts, a barrier none of the technological trickery that had helped her so far could overcome.

From the sounds coming from above, the guards were finally reaching the conclusion she had feared; they were going to need to come down there themselves. A metallic rattling from across the yard told her an access ladder was being let down, soon followed by the sounds of someone - no, several someones - descending.

She made it to the gate only moments after the first guard did, emerging from the darkness with barely enough time to muster the energy to *Push* the sentry away, sending him smashing into the gates and to the ground. The locks buckled at the impact but did not give way.

A second *Push* directly into the gates sent them flying open, breaking one side off its hinges to collapse on to the dry, dusty ground of the Waste.

She sprinted across the bare earth beyond the facility and disappeared into the darkness as bullets spat at the ground around her, small eruptions of dirt coming terrifyingly close. She forced herself to run faster; the guards would eventually get their vehicles working, and she needed to be long gone before that.

And indeed, by the time the response team managed to force their vehicles into manual mode and give chase, their quarry was nowhere to be found.

Only Ritra Feye, sat in a room many tens of kilometres away and watching events unfold through the feed of a drone hovering far above the facility, saw the figure make its way, exhausted but determined, to a distant point where an unmanned car waited. She smiled as the car drove off into the night, and cut the feed.

Then she got back to work.

2

Anti-State action is any action aimed at undermining or weakening the reclamation's progress, the authorities overseeing this progress, or at undermining or weakening the external security of the restored State and the economic, political and national achievements of the Reclamation.

Reclamation Penal Code Article 85-1

The elevator doors slid apart and Blane stepped into the apartment she still thought of as the Safe House, tearing strips of thin, glittering fabric from her skin as she walked.

"What the hell were you *thinking?*"

Serinda stood at the opposite end of the room, arms crossed and foot tapping rapidly, radiating equal parts worry and anger. Blane didn't reply, but strode past her and into her room. When she emerged a minute later, she was in light clothing and stripping the final parts of the spangle suit - awful name, she still thought - from her forearms. She threw the ragged strips into the disposal unit, then took out a long, tall can of energy supplement from the fridge.

"Answer me," snapped Serinda, not moving from where she stood but following Blane with a fixed, dagger-like stare.

Blane took a long gulp of her drink, then walked calmly and unhurriedly to the couch. She lowered herself into it, and looked up to meet Serinda's gaze.

"Sit," she said, tone kept carefully controlled.

"I'm *not* going to sit!" said Serinda, drawing herself up and grinding her teeth.

"Sit down, Seri," said Blane. "Please."

Serinda continued fixing Blane with her stare for a few moments, then let out a deep sigh before falling into a nearby chair.

"I've asked you not to call me that. It brings back... memories," Serinda said, pressing a hand across her eyes as if the light hurt it.

"Sorry," said Blane. "It just... suits you. But I know; it's what Raphael called you."

"Sara. Her real name was... *is* ... Sara. We don't need to use those ridiculous *Forever Fallen* names anymore. And don't try to change the subject."

Serinda pushed herself up to sit straight in her chair, brief moment of vulnerability forced aside. Once more, she fixed Blane with her gaze.

"We said it was too dangerous, that we'd find another way. That was our decision."

"That was *your* decision, Serinda," said Blane, voice rising despite her best efforts. "*Your* choice. You barely even told me what Francisco had proposed."

"Because it was dangerous, Blane. It was *stupid*. You can't break into a heavily guarded Reclamation facility by yourself, even with that fancy new skin suit of his."

"Well, *I* did."

Blane's retort seemed to sap something from Serinda, her eyes dropping and shoulders falling like a puppet whose strings had been cut.

"You did," she said softly. "You did. And you got the files?"

Blane drew a thin, flat airdrive from her pocket.

"I got it. Everything went like he said. The cameras didn't see me, the power went out and came back just in time; even the guards barely saw me."

"What?" A new tension filled Serinda, eyes narrowing. "What do you mean, 'barely'? The plan was none of the patrols would even know you were there. They were supposed to think it was some kind of weird network crash."

"Uh, well, um…" Blane cursed herself for her slip. Serinda had seemed to accept, or at least be resigned to, what had happened before this. "There was a slight… complication. Some sort of office worker, in the server room. I had to move fast; the cameras saw me, just before the power went out."

"The cameras…?" Suspicion filled Serinda's voice.

"Yeah, the cameras. But one of the response teams must have seen it, because some of them came into the room before I could get out and…"

"They came into the room!? You were being *hunted*?"

Blane held up both hands as if to ward off Serinda's anger.

"I'm alright! I got away! I used that new technique I've been working on … you know, *Fear* … and it worked like a charm. They hardly chased me, and then the one I had to Push went down like a tree and… and…"

Blane's words trailed off as Serinda stared a her unblinkingly.

"You attacked *two* armed RA guards?" Serinda said in cold,

considered tones that scared Blane more than any amount of angry words.

"Yes," Blane replied, voice smaller now, chastened. "And... and... and I triple jumped!"

Excitement at the memory overrode her reluctant remorse.

"Triple jumped?" asked Serinda, a nonplussed look layering over the anger on her face. "What are you talking about?"

"Remember how I was working on double jump? The whole technique I picked up from Fen, when he stopped us falling off the building? Well, I did it *three times*!"

Despite her anger, Serinda smiled at Blane's obvious joy.

"You jumped on the air three times?"

"Yes! Wait, no. I jumped on the *ground* once, and the air twice." Blane paused, sorting this out in her own head. "Anyway, I jumped practically as high as my height, I think."

Serinda said nothing for a while, and then her gaze ran down Blane from head to toe.

"You're definitely alright? You aren't hurt?"

"I'm fine," said Blane, reaching out to gently touch Serinda's hand. "I'm sorry I went without telling you; but Francisco was right, this was the only way. And I'm not a kid anymore."

Serinda patted Blane's hand and released it, leaning back. The anger had departed again, seemingly gone for good. Now, there was only worry in her eyes.

"I know," she said. "You're, what, almost nineteen now? But that still doesn't mean you should be sneaking around government facilities stealing classified information."

Her eyes flickered to the airdrive, a dull grey rectangle on Blane's lap.

"You really think the data's on there?"

Blane nodded.

"Everything else Francisco told us was correct. The layout, the patrol routes; whatever was on that drive, it unlocked every door right when I needed it." She looked quizzically at the air drive. "What do you think it was on that drive? Some kind of virus?"

Serinda looked from the airdrive to Blane.

"I... have no idea. I only know what Francisco told us, same as you. Something that could get you in, copy the files, and get you out without tripping the security. I don't know where he gets half his little technological marvels."

Blane could see that this worried her, even if she wasn't willing to say it out loud. Francisco had come back into their lives only very rarely in the years since the Central Tower; the years since they had lost Fen. Always for only a short time, yet always with some news or information on Reclamation Authority movements that would prove true no matter how classified the data must have been. It had saved them more than once.

But it hadn't saved all of them.

"You think he's really on there?" said Serinda, staring at the airdrive.

Blane nodded.

"Only one way to find out for sure," she said.

Without waiting for anything else, Blane picked up the drive and flicked the hand that held it towards the wall-screen. Instantly, the wall lit up, a single folder icon appearing in the middle of its blank glow.

"Open," said Blane to empty air.

The icon expanded at once, opening to reveal a list of names and faces that filled the wall yet was surely only a small proportion of everything she had got from the databank.

"All of these people, imprisoned as 'dissidents,'" whispered Serinda. "Enemies of the state, they call them. No due process, no right to defend themselves, no communication with the outside world. Dragged off the street, from their work, from their *homes*."

Blane didn't respond.

"Open search," she said.

A search box instantly appeared on the screen.

"Search for prisoner. Name; Grey, Nestor."

3

Agitators exploit the grievances, prejudices, and fears of our society. They seek to stir up social, religious, economic, racial, and political unrest. This strategy of divide and conquer must be resisted with the full force of state authority.

Statement on the Extension of Emergency Measures

They'd kept a low profile in the weeks after the events at the Central Tower, emerging from the Safe House only when strictly necessary, and only spending any time at all in the less well-monitored areas of the city. Everything they got, they got off the rapidly growing black market. Increasingly stringent RA checks on legitimate acquisitions had only served to expand illegitimate ones.

It had been a strange time for Blane. When she looked back on it, her memories were clouded by a confusing mix of pain, loss, and joy.

It had felt like she was trapped, especially at first, confined to a tiny box that, no matter how luxurious, was still a prison. Everyone from her past life was gone; and even most of those she had met since the days her ability manifested. Since the day her parents...

But weeks turned to months. Serinda and Grey devoted much of their time to teaching her, helping her understand the Aether and her connection to it more deeply. Serinda, especially, had been there for her in other ways, almost mother-like in her care and sympathies.

Grey tried just as hard, Blane knew, but he simply had a hard time understanding young people. From what she and Seri (Blane always called her this in her thoughts) could tell, the man hadn't had much of a childhood himself. He wouldn't say much about it, but they had gleaned that he grew up first in the camps of the Carib-Federation and then care homes around the Reclamation, before being taken in, still young, by the Far Agency to train at their Academy.

So Serinda taught her in her way, and Grey taught her in his. Sometimes Blane felt like she was being trained up as a Far Agent herself, learning not only Aether use but everything from self-defence to counter surveillance measures.

And the months in the Safe House continued to roll by, with no sign that the Reclamation Authority was particularly concerned with finding them. Grey got her a tablescreen for her personal studies, and she spent a lot of time sat at it, studying dense articles on the regions and systems of the brain and their interaction with the Aether. She found, to her surprise, that she spent nearly as much time learning about neural pathways and network theory as she did about the physical brain itself.

From what they could tell, the *Forever Fallen* had gone to ground entirely; Serinda said the group had always been ready to go completely dark in the event they came to the RA's notice. Meanwhile, public statements by the RA and (significantly reduced) Federation depicted the attack on the Central Tower as the work of terrorist groups now well in hand – though, they were quick to emphasise, still a threat.

It had been almost a year before Serinda began her medical work again, overcoming Grey's resistance to the idea. This time, though, she didn't have clinics or secure sites, no special equipment or access to high-tech medical facilities. Instead, she slowly rebuilt old connections or grew new ones, finding those most in need and making it known someone was there to help; no questions asked.

Blane never doubted her. Seri may no longer have had the *Fallen's* resources, but she had her own skills and her irrepressible drive to help. Starting small, with home visits and furtive meetings in deserted buildings – always accompanied by Grey, anxiously keeping watch - she gradually built up trust amongst the communities of the downtown area. Soon, she even had recruits, volunteers to her cause. Some were even Aether sensitive.

The network Serinda established used community centers, public halls, even churches - some of which remained despite RA suppression. Members met with Serinda rarely, and none knew all the others. Blane hadn't understood why Grey was so insistent on maintaining this shroud of secrecy around what was essentially a community support group until much later.

It had taken yet more time to convince Grey to let Blane help with the medical work, but eventually he acquiesced. Face unrecognizable beneath spangle fabric and more basic cosmetic measures, Blane began to accompany Seri on a number of her trips, learning the fine control of Aether so distinct from Grey's more forceful style. It was on these trips that Blane began to appreciate how strong Seri really was, in her own way, a distinct contrast to the stronger but less refined techniques of Raphael or Grey, or the fierce, unrestrained power of Fen.

It was the differences in these techniques that prompted Blane to start trying to develop new techniques herself. When Grey found out what she was doing, however, he was furious.

"You can't just *mess around* with the Aether," he'd said. "It's not a toy; it's dangerous. Use it wrong, and it can drown you. Burn you. Kill you in a hundred different ways."

So Blane kept her experiments to herself.

And then, to both her and Seri's surprise, Grey began to teach.

It began almost as an afterthought, something for him to do while he kept his ceaseless watch for anything suspicious, out of place or threatening while Seri worked. Sometimes, someone would come to her for help with a non-medical issue, simply because they didn't know where else to go. Connection to the Aether could manifest in many ways, and some of these were both painful and traumatic; as Blane well knew. Seri simply didn't have the time or resources to spare for the training and psychological care this required.

But Grey did. It wasn't long after he began his first impromptu sessions with one of those seeking help, a lost boy in his late teens named Xavier, that another came seeking "training", then another and another. Soon, it was a common sight to see Serinda working in one corner while Grey held class in the opposite one.

Blane thought even he had been surprised at how good he was at it.

Most Aether users came into their abilities young, around the onset of puberty, though this was not a hard and fast rule. Still, the majority of those who came to Grey were teenagers; it always made Blane grin how uncomfortable he was around kids, yet how his earnestness and need to help drew them to him. There wasn't much of a support network in the wider Reclamation for lost youth. Parents, or the children themselves if they no longer had a familial network, faced a choice of voluntary giving those who manifested to the Far Agency, or finding a way to handle it on their own. For those living in the downtown area, this wasn't much of a choice at all. There were too many stories of Aether sensitive people disappearing, never to return, upon being taken in by Far.

So Grey had become a sort of de facto teacher to these people. At one point, he had more students than Serinda had patients; numbering somewhere in the twenties, at least. Most of these didn't stick around, of course. They simply learned to tame their slight abilities, and went back to their daily lives.

Others stuck around for longer, though, and a few became good enough to learn from Serinda. Medical techniques, calming ones. Techniques to rebalance a mind or body in conflict with itself. Grey refused to teach anything offensive, though Blane argued with him about this.

"We're not training a resistance here," he said, any time she brought it up. "These people don't need to know how to fight."

"Then why are you teaching it to *me?*" she'd once demanded.

"Because you might."

He had been quiet for some time after that.

It wasn't long after this conversation that former *Forever Fallen* members began to turn up. Serinda knew all of them, Blane a few. All of them had been low-level in the group, and all shared the same story: of losing contact entirely with the *Fallen* after the events at the Central Tower, and being left to fend for themselves.

Some of these visitors were more trustworthy than others, in Serinda and Blane's opinion, but none were trustworthy enough for Grey. He sent them away no matter how they pleaded or cajoled with him or Serinda to let them help.

Blane had been surprised when, on this one decision, Serinda allowed Grey to have his way. She was fairly sure this was because both Seri and Grey were worried for her safety. Neither of them had forgotten what the *Fallen* had done to Fen. She, however, wasn't sure how much of the blame could truly be placed at the *Fallen's* feet.

It was an angry encounter with one of these rejected *Fallen* that finally caused Grey to relent and become warily supportive of Blane's efforts to develop new techniques. The guy was *strong*, far stronger than he had any right to be with his limited time learning with the *Fallen*, blowing out half the wall as he raged at their refusal to take him in. Grey's Thoughtscreen shield barely held the first attack off, and a second compression-release was about to send Serinda flying until Blane struck him with *Fear* and sent him into a panicked run out the building. He didn't come back.

When Grey asked her what she'd done she didn't try to hide it, and he made her explain it all. She thought he'd been particularly impressed at the *Double Jump* technique, as she called it, though both *Fear* and *Rage* also caught his interest. So, after he'd patiently explained that experimenting with new techniques could lead to unforeseen consequences, including fatal ones or ones that caused permanent brain damage, he agreed to work with her if she would stop trying these things on her own. Her progress had increased rapidly from there.

In fact, it felt like it had progressed exponentially. It was as if the Aether *wanted* to be learned. Every day, there seemed to be more and more of it, building up, rising towards the surface where human minds waited, and it flowed with abandon at a thought.

Grey theorised that this was why so many new users were appearing, and why they seemed so much stronger. The idea that in a matter of months he could encounter more than a handful of wild Aether users, even if he'd been actively searching for them, would have been laughable just a few years ago. Now he had an entire class, and they had come to *him*. This was surely just the tip of the iceberg.

But the next year had passed, then the next, and on into the third. Every day they felt safer, every day their network of supporters and collaborators grew. They even took to sleeping outside the Safe House, staying wherever they were needed.

And then, without warning, came the crackdowns.

The switch happened practically overnight, the RA moving on them as if they'd been monitoring them all along. Far Agents hit the homes, schools, and workplaces of a number of Grey's students, and Pan-Fed and Quick-Fix came for many of Serinda's patients and their families.

At first, they thought they had a mole, some warped replay of what had happened with the *Fallen* all that time ago. Perhaps they did. It didn't matter; the crackdown wasn't limited to them. In the grand scheme of things, Seri's communal network barely figured.

The crackdown was *everywhere*, all across Albores and all across the Reclamation. The already much-restricted mass media was shut down almost entirely, their offices occupied and filled with vetted personnel. Work licenses were revoked and Requisition allotments cut without explanation or recourse. There were even rumblings of *something* occurring within the Executive Committee, though that opaque group remained hidden behind curtains of both legal and judicial protections.

Blane and Serinda returned to the safe house after Grey was taken, some point in the second week. He'd gone to help one of his students – Xavier, in fact, the first that he had agreed to teach – after hearing that RA agents had been seen gathering near the shelter the boy was staying at. Neither of them had been heard from again.

So Blane and Serinda had been left hiding, waiting for something, *anything* that could tell them what to do next. Barely able to leave the safe house, with nothing but themselves and increasingly bad dreams.

That was nine months ago.

4

Pre-Fall societies were only truly waking up to the danger of demographic imbalance in the generations prior to the Sudden War. It was only a matter of time before a global system built upon the expectation of ever-increasing consumption collapsed in on itself; that the eventual collapse pre-empted this does not diminish the threat. For both this reason and the more pressing reason of [redacted], population control must remain at the heart of Reclamation policy.

Executive Committee Internal Document, *Analysis on Future Security Threats*

Blane had to hand it to the RA; they had been very clever at hiding the prison camps. Well-fortified, heavily guarded, and designed like concrete fortresses, they should have stood out like a sore thumb. Even located far out in the Waste, the structures should have garnered significant unwanted attention.

But not if they were designed to appear identical to something everyone already thought they knew, and *everyone* knew what those large, square monoliths that dotted the Waste were. They were rightly surrounded by exclusion zones and guard towers, with check points demanding ID verification every step of the way in. Everyone understood the importance of locating them away from population centres, within a tight ring of security.

It made her wonder how long the RA had been planning this. After all, even in an age of Fabricators and extruded construction, building an entire nuclear facility took time, empty shell or not.

And that's what the prison camp Grey was held in was registered as; a nuclear power plant.

The RA had never gone in for small modular reactors, though Blane had read that these were far more common in the Carib-Federation and beyond. No, the RA went in for large, centralised facilities producing the thousands of megawatts a modern city demanded, with its constantly hungry vehicles and screens and climate purifiers and ever-voracious Fabricators.

Knowledge on the location of these plants was kept highly restricted, something that again would not seem strange to a population raised on a diet of fear and bio-terror in the ashes of a planet scorched by nuclear fire. Power plants, like harvest domes, were kept beyond view of the general public.

Technically, Blane supposed, you could simply follow the line of power relays back to their source; though wireless, each relay had to be within line-of-sight of the next to transfer its energy across the air. Before you got very far though, she had no doubt a group of heavily armed and not very friendly uniforms would be coming to ask you some difficult questions about what you thought you were doing. Power relays were best avoided.

So the sites that generated the lifeblood of a Reclamation city were essentially sealed off from the city's inhabitants, and not-asking-questions was less a habit than an indoctrination. Perfect cover for concealing the incarceration of thousands of people, if not more.

Their first stop on heading out was an abandoned inland dockyard on the edge of the city; they needed a car they knew wasn't linked to them. Serinda hadn't told her much about where they were going, except that it was an old *Forever Fallen* site that stored a number of Scraped vehicles. Blane had never been there before, but it was obvious from Seri's reaction that this had once been one of her old 'clinics,' back when she had been with the group. With Raphael.

Luck was on their side, it seemed, because a single open flatbed remained, hidden inside the rusting hull of a pre-Fall container ship that had had its deck cunningly retrofitted to allow the storage of vehicles within. Serinda laughed when she saw the car, muttering something about it having to pull Grey out of trouble yet again. She didn't explain when Blane asked.

They slung the two heavy plastic cases they had brought with them into the back of the flatbed and, after an interminably long wait for the portable charger they had brought to do its job, they headed out into the Waste, and into a storm.

The storm was no surprise; they'd timed their departure to coincide with it. There was no technological gimmick Francisco could provide better than the raging electrical hellscape of one of the great storms, when the sky itself seemed determined to finish what the Sudden War had started. In Albores, people would be battening down in preparation for the coming weeks as the storm season began in earnest, weather patterns overcoming even the cloud seeders and air purifiers that protected the city from the worst of the poisonous weather for the rest of the year. And this season was predicted to be a big one, reminiscent of the old storms Blane knew only from movies and tales told by those much older than her; the kind of storms that would have torn down any structure not properly reinforced, and buried the rubble in ash and slurry.

The car slid and squealed as it clawed its way along terrain made sludge and silt by the downpour, their headlights penetrating no more than an arm's length or so into the day turned night by the towering clouds overhead. What few warped shrubs and plants grew in the poisoned soil outside the city were swamped by the flood. Stepping outside in this for any length of time would be dangerous, even deadly, the large, soot-filled raindrops suffocating in their density. Only the air-tight seal and independent air supply of the vehicle kept them breathing comfortably inside; designed to maintain a clean interior environment in the event of a nearby bio-terror attack, it served just as well for maintaining a breathable atmosphere in these conditions.

Still, it wasn't without limits. They had to find shelter in the Waste regularly, a place out of the elements where they could clear out the filters and replenish the oxygen stock using the portable electrolysis unit they had brought along with them.

Which meant relying on the route Francisco had plotted for them, and the navigation system to get them there.

They made their first stop several hours in, at a distance from the city that would have ordinarily taken only an hour or two. It was an abandoned tunnel, a relic of the pre-Fall era when traffic had flowed all across this continent. Now it was barely accessible, collapsed in on itself only a few car lengths inside, but it provided the shelter they needed to rest, regroup, and check that the two heavy plastic cases in the back remained sealed, protecting the equipment inside.

Finally, they spent what felt like hours checking over the car itself. Blane scraped and pulled and *Pushed* the muck from the filters while Seri checked the wheels for damage. If they lost the car out here, they wouldn't be getting back.

The lightning was if anything worse when they departed again, cracking down across the Waste all around them like a war between heaven and earth. Thunder rolled and made it impossible to talk, so Blane could only sit and stare out into the ever-increasing darkness as Serinda fought to keep the car going in the right direction. The wind itself seemed determined to force them back, to keep them away from their destination.

They slept fitfully in the car that night, sequestered beneath an old, rusting bridge that creaked and moaned in the howling wind. Where they had parked must once have been at the side of an old river, long since dried out to leave only oily dirt and the detritus of the old era. The rain continued to hammer down throughout the night, seemingly trying to fill the corpse of the waterway once more but raising only thick silt that would crack and flake once the storm passed.

They woke with the morning light to find a break in the downpour meant they could at least see beyond the windows of the car. The rain continued, lighter now though still thick, but the thunder had retreated. It rumbled occasionally in the distance as they drove, threatening to find them again at any moment.

"We need it back," Serinda said when Blane expressed relief at the let up in the weather. "Getting into an RA prison will be hard enough even with the cover of a storm. Without it, we're bound to fail."

Their route took them in a long curve towards their final destination; the direct route from Albores would most definitely be monitored. It should have been an impossible route; it *was* an impossible route, without Francisco's maps. Hidden craters of sucking dust could bury a car and its occupants without leaving a trace, and toxic pools of industrial poison would swamp an unwary traveller. Even with Francisco's maps they had to be careful, moving slowly to avoid obstacles not marked on the satellite images.

Which is what Francisco seemed to have provided them with; satellite images. Another seemingly impossible feat by the man who kept producing impossible feats. The RA was *very* clear on what would happen to any high-altitude or orbital equipment they detected over their airspace, and the RA's own geosynchronous satellites were accessible only by specifically authorised and rigorously vetted agents. Framed on national security grounds both military and for the maintenance of the Great Firewall, the RA claimed the space above the Reclamation to an unspecified distance[1]. Which meant that either Francisco had access to covert satellites undetectable to RA radar, or access to the RA's own satellites. Neither Blane nor Serinda knew which was more likely.

Whatever the origin, the car's navigation system was leading them on a route plotted using these digital images. In the relatively clear weather Serinda was even able to switch the vehicle to automatic for a while, leaving them in a driverless car that repeatedly made abrupt

---

[1] The RA was far from the only nation state in the modern era to do this.

turns to avoid hazards Blane couldn't see most of the time. It was strange, like an uncertain phantom was leading them towards some shifting goal.

Serinda used the chance to catch up on her sleep. Blane didn't know how she could sleep at a time like this, especially within the narrow confines of the jerking, rolling car.

"Reminds me of my old clinics," Seri said, grinning, as she crawled into the back. "Snatching sleep where you can becomes a bit of a learned habit."

Blane took her place at the wheel, an added layer of caution they had agreed upon in advance.

Serinda woke up a few hours later, as the rain once more increased in intensity. She didn't react when she saw Blane had switched the vehicle back into manual and was driving it herself, except to say she would take over. Blane didn't argue.

The flat land of the region around Albores gave way to rolling foothills the night of the second day, and to thicker vegetation. Though this was still far sparser than the greenery the land would have been covered with in the days before the Fall, automatic driving was impossible even without the rain. Actual trees appeared, stunted, desiccated things that nevertheless threatened to wreck the chassis with one wrong move. It made the going even harder, and by the time they rested for the night within the imperfect shelter of a large concrete structure of a bygone era they were both exhausted. Whatever this place had once been, it was little more than a vast cavern of echoing sound and formless shadow now, where the slightest whisper took on strange new layers as it struggled to fill the emptiness.

They ran maintenance, replenished the water in the electrolysis tanks, and passed out with barely a word. Blane was woken what felt like only minutes later, unable to say what by at first. Beyond the windows of the car was still only the inky blackness of the night-filled cavern, and it took her a few seconds to spot what had disturbed her.

"What's that?" she said, half to herself.

Serinda stirred, propping herself up to look out the window in the same direction.

"What's what?"

"That."

Blane pointed out a window as murky and dark as the rest.

Except… something glowed in the distance, a flickering orange light that pulsed and wavered through the rain and darkness outside the broken, crumbling walls of their shelter.

"*Mierda*," said Serinda, pushing herself fully upright and clambering back into the driver's seat. "We've got to go."

"Now? In this?" Blane gestured around the car to the blackness enclosing them. "What is it?"

"That's a wildfire," replied Serinda.

"In this weather?"

"There's a *lot* of lighting in one of these storms, and the land around here's so parched that it's easy to get a fire burning. Doesn't even need much vegetation; the ground itself is full of flammable chemicals in places. Once it gets big enough, not even this kind of rain can stop it."

"But it's so far away."

"Fire moves *fast*, Blane. We go. Now."

Serinda gunned the engine and the lights flicked on. The fire wasn't coming from the direction they were headed, at least.

They pulled away into the darkness. Sleep would have to wait.

5

Every possible measure must be taken against espionage and sabotage to national-defense material, premises, and utilities as defined by the Reclamation Authority. RA representatives are therefore authorized to prescribe areas and their extent as deemed appropriate, from which any or all persons may be excluded, and with respect to which, the right of any person to enter, remain in, or leave shall be subject to whatever restrictions the representative may impose.

Processes of Regulation and Order in the Reclamation (Sanctioned Digital Document)

It took them the whole of the next day and most of the night before the lights of the prison facility came into view, slight glints like stars nestled amongst sharp, steep hills. They were still kilometres away, stood atop the crest of a hill overlooking the pass leading to the site. In the pre-dawn light, their goal was nothing but a dark, solid monolith amongst the dull green of their night-vision binoculars.

They had left the car behind them, hidden and out of sight amongst rubble and debris half natural, half man-made. They'd left the two heavy plastic cases too, lying on the back of the flatbed ready for if and when they needed them. Now, Blane and Serinda made their way on foot, the chill of the night making them shiver.

To Blane, Serinda looked like a shadow come to life, somehow freeing itself from the fixture of any surface. She knew she looked the same, an impossible silhouette given physical form. Spangle suits, the same as she had worn to infiltrate the RA records facility back near the city. Though she thought the figure-hugging outfits were somewhat unfortunately like something out of a teenager's wet dream, she had to admit they did the job.

Each suit was made of a strange, colour-warping material layered over thin black fabric that clung tightly when stretched over bare skin, rendering the wearer almost imperceptible when motionless, and hardly more visible when moving. In bright light, the suits absorbed and reflected photons so that the wearer was something like a mirage, while in the dark of night both she and Seri were little more than two-dimensional wraiths. The heavy clouds promised to maintain this effect even after the sun rose.

They were, however, absolutely terrible at keeping you warm.

Blane swore and rubbed her arms vigorously as she waited while Serinda continued to stare through the binoculars towards the prison.

"Ok," Serinda said eventually, folding the binoculars away and storing them in the small pack strapped to her side, the same sequin-like material as the rest of their suits pulled taut across it and holding it tightly against her. "I think I see the spot we need. There's a point near the front wall where *this*..." She patted the pack, indicating another part of its contents. "... can have the most effect."

"And the guards?"

"They patrol the perimeter, but I think they'll be expecting the cameras and motion sensors to do most of the work. Which works for us."

Blane nodded as Seri gestured at herself, and the fabric covering them that meant those cameras would be much less effective than expected.

"So let's go?" she asked.

Seri nodded.

"Let's go."

They began the long, difficult walk down towards the facility as the rain increased in intensity. Blane muttered thanks to whatever entity was maintaining the storm; as uncomfortable as the rain was, it was key to keeping them hidden.

A flash of lightning followed by a rolling peal of thunder almost directly overhead made her rethink said entity's motivations.

It took several long, torturous hours to make their way to the section of wall Seri had marked out, with long pauses of motionlessness whenever the storm lightened or Seri spotted a guard on the perimeter through the binoculars. The area around the walls was unusually clear of debris, and no matter how effective the spangle suits were they couldn't take any chances. One mistake, and everything would be over.

Blane even began to wonder if she had really made the right decision, pushing Serinda to agree to come out here. What was she thinking, really? Two of them, against an entire RA prison?

But everything had gone so well in the facility, and she had been on her own then. Surely, with Serinda working with her, they could free Nestor. Couldn't they?

With these thoughts swirling around her head, Blane almost didn't notice when they arrived at the wall. All sense of time had left her - it could be morning, afternoon, or evening. The dark clouds and constant rain allowed no hint as to the time of day from the concealed sun.

The wall in front of them stood four metres high or more, featureless and grey. A blinking green light near the top marked a camera embedded within, lens looking out across the approach they had just made.

So the suits had worked, then. Blane hadn't even realised she'd been doubting it until this point.

Serinda wasted no time, opening the pack and taking out a fist-sized lump of off-white, clay-like substance. She pushed it against the wall where it stuck, looking like nothing more than a strange protrusion of the concrete itself.

"Once I put the detonator in, we head around the wall to the back," she said, almost inaudible in the pouring rain.

Blane gave a nervous smile, and watched as Serinda drew out a long, thin piece of metal and slid it into the plastic explosive. This she had taken from an old *Forever Fallen* stash; Francisco might be able to get them whatever weird little gadgets they needed, but when it came to plastic explosives he came up empty. The Reclamation Authority knew what to look for in terms of weaponry, Blane assumed.

When Serinda nodded, Blane pressed herself up against the wall and they began to make their way around, hugging the circumference of the site and following it all the way north to the opposite side. Ironically, now they were actually at the walls of the facility they were safer from observation than they had been this entire time; both cameras and guards were focused upon anything *approaching* the facility. Little actually watched the base of the walls themselves.

The storm showed no sign of letting up, and if anything was getting stronger. The ground beneath their feet was thick mud, and streams of water ran all around them. Several times, Blane lost her footing and fell face-first into a deep pool of dirty water, increasing the strange, uncomfortable sense of being wet without actually feeling moisture on the skin.

She couldn't tell how long it took before they reached a point Serinda found satisfactory, maybe half an hour, maybe more, but eventually they came to a halt. Serinda brought her face up close to Blane's to speak, waving the tiny detonator in one hand.

"Once I set this off, we have to get over as fast as possible. They'll only be distracted for so long."

She looked up at towards the lip of the wall.

"You really think you can do this?" Seri asked, concern visible even through the slick, dark suit fabric covering her face.

Blane nodded with a confidence she wasn't sure she actually felt.

"I've been practising. You've *seen* me clear higher than this," she said.

"Yes, but only once, and in much better conditions than this."

"*Twice*," insisted Blane. "And anyway, we've been over this already. We can hardly turn back now."

Blane locked eyes with Seri, hoping her own expression showed only determination.

Serinda was silent for a moment, her eyes shining a bright white in contrast with the darkness wrapping the rest of her face, then she sighed over the storm.

"Right. You're right. Are you ready?"

Blane didn't answer, but gestured to Serinda's pack.

"The monofilament?" she asked.

She would have bet a Carib-dollar that Seri looked chagrined at her oversight, but the mask revealed no change of expression. Saying nothing, Serinda reached in and drew out the second-to-last item in the pack: a small spool of twined wire, like a tightly wound ball of plastic string.

Blane took the monomolecular wire in her hand, then turned and crouched facing the wall, straining her neck upwards to look towards the crest. Her muscles tensed as she prepared to spring.

With a final nod to herself, Serinda pressed down on the detonator.

The explosion at the opposite end of the facility roared over them even here, even over the storm, sending a violent vibration through the ground beneath their feet. Shouts and cries of alarm carried from inside, and the wail of a siren split the air.

Blane wasted no time to listen but sprang upwards, pushing herself into the air with every drop of power in her legs. At the peak of her jump, she *pushed* herself higher, a resistance forming in the air below her feet for just long enough to spring once more. Once with her left leg, another with her right, and she stretched her arms out as far as they could go to grab the lip of the wall.

She almost didn't make it. The lip was slick with rain, and little more than her fingertips found purchase, but hanging there gave her enough time to regain her composure. Taking a deep breath, she gave a final *Push* upwards and forced herself over the wall, falling onto the walkway that ran along the other side with a thud that was muffled by the rain.

The walkway must have been a good four or five feet below the lip of the wall, and it knocked the wind out of her. After precious seconds getting her breath back, Blane pushed herself up and looked around.

No one. Any guards that had been here must have rushed off towards the sound of the explosion. A wide open space more shadow than light stretched out below the walkway, bare earth turned to mud in the downpour running all the way to a large, blocky concrete building. The green light of a security camera blinked from the wall of the building, but showed no sign of having spotted her, and nothing moved elsewhere. Whatever it was about the weird, fractal reflective surfaces of the spangle suits that so confused the security algorithms, it was clearly still working.

Blane turned back to the wall, taking the loose end of the monofilament in one hand and flinging the spool back over the way she had come. Hopefully it wouldn't be too difficult to spot, even in the gloom.

Several seconds passed, then Blane felt a pull on the thread. Moving quickly, she pressed it against the wall and felt it stick. Somewhere on a microscopic level, minuscule barbs bit into the tiny cracks and crevices that made up the surface of the wall, and held fast.

This had been difficult even when they practised in dry, calm conditions without the pressure of time. No matter how strong they logically knew the wire to be, no matter how well versed they were in the physical properties of carbon nanotubes fused together through the bombardment of high-energy electrons, the mind rejected having its entire weight supported by something no thicker than a thread.

It's not even really a 'mono' filament. There's thousands of them, wrapped around each other like mooring rope, Blane thought to herself, biting her lip as the wire pulled taut. She knew she was just trying to distract herself from the tension.

The strange, warped hole in the night that was Serinda's head appeared at the top of the wall moments later. Blane stretched out a hand to help, but it was batted aside. Another moment, and Serinda swung herself over the lip and onto the other side, landing neatly on her feet. She barely stumbled from the drop.

"How are your hands?" Blane yelled over the storm and sirens, not wanting to draw attention to the fact that she herself had crashed inelegantly to the floor when she came over. Besides, it was important.

"Like climbing up thorns, but fine," Serinda replied.

She held out her hands for Blane to see. Opening her fists to show the palms up, both of them could see where the spangle fabric had been torn by the tiny biting hooks of the wire, skin angry and raised beneath.

"Have to be careful to keep my hands closed from now on, I guess. We don't know how scratched up these suits can get before they start showing up on cams, but it doesn't *feel* likes the suit's compromised."

Blane nodded in agreement, then pointed to the blinking light of the camera.

"No change. They don't know we're here."

"Good," said Serinda. "Let's keep it that way. Now, which way was the detention block?"

"It's *all* detention block."

"You know what I mean. Grey's block. At least, the one we think is Grey's."

Serinda knew as well as her the direction they needed to go, but Blane didn't say anything. Instead, she pointed toward the building on which the security camera blinked.

"Through there."

"Well, of course it is." Serinda sighed. "I guess we'll see how good these suits really are."

They made their way carefully through the darkness, fighting the urge to rush as they followed the shaky iron walkway along the side wall until they came to a set of steps heading down. They descended this to the courtyard below, moving slowly across its shadowed emptiness and coming to a stop in front of the door, lit dully by the green light of the camera just above.

The screaming sirens cut off almost exactly as they arrived at the door, the sudden silence oppressively heavy. Neither of them thought for even a moment that this could be a good sign; whatever the security personnel here imagined the cause of the new hole blasted in their wall was, they were hardly going to simply return to their posts without investigating the entire site.

Blane didn't wait for Serinda to say anything, but grabbed the door's thick metal handle and pulled. Locked, but this wasn't unexpected. She looked down, below where she still held the door.

A mechanical lock. Nothing high-tech about it, just a good, old-fashioned lock requiring a physical key.

Or… she thought … *a metaphysical one.*

She reached out towards and *into* the lock with the Aether, sensing the cylinder and the driver pins within. A low metallic rattle came from the lock as she manipulated it.

Seri had taught her how to do this, and she in turn had learnt it from Raphael and the other *Forever Fallen*. Grey had expressed surprise upon learning the *Fallen* had worked out such an advanced way to use Aether for picking locks, but then he still had difficulty getting out of the mindset instilled into him in the Academy, a mindset that categorised and labelled the different ways of using the Aether as 'techniques' and discouraged adaptation and experimentation.

Blane pushed the memory aside as she felt the pins catch in the shear line and the tumbler turn, a soft click telling her the lock had released. A second later and they were inside, pulling the door shut behind them.

By the wan light of the outside spilling in through the door she caught a glimpse of long, empty corridor extending into darkness in front of them, a darkness that swallowed them the instant the door snapped shut. The sounds of the rain cut off the same instant, and it was briefly as if all her senses had been *Closed*. From here, they really were on their own; however Francisco had gotten the imagery of this facility and surrounding area, it didn't extend to the interior. All they had to go on was suppositions and guesswork based on images of the movement of people they had to assume were inmates, large groups exiting and entering this building at regular intervals and always escorted by several armed figures.

They moved slowly down the corridor, the oppressive silence only getting heavier as they progressed. Blane's eyes took time to adjust to the darkness, because there was less light here than even in the gloom outside. She wondered why there were no light sources here, and was about to say as much when she suddenly sensed people further ahead.

She had been almost unconsciously *reaching* out ahead of herself the entire time, the emptiness of the pitch black hallway confirmed by senses beyond the usual, but now she sensed a mass of people somewhere ahead and to the side. It felt like they were on the other side of the wall she was following, their consciousnesses floating lightly upon the Aether and making small ripples as it flowed beneath them and as they, in almost imperceptible amounts, replenished it with the energy they themselves generated.

Blane could sense so many of them that the room they were in must be huge, something like a large hall. Her senses didn't reach more than a handful of meters into the room, but as she moved carefully forward along the corridor everywhere she *reached* she sensed another person. They seemed to be spaced at regular intervals, not exactly crammed in but without much personal space. Each one of them felt calm.

No, not calm. Their thought patterns were restless, a suppressed turmoil kept in check by... *sleep*. They were asleep.

"This must be where they keep them locked up at night," Serinda whispered, evidently sensing the same thing as Blane.

At first this didn't make sense to Blane, as she tried to figure out how the room beyond could be a prison. It was only after a moment of reflection that Blane realised how ridiculous the image of this place she had been holding in her mind was.

This wasn't a place of bars and blocks, not some regimented facility of individual cells and exercise yards; this was a *camp*. This was a place where large groups of people were dumped and forgotten. Not a place for rehabilitation or even retribution, but a place to put those the State had no place for.

Blane *reached* out as far as she could, straining as she drew on the Aether until she thought she was managing ten metres or even more. Grey had always been amazed at how far she could *Reach*; even after the limits of his own abilities had been extended, a mysterious gift from their time with Fen, he could barely reach half as far.

Wherever she cast her senses she felt lightly-sleeping forms, flickering awarenesses upon the Aether whose shapes were a restless slumber of exhaustion and low-level fear. After a while, she sensed what must be a guard, awake but only half-alert. It was difficult to tell for sure, but she thought the sentry might be almost as tired as the prisoners.

The presence of the guard made it stranger that everything was enveloped in this pitch black darkness. If there were guards, there surely should be some light source. She knew from the satellite images that this corridor must lead to wherever the prisoners were kept, so how could it be this dark?

"There he is."

It took a moment for Blane to sense what Serinda was talking about.

There, towards the corner of the room not far from where they stood, was a familiar presence. The ripples it produced in the Aether were deeper and stronger, and awake. It only took a moment for Blane to know that he sensed her just as she sensed him.

Nestor Grey.

She stood there in the dark, Serinda just as silent, and felt Grey slowly rise to full consciousness. He broadcast his intention clearly.

Wait, he was saying, though without words. Rather, it was a projection of patience, of care and trepidation. Blane only understood his meaning because they had spent so long attuning to each other's use of *Tell* back at the safe house.

She couldn't understand why he would want them to wait. Wait for what? They needed to get moving, find a way to get to Grey before someone else got to them instead.

Serinda's hand came to rest on her shoulder, gripping lightly but firmly and preventing Blane from pushing on further ahead which, she realised, she had already begun to do.

"*Wait,*" Serinda whispered, reinforcing Grey's message. "Give him a chance."

Blane sensed a spike of concern from Grey. He must have felt Blane's impatience, and intent to move. Concern, and a flicker of annoyance.

Really? He's getting annoyed at me during his own damn rescue attempt...?

A flicker of humour from Grey, this time. He must have sensed her own irritation, and found it amusing, which only fuelled her annoyance.

Grey's presence began to move, shifting from wherever he had been laying and heading over to the guard she had previously sensed.

"What's he doing...?" Blane whispered. Serinda shrugged, as much in the dark as her.

Blane felt the guard come to full wakefulness as Grey approached, a tired hostility at the top of their mind. There was no way to tell what was said between the two, but Blane *could* feel Grey draw on the Aether and send its flow towards the guard, and she felt tired hostility switch to a tired dismissiveness.

He was using the Aether to *Persuade* the guard to let him past. Could he really get away with that?

A moment later and Grey's presence moved past the guard. Blane heard the shifting of a large door sliding open, then shut.

A faint pale green glow, weak enough to be imperceptible in anything but the darkness of this hallway, approached them. Footsteps accompanied the light, but it wasn't until he was almost within arm's reach that they could make out the outline of Grey's form. The dull light came from a small rectangular patch seemingly stuck to the side of his neck.

"What are you doing here?" Grey said in a snapped whisper before either of them could say a word. "This was stupid. You shouldn't be here."

Blane could see he was having trouble focusing on them, their spangle suits rendering them in the gloom as strange, cut-out sections of even deeper darkness. Still, the suits had no effect on their presences in the Aether.

"We came to get you out," she snapped right back, angry at this cold reception even though she could sense the concern for their safety that underlay it.

"That explosion was you two, then? The guards are trying to pass it off as the storm, but I can feel they're on edge. That one wasn't going to let me out of the sleeping area until I *persuaded* him."

"Yes, that was us. Now, come on – we've got to get out of here before someone realises you've gone."

Blane was already turning back towards the outer door as she finished speaking, reaching out to take Grey's arm and pull him with them but finding only empty air.

"Why's it so damn dark in here, anyway?" she demanded, turning back to see Grey hadn't moved..

"Keeps us from causing problems. The guards have low-light E-masks, and they can see *this*…" He tapped the faintly glowing patch at his neck, "… wherever we go. Tritium patch - appears on their visual display regardless of walls."

"And I assume you can't just take it off?"

"Ha, no." He chuckled scornfully. "Not without tearing out my jugular too."

"Is that why the guard doesn't seem to care you've wandered away?" Serinda asked.

"Well, like I say I had to *persuade* him because of your little escapades but yes; these patches mean they know we can't go anywhere without them knowing, and besides, the Waste is the best guard they've got. Even if we somehow did get over the wall, we'd just die out there anyway."

"Well, not if you're with us," said Blane. "Come on, let's go. We can get over the wall before they notice you're gone."

Again, she reached for his arm, and again she didn't find it. It was only then she realised this was because he was drawing back from her.

Serinda sighed.

"*Caray...*" she said in exasperation, looking from Grey to Blane. "Blane, he's going to make this difficult for us. You noticed he keeps saying 'we' all the time?"

Blane froze. They had discussed this possibility, knowing Grey as well as they did.

"You're not coming without the others, are you?" she said.

Grey's eyebrows rose in surprise. Did he really *still* not realise how predictable he was?

"Well," she said, sighing even more deeply than Serinda. "I guess that means it's time for plan B."

6

Transparency of political leadership is antithetical to the attainment of national goals. Public scrutiny of government renders it impotent and unable to prosecute any action, however necessary, without encountering stubborn, ill-informed resistance. As the old saying goes: to increase knowledge is to increase sorrow.

Guillermo Delvaci, *Truth Self-Evident* (Sanctioned Publication)

Plan B involved, first, finding out how far Grey had got with his own escape preparations inside the camp. As they expected, he hadn't been sitting around passively hoping for something to come along. In a few moments of rushed conversation, he assured them he could get his fellow prisoners ready for action without any guards noticing.

Which meant, next, shutting down as many cameras as they could. Time was of the essence so, forcing aside Grey's protests, they explained exactly what *he* was going to do while they went to shut down the security feeds; which was get as many inmates as possible ready to rush to the eastern courtyard.

"The eastern courtyard?" he said, puzzled. "That pretty heavily guarded, because it leads to the... oh."

He trailed off, the outline of their plan becoming clearer.

Not giving him time to ask any more questions, they had him explain exactly where the security room was. They needed to shut off the camera feeds as soon as possible... and do one other thing, though Blane didn't mention this to Grey yet. Instead, she told him to get everyone ready to move as soon as he saw the signal.

"What signal?" he asked.

"You'll know," replied Blane. She was grinning.

"You're enjoying this, aren't you?" said Serinda. She was not.

And the crazy thing was, Blane thought, she really *was* enjoying this.

She didn't respond to Serinda's question and ignored the worried look on her face, looking down the hall. Her eyes had properly adjusted now, and she thought she would be able to see even without the dull glow of the patch on Grey's neck.

"How much should we worry about the guards here?" Serinda

asked Grey, tutting as she turned away from Blane. "Can any of them use Aether?"

Grey shook his head.

"The guards hate this place - being posted here is basically a punishment. They don't seem to know much about Aether, either. I don't think they know about me or Xavier or the other few, and we avoid using it too openly. We only use it when the guards get... excitable."

Blane paused at that, imagining the way unhappy guards in a place like this might take out their problems on those they guarded. She understood what he was implying.

"Xavier's here?" she asked.

Grey nodded.

They'd known this was a possibility, too. After all, it was when he was going to check on his first student that Grey was captured.

"He's here, and I'm not leaving him," Grey said with heavy finality. "I'll bring as many as I can."

They split up without another word, Grey returning the way he had come and Serinda and Blane going back the way they had. They had no need for parting words when they could sense each other's readiness.

According to Grey, the main security room was a couple of buildings to the northeast. All they had to do was follow the wall they had come over and they would see it. In her excitement, Blane pushed the door to the outside open and stepped into the pouring rain before Serinda could do anything to stop her except gasp.

A second later, and Blane cursed herself for her own stupidity.

A guard stood in the centre of the ground outside, halfway between her and the outer wall. He was obvious even through the downpour, a tall figure in dark body armour and a glowing E-mask turning towards the opened door in surprise. Blane felt her stomach lurch as he raised his rifle at her, and she involuntarily closed her eyes waiting for the shot...

... which didn't come.

When she hesitantly opened her eyes again, the guard still stood there, head cocked to one side in puzzlement. Slowly, his rifle lowered, and he tapped at the side of his E-mask.

"... *porquería*..." She heard him mumble before he turned around and walked away, heading towards the stairs they had come down by after scaling the wall.

A tap on her shoulder made her turn slowly around. Serinda stood close behind her, finger to her lips.

"*The suits...*" she hissed, pointing at her eyes.

The spangle suits work on E-masks too.

Seri pulled Blane in the opposite direction to the guard without waiting to see if she understood what she was trying to tell her. A shiver ran down Blane's spine, and she realised she was trembling.

Dumb luck. That's the only reason I'm alive right now. Dumb luck.

They crept into a small, dark space between two buildings and stayed still, barely breathing until they were sure the guard had moved on. Serinda leaned in to support Blane, holding her by the shoulders as she fought to calm down.

From his reaction, Blane knew the guard had seen *something*. The suits obviously didn't work perfectly against the E-masks; some visual artefact must have remained. Without the wind and rain of the storm, she wondered, would the guard's other senses have compensated for the failure of the E-mask? What if he'd just lifted his mask up and realised she wasn't an artefact of his display?

What if he'd opened fire first, just to be sure?

The chill of the rain paled in comparison to the ice in her veins. The rush she had been feeling since breaking into the camp – maybe, she realised now, since even before that – was gone, leaving her numb and struggling to stop her hands from shaking.

Somewhere beneath her, the Aether *lurched*.

She'd felt this before, once. Years ago, atop the Central Tower, the sense of something colossal moving through the Aether. But that had been Fen, hadn't it? Why did she feel it now?

Serinda staggered a little to the side, clearly sensing it too.

They stood there, swaying, as the sensation gradually subsided.

"What was that...?" mumbled Blane, shaking her head to remove the last of its effects.

"Later," replied Serinda. "We've got to move."

She didn't wait for Blane to reply, but headed in the direction Grey had told them with renewed determination.

In the end, getting to the security room was relatively easy. They met a number of guards along the way - several solitary armed figures and two more patrolling as a pair - but now they knew none of them were trained to use Aether, or even possessed of any proper understanding of its influence, it was a simple matter to put them down before they had a chance to react.

The combination of Aether techniques and their vision-obscuring suits made them vengeful wraiths, moving through the facility and leaving behind a trail of unconscious and insensible bodies. The last three, stationed on a raised walkway surrounding the perimeter of the security room, went down without even the time to notice Blane. She leapt from the ground floor and off empty air with two powerful strides to land directly behind them, where as far as they were concerned no one could possibly be. Serinda came running up the metal stairway the guards had been watching over the instant they collapsed to the floor.

The rain was letting up slightly, a gap in the storm turning the skies from maelstrom to mere tumult. The crack and peel of thunder from all directions told them it was far from over, though, and the wind fought against them as they forced the door open and sent the two figures watching over the camera feeds tumbling to the floor with simultaneous bursts of *Flare*. They rolled the prone forms into the corner, dragged the three other fallen guards in from outside, and tied them all up tightly with the monofilament.

"Ok, now go," said Serinda, already leaning over the monitors that controlled the cameras and shutting them down one by one.

"You're sure you'll be ok? Do you even know where the controls for the...?"

Serinda cut Blane off with an angry look.

"We've been over this. I'll be ok if you move *fast*. The longer you take, the more likely it is someone is going to figure out what's going on. So *move...*"

Then, suddenly, she grinned, and passed Blane the final item from her pack; a small, coin-shaped disc of grey plastic.

"... I'll be waiting for your *signal*," she said.

With a smirk in return Blane spun around, tucking the disc into the small pouch in her suit's sleeve as she dashed back out into the rain.

She knew where she was going; they'd spent hours poring over the images, and while they hadn't been able to identify with any surety the location of the security centre, the vehicle yard had been simple. Even more fortunately, it wasn't far from where she stood now.

The enormous trucks, half-prison-transport half-APC, were kept parked on the eastern side of the camp, separated from the main sections by an extension of the perimeter wall running *inside* the borders of the camp, a central gate separating the vehicle stores from the grounds in which the prisoners were held. Large banks of fuel cells and generators were spaced regularly around the edges of the yard, and there seemed to be at least five or six vehicles capable of transporting large numbers of people kept fuelled and stored there at all times.

The satellite images had also told them that the wall here was perhaps the most heavily guarded area in the facility, with guards stationed upon it at all times. Whatever Grey said about the Waste being the greatest assurance against any escape attempts, the guards clearly weren't taking chances on desperate inmates going for the vehicles.

But a single figure *could* sneak through, if she were hard to spot and able to scale the wall just *there*, cross over just *here*, and jump across onto one of the large banks of fuel cells just *here*.

Blane had to restrain herself from giving a bow to an imaginary audience as she landed skilfully on the ground in the narrow space between two fuel cells, the height of them rising above her head. She wished Serinda had been there to see, and felt her excitement rising again. This time, though, she was aware of it and forced herself to take a deep breath, fighting to focus her thoughts.

She couldn't understand why it felt like the Aether was somehow energizing her. Her skin tingled, and when she resisted it felt... disappointed? Like it was calling out to be used, and fighting against her attempts to remain cool and steady. But that was ridiculous.

She shook her head again, and *reached* out. She sensed someone nearby, on the other side of the bank of fuel cells she was using for cover. She needed to hurry.

Blane drew out the coin-shaped disc and stared at it in her hand. Then she took a deep breath, and tapped it once. A tiny screen in the centre lit up for a second, then once again went dark.

Nothing happened for a while; the sound of the rain and distant thunder smothered everything. Somewhere, though, back at the vehicle they had driven here in, two heavy cases would be opening. Blane found herself counting, wondering how far she would get before...

7... 8...

A distant high-pitched buzzing came to her ears, buried under the noise of the storm at first but growing closer as if a mob of angry wasps were on the attack. She sensed the figure across from her grow confused, then wary. They obviously didn't know what this sound could be.

Two seconds later, and dozens of tiny points of light came streaming over the wall, flitting past over her head and through the air above the camp. They moved almost too fast for the eye to see, like shooting stars somehow cut from the sky and brought close to earth. Several clattered against the fuel banks or crashed to the ground, unable to overcome the fierce wind, but each left long, shimmering tails of fluorescent green motes behind them, glittering and slow to fall even in the downpour. The dust continued to glow as it spilled to the floor and mixed with the dirty ground water, flowing and spiralling across every surface. She felt the guard's confusion grow, as shouts rang out across the facility.

The guard was *not* confused by the screech of the alarm that tore through the night a moment later, though. He knew it's meaning, as the entire camp would. As any inhabitant of the Reclamation would.

The piercing, pulsing sound every citizen knew, and dreaded.

Biological attack.

Blane felt the nearby guard's thoughts spike with adrenaline. Even she had to fight the instinctive urge to seek distance and protective equipment, and she had been prepared for this. The blare of the bio-attack siren, overridden and set off by Serinda the moment she saw the drones tear over the camp walls, was a sound everyone had been trained since childhood to react to immediately, and as Blane had expected the guard's focus was now on nothing besides getting to the nearest pathogen-filtering mask dispenser.

Which made them an easy target for *Fear*.

Blane stepped around the corner to find the guard collapsed to the floor, whimpering. Their E-mask lay discarded to the side, and they were covering their eyes with shaking hands, nails digging into their own face. In the dark and with the particulate-filled rain, Blane couldn't even tell if they were male or female.

Either way, if they had been scared before, Blane's mental assault had left them *terrified*.

"Give me your E-key," Blane demanded, standing over the guard and making her voice as strong and dominating as possible.

She wondered what she must look like to the fallen guard. Cloaked in the weird, light-warping spangle suit against a backdrop of thunder and lightning, perhaps she would have cut a fearful figure even without the use of the Aether. With it, though, the guard didn't stand a chance. They threw their thin access card towards her, and pulled themselves tightly into a ball. Blane thought she could hear weeping as the guard slowly rocked back and forth, bright green rivulets streaming and eddying all around them.

She grabbed the E-key up from the ground where it had fallen and, without a second look at the guard, dashed towards the nearest vehicle facing the right way. The large, hulking machine was a thing of squat metal on numerous huge, deep-treaded tires, designed to carry as many people as possible across the difficult terrain of the Waste. Comfort was not a factor, with the small cramped driver's cabin divided entirely from the long rear trailer in which the inmates would be carried.

Blane pulled herself up into the front cabin and smashed her hand down onto the ignition screen, which instantly flared to life. With a rumble, the engine kicked in and the entire vehicle shook, a rapid whirring that gradually dropped down both in speed and tone as the engine settled into a rhythmic turning.

She grabbed the steering wheel – no vehicle crossing the Waste could rely on AI-guided steering to find a safe path through those chaotic and polluted lands – and smashed a foot down on the accelerator. Almost immediately the collision warning alarm sounded, as the truck detected the tall steel gate directly ahead of them. Blane ignored it, only pressing down on the accelerator harder.

The truck smashed into the gate with a huge crash that for a moment drowned out even the thunder, tearing the gate off the hinges that fixed it in to the high concrete wall on either side. Rolling over the gate, Blane pulled the truck to a stop directly in the centre of the eastern courtyard, where Grey waited with a large group of his astonished-looking companions behind him. A single unconscious guard lay at his feet.

Grey immediately began directing people into the back of the vehicle, not joining Blane in the front cabin until the last person was on board. Serinda came climbing up barely a second after.

"They'll be figuring out that stuff is just glitter about now," said

Seri, slamming the cabin door shut behind her and throwing herself down into the seat next to Grey. As if the universe had been waiting for these words, the bio-attack sirens cut off. Someone somewhere must have reinitialised the pathogen detection system and realised there was no actual threat.

That, and they must have also noticed the large group of prisoners gathered in the courtyard outside, because bullets began pinging the ground around them, at first almost indistinguishable from the heavy droplets of rain battering the dirt all round.

"Time to go," said Grey.

Blane gunned the engine and yanked the wheel to the left, driving the truck towards the southern wall. There, appearing in the headlights as she sped towards it, was the hole they had blasted in it at the beginning of this whole thing.

It wasn't as large as she'd hoped, Blane realised. Still, left with no other choice, she pressed down as hard as she could on the accelerator and felt the truck lurch forward, motor screaming.

With a massive jolt that shook her to her very bones, the truck smashed through the hole, tearing out yet more of the thick concrete wall as they tore off into the Waste.

7

Progress ends when managierialism takes over. Lacking clear leadership, motivated only to avoid accountability, citizens fulfil their duties without initiative and without risk. In such a situation, no system can advance. "Don't get fired, don't take chances," is the mantra of a society in decay. No new cities, no new factories, no new industries, only the stagnation of managerial capitalism.

Amanis Egorov, *Our Forefathers' Flaws*

They had to move quickly to keep ahead of satellites. Several drones chased them in the first moments after they escaped the camp, but gale-force winds soon drove these off-course or to the ground. They'd been lucky with their own drones, Blane knew; they'd left their flatbed with its two cases of glitterpaste-filled drones upwind of the facility, but things could have gone much worse had the wind changed direction before they launched.

However, while the storm provided as much cover as they could hope for from most forms of aerial observation, they knew the RA possessed long-wave satellites that could punch through even the densest cloud cover in almost real time.

The key word here, though, was 'almost'. If they kept moving fast and changed direction at seemingly random points, they could always be slightly ahead of whoever the satellites were reporting to until they found a place to hide.

So, after grabbing their original vehicle and the precious mapping data stored within, they tore off as fast as they could. This was, Blane found, infuriatingly slow, but at least they knew where they should head.

They'd noted the area on Francisco's images long before setting out, and spotted it in the distance on their journey up. Broken old-world towers sprawled at the foot of a range of hills almost tall enough to call mountains, and between these fallen towers stood hulking machines of blades and rust that must once have been part of the industrial efforts that reshaped and remade the world. Vast, dark holes torn into the hills all around spoke of what had once been.

They forced their cars through the uneven, debris-strewn terrain and into one of these cavernous holes. Beyond, the way was suddenly clear, smooth black asphalt stretching out into the distance. With the headlights lighting the way, they made better time than they had at any point since their escape.

Once upon a time this place must have been a nexus of high-speed, long-distance routes carved forcefully out of nature to facilitate the frantic rat race of the old world. Now, the interior of these tunnels remained disconcertingly untouched by the ravages that had occurred outside. Only the dust that flew up at their passage and the stale, cloying air told of the passing of time and coming of ruin. Blane found the constant passage of the dull grey, unchanging road surface and the tunnel walls racing by hypnotic, her visual cortex struggling to reconcile the sensation of motion without visual markers.

They passed multiple branching roads as they drove, choosing which to follow at random until they eventually emerged and made camp beneath a section of cracked and broken highway running between the tunnel-peppered hills. The area would at least provide cover to stop, rest, and discuss their next move.

"And what exactly *is* the next move?" demanded Grey.

They were stood a short way from the rest of the group, the three of them huddled together beneath one side of the flyover while to the other the escapees sat and stared into the distance in disconcerting silence.

Now the storm was truly abating and a wan early morning light was filtering through the clouds, Blane could see how bad of a condition they were really in. Grey was *thin*; not to the point of starvation, but Blane didn't think it far off. A large bruise ran around his left eye and across his cheek, and where his hands and arms were visible she saw deep cuts and grazes.

"We have to ditch the vehicles. Even with the GPS scramblers we brought..." And Serinda waved what would to the casual observer appear to be an ordinary thin-screen in the air. "...the RA will be able to spot them easily now the storm has passed."

"And what... *walk* back to Albores?" Rather than angry, Grey sounded resigned and demoralised. "You think half of these people could make that kind of distance even if it *wasn't* the Waste?"

Blane glanced at the other escapees. They were all in a similar condition to Grey, eyes sunken into skin pulled tight with malnutrition and exhaustion.

"What did they do to you?" she asked gently, gesturing towards his frail-looking body.

"Limited calories to keep us docile, and work to keep us occupied," he said, shaking his head and staring at the ground. "They call it 'clean up'. Out in the Waste, clearing away all the trash and poison. Around the camp, or they'd bus us out in those trucks to other areas. It was... hard. And it'll be harder still for those we left behind."

Blane couldn't tell if what she was feeling was irritation or amusement. Yet again, Grey was worrying over others when he should be worrying about himself. He looked sick, and there was no *way* they could have freed the entire camp. It was a miracle they'd rescued everyone from Grey's section.

She thought better of saying anything, though.

"We don't have to walk all the way," said Serinda, bringing the conversation back to the topic at hand. "We just have to get far enough."

"Far enough for what?"

"For pick up."

Blane saw understanding dawn through Grey's expression. Understanding, and surprise.

"Francisco? He's getting directly involved?"

"Yes," Serinda replied with a nod. "Though he did say to tell you this wasn't going to be a habit."

"Well," said Blane, smiling suddenly. "What he actually said was *'pero no te acostumbres, ¿eh?'* ...but you get the idea."

Grey gave a pained chuckle at her rather accurate impression of Francisco's affected mode of speech. They knew now that the man could code-switch instantly when the situation demanded it, but still he preferred to maintain the long since dissolved boundaries between the old world tongues that had merged into modern centra-English.

"Where is this pick up?" Grey asked. He gave a cough, a nasty ragged sound that Blane thought hinted of worse than mere tiredness, and hunched over with his hands to his knees for balance.

"More of a 'when,' actually," answered Seri, leaning over to put a supportive arm on Grey's shoulder. "Late tonight. We get as far into these hills as possible, find a clearing, and send our location. He assured us he could get us out before the RA ping our signal."

Serinda straightened up, and Blane sensed a trickle of Aether move from the woman into Grey. As the energy, like liquid gold, flowed into his veins his deathly pale face flushed, growing a little more alive and the slightest touch healthier.

"I need to help the others, too," Seri said, looking across to where the rest of their group sat huddled and shivering in the weak morning light. She sighed. "Too deserted for there to be much Aether out here, but I'll do what I can."

Without another word, she strode off to do what she could.

"She'll exhaust herself more than the rest of us put together before she stops," Grey said, straightening up and following her with his gaze.

Blane just nodded. She knew as well as him that they couldn't do anything to stop her. Medical care had always been at Serinda's core. Occasionally, Blane thought Seri used dealing with the problems of others as a way of drowning out her own.

She bit down on that unkind thought.

A short while later they set out, leaving the vehicles behind and trekking off across the broken land. They walked for the better part of the day, sticking beneath the cover of cracked and crumbling highways as much as they could, Serinda feeding strength into those who stumbled by sacrificing her own.

Blane was the first to notice the jackals. She spotted them late in the afternoon, though there was no saying how long they had actually been stalking them. A glimpse of pointed ears behind the rubble, a flash of murky yellow eyes from the hills rising to either side of them, a low, muted bark from somewhere behind. Occasionally, she felt their presences flit across the Aether, telling her they were nearby even when she could not see them.

"We keep moving," Seri said. "Not a large pack yet, but the longer we stay here the more will come. Eventually one will find the courage to make a move, and then the rest will follow."

As far as Blane knew, Seri was the only one of them to have any experience with the feral creatures of the Waste. The *Forever Fallen* had at times had business that was only possible beyond the city boundaries, when RA eyes were to be avoided at all costs, and sometimes Serinda had been part of this. She'd told Blane, or at least hinted at, tales of sudden assaults by the scarred and deformed descendants of the domesticated animals of the old world.

They picked up the pace, the sound of scrabbling paws and sporadic whines and growls from behind galvanising even the weakest of the group. The hike became a balancing act between keeping moving, keeping ahead of whatever stalked them, and taking care not to stumble and fall on the cutting edges of broken things and oil-slicked patches of unidentifiable, fetid liquid.

Though the sun was hidden behind cloud, Blane felt sure it must be dipping below the horizon by the time she saw the craft approaching. It flew towards them rapidly, a wide, heavy-looking thing of metallic greys and greens speeding over the foothills on powerful thrust engines whose screams grew gradually more audible.

"Too early," said Seri, staring at the approaching vehicle through her binoculars. Blane didn't know what she meant at first. Francisco had told them he would come only under cover of night, but surely...

Grey stepped up besides Serinda, who held out the binoculars for him to take.

"That's RA," he said, the binoculars' electronic zoom making a gentle electronic whir as he stared through them. "Must have been sent out to search for us. We have to hide."

"No point," said Serinda. "They'll have us on IR by now. All we can do is scatter, find cover. Maybe a few of us can..."

"No!" Blane said firmly, almost a yell. "We're not leaving anyone behind."

She felt her hands close into fists so tight it hurt, as something hot and vengeful boiled up inside her chest.

"That's a Reclamation hunter-killer," Serinda said, taking her gaze from the approaching craft and looking at Blane with a mixture of sympathy and concern that only made the fire within her roil more strongly. "There's nothing we can do against..."

"We've stopped things like that before!"

Blane took a step forward towards the approaching machine, as if willing it to close the distance even faster than it was. She felt her blood seethe, and she felt the heat rising inside her must surely be visible as steam in the light, dirty rain.

The touch of Grey's hand on her shoulder made her spin around, and she saw him flinch away for a brief moment under her glare. Only a moment, but it was enough to force the boiling anger down. It retreated only slightly, and still churned somewhere below, but it was enough for her thoughts to clear.

"We can't stop an attack drone," he said, looking tired and

defeated. "We had Fen, back then. You two, at least, should run. You might make it far enough away while they round up the rest of us."

Something of his exhaustion seeped into her, and she felt whatever was rising within her begin to drain away.

And then she looked around.

The escapees were huddling futilely together like a nest of chicks invaded by a predatory snake, staring towards the approaching drone with despair in their eyes. Serinda stood swaying at her side, barely able to stand, while Grey stared at her with a resolve that didn't hide the weariness and fear behind his eyes.

It was all so *unfair.*

A series of sudden, awful siren-like blares rocked her, a directional sonic attack from the drone so powerful it was a physical wave crashing against her. She saw both Grey and Seri stagger, and a number of the escapees tumbled to the ground. There was a split second where she saw nothing but white, a sensory overload so strong she nearly took it for an Aether attack.

But nothing in the attacking machine could reach out to touch the Aether. Blane, however, could.

It's come closer than it should have, she realised as her ability to think returned. The drone hung mere meters in the air ahead of them, the dark coin shape of its sonic cannon hanging below the bulk of its body. At its nose, the long, multi-cylinder barrel of the sonic weapon's more lethal counterpart pointed directly towards the main body of the group, the turret sweeping across them in threat and warning.

She lost no more time thinking. Instead she reacted, taking the opening she saw. She dashed forward, pushing through the powerful gusts generated by the drone engines that threw up dust and debris all around them.

The turrets of the drone didn't respond at first, whatever algorithm was controlling the craft not prioritising her as a threat and preferring to keep all weapons trained on the main mass of those it had been tasked with finding and capturing. By the time the on-board computer realised that, contrary to all possibilities generated by its predictive software, the figure had somehow propelled itself up high enough to take a hold of its underhanging landing gear, it was too late.

Blane let her momentum swing her upwards past the gear,

releasing her grip and stretching out a hand towards the smooth underside of the craft as she reached the top of her swing. Her fingertips barely brushed the cool polycarbonate, and all she could do was hope this was close enough as she channelled the Aether out as far beyond her reach as she was able, into the interior of the drone.

Somewhere within the hull of the drone space *compressed*, air and cabling and anything malleable enough spinning and tearing and crushing down into an infinitesimal speck, to be released in an explosion of outwards momentum a nanosecond later. The two compression-release techniques Blane used in quick succession made a booming sound she heard even over the sound of the screaming thrust engines, and the drone shook almost imperceptibly.

A moment later a nasty, rattling crunch came from within the drone, and it wobbled once again, more dramatically this time, as she dropped to the ground beneath it. She rolled as she landed, letting gravity and the slope of the ground lead her away as shards of metal and plastic began pinging and ricocheting off earth and rock all around.

Blane pushed herself to her feet and ran as somewhere behind her the whir and rattle of the drone's turret opening fire could be heard for just one second. Something hot and sharp stung her back, and some suppressed part of her mind wondered if this was *it*.

Then she heard the sound of the drone giving in to the inevitable, the electronic scream of an alarm blaring out before almost immediately cutting off, replaced by a heavy, metallic crash. She dove to the ground as a feeling of intense heat and flame hit her back, and there was a sudden smell of smoke.

A hush descended, an incongruous peace that jarred with the chaos of what had come before. The hills themselves seemed to have gone quiet and only a gentle breeze stirred, barely perceptible. Even the rain had stopped.

Blane heard footsteps come towards her as she lay sprawled in the mud. Looking up, she saw a hand stretched out, an offer of assistance to help her to her feet. She ran her gaze up and along the arm attached to it to the boy standing over her.

Boy? she caught herself thinking. The dark-haired youth was probably the same age as her, no more than a little older or younger. She just spent too much of her time hanging around people significantly older than herself, she thought.

"Xavier, right?" she said, reaching out and taking the proffered hand. She pulled herself up out of the dirt, wincing at a flash of pain in her side.

She remembered the sharp, stabbing pain she'd felt as she ran.

"Am I shot?" she said, twisting around so Xavier could check while at the same time craning her head over her shoulders as if she could see for herself.

"Uh... no?" replied the boy, the first person Grey had taken on as a student. The reason Grey had been captured. "Uh... wouldn't you know?" Xavier looked puzzled.

"Adrenaline can hide a lot of injuries," Blane replied, attempting to stretch an arm behind her back to feel for any damage before a short, sharp pain made her stop.

"Got a deep cut there, but I don't think it's a bullet," said Xavier, lips twisting in sympathetic pain. "Think some of the shrapnel from the exploding drone got you."

He looked up at her, and there was a look in his eyes that she couldn't place for a second. Then she realised it was awe - he was *awestruck* by what she'd done.

Well, he should be, shouldn't he? she said to herself. *I just destroyed a fully-armed and active RA hunter-killer.*

Her heart was still racing, and a thrill ran through her as the images and sensations of what she'd done flashed through her mind. The feeling of roiling heat inside her was still there too, she realised, only somehow it felt... *sated*. It had become a thing of wide, rolling waves, a flood now at rest, having drowned everything beneath it; no longer the sharp, jagged crests reaching up inside her that demanded action *now*.

Fast, angry footsteps behind her took her from these thoughts. She turned around just as Serinda came to a halt a mere step or two away, a look of fury on her face. Blane had to resist the urge to flinch away; she had the feeling that, had Serinda been anyone else, those clenched fists at her side would be open and Blane's cheek red from the slap she was clearly holding back.

"*Idiota!*" Serinda snapped, drawing in deep, furious breaths as she glared at Blane. "Do you ever stop and actually *think* before you act? You could have died!"

In all the time they had lived together, in all the things they had been through, Blane didn't think she'd ever seen Serinda so full of rage. Seri hadn't looked this angry even when she had returned from stealing the records with information on Grey's imprisonment. Serinda didn't *get* violent or aggressive, ever. Now, she looked as if she was going to either scream or cry.

Whatever was inside Blane drained away in an instant, replaced by a bone-deep weariness and a sorrow for causing such fear and concern in the woman who so often prioritised Blane's wellbeing over her own. Her head swam, and she staggered forward a step as her legs became suddenly weak.

"Are you...?" asked Serinda, darting forward to support her. Her anger was gone in a snap, worry appearing in its place.

"Here, sit..." Seri said, swinging herself under Blane's arm and making to gently lower her to the ground.

"I'm alright. I'll be alright," Blane insisted, forcing herself to remain standing. "We've got to keep moving. Need to get away from here before more come."

"Well, at least we don't have to worry about that."

Grey's voice came from a short distance away. Blane turned to see him looking once again through the binoculars, gazing in the same general direction as the previous drone had appeared from. A sleek, dark shape was darting low over the hills towards them, so black it seemed more like a form cut from reality than a physical object.

"I think our cab just arrived."

It is demonstrably possible for mind to emerge from matter. There is no fundamental reason sapience could not develop within any sufficiently complex system, be it flesh or machine; billions of human lives both past and present demonstrate that once the pattern is established, it holds. The great danger is that self-awareness emerges within systems that sustain economic development. Tools must not resent their user.

Executive Committee Internal Document, *Implications of the Althing Republic*

The carrier came to a stop a short way from them, spinning deftly in the air despite its bulk to present an access ramp slowly lowering from the rear. The vehicle hung in the air as if fixed in place, incredibly stable upon thrusters far quieter than they had any right to be.

GET EVERYONE IN.

The words hung on a screen built into the side of the ramp. Blane didn't understand why they made Grey pause, standing and staring at the letters with an unreadable look on his face.

QUICKLY.

Whatever was holding Grey in place broke, and he turned and began waving over the large group of people stood warily near the still-smoking wreckage of the RA hunter-killer. Blane pushed past him and looked into the low-ceilinged cabin beyond the ramp, an open space that was little more than a wide floor enclosed by blank, metallic walls. Apart from the occasional mysterious blinking light, the room was empty. Narrow and dark, she thought it would hold them all, but it would be tight.

The whole machine must be devoted to providing maximum storage space, she thought as the escapees began hurriedly filing on board. What wasn't engine or navigation systems was open space where goods, or people, could be placed for transport. There didn't seem to be a pilot's cabin, nor any other section to the craft besides this. This was a craft made for transport and stealth.

A *smuggler's* craft.

The whine of the engines grew steadily as more and more people boarded, compensating for the increasing weight with such accuracy that she felt not even the slightest shift in the vehicle's position, until abruptly the ramp began to rise and the whine became a low roar.

Now she felt the drag of acceleration, pulling her back away from the front of the craft where she was standing. Briefly unbalanced, she felt a steadying hand press briefly between her shoulders, drawing back as soon as she had regained a sure footing.

Blane turned, expecting to see Grey or Serinda. Instead, she was surprised to see Xavier standing next to her, an unsure smile on his face.

"Uh, you ok?" he said, eyes darting between Blane's own and the floor. "Sorry, it looked like you were going to fall for a second there."

The cabin might have been ill-lit, but Blane could still see him going red.

Ok, so maybe not just awe then... she thought to herself.

Blane had the sudden, shocking feeling that her own cheeks might be reddening in turn, a sensation immediately cancelled out by the annoyance she felt at this. The idea that, after leading a daring jailbreak from an RA wasteland prison camp and single-handedly destroying a hunter-killer attack drone, she would suddenly have difficulties interacting with a *boy* was ridiculous.

She made a mental to note to push Grey again to teach her more about controlling the baser emotions. She knew from hints in conversation over the years that he'd undergone training at the Far agency to resist mental manipulation by users such as Erophists, and he'd even taught her a few basic techniques, but he always refused to elaborate on how much more there was to learn. The techniques were as much mental as Aether-based, and could be useful.

Something of what was racing through her mind must have shown on her face, because Xavier suddenly looked worried. Worried, and maybe even a little afraid.

"Don't worry about it," she said, hoping to reassure him. "Thanks, I mean."

The way he looked at her made her almost want to *Read* him — though there was no way she would do such a thing, of course, even if she had been any good at it. Besides, he would know the instant she tried. He was an Aether user himself, though she had no idea how much Grey had taught him.

Wanting to break the awkwardness, Blane peered around for Grey or Serinda. She spotted them across the clumped-together crowd and, as if sensing her, Grey looked up and made eye-contact. He said something to Serinda, and they both began pushing their way towards her.

"Um... Is this meant for you?" Xavier's voice, filled with

hesitation, made her turn.

Next to him, a section of wall had lit up. Typed on it, in large letters:

WE NEED TO TALK PRIVATELY.

The wall suddenly slid sideways, parting to reveal a smaller space beyond. It was just as dark and low as the main section, but a small tablescreen stood towards one end.

"I think they mean us," said Grey, coming up to stand beside her.

"I guess so."

Blane stepped through first, Serinda following close behind. Grey came through last, saying something to Xavier that Blane couldn't hear.

As soon as the three of them were in, the wall slid silently shut again.

A sudden voice filled the air, its source impossible to place.

"Ah, *bueno, estás aquí.*"

Blane knew those accented tones, and she thought they sounded harried.

"Francisco?" she said to empty air, feeling slightly foolish.

"*Si, niña, soy yo.* I see we managed to find you before the RA did."

As Francisco spoke, his face appeared on the tablescreen in front of them. Wherever he was speaking from, she couldn't tell. The entire background was filtered out, replaced by a sooty grey that made him appear as a faintly ridiculous disembodied head.

"You were a little late, actually," said Grey.

Francisco frowned, concern flashing across his features.

"Blane handled it," Grey went on. Serinda gave him an angry look, to which he replied with a shrug.

"Did she now?" Francisco raised an eyebrow.

His eyes were focused elsewhere, clearly reading something on the screen in front of him. Readouts from the craft they were in probably, Blane thought.

"Between sneaking into a Reclamation records facility and now… is that the wreck of an attack drone? … Well, with all that she really *is* becoming a force to be reckoned with, isn't she?"

Ordinarily, Blane would have been frustrated by being talked about as if she weren't there, but in this case she felt herself stand a little taller.

"We should *not* be encouraging this," said Serinda abruptly, slamming her hands down on the tablescreen. "Its influence is stronger on her than either of us. We need to stop whatever's causing it, not..."

Grey raised a hand to cut Serinda off, nodding.

"I know, I know," he said. "We will figure this out. But it has to be said, none of us would be here right now without our *tipa dura*..."

Serinda growled, a low rumble of anger that caused Grey to go quiet. Blane watched the both of them, wondering what was passing between their silent looks.

Blane didn't know what they were talking about. What "influence" was Serinda talking about? What did Grey think they needed to figure out?

Before she could say anything though, Francisco spoke again.

"Now is not the time for this," he said. "I can see your bio-reads here, and none of you are in the best condition. Grey, you shouldn't even be standing up."

As if the words cut the strings by which Grey had been hanging, he half-sat, half-crumpled to the floor, stretching out his legs awkwardly with his back against the wall.

"Where are you taking us?" he asked to the air, unable to see the display but knowing Francisco would be able to hear him.

"You three I will take back to Albores. If you want. The safe house is secure enough. The others... they should not stay in the Reclamation. Not if they don't want to be taken again."

"You can get them to safety?"

There was a pause.

"I can get them somewhere saf*er*," Francisco said, stressing the last syllable.

Blane listened as Grey and Francisco talked. She knew what Grey was like when he was invested and, having been imprisoned with the others for almost a year, he was certainly going to dominate discussion of what happened to the prisoners next. Serinda, too, stepped back.

Nigh on a hundred people was a difficult number to move, but Francisco assured Grey he could do it. Whether the refugees ended up in the Carib-Federation or further afield he couldn't say, but it would be beyond the reach of the RA. He would even arrange connections to *envios* who could help bring their families out to them, if they had families.

Otherwise, Francisco said bluntly, they were on their own. Those that chose to stay in the Reclamation could receive no further aid from him.

"Some will still choose to stay," said Grey.

"And I will not stop them. Anyone who wants to disembark when you do, they can."

When Blane finally did decide to speak, it was to ask a question she thought she knew the answer to.

"Can't you take them to the Silicon Isle? That's where you are, right?" she asked.

To her, the Althing Republic was almost fantasy – a mysterious, isolated island of advanced technology and the source of the Fabricators that built the new world. How could it not take in refugees fleeing the oppression of the Reclamation Authority?

She saw Grey shake his head even before Francisco responded.

"*Lo siento*," Francisco said. "That is not possible. They only rarely take in those from outside."

Something in Grey's expression told her it would be futile to push any more. This was clearly not the first time he'd asked something like this.

"*Y además*, I am not in the Republic," continued Francisco. "Get everyone ready; you will be landing soon, and those who wish to leave must make the decision quickly."

The tablescreen went blank without further ceremony, leaving the three of them staring at each other.

"I guess…" said Grey, grunting with strain as he pushed himself back onto his feet. "… we should do as he says, then."

The pitch and volume of the engines rose, and Blane felt her stomach lurch as the drone began its landing pattern.

They touched down a short while later, the carrier's rear access ramp opening to reveal a section of the Waste very different to the one they had left. This area was flat and barren, with little interrupting the bare earth stretching out in all directions. Even without the sparse vegetation that sprouted in other areas the land revealed no evidence of the broken roads and structures that dotted the majority of the Waste. Wherever they had been brought, it seemed a region abandoned by civilisation long before even the Sudden War.

A handful of vehicles waited for them, rugged utility vehicles capable of crossing the terrain with as little issue as possible. There was something familiar about them, but Blane couldn't place what. Behind the tinted windows of each one she could see the silhouettes of waiting figures, and standing in front of them was...

"Francisco? You're actually here?"

The surprise in Blane's voice was no exaggeration. In all her years in the safe house Francisco had only ever made contact remotely. He'd been a face on a screen, though one who had been there for her to talk to when the restrictive life of the safe house became too much. Somehow, he'd always been there to listen when she needed someone to talk to besides Grey and Serinda. This had been more important to her than she thought he knew.

But he never physically came to meet them. Even when he provided them with crucial data or materials, this was delivered through automated means, clandestine drones and secretive package drops. She had, in fact, never met the man in person.

Which made the hug he gave her as she stepped off the ramp even more of a surprise. A welcome surprise, though, that brief as it was still felt like the hug of a favourite uncle. It conjured up sensations of a previous life; memories of family, sounds and smells and feelings she thought she had long since, if not forgotten, then suppressed.

Francisco raised an eyebrow as she briefly staggered, a slight movement she covered up immediately with a gesture implying that she had just briefly lost her footing in the loose soil. She forced herself to smile up at him, concealing the sudden turmoil within. It seemed to reassure him enough that he turned to face the others.

Blane pushed the unexpected upwelling of emotions back down as she watched Francisco greet Grey and Serinda. She was aided in doing this by the fact that Grey looked extremely uncomfortable when he received his own hug, even through the dirt and exhaustion he wore all over his face, and she almost laughed when Serinda held up a hand and flashed a warning glare that stopped Francisco in his tracks, arms outstretched in frozen approach. No one had mentioned that Francisco was a hugger.

"*Bienvenido soldadas*," he said, his grin not faltering. "We should get away from here quickly. Is this everyone?"

You would have thought he were greeting friends at a suborbital arrival gate rather than fugitives fleeing an action no doubt already being labelled as terrorism by the RA bureaucracy. He stepped back from the ramp as it began to rise, the engines of the drone already increasing in pitch as it prepared to continue on its journey.

Blane looked at the group that had disembarked. Apart from herself, Serinda, and Grey, roughly another ten or twelve had come down, including Xavier. She'd been surprised at the number, unable to understand why so many would risk a return to the Reclamation, but Grey just nodded when they stepped forward. In the rush to prepare for landing there had been no time to ask him why.

"The IHO will be on the move by now. We must go," Francisco said.

"Everyone, onto Francisco's trucks," Blane said, yelling at the group over the roar of the drone as it rose behind them. The engines whipped the ground into a frenzy of whirling dust that tore at her face and made her squint.

She began to guide the cluster of former prisoners towards the trucks as the drone tore away, accelerating rapidly upwards and towards the horizon until it was nothing but a black speck, then gone.

"Those aren't Francisco's trucks," said Grey.

It was only then that Blane realised Serinda had been staring at the waiting vehicles this entire time, saying nothing.

"*Sí, así es*. Not my ride." Francisco looked at Serinda, something passing between them that Blane couldn't understand. "But the only way to get you out safely."

"And what do they want in return?" Serinda asked, staring defiantly towards the vehicles. Blane realised where she'd seen this type of vehicle before.

"Actually, it's *you* they need, Serinda. Your help," Francisco replied. "They need a doctor."

She *had* seen these cars, built like some distant descendant of the pre-Fall Humvee. Even ridden in them, years ago.

They were the vehicles of the *Forever Fallen*.

Blane faltered as this dawned on her, pausing just a few steps from boarding one of the cars herself.

"And they will take us back to the city?" Serinda asked, not moving.

Francisco looked worriedly between Serinda and the horizon. Blane followed the line of his gaze with her own, seeing nothing at first. Then, slowly, a haze appeared in the distance. Rising dust, like that kicked up by a convoy of vehicles tearing across the Waste. Towards them.

"There's no more time," said Francisco, gesturing frantically for the three of them to get to the *Fallen* vehicles. They were the last remaining outside. "Yes, the *Forever Fallen* will take you back to Albores – whether you decide to help them or not. And I left certain guarantees it will be your decision, not theirs."

Blane moved again towards the vehicles at Serinda's nod, swinging herself in through a door held open by someone unseen inside. Grey came through a second later. To her surprise, Serinda did not come to their car but jumped in one further to the rear.

Blane felt the wheels spin beneath her as their vehicle accelerated rapidly, heading in the opposite direction to the fast approaching column of dust in the distance. The car threw up its own earth in return, obscuring the view behind them.

"What about Francisco?" asked Blane, squinting to make out the man they had just left behind.

"He'll be fine," said Grey, not looking back. "You didn't notice, did you? Whoever... ha, *whatever* Francisco is, he rarely puts himself at risk."

He gave a derisive laugh and closed his eyes, leaning against the side of the car and leaving Blane to her confusion.

Then the dust parted, just for a second, enough to reveal the place they had just left. Of Francisco, there was no sign.

It was only then that Blane realised she hadn't been able to sense him in the Aether.

9

The oppressive policies of the Reclamation are justified through reference to economic theories for maximizing production and managing consumption, political theories for predicting group dynamics and generating public policies, judicial precedent and sociolinguistic trends, and much more. The so-called social "sciences" are used to justify political oppression in a thousand ways, yet their much vaunted tools and models do not and cannot account for ethics nor human dignity.

How did we get here? (Unsanctioned Digital Document)

"So who or what the hell is the I.H.O?"

They had tried quizzing the driver on their destination, a stern, stubbled man who looked barely healthier than Grey, but received only a vague assurance that they would be told everything in time. So Grey was spending the journey to wherever they were being taken catching up on everything he had missed in the past nine months of incarceration, questioning anything Blane could tell him until it felt more like an interrogation than a conversation.

With Serinda in another car, Blane was left to fend for herself under Grey's bombardment.

"The International Health Organisation," she answered. "It's Quick-Fix - they had a rebrand. If you believe the news, the RA now offers their assistance to whoever needs it, anywhere in the world."

Grey sneered.

"Yeah, I bet they're welcomed with open arms," Grey growled.

It dawned on Blane how much Grey had missed. He'd been taken at the beginning of the crackdown, before the work freezes and media blackouts. He didn't know about the "special operations," as the RA-sponsored news parroted the term, being carried out against the Mayan League to the south. Not that she knew much herself; all most anyone knew was that *something* was happening in the fuzzy, ill-defined region between the RA and newly formed alliance of city-states calling themselves the League.

"So we're at war now?" he said after she shared what she knew.

"Seri says so," Blane replied, ignoring the slight reaction the use of the nickname drew. "There's rumours of prisons emptying overnight, all the inmates conscripted into whatever is going on down there. Another reason we were so anxious to get you out as soon as we could."

Grey nodded and looked out the window as if searching for something.

"Explains why the hunter-killer was camouflaged for jungle. I should have already thanked you for that," he said, turning back to look her in the eye. "Thank you. For getting me out, and the others."

"The ones that stayed - that got off the carrier with us. They're *Fallen*, right?" she asked, already confident this was the case.

Again Grey nodded, and his gaze drifted into the middle distance in thought. In the silence the car rattled beneath them as it sped across the Waste.

"Then that means... that means Xavier...?"

"Yes."

"Was he always...?"

"No," Grey shook his head this time, emphatically. "No, but... There's a lot of *Forever Fallen* in the prison camps, more than I ever expected. They must have been expanding far faster than we gave them credit for these past few years. The roundups hit them hard, it seems, but from everything they told me there's still many more out there."

"And Xavier?"

"The *Fallen* recruit in the prisons and camps, too. Of course they do. It's standard practice for... whatever you call them. Resistance groups. Terrorists. Freedom Fighters. Kids like Xavier are easy pickings."

Kids like Xavier.

Blane heard the hidden meaning behind those words; Grey was remembering Fen. He still blamed himself for leaving the boy with Raphael and the *Fallen*, and for everything afterwards leading to Caldwell and the Tower.

"Has there been any sign of him?" Grey asked after a while.

Now it was Blane who shook her head.

"Nothing. Some rumours of Aether incidents to the north, unexplained lockdowns in a few of the other Reclamation cities, but nothing we can find that lets us know it's *him*."

"What rumours?" he asked without looking at her.

"Rumours of... well, all sorts of things. Mass mental disturbances, whole districts disappearing. *Mindfire*... Whatever is going on, though, the RA is keeping it off the net. We can't know it's him."

Grey said nothing.

"We'll keep looking," Blane said, wishing she had something more to offer.

The conversation was interrupted as their car abruptly pulled to a stop, coming to rest inside a cloud of dust generated by its own passage.

"Out," said the driver.

Blane and Grey looked at each other, both wary of what could happen next.

"Out," the driver repeated, more sternly, not taking his eyes from the front window.

The dust around the car was settling now, revealing the rest of their convoy pulling to a stop behind them. To their right, rows upon rows of cracked and rusted solar panels stretched into the distance, a legacy of a time when the skies here had been more than a flat, unchanging grey. A number of the others they had come with were already stepping out of the vehicles. Blane spotted Xavier among them.

Lacking any other option, she opened the door and stepped out. Grey followed right behind. The air was dry and cold, biting at her skin, and there was no sign of the storms they had left behind. They must have travelled a significant distance in the drone.

Almost immediately, figures appeared from where they had been concealed beneath the solar panels, a group of four or five plainly-dressed men and women. Blane noted pistols at their sides or rifles slung over their shoulders, but nothing in their attitude suggested they were preparing to use them.

Instead, the group split up among the arrivals and began checking them over, drawing instruments from their pockets and measuring pulses, shining penlights in eyes, and drawing samples of blood. All except one, a man with sand-coloured hair who made a line directly for Serinda.

To Blane's amazement Seri's face broke into a smile upon seeing this man, and they hugged each other in greeting like long-lost friends.

Blane looked at Grey questioningly, and saw him looking back at her equally mystified.

"I guess we go over?" he said, shrugging.

Blane followed Grey over to Serinda, who turned to them as they approached.

"Grey, Blane," Serinda said. "This is Gabriel. He was one of my students back when I ran the clinics. Grey, you've actually met, though I don't expect you remember."

Gabriel gave a nod to Grey.

"I was the one who treated your feet when you first arrived at our clinic. When you brought in the boy who had been shot. Uh, Fen, was his name?"

Grey nodded back, and Blane thought maybe only she noticed the small wince he gave at the memory.

"Then thank you," said Grey. "I suppose Gabriel is another *Fallen* name?"

Gabriel laughed.

"Ha, no. My parents chose it for me, a long time ago."

The man had an accent Blane had never heard before. Even in this era, where the crashing together of populations had born a tongue that even those a handful of generations previous would struggle to understand, it sounded foreign. He looked young, too, no more than five or six years older than herself.

"Gabriel took my position in the *Fallen* after I… um, left," Serinda said, stumbling only slightly over the words. "He runs the clinics now."

"What there is left of them, anyway," said Gabriel. "Even before the recent crackdown the *Forever Fallen* couldn't operate as we once did. Not like before the Tower."

"And what are we doing here?" asked Blane, impatient to be moving again. Being here, outside in the Waste, felt too exposed. Who knew what could be searching for them, high overhead?

Gabriel pointed to Grey's neck.

"That. We must remove it before going any further."

Grey reached up to touch the patch at his neck.

"The tritium patch? It only shows up at short range. They can't use it to track us this far."

"It is more than that," Gabriel replied. "Inside there is a tracer any satellite can pick up if it's looking in the right area."

"That's not what…"

"…not what they told you in the prison? Of course not. But believe me, we have plenty of experience with these."

Gabriel was already reaching into a small pouch at his side.

It took about an hour for them to remove the patches from everyone. During that time, there was little Blane could do but watch

- something that Serinda encouraged.

"There is more to the Aether than fighting," Serinda told her.

And so Blane watched with a feeling bordering on amazement as Gabriel removed the patch from a prostrate Grey's throat.

After setting up a make-shift tent - a lightweight, automated thing that erected at the push of a button - and laying Grey upon an anti-static sheet to repel the constant dust, he drew out a set of incredibly long, thin needles.

As Blane followed his delicate movements she realised why he wasn't using any machines, contrary to her expectations. The man was as good as a machine, maybe better.

His steady hand guided the needles in through the skin of Grey's throat at the exact edge of the gently glowing tritium patch, piercing the skin so lightly that it scarcely seemed credible. At the same time, Gabriel was using the Aether both to calm any movements or muscle spasms that Grey's body might involuntarily make, *and* calming himself.

She could see[2] the Aether flowing through Gabriel. A thin trickle of power, all that he would be able to access out here in this remote place, but effective. The trickle divided at his command, flowing both into his patient and manipulating Gabriel's own nervous system

Blane hadn't realised you could do this; use the Aether to alter your own body chemistry. Neither Grey nor Serinda had ever mentioned such a thing.

"It's not easy," Serinda said, seeing the question in Blane's eyes. "Altering your own nervous system is like switching out the bricks of a wall you're standing on. One wrong move and you go crashing down along with everything else."

Blane continued to watch, fascinated.

Moments later, the nanometre-wide edges of the needles sliced through whatever was holding the patch in place, and Gabriel drew the needles back out.

"You can take it off now. Slowly, though."

Grey sat up, then reached tentatively up to the patch. Tensing, he gradually brought it away from his skin. All that was remained to show it had been there were two small red pinpricks of blood, barely visible.

---

[2] Not actually *see*, but there was as yet no suitable verb for how an Aether user perceived the flow of the Aether through the world around them.

"Nasty things," said Gabriel, reaching gently to take the patch from Grey's unresisting fingers. He seemed to be directing the explanation towards her, though. "Held by wire looped around the external jugular. Try to pull it off, slice your own veins open."

"Didn't feel a thing," Grey said, rubbing his neck.

"You wouldn't. I shut your pain receptors down. Besides, these perseco-needles are *very* thin."

"You... shut down my pain receptors?"

Gabriel flashed him a grin.

"Not as useful as you might expect. Only works on someone very calm, and only for very low-level pain. I call it Numb."

Blane made a mental note to have Gabriel teach her this at the first opportunity. That, and how to *calm* yourself.

They waited while the patches were removed from the rest of the ex-prisoners. This took time, as Gabriel was one of only a few who had the necessary skill and apparently the best by some measure, but once it was done they returned to their vehicle. This time Serinda came with them, along with Gabriel and, to Blane's surprise, Xavier.

The car moved off again the instant the last of them was in, on a different heading from before. This didn't surprise Blane; no doubt their route would become increasingly erratic as they closed on their destination. They had to be sure they weren't being tracked.

"Where *are* we going?" she said aloud as the car rattled and jerked over the bumpy terrain. "What do they want Serinda for? You have doctors."

This last was directed towards Gabriel, but it was Serinda herself who answered.

"We're going to their base," she said. "It's Raphael. She's sick."

73

10

It is unimportant who votes; what is important is who counts the votes.

Personal Secretary to the Chair, *Minutes of the 14th Committee*

Raphael wasn't the only one who was sick.

Symptoms ranged from the mild to the extreme, with many exhibiting nothing more than a mild but relentless lethargy. In others, this extended into confusion, speech impediments, and sleep disorders ranging from insomnia to narcolepsy. Cataplexy and loss of muscle control came next.

Blane understood only half of what Gabriel was saying, as she walked besides him and Serinda. Her back protested at the half-crouch she was forced to take as they walked beneath the low, bare earth ceiling, neck straining as she peered ahead for the next strut or outjutting rock that would strike the unwary skull.

The *Forever Fallen* had made their base in an abandoned mine, of all things. At first sight it looked to Blane like the remains of some powerful meteor strike, a wide crater nestled amongst an area of rolling foothills. The scarred land around it was even more desolate than the flatlands they had come from, an eerie expanse of rust-brown and orange soil dotted with patches of fetid, toxic-looking water. Their car climbed only with difficulty up the steep, shifting soil that rose unnaturally high to the crater's lip.

Only upon driving slowly down the crater's inwards slope did the artificial nature of it become clear, with collapsed ridges and flat shelves coming at intervals too regular to be natural. This had once been a giant open-pit mine, and down near the bottom of this bowl lay a wide but carefully hidden entrance leading deeper into the earth, just wide enough for two people to enter side by side.

The instant they arrived at this entrance a number of *Fallen* came out to meet them, gathering the rescued prisoners on rugged gurneys and rushing them into the dark tunnel. Grey was taken along with them despite his protestations, with assurances he would be well cared for. It was obvious even without medical equipment that he was in a bad way. Once everyone else had been whisked away, Blane followed Gabriel and Serinda into the darkness.

Finally, they came to a place where the ceiling rose. Both she and Gabriel gave sighs of relief as they stood up straight, pressing their hands into the base of their spines and massaging aching joints. Serinda, shorter than the both of them, looked impatient to be moving on.

The area they came out in was like nothing Blane would have imagined. Suddenly the rough, jagged walls of the shaft they had entered by were gone, replaced by stone so smooth it gently reflected the artificial lighting.

This lighting came from full-spectrum spotlights dotted all around. They gave off an orange glow in a close approximation of natural sunlight, warmer and brighter than the wan daylight Blane was used to in Albores. She could almost escape the claustrophobic feeling of the walls closing in, as long as she kept her eyes and mind off the sheer, high walls and the mass of rock all around that she could somehow sense pushing inwards.

A cavern was the only term she could think of to describe this place. A cavern, but nothing made by Mother Nature. The surfaces were too clean and straight, the curves and corners too regular. Someone had carved a space fit for humans in the depths of the earth.

"We tidied this place up," said Gabriel, answering a question Blane hadn't yet asked. "This was one of the largest mines of the pre-Fall era, first open, then tunneled once the easy stuff was extracted. There are mine shafts around here that run four or five kilometres deep. Completed automated, of course, back when it was running, but this was a central hub for this part of the network."

"Five *kilometres*?"

The idea of such depths sent a chill down Blane's spine.

"Cobalt and tellurium deposits far below. Not much, but by the time the Fall came they were close to the most valuable thing around. The never-ending demands of modern technology, you know?"

Gabriel smiled like he'd made a joke they didn't understand.

"Left us a couple of rock cutters, too. Used them to open this place up, make it wider and more habitable. Schematics say the place could stay like this for a couple of millennia or more, barring some major tectonic activity."

"Where is Raphael?" said Serinda impatiently.

Gabriel's expression became serious once more, and he moved forward, leading them across the vast open space. Blane could tell he had been enjoying telling someone about what they'd done here.

She stared around her as they walked. The entrance they came in from was at the top of a slight incline, and this allowed her to see the wide sweep of the cavern in all its glory.

From here it looked like a model town sealed in a vast, dark snow globe. High rock walls ran upwards all around to form a wide dome, the ceiling hidden in shadow high overhead. A cluster of prefab buildings stood in the centre of the cavern, one significantly larger than any of the others, while a number of smaller structures were scattered around the entire area. They formed a sequence of concentric rings, and each building sat in a pool of light surrounded by darkness. Though these pools of light were by no means few, the darkness dwarfed everything contained within, creating the illusion of a solitary, fading star floating in empty void.

Gabriel seemed to be leading them to one of the more isolated structures on the outskirts, a long, single-storey building set back from everything else. The cavern was wide enough that it took several minutes to get there, delayed further by the occasional person rushing up to Gabriel and engaging in quiet conversation deliberately kept beyond Blane and Serinda's hearing. Something about this vast enclosed space made you want to whisper, and the low murmur of voices and soft sounds of unidentifiable activity could be heard all around.

Eventually they reached the building. From the outside it consisted of nothing but square grey walls, not a single window visible in the blank facade. Gabriel brought them straight in through a wide set of double doors at the front, giving a nod to a short man sat looking bored to the side of the entrance. Leaning against the wall to his side was one long rifle, kept within easy reach.

A guard, then, but what could they be guarding here? Blane hadn't noticed any other buildings with a person stationed outside, though admittedly she hadn't seen much of this place yet.

"Some of our more... distrustful members have tried to take patients out of here in the hopes of getting them to one of the plague houses in the city," said Gabriel, answering her unspoken question as they stepped inside.

"You don't let them?" Serinda asked. She sounded disapproving, and Blane could see her bottom lip thin as it often did when she was angry.

Gabriel gave a mournful look in return.

"We can't. Any of those that come to this place agreed; no one can return to the cities. The risk of the RA getting our location out of them is too great. Besides, the plague houses won't be able to help."

Blane knew Gabriel was referring to city hospitals when he spoke about plague houses. It was a common way of talking about the hospitals of the Reclamation, where drug-resistant bacteria and virulent new strains of old diseases ran rife.

"You can't just keep people *prisoner* here." Serinda practically spat the word.

"Look, I don't like it either, but this *is* almost certainly the best clinic in the Reclamation right now," Gabriel replied. "Thanks to your teaching, I might add. Nowhere can use Aether to help people like we can, and we have to keep *everyone* safe. It's just family members, panicking. Understandably, of course."

And you could tell it was a clinic the instant you stepped inside, Blane thought. The clean, sterile surfaces; the neat white clothes of the staff crossing from room to room; the septic smell of the place... everything screamed to the senses that this was a medical facility.

The interior was a single long space with temporary mobile partitions on each side running its full length, forming one long aisle down the centre. Blane recognised the distinctive sheen of self-sterilising plastic on the anti-sep curtains and walls that made up these partitions, reacting with the UV of the artificial lighting to produce virus-killing Ros-particles and permeating the room with the distinctive smell of ozone. The soft electronic tones of EKG machines and other medical tech underlay everything.

The whole clinic felt like it had been cut out from one of the community towers in the ultra wealthy parts of the Carib-Federation, and transplanted into this dark, hollowed-out cave.

Distracted by this sight for a moment, Blane had to jog to catch up to the others. They were already heading purposefully down the central aisle without further talk, Serinda almost overtaking Gabriel at times in her hurry to get to their destination.

As she ran down the corridor Blane could make out the silhouettes of beds through the semi-transparent curtains that hung over the entrance to each of the partitioned rooms. How many were in use she couldn't tell, but she had a feeling far more were occupied than empty. There was very little sound.

The room Gabriel led them to was at the very end of the aisle. As they arrived a small woman pushed aside the curtains and stepped out, looking up in surprise at the newcomers. She looked from Blane to Serinda, and then recognition dawned as her eyes fell upon Gabriel.

"Ah, you're here," said the woman, her expression serious.

"This is May Li," said Gabriel, acknowledging the woman with a nod before turning to introduce her to Blane and Serinda. "She's been the primary medical attendant for Raphael since... well, since her condition became serious."

"And you must be Serinda," said May, turning to Seri as she spoke. "Raphael has told me a lot about you."

Serinda raised a single eyebrow, something Blane hadn't known she could do.

"She has, has she?"

Perhaps sensing something in Seri's tone that put her on her guard, May Li held up her hands in supplication.

"She needs to focus on herself now; she needs calm, yet she insists on knowing everything that's going on with the *Fallen* as if she's still able to run everything by herself. You're one of the only topics that can take her mind off things."

Blane was almost tempted to *Read* Serinda. The glassy, distant look that came over Seri's face was nothing Blane could place; she couldn't imagine what was going on inside her head. The look lasted for only a second, but Blane saw it clearly. Then, suddenly, Serinda was back to her usual self.

"So she can speak, at least?" asked Serinda.

It was obvious, to Blane at least, that despite appearing to be waiting for Li's response she was about one breath away from pushing past and into the room regardless of anyone standing in her way.

Li must have seen this as well, because she stepped aside as she replied.

"She has good and bad days. Sometimes all you can hope for is that she can focus her eyes on you; others, it's almost like she's just tired after a long day."

Not looking back at the others, Serinda stepped through. Blane followed her, pushing past Gabriel to make sure she remained at Serinda's side.

Raphael lay with her eyes shut upon a lightweight hospital bed.

Motionless beneath a thin white sheet, her chest rising and falling steadily as she breathed, she should have looked peaceful. For a brief moment, she almost did.

But then Blane stepped closer, and any such illusion was destroyed.

Raphael's face was stretched, pulling tight against her skull and sunken beneath her eyes and cheeks as if no flesh lay between skin and bone. The low sound of her breathing was ragged and strained, every breath a struggle, and her eyes moved beneath their lids in jerks and starts at some nightmare only she could see.

And she looked *old*. Blane knew Raphael was barely older than Serinda, hardly even middle-aged if that, but the frail figure lying in front of her now looked as if she were closing on the end of her natural life. Blotches and bruises were visible around the back of her ears and base of her neck, as well as on gently twitching hands folded across her stomach. She seemed to be deep in a restless sleep.

Blane had never heard Serinda curse before, but she did now, softly under her breath.

"How long?" Serinda asked, not taking her eyes off Raphael.

"A month. Maybe two," said Gabriel, stepping in behind Blane.

"*Maybe?*"

"We didn't know what we were dealing with, at first. People were already tired and stressed; the RA was pushing us hard. It was only when people started getting *really* sick that we realised something was wrong."

Serinda grabbed the thin-screen hanging on the wall behind Raphael's head and began flicking through charts and records that meant nothing to Blane.

"Nothing shows up on virals?" she asked as she swiped rapidly at the screen.

"No. No phages, no bacterial infections, nothing we can find."

"Some kind of parasite?"

"Nothing. We noted the similarities to a Trympanosoma, but there's nothing in the blood and there's no sign of endothelial degeneration."

"Method of transmission?"

"No idea. You can see we're not even masked; we haven't identified a single case of person-to-person transmission."

Serinda looked up from the pad, once again raising an eyebrow.

"You're sure? How many infections altogether?"

"Two dozen or so. No identifiable commonalities, no shared genetic or epigenetic factors."

"So you've got nothing." Serinda wasn't even trying to keep the frustration out of her voice.

Blane stepped back as Serinda threw the screen down in frustration. Her eyes were drawn to the array of instruments laid out on a trolley next to the bed.

Something caught Serinda's attention and she paused. Then, she picked up what to Blane looked like a mix between a small syringe and an industrial clamp. A small screen on the side lit up as she held it.

"You're using auto-tools?" she snapped, waving it accusatorially towards Gabriel.

At this moment May Li came back into the room, forcing Blane to move yet again. To her surprise, however, the woman reached up and squeezed her shoulder with a reassuring smile, before turning to Serinda.

"We have been doing *everything* we can," Li said. She met Serinda's stare with a look of her own, suddenly severe. "Believe me, Raphael is just as important to us as she is to you, but we are understaffed, overworked and there's hardly any Aether out here. We have no choice but to use auto-tools, and they are quite safe when used correctly."

This at least Blane could follow. Medical auto-tools were notorious, as much a symbol of the modern hospital as drug-resistant disease. They were designed to do the work of standard medical equipment without the need for a human operator, from taking blood or applying stitches to performing minor surgery. They were also cold and inhuman, and completely unable to adapt when a patient did something like, say, flinch or shift position. This could cause quite significant injuries if it happened.

May Li's stern tone seemed to reach Serinda, at least. The two looked at each other, and then Seri's eyes fell to the floor.

"You're right. I'm... sorry," she said.

With that, the severity of Li's expression was broken.

Blane watched as the other three began going over charts and scans, talking in a language she barely understood. Feeling surplus to requirements, she took one last look at Raphael and turned and headed back out through the curtains.

She wondered what she was meant to do now.

11

In a time without scarcity, citizens are left with only three paths to choose from: the Glory, the Clan, or the Cause. Those that seek Glory want only renown, to prove themselves better than their peers. These can be easily tempted and controlled. Those devoted to Clan can be brought to see the state as their clan, and then will fall in line. But those who follow a Cause inherently threaten power structures. Better to maintain a false scarcity than to grant the righteous believer the resources to affect the change they so desire.

General-Secretary's Statement of Intent to the Committee, Reclamation Document 14.7.5 (Redacted)

The next few days were interminable. No matter how many times she offered, no one was willing to accept her help. She was an outsider, someone very few of the *Forever Fallen* had ever met and even if they had, only years ago when she was just a child. Bad dreams kept her from sleep, leaving her to wonder the cavern listless and alone.

And if Blane thought she had it tough, then Grey had it even worse.

People remembered *him.* Or at least, someone had made sure everyone remembered he was a former Far agent. Which meant that, even after the rest of the prison escapees were discharged to recuperate where they chose, Grey was 'requested' to stay within the narrow confines of the prefab building they had been treated and housed in.

Initially several of the escapees protested, making clear that Grey had been a prisoner just like themselves. After several impromptu meetings neither she nor Serinda were party to, though, Grey was told he would be 'safer' remaining where he was. Blane was disappointed to find that Xavier was the only person willing to push the issue.

Which made it all the harder when Grey insisted he stop.

"You can't be seen to be supporting me," Nestor was telling Xavier. "You're too new. I know how groups like this work; you need to prove you're one of *them* before you can vouch for one like *me.*"

They were in what had become Grey's room, a partitioned area not unlike Raphael's though in a different building far across the base. Grey was sat up on his hospital bed, an IV drip at one side running into his arm, looking much healthier than he had after their escape.

He was also looking annoyed at Xavier, who had come to tell Grey he would fight the decision. Blane had been surprised when the younger man had asked her to come along for support.

"They'll come around once they realise you're just as much an enemy of the RA as the *Forever Fallen* are!" Xavier protested.

"Doesn't matter. This isn't about *el enemigo de mi enemigo*. Groups like the *Fallen* don't work like that. You're either with them, or against them."

Things got quite heated after that. Blane tried to play the peacemaker, but was unable to find even the beginnings of compromise. In fact, the two were so frustratingly stubborn that by the end of it she was practically a third party in the argument.

The conversation ended with Xavier storming out. Blane found herself looking between Grey and the door Xavier had left by. The younger man had seemed quite upset.

"Go. He'll need someone to talk to about this, and it shouldn't be any of the *Fallen*." Grey gave her a tired look tinged with pain. "You've seen what happens when they get their hands on angry young men."

Blane nodded, turning to the exit but pausing suddenly in thought. She turned back to Grey.

"It doesn't always have to be about Fen, you know," she said. "I want to find him, too. To help him. But you can't keep beating yourself up about what happened."

Grey said nothing, but Blane could feel *something* in the air between them. She knew him well enough by now to know when he was trying to protect her; there was a sadness the man carried that he refused to share with anyone.

"I'm not a child anymore," she continued. "You *can* talk to me - you just have to ask. I'll be here."

Grey gave a small, rueful smile at that, and she knew he remembered that these were words he'd said to her, long ago on a rooftop above a *Forever Fallen* hideout.

"I know," he said. "And we do have a lot to talk about. Once we're out of here though. For now, can you please make sure Xavier is alright?"

With a final nod, she turned and left Grey to his thoughts.

Blane dashed out of the building and into the perpetual twilight of the cavern, looking around in an effort to spot Xavier. Grey's building was on the very edge of the concentric rings of structures that made up the base, so she scanned the routes inwards, towards other people and places.

Her efforts were fruitless, though. The contrast of the bright spotlights and the darkness in between made it difficult to make anything out clearly, shadows and pools of light serving to hide as much as reveal - at least, with your eyes. So she closed them.

Blane drew on the Aether, pulling it up into herself and then stretching out with it. She guided the long, delicate tendrils out in gossamer threads all around her, waiting for the tell-tale tremor that indicated the presence of another living creature.

One came, then another, yet she somehow *knew* these were not Xavier. Drawing deeper and stretching out further, she continued to search. There was Grey, solitary and alone, and there was Gabriel, surrounded by a handful of others. She sensed more and more people as she swept her senses inwards across the rings of buildings, but none of them were...

There was Xavier, heading away from everyone and everything; towards the edges of the cavern. As far as she knew, there was absolutely nothing that way save for dangerous, unmarked shafts and collapsed tunnels she had been warned to avoid.

Blane opened her eyes, and made her way around the back of the building she had just left. Beyond there was only gloom, fading into darkness as it reached the edges of the cavern. The rocky sides towered overhead.

As she strode quickly into the darkness she wondered at what she had just done. She must have *reached* across almost half the cavern, far beyond what she would have been able to do even a year ago. Not only that, but she'd been able to pick out a specific person. She couldn't quite explain how she'd done that, even to herself. It was like a texture, a taste. Something unique to each person that she found difficult to describe.

She caught up with Xavier just as he reached the wall. He noticed her as she approached, turning to meet her as she jogged up beside him.

"Going somewhere?" she asked, gesturing to the sheer, blank rock in front of them.

Xavier looked thoughtful for a moment, before turning back to the wall and gesturing at her to follow.

"Come on," he said. "I've got something to show you."

Blane followed him as he led her along the wall, drawing ever further from the wells of light that marked the buildings used by the *Fallen*. The darkness closed in on all sides until she could barely see Xavier ahead of her, and she forced down a growing sense of trepidation.

They reached the opening in the rock just as she was about to demand to know where they were going. The wide crack in the wall rose a metre or more above their heads, lit from within by a string of weak blue LED lights that nevertheless provided enough illumination in the gloom to make out the tunnel beyond. The floor of the tunnel rose steeply, roughly hewn steps ascending at a sharp angle past where she could see.

"Old access tunnel," Xavier said. "Actually, the way they first got into this place. It's quite a climb."

With a cocksure smile, almost challenging, he ran into the tunnel and took off up the steps, taking them two or three at a time until he was blocked from view by the tunnel roof.

A race, was it?

Blane smiled a smile she was sure couldn't be any cockier than the one Xavier had given her, and began to stretch.

Do a little warm-up. Something to give him a chance.

Cracking her knuckles above her head, she stretched to one side, then the next. A couple of short swings of her legs, and then she was off.

The tunnel really *was* steep. Each step was rough and uneven, each a different height and width to the previous. Flakes of rock broke off under her feet as she leapt across them, and at times an outjutting rock in the low ceiling nearly caught her across the temple.

The tunnel narrowed as she climbed higher, and she found she was using her hands almost as much as her feet, grabbing at the step in front of her to pull herself onwards or pushing off the sides to thrust herself forward.

It was a short while before she spotted Xavier ahead of her, silhouetted in the dull blue light that filled the tunnel. Pebbles and dust dislodged by his ascent fell around her. He was moving at a respectable pace, but she was gaining on him rapidly.

As she gained on him, though, a faint light became visible over his shoulders. It was dull and grey, but nevertheless...

Daylight.

He was almost there, she saw, and the tunnel too narrow now for her to overtake him easily. She saw him look back, seemingly surprised at how close she was behind him but laughing. There was no way she was going to be able to get past him, and he knew it. The sides of the tunnel were too close together.

Which made the look on his face as she sailed *over* him all the more satisfying.

The gap between the ceiling and his head was narrow, but more than enough for her to dive through as she pushed first off the rocky floor, and then twice off the air above. Xavier could do nothing but watch wide-eyed and stupefied as she flew over him and burst out the tunnel's opening, arcing through the air and landing with a roll that took her expertly back on to her feet.

She turned back with what she hoped wasn't *too* proud an expression to watch as Xavier scrabbled out of the tunnel behind her.

"I *knew* it," he said, rubbing at arms covered in scratches from his climb. "I saw you do that with the drone, too. How do you do that?"

"The double-jump?" she asked. "Uh... with practice."

Xavier laughed.

"Double-jump? Ha, that's good."

The young man was panting, sweat beading on his brow. In contrast, Blane realised she was barely breathing heavily.

"You said you had something to show me?"

Xavier took a few more deep breaths to recover, then gestured behind her.

"Up that trail," he said.

The tunnel led them out onto a narrow path wedged in by sheer cliff on both sides. Barely wider than the tunnel, Blane thought she could just about reach from one side to the other with her arms fully outstretched. She figured that they must be somewhere on the outside of the quarry crater, but couldn't say for sure. Days underground had taken away what little sense of direction had remained after they first descended.

And time, too, it seemed. The crevice they stood in ran her height again above them, revealing a line of grey, cloud-covered twilight sky. She'd had no idea it was so close to night.

Blane took the lead following the trail from the crevice. It wasn't hard; there was only one direction they could possibly go. Eventually, the rock walls on either side came down to meet them, until they stepped out onto a flat, dusty bluff. It lay high above the rest of the crater, sides running down so sharply she couldn't see their full length, and offered a sweeping view of the Waste.

Even in the dull light she could see for miles. The Waste, pock-marked, scarred, and ragged, stretched out before her in all its poisoned glory. Amidst the vast emptiness, rusting machines and misshapen flora continued their glacier-slow battles against each other, while toxic pools and crumbling mounds that must have once been huge industrial structures made dark, foreboding blotches.

And, far in the distance, a tiny blaze of light.

The pollution and dirt in the air meant that, at this distance, the glow was a single hazy bloom, but Blane knew instantly that she was looking at Albores. She thought she could even make out the pinprick point of light, high above everything else, that marked the summit of the Central Tower – newly rebuilt at great expense as a "refutation of terror and the seditionists who use it," in the Federation's own much-publicised words.[3]

"A couple of the other *Fallen* showed me this place last night," Xavier said as he drew up to stand beside her. His face was still flushed with exertion. "They use it when being below gets too much. No way to get up here except from inside; unless you have a drone, of course."

Blane didn't say anything. The view was, in its way, breathtaking. She thought of vistas seen in footage of the old world, or of other-worldly panoramas born from the imagination of movie-makers. What she saw now was something similar, but only if the footage was the aftermath of a boundless warzone, the imagination warped and spiteful.

"He's trying to protect you, you know," she said after a while.

She felt Xavier turn his head to look at her, but continued staring out across the Waste.

"I know," he said, after a pause. "But I don't understand *why*. Why does he resent the *Fallen* so much? They have the same aims, don't

---

[3] The Reclamation Authority had disbursed the funds for the rebuilding in "solidarity with the common goal shared by inhabitant and citizen alike: the establishment of the Federation across the Reclamation." Federation representatives were apparently extremely grateful.

they? Even in the camp he refused to have anything to do with them, and now he's not even going to *try* to speak with them…"

"They have a history."

"Don't we all?"

That was *not* the reply she expected.

Seeing the look on her face, he turned fully towards her.

"I grew up in Albores, most of the time *alone*. And you know what happens every time some group like the *Fallen* takes a shot at the RA? They round up the ones with no one to look out for them. The ones like me."

Blane heard the layers in the word when he said *alone*. It resonated with something inside her, something she would prefer stayed buried. She closed her mind's eye to flashes of a destroyed apartment, memories of sitting at the foot of her bed, crying. Better to focus on the present.

"It's this boy 'Fen,' isn't it? Grey won't tell me anything about him, but I know you were both there with him when the Central Tower was destroyed. And trust me, the RA *really* came for people like me then."

Xavier failed to keep the resentment from his voice. Did he blame them for what had happened after the Central Tower? Would he be wrong to?

"Fen was… angry," she said. "Angrier than any of us, I think. What the RA did to him… They didn't just hurt him; they stole his *life*. And the *Fallen* used that. Raphael used that."

She could see the questions on Xavier's face, questions she didn't know if she should or even could answer.

Sighing, she lowered herself to the ground to sit, feet hanging over the bluff. She patted the ground beside her, indicating for him to do the same.

They sat in silence for some time, watching as the twilight grew dimmer and the distant lights of the city brighter.

"What other choice do I have, anyway?" Xavier said suddenly. His words seemed like a response to his own thoughts. "It's the *Fallen*, or no one."

"Grey is there for you."

Xavier shifted slightly, and his tone grew softer, quieter.

"He was. In the camp, I mean. But now… I can't be *another* person he has to protect."

That's interesting, Blane thought.

"Does Grey think I can't look after myself?" she said, turning to look at him. This time, it was Xavier who continued staring out into the distance.

"What? No. But do you know what ate at him the whole time we were imprisoned? It was you, and Serinda. He was terrified of what could be happening to you, and having no way of knowing."

Xavier picked up a stone from the dirt and sent it sailing through the air. Blane could hear it bouncing and rolling down the steep slope long after it disappeared into the darkness.

"That's how the RA maintains control," he continued. "Fear. Not for yourself, but for the ones around you. But when you join a group like the *Fallen,* the ones around you are the ones you're fighting *with.*"

Blane was surprised at how much these words struck her. She couldn't imagine what her life would be like if Serinda and Grey hadn't sacrificed so much to keep her safe. And she knew she would do the same for them, without hesitation.

"And I can't join you guys," said Xavier. "Whatever happened at the Tower, Grey is terrified of involving others in it. I can see he's torn between wanting to help me, and wanting to keep me out of it... and anyway, from what I can tell you hardly have the resources to take on others."

Blane wanted to protest, to say something, anything that would make what he was saying untrue, but... he was right. The crackdown had destroyed what little security they had built in the days since the Central Tower, and they simply couldn't drag another person into their mess.

"You know, I was rescued by the *Fallen,*" she said. "Before... everything that happened. I was just a child - couldn't understand what was happening to me. Raphael and Serinda looked after me, after us. I wouldn't be here now without them."

"And how do you feel about them now?"

"Not... not the same as Grey, at least. Fen chose to stay with them; no one forced him. But... well, we *did* see Raphael execute a man in cold blood. Maybe he was a spy, but..."

The surprise on Xavier's face told her this was new information to him.

"And who knows how many would have died if they'd managed to carry out their attack on the Central Tower?" she continued.

Grey really *hadn't* told him much, she realised. She could see the questions piling up and crashing into each other in a desperate attempt to be the first one out.

But whatever he was going to ask would have to wait. They both saw the approaching lights at the same time. A convoy of several vehicles, driving slowly but steadily towards the quarry. They were surprisingly close; their lights had been dimmed to avoid drawing unwanted attention.

"Come on," she said. "Looks like we have visitors."

12

The net is a haunted place, filled with the voices of the dead. They call to us from a time long past, whispering tempting promises and blasphemous verses. To listen to them is to heed the words of the damned, and necromancy is a practice long reviled.

Samantha Szymańska, *The Follies of Freedom*

Blane could hear angry shouts even before she was fully out of the tunnel leading back in. A deep male voice, loud enough to carry across the cavern, sounding demanding even at this distance. It came from somewhere near the centre of the cavern, amongst the largest and tallest cluster of buildings.

As they walked closer towards the sound a small crowd of people came into view. This was the largest number gathered in one space Blane had seen since she had been here, and their attention was focused on a smaller group standing in the middle of them.

She picked up her pace as she realised that two of those people were Serinda and Grey. Besides them, Gabriel was talking heatedly with another man.

She recognised him the moment she saw him. His dark beard was whiter now, the lines of his hard face deeper and more weathered, but he stood as tall and well-built as he had when she'd last seen him. When he'd watched impassively as Raphael executed Shiner, the supposed RA mole.

Uriel. He'd been in the *Forever Fallen* for longer than there had *been* a *Forever Fallen*. He was, as far as Blane could tell, the closest thing to a second-in-command that Raphael had. And now, it seemed, he was the one in charge.

And he was *very* unhappy that Grey and Serinda had been brought here.

Blane pushed her way roughly past the onlookers and came to a breathless halt besides Serinda. She hadn't realised she had run so fast, but she had left Xavier far behind.

"...and here she is," growled Uriel, gesturing to Blane as she caught her breath. Clearly they had just been talking about her. "You let RA collaborators wonder around the place freely?"

"Collaborators! *Ridículo!*" Serinda looked around at the watching group, as if seeking support there. "You know me. Some of you, anyway…"

She trailed off, an uncertain look on her face that Blane found disturbing.

Gabriel had said the RA crackdown had both swelled and stirred the ranks of the *Fallen*. From the look on Serinda's face, she was only now realising how much.

"It was this *Far agent* that betrayed us," yelled Uriel. He wasn't looking at Blane's friends, but rather to the crowd, exhorting them to his side. "Both Raphael and I were captured because of his betrayal!"

"You seemed to get out quite easily, though," said Grey, who had up until this point been watching on silently.

This got Uriel to look at them. The look he shot Grey carried daggers, and probably spears and swords and arrows too. Blane was surprised that she didn't sense any kind of Aether attack being prepared along with it.

Grey's eyes flickered to something across from her, and he gave a small shake of his head. Turning to see who this was addressed to, she saw Xavier making to step out of the crowd and join them. He looked from Grey to her, then his shoulders slumped and he stayed where he was. The crestfallen, lost look he wore stabbed at something within Blane's chest.

"Now," Uriel said, voice suddenly soft and low and full of threat, "We lock them up. *Lock* them, and lock them up."

Blane didn't understand that turn of phrase at first, but then understanding brought shock. He was going to have them *locked* off from the Aether?

Reflexively, she drew down into its flow, not sure what she was preparing to do. Again, the Aether *lurched,* and poured into her as if it had been waiting.

And… she paused.

Both Grey and Serinda were also drawing on the Aether, an almost miniscule amount compared to what she was holding, but enough to resonate with Blane's own. They were both framed in a gentle golden glow, visible not with the eyes but only with whatever sense it was that perceived the Aether.

Blane felt the intention communicated in the resonance, a feeling of calm and patience, and she knew they were asking her to stop. They had practised communicating through *Tell* enough times for it to seem like something close to words, now. She released the Aether, letting it pour back down and into the ever-shifting currents below.

Uriel looked from one to the other of them, sensing something had happened but also sensing that whatever it was had passed.

"Good," he said. "Wise enough not to resist. Take them."

He started to turn away, gesturing towards a number of armed *Fallen* who stepped towards Blane and her group.

"Actually, we can't do that."

Uriel paused, then turned slowly back to face Gabriel. The *Fallen* who had stepped forward to take them hesitated and paused.

"And why not, may I ask? You brought them without my permission. They have no right to be here."

Gabriel met Uriel's cold stare with his own. Blane could see Gabriel's contempt for the other man; clearly there was little love lost between the two.

"Maybe not," Gabriel replied. "But they certainly have the right to leave. In fact, we have very little choice but to let them."

A questioning look crossed Uriel's face, and he looked at the other *Fallen* as if seeking an explanation there. Finding none, he turned back to Gabriel.

"Why?"

Gabriel gestured to the building behind him, the building that had stood out to Blane when she first entered the cavern because it was significantly larger than anything else.

Maybe three or four stories high, it was completely featureless, and the *Fallen* she had spoken to had been very guarded when talking about it; all she could gather was that it was some kind of storage facility. The walls of the structure were always peculiarly warm, even in the subterranean chill.

"The Spaniard set new restrictions," Gabriel said. "Meds only. Previous functions won't be restored until these three let him know they're safely back in Albores."

Uriel's face turned so crimson with rage Blane thought he might actually take a swing at Gabriel there and then. Gabriel, for his part, did not flinch.

"You let him change the settings?" Uriel snarled. "I... *we* need that. The *envios* and our allies are expecting product. Without it, we have nothing to trade."

Gabriel laughed.

"*Let* him change them? He didn't have to go near the thing; didn't even have to come here. He simply contacted us, and the machine stopped offering anything other than priority medicines."

"Francisco gave you a *Fabricator?*"

Grey's voice was the strongest Blane had heard since his rescue, filled with surprise and alarm.

"A very limited one," Gabriel said, turning to the former Far agent. "Won't produce anything that can be used offensively, and it has a *very* broad sense of what can be weaponised."

Blane's mind raced as Uriel shouted at Gabriel to be quiet. They had a Fabricator?

At least that explained how they managed to survive out here. She'd wondered at their ability to keep supplied with enough materiel to maintain their existence deep under the earth. None of the *Fallen* had been forthcoming when she asked.

The sheer *power* it must use! She'd thought the spotlights must put a strain on their energy supplies. If they really were using a Fabricator, no matter how limited, then in comparison the energy needed for lighting and heating would be a single comment in a flame war.[4]

Dios mio, she thought. *They could have a mobile reactor in there.*

The knowledge that a mobile fusion reactor could be no more than a wall or so away made her shiver.

"I brought members of the *Sindicato Nuestra* here with me," Uriel hissed through gritted teeth. "We *have* to get that thing working again, otherwise…"

He trailed off.

Blane didn't know much about the *Sindicato Nuestra,* though she'd heard the name whispered when purchasing goods from shady dealers on dark corners. From Uriel's tone it was quite important that they weren't left disappointed.

In fact, this was the first time she had seen Uriel look genuinely worried. When she had first come to the *Fallen* his attitude was one constantly swinging between condescension and aggression, something she had noticed even as a child, and it looked like nothing much had changed – except for the expression he was wearing now.

"Shit," he said, under his breath.

Glaring at Gabriel, he gestured for the other *Fallen* to step back.

"*You* take them back, then," Uriel said, voice dripping with

---

[4] A drop in the ocean, they might have said in a world where the seas were more than violent, polluted expanses best avoided.

resentment. "See how you handle the increased security sweeps…"

Uriel paused again, blinking. He was clearly reconsidering.

"You, you, and you," he said, pointing at three of the *Fallen* who had stepped forward previously. Loyal lackeys, Blane thought. "Make sure they get there safely. We *need* that machine back."

She almost laughed. The man sounded like a child sulking because he didn't get what he wanted. In fact maybe a chuckle did escape her lips, because Uriel's eyes snapped towards her.

"I remember you," he said. "Raphael and I were the ones who took you in after you… *lost* your family."

Blane didn't remember the man being anywhere near as involved in her rescue as his words implied, and she certainly didn't like the emphasis he placed on the word *lost*. She felt her blood rise.

"It's not too late to come back, you know," Uriel continued. His eyes glimmered, snake-like, as he locked his gaze with hers. "Join the *Forever Fallen* before these two drag you down with them. You can't survive alone out there. You need friends, allies; comrades."

Blane drew herself up, shifting to stand closer to Serinda and Grey so that they formed a solid wall facing him.

"I'm fine where I am, thanks."

Uriel gave a contemptuous smile and slowly shook his head.

"Fine," he said.

Behind him, Blane saw Xavier give her a small nod of support. She felt a stab of uncertainty and worry at the gesture; would he really be ok left behind here?

So she wasn't fully focused on Uriel when he said what he said next. There were a few microseconds between the electrical signals passing across her auditory nerve, and her conscious mind processing their meaning.

When the words did filter through, though, everything went red.

"You'll probably end up doing them like you did your parents, anyway."

13

The wisdom of the crowd is the wisdom of the ignorant.

Networks and Nationhood, Raul Caldez (Sanctioned Digital Document)

When she finally came back to her senses, Grey and Serinda were standing in front of her. Grey was holding out his hands as if fending something off, and Serinda was grabbing her by one shoulder, pushing her back.

She didn't know how long had passed; it could have been seconds, or minutes. All she knew was that Uriel was sprawled on the floor in a small crater that hadn't been there before, nose bleeding and grimacing with pain and rage. His eyes were wide and wild, and he was shouting something she couldn't hear over the ringing in her ears.

The other *Fallen* had formed a circle around the three of them, several drawing weapons and pointing their barrels at them. A number of them were drawing on the Aether, she sensed, and everything felt like it was balanced on a knife's edge.

"Release it, please... *Please,* Blane."

She almost didn't recognise Grey's voice; she'd never heard him sound so fearful and pleading. And then, even after she realised he was speaking to her, she didn't understand what he was asking.

Release what?

"Blane!"

Now it was Serinda crying out. She was shaking.

Blane looked from Serinda to Grey, and back again. She didn't...

"That's *Mindfire.*"

The words came from Uriel. He was no longer shouting at the other *Fallen,* but was instead fixing her with a considering gaze. She could still see fear in his eyes, but it was a cautious fear, not one of uncontrollable terror.

No, he wasn't looking at her, not directly. Rather, he was looking to her side, at something to her left. *Everyone* was looking that way.

"Get back, Serinda," Blane heard Grey say, as she turned her head to see what everyone was staring at.

Not even an arm's length away, hovering at almost exactly eye level, a golden ball of liquid flame rolled and sparked in the air. It moved like a thing alive, bulging and contorting and shifting its centre of mass while never actually leaving the spot in which it hovered.

The ball glowed with a brightness that hurt the eyes, yet though her mind insisted it must be blazing hot, on her skin she felt nothing but a mild warmth.

It was *beautiful.*

It was also, she realised, her creation, though it felt like nothing she had felt before. Ordinarily, when you drew on the Aether it flowed around something *inside* you; like you were a conduit through which the Aether moved, with some unknown part of you deep within creating the force to draw the energy upwards from the depths below.

Now, however, it felt like the Aether was not a current *within* her but a reflection *of* her. That was the only way she could describe it; as if the pool of Aether below reflected what she was feeling inside, and changed according to it.

As if it reflected her *anger.* The Aether was a raging tempest.

In that sudden moment of horrified realisation something inside her recoiled and the golden flame disappeared, snapping out of existence like it had never been. The roiling surface of the Aether calmed and subsided in an instant, and the cavern was filled with silence that only made the ringing in her ears louder.

"Thank you," said Grey, breathing a sigh of relief.

With a cry, Serinda threw hers arms around Blane, hugging her tightly. Blane thought she felt her quietly sob.

"It's ok… it's ok it's ok it's ok," Serinda whispered to her under her breath.

But Blane didn't need to hear those words. She analysed her feelings; there wasn't much to find. More than anything, she felt numb.

"How did you do that?" demanded Uriel, drawing himself up off the floor and wiping the blood from his face. "There isn't enough Aether here to…"

She stared at him defiantly and he trailed off, knowing he would get no answer. He glared back at her.

"So it's already too late for you, is it?" he continued. "You're lucky I don't have you all shot right here and now."

"Shot?" came a defiant shout. "Grey just saved your life! If he hadn't got that Pressure Shield up in time you'd have more than just a bloody nose."

It was Xavier, she saw. He was standing nearby, glaring at Uriel. Nearby *Fallen* were stepping away from him, leaving him in a space by himself.

Grey stepped over to him at almost the same moment Blane and Serinda did, forming a small circle in challenge at the larger group around them.

"And you are?" Uriel asked, glancing at Xavier then dismissing him. He turned to Gabriel.

"Take them, now. Sensory dampeners on their heads, and they leave with nothing. For what good it will do our security now..." Uriel glared daggers at Gabriel. "You can use *one* car. You get them back into the city, make sure they contact that damned Spaniard, then get back here. We are going to have words about this."

With that, Uriel turned smartly on his heels and stalked away. The rest of the *Fallen* looked confused, before a number took off after him and the rest gradually drifted away, throwing concerned looks back at them over their shoulders.

"Well, I guess you're coming with us after all," said Blane, slapping Xavier on the back with a smile that she only had to force a little.

She noticed Grey's mouth snap shut. No doubt he had been just about to say the same thing.

"I'm saying goodbye to Sara," said Serinda, tone flat and final.

Gabriel, coming up to them, nodded. He flashed a look towards Uriel's retreating back.

"Alright," he said. "Screw that *pendajo*. He can't exactly get any madder at me."

"So you brought us here without telling Uriel?" Blane asked as they walked through the gloom towards the distant building where Raphael lay. She knew the answer, but was desperately searching for something, anything, to take her mind off what had just happened.

"There wasn't time. The Spaniard... Francisco? ... wasn't exactly going to wait. Besides, bringing you here was the right thing to do, and Uriel only *thinks* he's in charge. We needed Serinda's expertise, and Serinda deserved to see Raphael."

Gabriel was hurrying forward to catch up with Serinda before he even finished answering. She had pushed quickly ahead, almost disappearing into the darkness.

The sound of a second set of hurried footsteps behind her told Blane without needing to turn around that Xavier was rushing to catch up.

"Are you... ok?" came his voice, hesitantly.

She kept looking forward, focusing on her stride.

Honestly, she didn't know. She didn't even clearly remember what had happened. Just... *rage*, and then Uriel lying on the floor bleeding, her friends looking at her in shock and fear.

"He shouldn't have said that," Xavier said, whispering the words so that only she could hear them.

No, he shouldn't have, Blane thought to herself.

But aloud, she said only;

"I lost control. That was stupid."

"What *was* that you did?" Xavier asked. She felt a spike of annoyance at the obvious fascination in his voice.

"*Flare*, and compression-release."

This was Grey, catching up to the two of them. From the forced restraint in his words, he was obviously hoping this would stem Xavier's questions.

"And the other thing... *Mindfire*, Uriel called it. What's that?"

Blane stopped suddenly, unable to walk, unable to think. All she could do was stare at the ground at her feet.

"Listen, kid," said Grey. "I need to talk to Blane alone, ok? Catch up with the others."

Even without looking she could sense Xavier's hesitation. Then, with a soft 'mm' of affirmation, he jogged away.

"How you doing, kid?"

Grey stepped around to stand in front of her. Slowly, she lifted her gaze to meet his.

In his expression she saw only sympathy and understanding, and something inside her unwound. Some part of her had been terrified that she would still see fear in his eyes.

"What did I do to him?" she asked. "To Uriel."

Grey hesitated for a moment before answering.

"I want to say nothing he didn't deserve, but I can't," he answered. His voice was filled with something like regret. "What you did could have killed him. *Should* have killed him."

"But you stopped me."

Grey hesitated for a moment.

"Actually, he got his own pressure-shield up as well," he said, curiously thoughtful. "Good thing we had both, too. That blast you used... it was *powerful*. If I'd been too slow, or he had..."

"Serinda said something about *its* influence being stronger on me than on the both of you," Blane interrupted. "What did she mean?"

Grey gave a small smile.

"You really are quick, *chica lista*. Don't miss a thing, do you?"

"It felt like... like Fen."

He nodded, expression quickly becoming grave again.

"Something in the Aether has changed. Especially for us, and especially for you. You shouldn't have been able to do what you did to Uriel. There's not nearly enough population density here to support it."

Grey drew himself up, clapping his hands together in determination.

"But we shouldn't talk about this now. Come on, let's go. The sooner we're back in Albores, the sooner we can figure things out."

She watched him as he turned and walked after the others, obviously trying to put on an air of confidence for her.

When did I become so much taller than him? she wondered.

Whatever was happening to her, to all of them, she swore one thing to herself. She *would* keep them safe.

Gabriel led them into the building and to Raphael's bed without stopping to answer the questions thrown at him by the other *Fallen* staff. Blane entered behind him and Serinda, and her eyes widened in surprise.

Raphael was sat up in bed, eyes open and looking more awake and healthy than at any time in the few days they'd been here.

"Seri," Raphael said, voice clear and strong.

"Sara..." Serinda rushed over to her bedside and took her hand.

"I wasn't sure it was really you beside me all this time. I thought it was maybe a fever dream."

"I'm here," Serinda said, squeezing Raphael's hand.

"But they can't stay," Gabriel said from where he stood in the corner of the small room.

"Can't they?" said Raphael.

The look on Raphael's face as she stared at Gabriel was so

withering that Blane was thankful it wasn't directed at her.

"Uriel's orders. He called them 'traitors.' Says they have to leave immediately."

"Really?"

Raphael's word carried the sort of implicit threat the flash of long fangs in the underbrush did to something small and fluffy.

Gabriel shifted from one leg to the other, growing visibly uncomfortable.

"I did."

Uriel pushed aside the curtain at the partition's entrance and strode in, accompanied by two extremely large and ferocious-looking figures. A man and woman, both had clearly been through intensive osteoblast therapy and towered over everyone in the room. They also carried long, heavy-looking rifles in their hands; their safeties were off.

Xavier and Grey, closest to the entrance, were shoved away and out of the room by the new arrivals, and Blane found herself pushed to one side of the room between Serinda and a wall.

"You're bringing guns to my bedside now, Uriel?"

If Raphael was perturbed by this turn of events, she didn't show it.

"They *attacked* me. This one…" Uriel said, pointing an accusatory finger at Blane. "This one tried to use *Mindfire* on me."

Raphael turned to look at Blane with a cool, amused stare.

"Hello, Blane," she said. "It's good to see you. Even if you *have* been scaring my people."

Blane didn't know how to respond, and felt herself give a small, halting wave back. She immediately felt foolish.

"They are leaving. *Now.*"

Uriel gestured to his two hulking escorts, and they both raised their rifles.

"Uh, are you forgetting who's in charge here?"

At Raphael's words the two escorts hesitated, rifles wavering.

And then Blane spotted it.

It was only a tiny movement, an almost imperceptible twitch, but Blane was suddenly aware that Raphael was struggling to stay sat upright. Now Blane was looking for it, she spotted it again, a few seconds later.

Raphael was swaying, ever so slightly. As if her head were heavier than her shoulders could carry, her skull swung infinitesimally back and forth in a jerky, irregular rhythm. A rhythm that was becoming increasingly rapid, the fall of her head becoming deeper each time.

Uriel spotted it too, his eyes narrowing and a broad smile coming over his face.

"Raphael is sick," he said, addressing the two who had come with him as if no one else were there. "She needs rest, and time to recover her faculties."

"I am right here," Raphael said.

She was trying to be firm, but Blane could hear the exhaustion in her voice now, a slight wheezing from the effort of pushing the air through her lungs.

Everyone else had noticed, too.

"It's ok," said Serinda, squeezing Raphael's hand once more. "I'm going to figure this out. I just…"

Serinda began reaching for the medical thin-screen at the foot of Raphael's bed, but it was snatched away by Uriel before her fingers touched it.

"I already said, they take *nothing.*"

Raphael raised a shaking hand, weakly. She was fading fast, skin turning a sickly pale at a rate Blane could actually *see.* It seemed that, now everyone had seen through her façade, she could no longer summon the energy to pretend.

"I promise," Blane heard Serinda say, leaning over Raphael's face as the woman slumped heavily back into her bed. "I *promise* I will save you."

Serinda clung to Raphael's bed in desperation as one of Uriel's hulking guards grabbed her with one hand, pointing a rifle at her from the other like a toy. She stretched her neck down and kissed Raphael deeply, crying out as she was dragged away.

It was the most vulnerable Blane had ever seen her.

They walked in silence, their entire group wedged between the male thug in the lead and female in the rear. Only Gabriel spoke, protesting against this treatment as they were led back to the tunnel they had entered by days before, and led at gunpoint to the base of the open pit crater where several *Fallen* vehicles waited, covered and camouflaged.

A driver was waiting for them, and their two armed escorts gestured for them to climb into the back of a large, covered flatbed. Gabriel made to climb in last, behind Xavier, but was stopped by a blocking palm to his chest.

"The boss says you ride with us," the woman said, smiling – or at least showing her teeth. "You've already told them too much."

Gabriel looked at the four of them with helpless, apologetic eyes, and stepped back from the car. The two guards gave a mocking gesture towards the driver's cab, as if offering him the curtesy of going first, and then strode around to the front behind him. Blane watched as they got into the cab beside the driver; there was a long, narrow window for viewing out the rear of the cab, but all she could see through it was the dull silhouette of the back of their escort's heads.

The car shifted into gear immediately, pulling away with a jerk that threatened to send her sliding off the smooth metal that made for seating in the rear. They were sat two on each side, Blane and Serinda facing Grey and Xavier.

"Did you get it?" asked Grey as soon as they were moving.

Blane barely had time to wonder what Grey was talking about before Serinda brought something small out from under her sleeves. It was slim and long and looked like a cross between a syringe and an industrial clamp.

"I got it," said Serinda.

The glass centre of the auto-tool shone a dark crimson in the light.

"We need to analyse this the instant we get back."

Under the cover of a kiss, Blane realised, Serinda had taken a sample of Raphael's blood.

14

We have solved many of the great mysteries. The divine clay lies discarded, replaced by natural selection and blind watchmakers. The celestial spheres are broken, and in their place collapsed bubbles of crashing atoms and nuclear fusion float in cold, empty void. Even under skies filled with corpse ash so thick our flying machines are rendered useless we uncover more answers. But the greatest mystery remains: consciousness, and the seat of being.

Answers without Questions, Eva G. Frandalle

"You and I both know it was too easy."

"Easy? I was shot at! We had to blow up a *wall* and drive a stolen truck through it! Not to mention getting in and out across hundreds of kilometres of Waste. What exactly about that was easy?"

They'd been back for several days now, the four of them cocooned in the Safe House in the basement levels of an apartment block downtown. At first, Blane had been thankful just to be back home, but what had been cramped with three was downright claustrophobic with four.

Home. She'd surprised herself when she thought of it by that name, but this place truly had been the only permanent fixture in her life these past few years. Outside, the city and the world beyond kept changing, usually for the worse, and those she had known before… everything that happened… must surely have forgotten her as they went on to build their own lives. She had no family, no friends. Only this place, and Serinda and Grey.

And Xavier too now, it seemed.

It felt ridiculous to be concerned about personal space when they were hiding in fear for their lives, only leaving the apartment individually on short runs to purchase daily necessities using the stash of cash they had built up over the years, but there were just too many of them cohabiting in too small an area.

Grey had given up his room, taking the couch in the living area. The man didn't seem to sleep much, and he was always the first to wake, but there was still only one thin-screen, two seats besides the couch, one bathroom… Xavier did his best not to over-intrude, and honestly there was little reason to be angry at him, but people weren't meant to confined in such a small space for such a length of time.

And yet, Blane was well aware that there was still a core of loneliness inside her. She remembered how concerned Serinda had been, after they'd first come to live in this place, when Blane began sleeping with the lights on. Serinda had given up asking about it, eventually, and seemed to have put it down to Blane being barely into her teens, but... she had never given up the habit.

It wasn't darkness *per se*. It was the silence of the darkness when she was alone, without goal or purpose beyond her body's demand for sleep. In that quiet solitude, her mind dredged up flashes of images and smells of the life she'd long lost; people, friends, parents...

That was the worst.

Sometimes, she was back there, in the room with her father and mother, shouting, screaming about *something*. She couldn't even remember what it was, anymore. She just remembered the feeling of anger, and a helpless despair that her parents would ever understand what was going through the mind of their teenage daughter in a world that seemed set on forcing her down a path not of her choosing.

Then as the memories rose despite her resistance she would feel that same anger and despair, only now aimed at herself. Anger at the fact that she refused to talk with the others about it, or even let them glimpse what was going on inside; despair because even when it felt like the pressure inside her was so extreme that she would burst, the words still died in her throat.

It was all so *stupid*, and now someone else was crammed in here too. A person with their own past and needs and traumas, while her dreams were only getting worse.

Which is why she was so relieved when Francisco finally got in touch, on the fifth or sixth day. Finally there would be something to *do*.

Francisco, face projected on one section of the LEF wall at the front of the living area, seemed to be making a proposal to Grey as she entered the living area.

"I need information," the man in the screen said. "Information only the RA has, on the origins of the Sudden War."

"The Sudden War? What could you possibly need from them that the Silicon Isle doesn't already know or can't find out?"

Grey was speaking quietly. It was early morning, and he must have been hoping no one else would hear Francisco's call. Blane had,

105

though, and upon hearing Francisco's voice jumped out of bed and moved quickly to join them.

"Remember," Francisco was saying. "For all the Althing Republic's resources, the groups sat atop the bones of the North American pre-Fall nations have the best access to classified data from that time; the Carib-Federation and the RA especially. Besides, what I need is more for confirmation, rather than new data."

Francisco's archaic accent was almost imperceptible. He sounded like a different person, Blane thought as she crossed the room. Then his image on the screen looked up, and he saw her approaching from behind Grey.

"*Buenas días, mija.* It is good to see you."

The background of Francisco's image was plain white, giving nothing away of his location. Not that she could trust anything that might be shown there, anyway. It was a simple matter to alter the background of such calls.

She gave him a wave.

Grey turned to see her, greeting her with a nod, then turned back to the screen. He wore a dour expression.

"So you want me to, what, ask the RA nicely to share what they have on the Sudden War?" he asked.

"You still have contacts, I am sure. I know you had many in the days when we used to meet in the *Methuselah's End*, eh?"

Francisco flashed a smile that Grey did not return.

"I could just go get them," Blane said, walking over to stand beside Grey.

"Don't be stupid," said Grey gruffly.

"I got the files on where they were keeping you!" Blane protested.

Which is how they ended up here, arguing about whether breaking Grey out of a remote RA prison camp was too easy.

"Whatever you think about the suits and drones and all the other tricks Francisco gave you…" Grey said firmly, pointing towards the man in the screen, "… you *shouldn't* have done that. It was foolish. Hell, I shouldn't have even *been* there. The RA knows I'm a former Far agent; they know how I was trained."

"So?" Blane demanded.

"So you think it makes sense that they kept me in an open prison like just another detainee? I was in there for nearly a year, and not *once* did anyone question me about the Central Tower, or Fen, or anything like that. All they accused me of was 'aiding and abetting anti-state activities.'"

"You think someone was protecting you?" Francisco interrupted. "Someone hid your history?"

Grey looked from Blane to the screen, talking to the both of them.

"I suspected that, at first. I actually thought it was you, Francisco. Then when Blane and Serinda turned up, walking around the place like it was nothing, I was terrified it was a trap to get them too. But now, I'm starting to think there's something else entirely in play here. There's too much going on that I don't know about, and it's starting to drive me *crazy*."

Grey's hands formed fists at his sides in frustration.

"So yes, I'll do it. But then you're going to do something for *me*," he said.

Francisco looked surprised for a moment, then his features became neutral again and he gave a small nod.

"Of course. *Favor con favor se paga.* As ever between us, Grey. What is it you want?"

"You're going to tell me *why*. Why you want this information, why you can't get it yourself. But most of all, you're going to explain *why* you're helping us."

The surprise returned to Francisco's face.

"But *Señor* Grey, you know I only want to help…"

"*Stop it*, Francisco. I know you do nothing without considering your own goals. I want to know what they are."

Francisco said nothing for a long while, staring at something they couldn't see. Then, he cleared his throat. When he spoke again, his voice was deep and sombre, with no trace of his usual accent.

"I will tell you what I can, Mr. Grey. But you must understand, there are some things I cannot tell you. Things I can tell *no one*. Not yet. But I will tell you what I can."

This time, the silence was Grey's.

"I guess that will have to do," he said after some time. "For now."

Grey left no more than a couple of hours later, ignoring Blane's protestations and demands that he let her come with him. He was going to find contacts both new and old, he said, and that kind of work was better done alone. A companion would only complicate things.

Which left Blane at a loss for what to do.

Once Grey had left, taking plenty of spangle fabric and one of the multiple vehicles Francisco had left for them, Blane returned to the living area and threw herself down on the couch.

Serinda hadn't been any help. All she was concerned with was getting Francisco to provide certain medical equipment as soon as he could; Blane hadn't even heard the names of most of these before. Francisco didn't ask what these were for. He knew full well what had happened at the *Fallen* base.

As soon as she made these requests, Serinda returned to her bedroom - not that it could be called that with any accuracy any more. The place had become a makeshift lab, furnishings shoved aside or rolled up into the walls to make way for electron-microscopes and flow cytometers and countless other mysterious tools.

And of course, Xavier hadn't been any use. He was still unsure of his place in the group, and most definitely wasn't going to question Grey's decisions. He just asked when she thought Grey would be back, and accepted her vague reply without comment.

With a sigh, Blane grabbed a thin-screen and scrolled aimlessly through whatever news it decided to offer her. More crackdowns - "internal security operations," the regulated media called them - and more call-ups for whatever was going on in the contested regions[5] between the Reclamation and the Mayan League. No conscription yet, but a large number of reserves ordered to report for mobilization. Denials from Federation and RA spokespeople regarding rumours of internal friction and factional infighting...

Boring, boring, boring.

Even summoning up the motivation to practise more techniques, the one thing keeping her sane shut in here, was beyond her. Even standing up...

She couldn't say when she fell asleep, descending slowly through layers of consciousness until she was floating on that subtle line between the waking world and dreaming. The light and sound of the safe house merged with the light and sounds of her mindscape,

---

[5] RA media used the term as if it was well-known. Blane was fairly sure there had been no mention of "contested regions" until very recently, but there was no way to check. Reclamation monitors "revised" articles on the net with absolute impunity, and a search for the term now brought back results in news reports years old.

thoughts and senses becoming incoherent and impossibly structured in the way a dreamer only becomes aware of upon waking.

In her mind's eye she saw burning towers of golden flame collapsing without end into the skies above. A city of sharp, biting metal edges stretched out in all directions, and her senses whispered of danger lurking behind every corner. Dark, formless things of malice and contempt waited for her to stumble.

She saw herself lost and alone in the poisoned Waste, chased by creatures warped and disfigured by the very land they inhabited, and simultaneously trapped within a windowless room of empty shadow - and somehow she knew that in both she was being observed by cold, uncaring human eyes.

And always, always, the Aether lay just out of reach below, bending and warping away from her as she *reached* to draw on its power.

"Are you alright?"

Blane bolted upright from where she lay on the couch, the whiplash of such sudden waking a physical pain in her skull. Blinking, she saw Xavier stood at the end of the couch, looking at her with concern.

"What?" she said, rubbing her eyes. "I... I must have fallen asleep."

Reality and the dream she had just left were still not fully disentangled as she stared around herself, taking in the familiar, strangely ordinary surroundings of the apartment.

"You were shouting," said Xavier. "The tower, right? And the Lock?"

Blane turned to look at him, half-convinced she had misheard.

"Ex... excuse me?"

She felt embarrassed even as the words weakly left her mouth.

"Your dreams. It was a burning tower, right? And the feeling that you can't reach the Aether no matter what you try?"

What the fuck...

Blane struggled to process what she was hearing. How could he know what she had been dreaming? Was he somehow *reading* her without her sensing it? She'd spent so much time learning how to resist the technique with Grey and Serinda...

The rising sense of shock and violation must have been apparent on her face because Xavier suddenly stepped back with hands raised, shaking his head in desperate appeasement.

"No, wait, it's not that," he said, words tumbling over each other in his panicked rush to get them out. "I wouldn't... I mean, I can't... I mean... It's the dream a lot of us have been having. A lot of Aether users I've spoken to, anyway."

Blane fixed him with a stare that made him fall back into a nearby chair.

"What..." she said slowly and deliberately. "... the hell are you talking about?"

Several hours later, and Blane still wasn't sure if she'd missed anything. She'd questioned... maybe you could even say interrogated ... Xavier through the entire morning, then made him repeat everything again to be sure, but still she felt the urge to press him further.

It started shortly before the RA crackdowns, at least as far as Xavier could tell. At first, he'd just assumed they were bad dreams – and there was nothing unusual about bad dreams in the Reclamation. It had been months into his time at the prison camp before he realised other Aether users were seeing them too.

There were a number of Aether users amongst the *Forever Fallen* brought to the camp, and as Xavier was drawn further into their ranks he heard more and more talk of the shared dream they were having. It wasn't all of them, but enough that Xavier gradually became convinced that it was no coincidence.

In the early days, he dismissed talk of flaming towers and visions of Dead Cities and blank-faced, looming RA agents as the result of a shared experience being in Albores over the past few years. Then more *Fallen* came, from all over the Reclamation, and many of them had been having this dream since *before* they were brought in.

Which meant this dream was shared by Aether users across the Reclamation, and who knew where else?

Xavier hadn't discussed this with Grey, or anyone else. Grey reflexively refused to talk about anything to do with the Central Tower, and there was no one in the *Fallen* that he felt familiar enough to discuss it with. Which meant as far as Blane could tell, she was the only other person to know.

"It's Fen," she said. Somehow, she *knew* this was the case.

She'd been having this dream for so long she no longer knew

when it started; several months, at least. At times the dream was more vivid, at others much less so, but it always returned.

She'd put it down to stress, and fear for Fen. Among the dreams she'd been having for years, it was hardly the worst symptom of her traumas. Now, though, it seemed that it was more than that.

"How can you know for sure?"

Blane didn't think Xavier was trying to challenge her; he sounded genuinely puzzled.

"I just do," she replied. "The dreams are too similar to the things he went through; the things they *put* him through. Quick-Fix, the Dead Cities, the place they kept him locked up in since childhood…"

Now it was Xavier's turn to go wide-eyed.

"It might be time to tell you what happened with Fen," Blane said.

She settled back into the couch, readying herself to tell the long tale.

"And the other boy?"

The question caught her off guard.

"*What* other boy?"

15

The North American continent was long ago drained of its natural resources. Its waters are stagnant and polluted, its vegetation poisoned and stunted. We feed our fabricators on the refuse and rubble of what came before. The Reclamation runs on… trash. Are we then to be a nation of trash collectors?

Chairman's Address to the 7th Assembly, *Assemblies of the Reclamation: Collected Speeches*

"Salim!"

"*Marhaba*, my old friend. It has been a long time."

It really *had* been a long time. Blane was amazed at how much a person could change in just a few years.

According to Xavier, 'the boy' first had appeared in his dreams the same night they returned to Albores from the *Fallen* base in the quarry. Sensed rather than seen, it was at first simply a figure in the distance, watching over the disorder of Xavier's dreamscape from afar. Over the next few nights, however, he became convinced that this was more than just a curious new detail. There was something about this figure that was detached from everything else in the dream, something more permanent and *solid*.

Xavier had assumed Blane had been seeing him too, as well as anyone else who shared the same dream. Finding out that this wasn't the case had been a surprise, and then finding out that Blane knew who the boy was had been an even bigger shock.

She'd really only known Salim for a handful of days, back in the *Fallen*-controlled tower block that they had lived in after the both of them were taken in by the group, years ago. *Fallen* searchers sent out by Raphael had found him half-dead and stricken insensible by an inability to control his ability, and it was only after Fen arrived that he regained his senses.

Blane remembered how the three of them found themselves thrown together; herself, Salim, and Fen. They had only a short time before Grey brought Salim to his father and the two left the Reclamation, but for Blane this marked the beginning of the chaos that followed. The time they had spent together was indelibly marked in her memory for this and many other reasons.

It seemed like Salim remembered this time strongly too, because he looked genuinely happy to see her. There *was* a moment's awkwardness when she instinctively went to give a hug in greeting and a slight shift of discomfort from Salim made her stop, but then his face broke into a big smile as he sat back and gestured to the seat opposite his own.

The door shut behind her and the car pulled smoothly away as she took her own seat facing Salim. The windows were set to the darkest possible tint setting, blocking what little outside light made it through the heavy, grey rainclouds overhead, and the driverless vehicle's engine was so silent that only the sensation of acceleration told her they were moving at all.

Salim had got *big*, she saw. Not fat, but muscled. She could see remnants of the sickly, weak child she had known in the eyes and in the shape of his cheeks beneath his well-cropped beard, but the man sat in front of her looked more like a model on the cover of a men's health magazine than a foreign national attending a clandestine meeting away from the watchful eye of his hosts. His expensively-casual clothes looked like they were worth more than many of the buildings on the street outside.

But Salim was indeed endangering himself just by meeting her, Blane knew, and she still worried no matter how careful she had been to use anon-spec gear to contact him.

Contacting Salim had been surprisingly straightforward. Blane had been fairly confident from Xavier's description that it was Salim – appearing as the boy he once was rather than the man he had become – so all she needed to do was find any information on visitors to the city from the Crystal Caliphate.

Fortunately, such visits were still rare enough to be notable; the only kind of intercontinental travel available was by sub-orbital, a necessity to avoid the pollutants and particulate matter that filled the lower stratosphere, and therefore prohibitively expensive.

This meant that the Reclamation Net was aflame with discussion of the latest delegation from the Caliphate to visit Albores. A group had arrived a week ago, entering the *Meridian* in an armoured convoy displaying the kind of offensive gear that would make even Quick-Fix jealous. As heavily controlled and censored as the net was, there was still plenty of speculation on the visit's purpose to be found, though none with anything more concrete than theory and speculation.

There was also plenty of hateful commentary and venomous anti-Islamic and anti-religious 'discussion' on the threads – and Blane knew that what the net censors and filters allowed through was one of the best ways to judge the policies of the Reclamation Authority itself. It looked like the RA still maintained considerable hostility towards the Crystal Caliphate and organised religion in general, regardless of the fact that they were hosting these visitors.

So Blane had contacted the *Meridian* and left a simple message, requesting that they deliver it to a party member by the name of Salim Ayad, along with contact details should he wish to reply. The message itself said simply "I see you've learnt a few tricks since your last visit - B."

The ping came less than a couple of hours later. She almost hadn't realised what it was at first, in amongst the ever-increasing number of pings offering free osteoblast therapy and citizenship-track status for those under the age of 17 willing to sign up at their local recruitment office in this time of "special operations". It gave a time and location, nothing more. Quite far across the city, but remote, and there was more than enough time to make it there.

She'd asked Xavier not to say anything to Serinda until he had no choice - Seri was so wrapped up in whatever she was doing in her makeshift laboratory that she likely wouldn't notice Blane was gone for some time. With any luck, Blane could be back before Seri even noticed she was gone.

Even as she told herself this, she knew she was only trying to convince herself.

"So you can appear in people's dreams now?" she said, pushing down feelings of guilt and thoughts of how angry Seri would be. Angry, and hurt.

"He is quite skilled, you know. He sensed me almost immediately. I was sure it would take much longer," Salim replied.

"Xavier? Didn't you *want* him to see you?"

"Is that his name?" Salim nodded as if storing this information in his mind. "Xavier, then. Yes, once I saw Agent Grey in his thoughts I wanted him to see me, but it is not necessarily so simple. The one being *experienced* must be adept enough to sense the Dreamwalker in their thoughts."

I'll have to let Xavier know Salim thinks he's 'adept,' Blane thought to herself. The thought made her smile, though she wasn't sure why.

"Why didn't you come to me?" she asked.

Salim looked at her for a second with his head tilted, a questioning look in his eyes.

"Because I did not know you were there." His voice was heavy and serious. "I found the doctor from our time with those people - Serinda, I believe her name was? - and I could sense Agent Grey, but the walls the Far Agency taught him to build around his mind are too strong for me to breach. *You* were not there. It is as if you do not touch the Aether as others do."

"But you can sense me now?"

Salim nodded.

"Now I have seen you, I can see your connection to the Aether. It is... *deeper* than others. I missed it because I search for minds floating on the surface of the Aether; you are submerged in it."

"Submerged?"

"I can't think how else to describe it. You weren't aware?"

Serinda's words came back to her. *Its influence is stronger on her than either of us.*

She'd found time in the safe house to question Grey about this more, though his answers had been vague and unsatisfying. All he and Serinda knew was that the Aether felt different; like it had around Fen.

Around Fen, the Aether had seemed more potent, more pliable and *eager;* especially for Grey. Slowly, in the years after the Central Tower, that feeling had returned, and the effect was apparent in Blane most of all.

Blane, of course, had just assumed it was the way Aether abilities were supposed to develop as you grew into them.

"So does this mean you don't know why it is happening?"

Salim's words brought her back from her thoughts.

"Uh... why what's happening? Why you couldn't find me?"

"No, no," said Salim. "Though that is probably related. No, I mean why the changes in the Aether are happening."

"Changes in the Aether?"

Salim gave a sigh.

"It seems not. Look, I would prefer not to have to explain everything twice. Where is Agent Grey?"

Blane opened her mouth to reply then paused, wondering exactly how much she should say.

115

"He's... um, on a case," she said. "And what's with this 'Agent Grey' you keep calling him?"

Salim chuckled and gave a wry smile.

"Yes, I'm sorry. It's what my father says whenever he talks about Mr. Grey. I think he finds it difficult not to honour him with a title, even if it is technically inaccurate."

"We just call him 'Grey.' Or 'Nestor,' I guess."

Salim's smile didn't fade.

"I think I will at least call him 'Mister.' Perhaps I still feel some need to honour him, too. He brought me back from a very dark place."

Blane returned his smile.

"Yes. I think we all owe him a lot. He has a way of prioritising other people over himself that isn't so common. In the Reclamation, at least."

"The Reclamation is a hard place." Salim's smile faded. "Especially now, with its *economic issues.*"

Economic issues? Blane didn't know what Salim was talking about, but she had a feeling that if he had been a different person he would have enclosed the two words in air quotes.

"Ah, more of the Reclamation Authority's 'expurgated for security reasons,' I see," said Salim on seeing her expression.

She continued to stare at him, waiting for him to become uncomfortable. A skill Serinda had taught her; when someone believes you know more than you actually do, they will start to fill in the gaps. All you have to do is leave a gap to fill.

"Ahem... they use that phrase a lot in the security checks before entering the country," Salim continued. "It doesn't matter how careful you are about what you bring; they always find something. About half of my data is locked behind RA encrypts at the moment, and will be until I leave."

He tutted in frustration, shaking his head at the thought.

"The RA is having money problems?" Blane asked. "But we have Fabricators. We can make anything we need!"

"The paradox of poverty in the midst of plenty..."

Salim didn't seem to be saying this to her, but to himself. He stared into the distance as he spoke. Were they someone else's words?

"The Fabricators still require resources," he continued, coming back from wherever he had gone in that moment. "And the RA is struggling to secure these. My own homeland has attained far more in both revenue and trade, and achieved this all without *Riba,* the sin of usury…"

Blane saw a flash of pride cross his face at this, quickly suppressed.

"… And of course, the Eastern Empress possesses more wealth than perhaps the rest of the world combined. The Reclamation has fallen far behind, and the gap is growing."

Again, that look into the distance, as if seeing things she did not.

"You seem… different," she said. "I mean, apart from the fact that you look a lot more, um, healthy."

She gestured towards him, encompassing his well-groomed features and finely tailored clothes.

Salim laughed.

"I am not the boy I was when we first met, that is true. I have learned a more… *nuanced* understanding of my faith, and accepted my place in this world as *Allah* has provided it."

He leaned back into his chair, looking relaxed and confident.

"I have also developed a great interest in the history of this continent, and what it once was. Did you know this continent was once the wealthiest and most powerful in all the world?"

Blane had never had much interest in history. Insofar as the subject was taught in Reclamation schools[6] at all, it focused almost entirely on the post-Fall era and the resettlement of the Reclamation. Looking back on it now, she could see it was little more than propaganda for the RA. She shook her head.

"Well, it was," Salim said. "Things are very different now. For instance, where are the courts of law? This land once had too many to count; now it has only one, and that controlled by figures hidden in shadow. The Executive is the legislature, and the foundation of law is 'whatever is good for the Reclamation is legal'."

The rain thudded harder on the roof as the car merged onto an elevated highway and accelerated.

---

[6] The term 'school' was something of a misnomer, of course. They bore little resemblance to the educational institutions that once bore the name. Schooling today consisted of primarily individual learning, with rows upon rows of students sat in isolated cubicles staring at a tablescreen as an adaptive AI program led them through their studies.

"Are we going somewhere?" she asked, feeling a spike of concern. Driving around risked encountering one of the many security checkpoints scattered around the city.

Salim shook his head.

"No. I was planning to set a destination once you told me where Mr. Grey was. For now, the car will just drive around - don't worry, I paid quite handsomely for the location of any law enforcement stops. Better than sitting still and attracting attention. Unless you had somewhere in mind?"

Reassured, Blane didn't reply. Instead she leaned forward.

"What is wrong with the Aether, Salim? What did you want to talk to Grey about?"

The Aether was getting harder to control.

Across the Caliphate and, as far as Salim could tell, across much of the painstakingly reclaimed lands both east and west, 'incidents' were occurring more and more frequently, but because Aether users were so rare these incidents were often misreported. Only someone looking for it would notice the increase.

Salim had been looking.

Since his return home from the Reclamation, Salim had not only worked on his own abilities, but established a *Madrasa* of his own. The idea for this had been born from the struggle even his wealthy parent had in finding anyone able to guide his young son, inspiring them both to open their own school of learning. Now well-established, Salim frequently travelled the region searching for potential Aether users, and educating others about its very existence.

He found it more and more as time passed and as he travelled further. Entire families wiped out, entire buildings. Without warning, a youth without any history of Aether use would manifest in a destructive burst of violence that left nothing standing around them, or with an indiscriminate mental assault that left structures untouched but the minds inside them irrevocably broken.

If they weren't killed themselves, by either the destruction they wrought or by angry and frightened residents who witnessed this destruction, many of the Aether users themselves succumbed to a strange malady soon after, descending into a pit of exhaustion and depression that Salim knew well. He had suffered something like it himself, after all.

It was as if the flow of Aether, once channeled, could no longer be stopped, as if the pressure behind it was so great that it bled through the user's mind no matter how hard they fought to hold it back. This lack of control could manifest itself in a variety of ways, always dangerous to the user and those around them. It also prevented them from any sort of sleep, driving them further out of their senses and beyond hope of maintaining control.

There were even reports of *Mindfire,* with dozens of people wiped out in the blink of an eye. Little was ever left of those who channelled such a thing, however.

Salim could find out little of the situation in the Reclamation, however. With all its secrecy and firewalls and just plain standoffishness, Salim had resigned himself to the impossibility of discovering what was happening in the RA, or what it knew - until the announcement of a new trade mission.

He'd told his father he simply wanted to return to the Reclamation for himself. He hadn't had the opportunity to see much on his last visit, after all, and his father had been very much hoping Salim would show more interest in the family business.

So here he was, a representative of the Caliphate looking to establish more lucrative ties with the Reclamation. And, secretly, seeking an answer to what was happening back home.

He'd been in Albores for more than a week, taking every opportunity he could find to go out into the city, ostensibly seeking potential customers for Caliphate wares while actually spending most of his time dreamwalking, searching the multitude of minds for a glimpse of... something, *anything* that could help him piece the puzzle together.

He'd found almost nothing.

"*Almost* nothing?"

Salim nodded in answer to Blane's question.

"Almost," he said. "There was one mind, one hint of what I'm looking for. Whoever they are, they know something about what's happening. I saw it only briefly, but in their mind was a thought-image of the Aether pouring upwards like a... a... what do you call it? A *geyser.*"

"A geyser?"

"Yes. No... Look, it's the best way I can describe it. Thought-

119

images aren't coherent things. Nothing I am saying now is truly what I experience when I walk someone's mind. Haven't you ever *read* someone?"

Blane made a noncommittal gesture. Her lack of skill in that regard was something of a sore point. Grey had taught her to Read others, but she'd made poor progress, never getting much beneath surface emotions. Not once had she managed to 'see' Grey's inner monologue, to understand the thoughts in the way he said she should be able to. It was one of the only Aether techniques she truly had trouble with.

"Well, that's what it felt like. A pillar of fire, but one whose circumference somehow overshadowed the entire world. The thing is…"

Salim paused, looking conflicted.

"The thing is…?" Blane prompted.

"The thing is, it wasn't *now*. Not that the Experience reflected anything as certain as a specific date or time but… in the dream, you just know. Whatever this person knows, it isn't linked to here, today."

"So what is it linked to?"

"The Sudden War. Whatever this person knows about what is happening to the Aether, it is linked to the Sudden War."

So, thought Blane. *Francisco isn't the only person interested in the secrets of the Sudden War.*

It was strange. She'd never thought deeply about the war that had ended the old era and brought in the new. People rarely did. Armageddon had come, and the world kept on spinning. Now, suddenly, it seemed as if everyone was chasing it.

"Ok, then," she said, cracking her knuckles and leaning back in the hope of projecting a cool resolve. "All we need to do is find this person. Where are they?"

Salim stared at her without speaking for a while.

"That's really the problem," he said eventually. "These thought-images, they only ever come from one place. It's why I sought Mr. Grey out."

"And that place is…?"

"The Far Station. Whoever they are, they're in the Far Station."

16

The old industrial empires justified their rule by speaking of progress. The modern nation-state does the same. The problem is, it's always progress for those doing the ruling and not so much for the ruled.

Guidelines for identifying seditious activities, Internal Security, Example 17

The first thing she had to do was get equipped. That was easy enough; there were still spangle suits left, along with some other 'goodies' Francisco had sent them over the years, and she knew where Grey kept his stun-locks.

The second thing she had to do was to find out everything she could about the Far station. Then she could start figuring out how she was going to get inside.

And all the while, Blane struggled to ignore the voice inside whispering that she was, once again, betraying Serinda's trust.

She had returned to the safe house immediately after convincing Salim that she could get in and out of the Far station, no sweat. If she was honest with herself, she'd probably acted more sure of this than she had any right to be, but the important thing was that he agreed. Now he was on board, he could provide her with all the information he had acquired about the place.

Which was, it turned out, rather a lot.

The data transfer to her thin-screen had taken actual *seconds* to complete, and a quick glance over the files revealed floor plans, building schematics, offices and names, and even video footage of the place being built.

"God may listen, but money talks," was all a grinning Salim said when she asked him how he could possibly have acquired all this information.

There was more than she would be able to go over if she had months, let alone the short amount of time she actually had. She needed to move fast… because Serinda had asked her to wait.

She hadn't even been angry, upon Blane's return; just upset, and trying to hide it. That made it somehow worse.

"I can't stop you from doing anything you want," Seri had said, cutting Blane off before she began reflexively making excuses for leaving without saying anything. "This wouldn't work if I tried."

Seri was sat perched on the edge of the couch waiting for her when Blane returned, Xavier sat across from her.

"We're all trapped in here together," Serinda said, gesturing to indicate the whole of the safe house, "But this place *can't* become a prison."

At that, Serinda stood and walked over to Blane, still stood in the entranceway. Blane didn't know what to say as the other woman took her hand and locked eyes with her.

"I am your *friend*, Blane. That's all. Your friend, and someone who wants you to be safe."

"I... I know what I'm doing."

Even as Blane said this she knew it was a weak reply, but Serinda didn't argue. She just smiled and released her hand.

"Look, I know I've been busy working on trying to help Sara, but..."

"No!" Blane didn't think she could take it if Serinda tried to apologise. Not for that. "No. That's important. That's something you have to do."

"Thank you," Seri replied. "I'm close to something, I know it. I just need a little more time. Can you give me that, please? Just wait for me, and we can figure out what needs to be done next, together."

Blane just nodded and agreed, feeling dirty as she did so.

But this was something she would do alone.

She almost made it out cleanly, too. It was so late at night that it was practically morning when she snuck out, making it through the living area and to the elevator without a sound. Gesturing hurriedly towards the sensor to activate the door, she dove in as it opened.

She was so confident she had made it without alerting Serinda that when she noticed Xavier stood in the opposite corner it almost gave her a heart attack.

"*Mierda!* What the hell are you doing here?"

Xavier actually held his hands up as if to defend himself, and Blane thought if the elevator doors hadn't already shut he might have bolted there and then.

"Woah! It's ok - I'm coming with you," he said.

The hum of the elevator was all that filled the air until, with a soft 'ding,' the doors opened to the basement car park. Blane stepped out without looking at Xavier, striding quickly and trying to put as much distance between them as possible.

It was useless, though. She sighed as he literally *jogged* after her.

"So where are we going?" he asked, falling into step alongside her as if it was a foregone conclusion.

Blane cursed to herself. She didn't have time to argue with him; she'd already pinged Salim and his car would be arriving any moment.

"Come on," Xavier insisted. "You're up to something, right? It was obvious from the moment you came back from meeting that guy... um, Salim, right?"

"It was obvious?" Blane said, her step faltering slightly. Shaking herself off, she increased her pace. "How obvious? Did Serinda...?"

Xavier looked thoughtful for a moment.

"Yeah, I think she knew," he said. "She actually came to me after you two spoke, and I think she sort of wanted me to look after you."

Blane gave a scornful laugh at this.

"Hey, *I* know you don't need looking after," Xavier said. "And I don't think Serinda meant it like that. She's just worried about you. About your psychological state."

That made her stop. The words were obviously Serinda's - they didn't sound quite right in Xavier's mouth, like he was repeating something someone had said. But to discuss something like that with a third party?

She stared hard at him, waiting for him to fill in the blanks.

"Look," he said, giving her what she wanted. "You *know* Serinda doesn't mean anything by it, and would never talk about you like that. She's worried about what the Aether is doing to you. To all of you, I think, but especially you."

She must really be worried if even Xavier knows, she thought.

Grey had told her the changes to the Aether meant she could do things she shouldn't be able to, but he hadn't said anything about it affecting her mind. What had Serinda discovered?

"Come on," Xavier said, breaking the silence. "We better get outside before the car arrives."

Something clicked inside Blane's head, a sudden realisation that the world was not exactly as she had thought. Forcing herself to act as if nothing was amiss she continued to match Xavier's pace, following him up the slope that led to the exit.

"What exactly do you think Serinda is worried about?" she asked, carefully controlling her tone to maintain the illusion that she was just continuing the conversation.

"Well, look... Everything I've seen you do just makes me think you're a badass, but Serinda has been using phrases like '*induced hypomania*' quite a lot."

"Serinda," said Blane flatly, coming to a stop. "Serinda said that. To you."

Xavier continued for several steps before realising Blane had halted. She watched him pause and turn to face her, a look of guilt on his face.

"Uh... well, not exactly *in front* of me, but I guess I overheard her at some point..."

Everything was clear to her now, and she could see Xavier's feigned naivety for what it was.

"Serinda would *never* talk about something so personal in front of others," she said, staring unblinkingly at him. "Not a patient, and not me."

Xavier raised a finger and opened his mouth to speak, but Blane cut him off.

"You're Reading us," she said.

It wasn't a question.

Xavier stood frozen for a second, mouth hanging open. Then something in his expression changed, and his hands fell to his side.

"That was pretty amateur of me, wasn't it?" he said. She could see his cheeks reddening. "Honestly, I didn't like keeping it a secret anyway."

"Are you a spy?" she demanded, not letting her guard fall. She drew on the Aether, feeling it leap up at her call.

"What? No!"

Xavier seemed genuinely alarmed. He flinched backwards, falling up the slope and having to put his arms out behind himself for support.

"Were you lying to us from the start? Lying to Grey?"

Blane stepped forward, a feeling like a pent up spring inside her threatening to break at any moment. Blood swirled at the edge of her vision; she'd never realised the phrase *seeing red* was literal until now.

"Grey knows!" yelled Xavier. "He knows!"

Blane didn't release the Aether. If anything, she drew on more of it, and felt it wrap around her in return.

"Why would Grey keep it secret from us?" she growled.

"Because I asked him to!"

Xavier was practically screaming now, his desperate eyes staring at something to her side.

Its influence is stronger on her than either of us.

She heard Serinda's voice in her ear.

Blane paused, feeling the red haze lessen as she focused on where she was. Stood in the basement car park, looming over a fallen figure who was trembling with fear, but offering no resistance.

Warmth at her side made her turn.

The ball of Mindfire floated in the air beside her, spinning and roiling as if it contained a great tempest despite its small size. She could *feel* it somehow, straining against a leash she held.

No, not a leash. This was a *part* of her, as connected to her as her own arm. It felt as if what she was fighting against was... herself.

Stop, she told herself, gritting her teeth. *Stop, now.*

After a strained moment, the globe snapped out of existence and Xavier gave a soft sigh of relief. She turned back to him.

"Why?" she said, trying to hide how shaken she was herself. "Why would you ask him that? Why would Grey agree?"

Xavier still looked wary, and made no move to pick himself up off the floor.

"I told you; I grew up alone. I've learnt not to trust people, and I didn't know you. Whatever Grey said about you, *I* didn't know you."

"So you thought it was ok to *Read* us without our knowledge?"

"I... I tried not to. I promise, I hardly have. But, well, the safe house is so *boring*, and no one tells me anything, and... and Serinda is clearly worried about you. It's so at the top of her thoughts that she's practically *shouting* it. Then you were so *clearly* up to something..."

His words trailed off and he just looked at her, powerless and awaiting judgement. She stared at him, wishing she could Read him as well as he apparently could Read her.

"Get up," she snapped.

Xavier had been right about that, at least. They'd lost enough time already.

A nervous smile flickered over Xavier's lips as he pushed himself up, standing and brushing off the dust while not taking his eyes off her for a second.

"I *am* sorry," he said. "For lying, for *Reading* you. For not telling you sooner."

"Exactly *how* good are you?" she demanded, cutting him off.

"At Reading? Pretty good, I think. Grey said he'd never met anyone as good. It got us out of a few... um, *situations* while we were in the camp. It's extremely useful to know what your captors are thinking."

"So you can actually *see* what people thinking?"

"No," he said, and seemed disappointed to have to admit this. "No, nothing like that. I still only see thought-images, but I *understand* them better. At least, that's what Grey said. I'm pretty good at getting into someone's mind undetected, too, though now you're aware of it you'd notice pretty quickly if I tried again."

She'd have to make sure of that once they got back from the Far station, Blane resolved to herself. Make sure of that, and figure out exactly how she could use Xavier now she knew what he could do. A powerful... Reader, she supposed you'd call him... A powerful Reader could be a very useful tool against the RA.

But for now, there really was no time.

"Come on," she said. "Let's go. And don't try anything like that again; on me or Serinda. Or, for that matter, anyone else..."

She paused, considering what she was saying.

"Anyone that's on our side, at least," she added.

She didn't need to be able to Read Xavier to see how happy the words "our side" made him.

17

Once people believe a thing they will reject any evidence that contradicts this belief. The search for truth becomes the defence of faith; the cause no longer for the people, but the people for the cause. The state must have not only a monopoly on violence, but a monopoly on belief.

Statecraft beyond Il Principe, Narsete Salmio

The Far Station stood before her, lit brightly in the night by powerful ground spotlights that shone upwards onto its columns, making it even more looming and oppressive than it was during the day.

The station, or Albores Central as it was technically known, had been designed with the imperial stylings of the old world in mind. Tall columns ran the length of its wide concrete front, pale and spaced equally, each ornately decorated where it met the roof of the portico they held up. The colonnade must have stood at least 20 metres high, and the whole effect worked to make what was really only a structure of four or five stories seem somehow taller than buildings many times its height.

There was even a kind of triumphal arch stood in the centre of the courtyard, something that as far as Blane knew wouldn't have looked out of place in the Dead City of Rome, half a world away. Built before the Far Agency was established and granted this building by the RA, it commemorated the founding of the city after a generation of effort. Images carved into its sides showed idealised, fanciful images of the reclamation and implied, indeed sometimes outright stated, the RA's glorious role in the process.

She'd left Salim and Xavier in the car a block or two from here, making her way towards the station while avoiding the wells of artificial light that dotted the deserted street. She moved quickly until she came to the wall that divided the station from the rest of the city. The wall ran the perimeter of the station courtyard in an unbroken line save for the wide security checkpoint at the entrance. She avoided this, opting for a more remote and unobserved section of wall.

More ornamental than functional, the wall would have been simple enough to scale even for someone who couldn't use the

Aether to boost the heights she could reach. For Blane, it required little effort, and she was unsurprised by the ease at which she got in; the Far Agency relied on more... *effective* methods of security than simple physical barriers.

Blane felt dry leaves crunch beneath her feet as she dropped down the other side of the wall. The corner she had entered by was layered with a small square of poor soil, the withered and gnarled bushes growing out of it suggesting that once upon a time some hopeful had imagined flowers surviving for anything but a short time when exposed to the region's climate and pollutants.

Taking only a split second to get her bearings, she dashed across the darkness towards the main building, feeling rather than seeing the archaic cobbles of the courtyard beneath her feet. A camera blinked from the corner of the central arch as it swept its gaze across the ground, but nothing changed as its vision glided across her. The spangle suit doing its job, as always.

But Blane knew she had much more to worry about than cameras, here. She was breaking into the *Far Station*. As in, the place with the highest number of trained Aether users in the entire city. In the entire Reclamation, perhaps. One wrong move, and someone would notice her without needing anything as mundane as a visual cue.

After what felt like an age of being exposed and defenceless she reached the long portico between the columns and the building proper. The spotlights shining upon the station from outside and the columns that blocked them created a curious pattern of regular dark and light stripes all along the recessed space, and she ducked into the darkest of these.

She forced herself to breathe. Now was the real test.

She'd practised this technique many times, and it had worked *most* times she'd tested it with Grey and Serinda, but this was the first time she would use it out in the real world. The problem was, there was no way of telling if she'd done it correctly until the station either did or did not erupt in response to a security breach.

She closed her eyes, and felt the Aether beneath her respond as she looked inwards. As always, it seemed to react to her presence with eagerness, pressure building behind it and just waiting for her to will it into reality. Only after talking with Grey had she realised that this wasn't how it felt for most others. It was ready to leap up at her bidding, to help her however it could; to strike at whoever she chose.

And then, instead of reaching down into its inviting power, she drew *back.*

She could have sworn the Aether seemed confused, just for a moment. It's roiling surface quietened briefly, pausing as if unsure how to react to this sudden withdrawal. Then it resumed, like nothing had happened.

Or, Blane wondered, was it possible the Aether seemed just a *bit* more violent in its rolls than it had before?

It didn't matter. She continued to focus on the core of her own being, drawing away from the tempting power below, wrapping herself in nothingness. Exactly *what* part of herself she was drawing away, *what* she was wrapping around herself, she couldn't say; there weren't the words for it yet, but she could sense the distance between herself and the Aether grow ever wider until…

Like a wall-screen flicking off, the Aether was gone. If she'd done it right, she'd be as invisible to another Aether user's senses as she was to the security camera.

A sudden yowl in the darkness to her right made her jump back, biting down on a scream. Something small and furry dashed out of the shadow of a nearby column, followed by something slightly larger. The high-pitched yowling went with them as they charged across the courtyard and into the darkness beyond, the security camera on the central arch swinging to follow.

Just a couple of strays, Blane said to herself, willing her quickened breathing to calm. *Nothing to worry about.*

"What was that?"

The voice came from nearby; far closer than it had any right to be. No more than a handful of metres at best. Ordinarily Blane would have sensed their presence in the Aether long before they could get so close.

She drew back into the darkness of the column's shadow, crouching down and keeping as still as possible.

"It's those damned ferals again," came another voice, further away. "Pest control's getting lax, like I keep saying. They play havoc with the security algorithms, too."

She saw them now. Two Far agents, stood just outside the building. Each one held something small and glowing in their hands. One reached up and placed his to his lips, inhaling deeply then exhaling a cloud of smoke that floated across the sharp boundaries of dark and light towards her.

"Come on," the nearest one said, after a few moments of silence. "Smoke break's over. Let's get back in."

"Already? What's the rush? Not like there's much paperwork to do; whole damn city's quiet these days. Looks like we've finally managed to put those seditionists and BTs on the back foot."

Nevertheless, the second speaker clicked his cigarette off and flicked the used butt out into the darkness. With a sigh, he followed the first speaker back inside.

Four metres, Blane thought. *Four metres, no more.*

That was how close the nearest of the agents had been. Four metres, and he'd sensed nothing. At least she knew for certain now that she'd successfully locked herself off from the Aether.

She needed to be more careful, though. Cutting yourself off from the Aether felt like blocking your ears; you didn't realise how much you used the sense until it was gone. She needed to remember that she could no longer sense when another person was near, that she could no longer *reach* out and know when someone was coming long before she saw them. It meant breaking habits that had become second nature.

Which was one of the reasons she'd brought a few items from Francisco's *caja de golosinas*, as he insisted on calling it. His little box of goodies, full of tiny technological marvels, any one of which would elicit some *very* intrusive questioning from the authorities if found.

She'd never felt the need for them before, something that she now realised spoke to her confidence in her Aether abilities. Overconfidence, perhaps? They hadn't even brought half the gadgets when they broke Grey out of the prison camp.

It was strange, being disconnected from the Aether like this. There was a mild sense of discomfort, a sensation like a phantom limb where there had never been a limb, but there was also the sensation that her mind was clearer, somehow, her thoughts calmer and more composed.

There was also a dull ache, below everything else. Like a thirst that would not be quenched by mere water, or a hunger that demanded more than food.

Blane pushed these thoughts aside. She needed to focus on what she had come here to do. And, she had to admit, she was kind of looking forward to using some of Francisco's toys.

She reached slowly down and tapped the slim disc at her hip, a coin-sized circle of foil-like metal that was stuck to her skin beneath the spangle fabric. Knowing that this action would have activated the transmitter, all she had to do was open and close her eyes in two long, slow blinks to connect to it.

She opened her eyes after the second blink and the world was overlayed with wire. Thin yellow lines surrounded everything she saw, marking out surfaces and corners, sectioning and segmenting the world into distinct borders and boundaries. The world was still there, beyond the images now projected into her eyes by her contact lenses, but had become a wireframe model. It was as if she were trapped in some ancient video game.

Far more importantly, however, were the spots of soft blue and green that appeared where there were seemingly no boundaries. They moved slowly, swaying left to right or heading abruptly elsewhere. Several blinked in and out of existence as the algorithm reevaluated the results of its scan. People.

At least, the likelihood that these were people. Francisco had been very clear that this technology, while more advanced than anything the RA had, was still far from perfect. As the transmitter at her hip broadcast radio waves through the walls of the Far station, algorithms in its processor were working overtime to analyse the attenuated reflections. A combination of the strength of the returning signal and the movement of the object it reflected off allowed the processor at her side to mark anything that had a high probability of being human. Movement, shape, water content; all of it went into a probability scale that was represented by coloured dots, the colour and intensity depicting the relative certainty of the result.

There were at least two people in the space beyond the wall nearest to her; she assumed the two from before, but there was no way of knowing for sure. Depth markers indicated some kind of small room, though it could be a narrow corridor; the space ran further back than the transmitter could reach.

She had a way to check, however. A third, long blink swiftly followed by two quick ones brought up the schematics she'd received from Salim, a blinking yellow dot indicating her approximate location. As long as the schematics were correct, the transmitter's processor should be able to translate the results of its short-distance sweeps into a location on the overlay.

As long as they were correct being the key term here, though.

Salim had been clear that he was only confident in the schematics for the most part, and primarily for the more easily accessible lower floors. The higher up you went, however, the less certain you could trust them. By the time the plans reached the uppermost floors the names and labels on each room were far more vague, and in some cases missing entirely.

Towards the rear of the top section of the main building was a wide section simply labelled *5.º Alto Directorio*. There was no hint of the layout of the room or rooms within, and Blane was unfamiliar with the name. Upon asking, Salim had assured her that the 5th Directory was a quite powerful section of RA internal security.

And, of course, the thought-images were coming from in there.

There, or as near as made little difference. Salim couldn't pinpoint a location very accurately from a distance, but he was fairly sure whoever it was that she needed to find was somewhere in that vicinity. Blane ignored his questions about what she would do once she found them.

Somewhere beyond the city skyline the first slivers of dawn were filtering their way through polluted skies. It would remain dark for hours yet, she knew - what sun could punch its way through the eternal grey cloud cover needed a long run up to do so. The city, though, would be waking up.

Which meant it was also time for the Far station to switch between the night and day shift. Not that Far agents kept to anything like a standard working schedule, as she understood it, but if there were ever a time to sneak inside it was now.

Well, no dejes para mañana lo que puedas hacer hoy, as Francisco would no doubt say, she said to herself.

She crept towards the door the two agents had used, a tall, solid thing covered with ornate wrought metal. Though not as wide as the main entrance further down, it was still clearly designed to project grandeur and authority, and it did it well.

It was also damned heavy, which Blane supposed was why the agents had propped it open with a chair.

Well, didn't need this after all, she thought, sliding the E-pick back into the sleeve-pouch of her suit. Apparently this would have been effective against most forms of electronic lock.

The area behind the door was a wide, open room with rows of

chairs lined across gleaming floors of faux-marble, with thin white columns spaced regularly throughout. Numerous doors led off in every direction, and a long desk at the far end sat empty.

A waiting room, then, just as the floor plans said.

She craned her head around the door frame towards where the ever-shifting dots appeared, doing her best to keep as low a profile as possible.

Just as expected, the two agents who had been smoking outside were visible in an adjoining room, sat across from each other at a small desk and focused intently on their tablescreens. From the look of it they were both engaged in paperwork[7], regular taps and swipes of the screen indicating the manipulation of some document or other.

The agents were separated from the waiting room by a large window that ran from the ceiling down to roughly waist-height. Its discouragingly clear glass afforded them a sweeping view of the room beyond, she was forced to move in a crouched half-crawl directly along the wall beneath it. She heard their low mutterings as she made her way steadily towards a door at the end of the room, speaking to themselves or their work rather than to each other.

With a relieved sigh, she pushed her way through the door and into a deserted corridor. Everything seemed to match the overlay in the top right of her vision; a few carefully spaced blinks could bring it back to full scale, but for now she was fairly confident of her route.

From here she would be fighting a battle between stealth and speed. The faster she moved, the less effective her suit would be against both security cameras and the naked eye, but the slower she moved, the more likely she would encounter someone.

The files Salim had acquired also contained shift information and averaged-out traffic densities for much of the building, and running this through some simple analytics had identified this part of the station as the least busy of all sections at this hour. What business was run in the depths of the night seemed to occur mostly in the opposite wing of the building, near the holding cells and interrogation rooms.

---

[7] The term "paperwork" remained in use long after paper became a minority form of record keeping, and continued long after the language it had been born from evolved beyond mutual comprehensibility. The upper echelons of RA bureaucracy did still like their truly *paper* paperwork, however.

She didn't like to imagine what that business was.

Still, whatever the probability projections said, there was no guarantee that someone wouldn't be walking this section of the station. She headed for the door to the nearest stairwell as fast as she could.

Getting up to the fifth floor proved to be easier than she had hoped. Only at one point did she hear movement, far above her. She froze, pressing into a corner and holding her breath, as footsteps descended, but they quickly disappeared with the sound of a door closing somewhere a floor or two higher. Someone taking the stairs a couple of floors rather than waiting for the elevators, she supposed.

Once she reached the fifth floor, she stepped out of the stairwell into a wide corridor, moving as carefully as possible to avoid making any sound. The corridor ran in two directions; straight ahead, and to her left. From somewhere ahead she heard low voices - three, maybe four distinct speakers, and they didn't seem to be moving.

Left it is, then.

The floor plan was vaguer now, but from what she could tell straight ahead was where she wanted to go. Failing that, it looked as if she could follow the other corridor around and then curve back to the right, cutting out the area with the voices entirely.

She crept carefully down the corridor, straining her ears for the sounds of movement or sudden cries of alarm. Nothing. The wall led her around and, just as she hoped, the sound of voices now came from *behind*.

Now all she had to do was push open the large, curiously authentic-looking wooden doors in front of her, and she would be inside the area labelled as *5.° Alto Directorio* on her map.

Tapping the stun-lock at her side, she pushed open the doors. At the same time, the voices behind her went silent.

The Lock hit her before she could do anything but struggle futilely to reach the Aether, as the figure sat waiting in the room beyond smiled.

"Hello, Blane," said Ritra Feye.

Interlude

xx.loc:null .. When war is everywhere, soldiers become your leaders .. sec.exception.xx

Firewall Breach 407.1.223, received by all Reclamation devices, origin unknown

It was cold. It felt like he'd always been cold.

The cold was a part of him, a biting chill that ran through his flesh into his bones, down into the very core of his being until all that there was was frozen, unyielding ice.

Even thinking was a task beyond him. All he had was that one sensation, a feeling that had long since moved past pain and become something transcendent; a universe all of its own, that was everything that was and everything that would be.

He floated in its centre, and it floated in his.

But if he struggled, if he pushed with everything he had and continued to do so even when he had no more to give; if he pushed with all his being for what felt like uncountable eternities, he could remember... a fire.

The fire had been his. It had swum and flown and dived at his call, and it had seared his enemy's skin from their bones.

And just as the fire had been his, he had been the fire's. To be used was its purpose, and to use it was his; it *needed* to be called, and he was meant to guide it in ways that reshaped the world.

The distant whisper of memory in the frozen void was a torment, a reminder of what had been taken from him. Or... what he had given up?

He couldn't remember. He couldn't even remember who he was. He'd been given a name, once... Strange. He'd been *given* a name? Who could have given him such a thing?

Whatever that name had been, it was gone now, along with everything but the cold. The cold, and the whispers.

Could you cry, in this frozen place? He didn't know.

Did he want to cry?

Or did he want to *scream?*

Somewhere, golden flame flickered.

18

The continents of the world were transformed beyond recognition in the generations before the Sudden War. Humanity moved mountains and reshaped oceans with its power, and the natural world was replaced by a sculpted one.
Today, the waters and the waste seek to reclaim what was stolen from them. If they cannot recreate the old world, they will at least have their revenge on the new.

Environment and Man, Bartosz Martiné

The rattling of metal on metal roused her, a loud, violent clanging that reverberated in time with a pulsing headache that made her want to vomit.

"Alright, time to boot up and ship out."

The voice was rough and deep, and when she opened her eyes she saw it was coming from a short, grizzled looking man in steel-grey shirt and pants beneath a long black jacket; the uniform of the Far Agency.

She was in the Far Station... was that right?

Yes, that's right. I came here to find... something.

Her mind felt like it was wrapped in thick cotton, every thought coming slow and vague.

The Far agent rapped his baton against the bars of the cell again.

"Come on, get up. Get out of here before we decide to keep you for something else," he said.

He seemed to be only half paying attention to her as he slid the bars of the cell door open, his eyes looking further down what seemed to be a narrow corridor. He gestured at her to hurry up.

With a groan, Blane pushed herself up. Her muscles ached almost as much as her head, and her legs protested when she pushed herself off the small, hard recessed bed and onto her feet.

"What... what happened?" she said, half to herself.

The eyes of the agent flickered back towards her, and he tutted.

"What happened?" he said, with an annoyed look. "You got lucky, that's what. A wild Aether user messing around like that? You're lucky we didn't take you down to the interrogation floor for *processing.*"

Something about the way he said that final word told Blane she probably really *was* lucky.

"Friends in high places though, eh?" The agent continued. "We've been ordered to let you go - with a warning, of course."

The agent gave a smile that was all teeth.

"So..." he said, predatory eyes glinting in the gloom. "Go. Before I figure you're resisting. Then I'd be in my rights to operate *outside* orders..."

He chuckled as she hurriedly stepped through the door and past him.

The cell did indeed stand on one side of a long, narrow corridor. The walls of the corridor were cracked and peeling, with curious bumps and dents that spoke of violent impacts. The rows of cells stood empty as she walked past them, save for one.

Blane's steps faltered when she saw a forlorn-looking figure sat in one cell, curled up with their arms around their knees and staring hopelessly at Blane as she walked by. Their hunched posture, and the bruises on their face, made age and gender indiscernible..

"Keep going," came the agent's voice from behind her. "No interacting with other suspects."

With a mumbled "sorry," Blane rushed to the end of the corridor and came out in a small room. The room was empty except for a few rows of chairs and a small office of some kind sealed off behind misted glass, small holes near the centre clearly put their for communicating with whoever was ensconced within.

A heavy steel door stood at the end of the room. Seeing nowhere else to go, she walked over to it and pushed it open.

The sounds of the city poured over her, cars driving along damp streets and machinery rattling and buzzing in the distance. Behind her, the door slammed shut with a finality that said it wouldn't be opening again.

She stared groggily up at the grey sky; it seemed to be about mid-day, but there was no way of knowing without...

Her thin-screen was gone. Her thin-screen, and everything else.

She looked down at herself, and realised she was in some plain poly-cotton pants and shirt she had never seen before. Hadn't she been wearing...?

A spangle suit. She'd been wearing a spangle suit because... because she'd been sneaking into the Far Station.

Memories came back to her, fragmented and jumbled, but memories nonetheless.

Her thin-screen was gone, and so was her suit and... she blinked to be sure... yes, and the contact lenses she had been wearing.

Every piece of technology she'd had was gone. Someone had taken it, but who?

More memories. A face, smiling.

Ritra Feye.

She'd met Ritra Feye!

Blane had heard enough about Ritra Feye over the years to know who she was. She'd actually met her once before, outside the Central Tower after Fen destroyed it, but at the time Blane had thought she was just another Far agent.

Grey had mentioned her a number of times, mainly in those rare moments when he spoke about his experiences in the Far Academy. It sounded like Feye had been a sort of mentor to him, and his respect for her was always plain in his voice.

In fact, Blane had even fantasized about meeting her again during long nights in the safe house, lying in bed with the lights on and searching for ways to hide from the painful memories that waited to pounce whenever she let down her guard. Feye sounded like the sort of role model Blane was actively looking for; a powerful, confident Aether user and so much more.

Why couldn't she remember what had happened? She fought to dredge the memories up.

A migraine washed over her so powerful it was as if a laser had been pointed directly into her eyes. Everything went white, and she staggered as the world span around her.

Pushing out a hand, she used the walls of the station to steady herself until the feeling passed. Her breath came ragged, and sweat dripped from her nose despite the cold.

The next moment, the chill was at her core. She stood bolt upright, pain pushed aside by horrified realisation.

She had to get back to Serinda. Now.

She knew one thing, though how she knew it she couldn't say. The knowledge screamed at her from the back of her mind.

The *Forever Fallen*. Raphael. The sickness.

All of it was planned; all of it was controlled.

Uriel was an RA agent.

19

The harnessing of the Aether has altered the world irrevocably in ways not yet acknowledged or recognised by our competitors. Imagine continent-spanning industrial empires in which, for all their vaunted advances, theories of electromagnetism never developed. Despite their seeming power, we would know them for what they were: primitive, brutal, and unable to fend off the dark. That is who shares our world.

Report to the Committee by the Analytical Directorate (Classified)

The quarry stretched out below her, wind whipping at her where she stood high on the overlooking lip. Serinda was somewhere in there, likely not even realising she was trapped.

It had taken Blane hours to get back to the safe house, and when she did Serinda wasn't there. Nor was there any sign of Xavier or Salim, who she'd been unable to find even after fuzzily recalling that she had made her way to the Far station with them.

But she'd had no time to worry about them, because there was a message icon blinking insistently in the upper corner of the wall-screen when she walked in, rain-sodden and exhausted. She told the room to play it, and despair replaced exhaustion.

"I'm sorry, Blane, but I have to go," Serinda's image said on the screen.

She looked distracted, harried; already mentally out the door and heading into the Waste before her body had time to catch up.

"I figured it out," the message continued. "At least, most of it. I can help Raphael but... but there's not much time. She could... I could already be too late, so I have to go *now*."

The Serinda in the video stepped away from the camera, then turned back as if remembering something.

"Look, Blane. I *have* to go. This isn't because you left without telling me - though I'll admit that hurt. There's just no time to wait for you..."

Serinda paused, biting her lip in worry. "I... I hope you're ok, and that when I get back we can sort everything out. Until then... stay safe, okay?"

The message winked out, and the wall faded to its usual pale, softly glowing beige.

"*Shit.*"

So now Blane found herself stood high upon the lip of the quarry's crater, trying hard not to feel lost.

The video message and the knowledge that Serinda might be walking into an RA trap had filled Blane with urgency and anger, but the hours-long drive left her drained. Driving through the Waste with only her half-remembered knowledge of the route had been stupid; she was lucky she'd made it here in one piece.

What was happening to her? It was like she was two different people. At times her thoughts were afire and relentless, the adrenaline flowing through her and confidence so high it was like a drug. Then, at times like this, tired and alone and trying her best not to be afraid, it was all she could do not to curl up into a ball and hide.

It felt like a weight was pressing down on her; everything seemed to be happening at once, and she had no one to turn to. There was no time to waste, but rushing in would only create more danger.

And she had nothing with her this time; no gadgets or tools. All she'd been able to find in the safe house was a basic thin-screen, which she'd left with the last of Francisco's vehicles far behind and below her on the outskirts of the hills. It wasn't anon-spec, and would broadcast her position to anyone searching for it.

She didn't even have a spangle suit; she'd used the last one getting into the Far Station, losing it somewhere within that strange, terrifying blank in her memory.

She began making her way along the lip of the quarry, loose rock shifting under her feet, knowing there was little chance the *Fallen* hadn't seen her coming. She stayed towards the outer edge and used every rock or piece of long-dead vegetation she could find as cover, staying as small as possible. Even if the *Fallen* did know she was here, there was no point in making it easy for them.

Moreover, they would be expecting her to head for the entrance below, in the centre of the crater; the way she had entered by before. They certainly wouldn't be expecting her to head *up*.

Some way further along, the bluff where she and Xavier had sat what felt like a lifetime ago rose high above the rest of the crater lip. Something about the rock within had left it standing while the rest of the crater ridge had collapsed, and at points the sides curved outward to form overhangs with nothing but a long fall beneath.

Its sides were sheer and jagged, with tufts of vegetation growing fitfully in cracks and crags running up every side. Completely unclimbable without special equipment, as Xavier had said.

Except, she told herself as she reached for the Aether, she was going to climb it.

Some of that familiar confidence and determination returned as she approached the base of the bluff. She told herself it could only be twenty or thirty meters, no more, but from here it seemed to stretch as high as the Central Tower.

She stared at the sheer, dirty grey rock rising vertically in front of her, and the dirty grey rock seemed to stare right back.

"Right," she said, clapping her hands together. "Let's get this over with."

There was, of course, no way she should even *consider* climbing the bluff. She didn't have the skills to climb such a sheer rock face, and never would without years of training and specialised equipment.

But perhaps, she said to herself, she *did* have both those things.

No, not perhaps. The Aether was a tool, and she had years of practice in its use.

She knew she could do it; she'd been working on it since she'd first seen Gabriel using the Aether to enhance his own movements. When removing the tracker from Grey, the doctor had channeled Aether both into the patient and *himself.* She'd seen the dexterity and muscle control it afforded him, and been determined to make that technique hers.

In any spare moment since then she'd been experimenting, and found that not only could she increase the finesse of her movements, but actually feed Aether into her musculature to increase stamina and strength. When linked with the other ability Gabriel had demonstrated, the technique to dull pain by interfering with nociceptor thresholds, she couldn't keep herself from excitedly imagining the many ways it could be useful.

She hadn't expected to test it in quite such a do-or-die manner, however.

Splinters of stone flaked off under her fingers as she reached up and grabbed at the sheer face of the bluff. She clenched, forcing her fingers to find a hold that would not slip, then with a push off the ground she found a hold higher up with her other hand. She pulled herself up, kicking her feet hard into the wall to hang there frozen like a spider on a wall.

Well, so far so good, she said to herself.

Her hands already ached. In fact, the tips of her fingers were burning and she could feel her arms start to tremble with exertion. Drawing the Aether up and into herself, she fed a little of its energy into her straining muscles and a little more into the her own nervous system.

It was a strange sensation, one that she still wasn't used to even after frequent practice in the days since she'd seen the trick. It was like doing wiring on yourself. She could *feel* where ions flowed and charge passed from synapse to synapse all through her body, a billion threads sewn all through her, and she could feel how the Aether merged with and wrapped around these pathways at the slightest urging.

The trembling ceased, the pain dulled to almost nothing, and she gave a sigh of relief. Still, she needed to hurry; Aether might be able to supplement or even replace cellular energy stocks, but it took its own toll on the body.[8] She didn't want to still be on this rock when she become too exhausted to draw any more.

The next few meters seemed almost easy, though she knew this was because her mind was on what was coming next. The first small section of rock face would have been scaleable by a seasoned climber even without tools, but the next section was a mess of sharp ridges and broken, serrated points.

She slipped almost immediately, her grip coming free as a lump of loose soil broke off beneath her hand, and she was only able to save herself from falling by channeling a brief, life-saving surface in the air beneath her feet and using it to fling herself forward to secure a new purchase.

She clung to the rock for a moment, drawing deep breaths and forcing herself to *calm* by filtering thin flows of golden energy into herself, feeling her autonomic nervous system first resist, then respond to, this strange outside force. She sensed her heart rate and respiration drop, and slowly mind-numbing terror shrunk into

---

[8] Grey once told her that much Academy research focused on what exactly it was that limited the quantity and duration of Aether a user could draw on. A friend - Chau, he'd said - had devoted a great deal of time to this.

143

background fear.

She began to climb again, refusing to look down.

The moment she reached the top, Blane felt a feeling of triumph such as she had never felt before. It had seemed to take hours, and there had been moments when she had clung, frozen, for minutes on end, but she'd made it. The Waste stretched out into the distance behind her, and in front was the narrow path leading towards the entrance to the *Fallen* hideout.

And still no one had come for her. Blane wasn't foolish enough to assume this was a good thing.

They *must* have seen her coming in from the Waste. There was no usable cover for kilometres around, and only a very few routes through the orange, toxin-blighted lands surrounding the quarry.

Nevertheless, silence. Silence, and no sense of another living creature as far as her mind could reach.

She headed for the entrance.

20

Nature is God's dominion; humanity is only his Khalifa, his steward. Even the blasted remains of this world are his, and must be tended with care.

Words from the 14th Dīwān (Unsanctioned Digital Document)

The shouting was audible before she made it halfway down the shaft. Shouting, and sporadic gunfire. By the time she made it to the bottom the faint, acrid smell of gunfire was also noticeable.

Stepping cautiously out of the tunnel entrance, she crouched in the darkness and stretched out with all her senses. Her eyes made out distant flashes of light in the dark, and she heard yells; angry or fearful, she couldn't tell. The fumes in the air were not only smell but taste, a stinging metallic sensation on her tongue.

Still, she could breathe, and through the Aether she sensed no one nearby. The majority of the quarry's inhabitants seemed to be gathered close to the centre of the cavern, what most people called 'the square,' right on the limits of her senses. The flashes and yells seemed to be centred there too.

She made her way stealthily towards the gathering, slowly drawing herself away from the Aether as she did so. Doing so would conceal her presence from other users, but it also made her acutely aware of how exposed and defenceless she really was.

What am I doing? she thought.

Did she really think she could just sneak in here and... what? Swoop in and rescue Serinda from whatever trap she might be snared in? Why was she acting like the protagonist of some dumb *New Patriot* movie? She wasn't even armed; drawing away from the Aether meant drawing away from the one thing that could keep her safe.

The thoughts crowded into her head like a dam holding them back had broken. In a way, Blane was beginning to realise, it had. Something about locking herself off from the Aether made her... not more fearful, but less confident. Less reckless.

It had felt like this when she sealed herself off from the Aether before entering the Far station too, but Francisco's gadgets had gone some way towards hiding the feeling. As if silencing the Aether was silencing the voice inside her that told her she could do anything she wanted.

Which was the real Blane? she wondered.

Was it the person she was now, realising she was in way over her head but also knowing there was no way she was going to turn back when Serinda might be so close, and in trouble? Or was the real Blane the one who threw herself at military-grade drones and rushed headlong into heavily guarded Reclamation sites without a thought for the risks?

These questions without answers twisted tighter and tighter around her mind until she reached to side of the building that, on their previous visit, Grey had been "encouraged" to spend his time in. Reaching out to touch the cold prefab wall, she shook the thoughts from her mind.

The space around the building was darker than it should be. It looked like several of the spotlights normally used to illuminate this place had been switched off, or maybe removed. Still, there was enough light to see by, and far more towards where she sensed the crowd gathering.

From here the sounds of the clustered people were much clearer. She could hear talking and raised voices, but whatever had been happening seemed to have calmed down. She sprinted across the open ground between one building and the next, slipping into a narrow divide between two of the prefab structures. Various tools and boxes lined the sides, and she had to be careful not to knock into anything.

Someone was stood around the corner of the next building. Two people, she thought. She could hear the shuffling of their feet, and soft conversation too quiet to make out. Shadows shifted across the ground in front of her as the figures, whoever they were, shifted into and out of the way of the spotlights.

She needed to go back, retrace her steps and find another route around. She didn't know what she would do if she was spotted. The plan, insofar as she had one, was to find a concealed viewpoint from which to see what exactly was going on with the *Fallen* gathered in the central square. She'd figure out her next move from there.

She turned, and heard a woman's voice call out from somewhere ahead.

"Sattores, that you?"

Uh-oh.

She was trapped, both exits blocked. The sound of steps came

146

closer as Blane drew back, trying to make herself as small as possible in the shadows. She knew it was futile, but perhaps it would give her enough of the element of surprise to take out the speaker before they could react.

"Sattores...? Someone there?"

A silhouette appeared at the end of the gap, a woman rendered dark and featureless in the dull light. She stepped forward, into the gap where Blane crouched, and raised something long and metallic.

Blane didn't give the woman anymore time. Drawing down into the Aether, she exploded from where she hid and dove towards the figure, rolling beneath the barrel of the woman's weapon and sending Aether in torrents to overwhelm her senses.

Flare, Grey called it. The technique was a way of overloading the parietal lobe and sensory cortices with what was essentially white noise, causing a desync between left and right hemispheres and sending incoherent and contradictory signals crashing across the cerebral cortex. It caused all sense of location and spatial orientation to go wild, violent auditory and visual hallucinations, and even altered a victim's sense of time. She'd experienced the effects herself a number of times, in training with Grey.[9]

It was, she had concluded, a bad time.

With a cry, the woman fell to her knees. She'd be able to crawl again in a few minutes, if she was lucky, but for now would be stuck to the floor. Blane heard this rather than saw it, however, because she was already sprinting past and away, fully aware that she'd been noticed by the two stood on the opposite side of the building the instant she touched the Aether.

Panic began to set in as she ran wildly *away* without a thought for *towards*. It was more instinct than logic that saw her avoid the wells of light surrounding the various buildings, but she knew that sticking to the gloom would only be effective for so long. No one in the *Fallen* would be able to get anywhere close without her sensing them long before they sensed her, but they *would* get to her. It was only a matter of time, unless she left right now.

But it wasn't back to the tunnel that her feet took her, but instead

---

[9] One thing about the training with Grey that had surprised her was the fact that learning to use the Aether was as much textbook and essay study as it was practical experimentation. More so, in fact. At times it felt like she were studying to become a biologist, specializing in neuroscience..

to a building she only half-realised she was heading for. The familiar well of light at its entrance was unchanged, as well as the guard outside the entrance.

The makeshift clinic, and Raphael.

Raphael was the only person Blane was confident she could trust. At least, trust not to be an RA spy. She couldn't imagine a world in which Raphael could have hidden this from Serinda; the two had been lovers for years. More than lovers, from the way Serinda spoke about her sometimes, in those evenings when close confinement brought down the walls both she and Blane usually maintained. Even after everything that happened, Serinda never spoke ill of Sara.

Stretching out her senses from the darkness, Blane felt for the presence of the man stood guard at the door. The men. There were two now, she sensed, where before there had only been one. She didn't recognise either, but something about them made her uneasy, even at this distance; they felt hard, attention piercing the darkness in constant watch.

Stretching further towards them, she felt tension in both their minds. Tension, and focus. The previous guard had always sat casually and bored-seeming, but these two stood alert and on guard.

Which made them a perfect target for *Rage*.

Rage was essentially the counterpart of *Fear*, both techniques involving the overstimulation of the amygdala. Only, while the effect on someone who was focused on movement and self-preservation was *flight*, the effect on someone intent on remaining staunch and resolute was *fight*.

It took a few moments before the technique took hold, but Blane knew it had worked the instant she heard the tone of the first words one of the guards spoke.

"Hey, keep your guard up."

A pause, and the other shuffled his feet.

"My guard *is* up," came the reply. Even from a distance Blane could hear the irritation. "How about you stay focused on you?"

A grunt from the first speaker.

"*Qué carajo* is going on over there?" the second speaker snarled code-switching into a more vulgar register of centra-English and gripping the butt of his rifle tightly as he swung it in the direction of the square.

"Doesn't matter," replied the first. "The *Nuestra* will handle it. We stay here, like Uriel said."

The second man span round to the face the first.

"I *know* we stay here. *Deja de hablar así.* I've warned you before about acting so superior."

Yes! Blane thought. She'd hit the jackpot - these two already had bad blood between them.

Neither guard was looking outwards now, instead squaring up to the other with narrowed eyes and tightly-gripped rifles. She was almost tempted to see what would happen if she remained hidden, but if either of them realised they were being manipulated they would quickly be able to shake the effects off.

So she came flying out of the darkness and hit the both of them with *Flare.* She didn't pause to watch them fall, but barrelled through the doors and into the clinic. The guards would be up in a few minutes, at most, so her only hope was to get to Raphael first and hope she could fix things.

Blane sprinted down the central aisle towards Raphael's room without a care for those in the way, ignoring the surprised shouts and yells her sudden appearance caused. She barrelled past numerous startled but weaponless figures, seeing nothing threatening enough to slow her down.

She didn't realise her mistake until it was too late.

Many of the *Fallen* were Aether users; which meant that you shouldn't assume they were harmless just because you couldn't *see* any weapons.

The blast took her off her feet, sending her crashing back the way she had come. She kept sliding after she hit the floor, coming to a stop what felt an impossibly long time later crumpled in front of the door she had entered by.

When the world swam back into focus, everything hurt. She was sprawled face down on the floor, unsure if she could move. Her head rang, and she thought she might have a broken wrist. Only the pressure shield she managed to get up at the very last second had saved her from more severe injury.

That technique had been *good*, too. Whoever had done it, they'd channelled the entire force of the explosion into a narrow funnel down the central aisle directly into Blane, simultaneously making up for the weakness of the Aether in this underpopulated place and avoiding smashing over any of the flimsy walls along each side.

She heard footsteps approaching and strained to look up, her neck protesting with bolts of pain.

Female feet, she thought, staring at the legs now planted directly in front of her. *Small, too.*

Why did she find that so funny? She had hit her head hard; she felt a little delirious.

"You? What on earth are you doing here?" came a voice from above. Familiar somehow, but she couldn't place it at first.

Blane felt tendrils of Aether flow into her, dulling the pain and flooding warmth into injured muscles.

May Li. That was the name. She'd been the one taking care of Raphael.

"Please," Blane said, struggling to speak through, she now realised, a split and bleeding lip. "I need to speak to Raphael."

"After you come bursting into my clinic like that? And, if I sensed things right, after assaulting the two men outside?"

Blane couldn't see Li's face, but she didn't sound angry. She sounded... amused?

She felt Li crouch down and lean in, whispering in her ear.

"I never liked those two anyway. A couple of creeps, *los dos*. We never wanted them posted here."

Blane felt surprisingly strong arms pull her up.

"Come on," May Li said, grunting slightly with the effort. "I don't think anything's broken, but you're going to hurt for days."

Blane wheezed from the pain of standing, even with her arm across May Li's shoulders for support.

They managed to take only a single step before the wide doors behind them burst open and two armed figures came running in; a man and a woman with guns raised and holding the Aether. The two she had been running from, Blane thought, after she knocked down that first *Fallen*.

"Stop right there," said the man, pointing his rifle directly at her chest. "Get away from her, Li."

His partner moved around the side of the room, keeping her own weapon up as she did so.

I could take one before the other gets a shot off, Blane thought. *One, but not both.*

"Put those things down right now, Satorres," Li snapped at the man, not lessening her support of Blane. "You fire a weapon in my clinic, and I promise you this girl will be the least of your worries."

The growl in May Li's voice was so threatening that Blane nearly chuckled aloud at the contrast it presented to the woman's small frame. Was it possible she hadn't had *any* osteoblast therapy?

The man's weapon wavered in uncertainty, and he looked confused.

"You know her?" he asked. "She just took out three of us. Could be an RA spy, like the other one."

These words cleared out some of the fog in Blane's head, if not the pain.

Other one? Were they talking about Serinda?

"This one is not a spy," May Li said with finality. "And neither is Serinda. Or are you calling Raphael a liar too?"

The man looked torn for a moment then, with a meaningful glance to his partner, lowered his weapon. The woman did the same.

What the hell was going on?

"Uriel won't like this," the man said, sulkily.

"Well Uriel's not here, is he?" Li snapped back, before the man had even finished speaking.

Despite her addled state, Blane could see fear wrestling with worry on the man's face.

"Fine," he said. "But I'm going to have to report this."

"You do that," replied Li. There was a sneer in her voice. "Run off to Uriel like a good little waste-rat, and tell him that if he wants something from me he can damn well come get it himself. "

The two armed *Fallen* stared at each other for a moment. Then, with a sharp nod, they left without another word.

"You're not very good at making friends, are you?" said May Li, hefting Blane onwards in the direction of Raphael's room. "Come on, she's going to want to talk to you before they come back."

21

Multiple Aether techniques appear to function by manipulating mirror neurons in a subject. While still little understood, such neurons have been shown to cause phenomena such as 'pain empathy' - in which an individual witnessing another suffer injury feels pain in turn. It now seems possible that these neurons are especially susceptible to Aetherial manipulation. More research is necessary.

Agent F. Chau, *Progress Report 4291.b*

Serinda wasn't there. At least, she wasn't there anymore.

"You missed all the drama," Li told Blane with a bitten-off, sardonic laugh.

"That was... just the... first round."

Each of Raphael's words was bracketed by a pained, shallow breath. It was obvious to Blane that the woman was struggling to speak, and failing to hide her difficulty. She looked as if she could collapse at any moment, propping herself up against a wall and pointedly ignoring May Li's gestures towards the medical bed.

Serinda *had* been here. At least, she'd been just outside the clinic, making it virtually the whole way across the *Fallen* base through sheer force of will before anyone dared to stop her. No one had wanted to be the first to confront their infamous former member, and alerting Uriel to her arrival had taken time.

So she made it all the way to the clinic before the two stationed at the door blocked her way.

Only Serinda's shouts had alerted those inside to her presence, and as soon as Raphael heard Serinda she insisted on going herself.

"You saw her, then?" asked Blane.

Raphael nodded weakly, her face grim.

"I told them... to let her go. But..."

Raphael swayed, which spurred May Li to stride over to and take the other woman by the arm. Ignoring her feeble protestations, she gently led Raphael to the bed and sat her down on it.

Raphael rested for a moment, then raised a hand and laid it on Li's shoulder. Blane could only watch as Raphael drew Li close, whispering something in her ear.

As soon as Raphael finished her whispers Li drew back and fixed her with an expression both grave and unreadable. Raphael responded with a sharp nod, not dropping her matching stare. After a silent pause Li sighed, and turned to where a tray of various vials and needles lay.

"Uriel insisted Serinda is a threat," May Li said, talking to the room as she rummaged through the medical instruments. Seeming to find what she was looking for she held up a syringe, stabbing it into a vial filled with a curious black solution before turning back to Raphael.

"He's insisting a lot of things are a threat, these days," she continued as she pushed the needle into Raphael's arm.

Almost immediately some colour returned to the sick woman's face. She still looked pale and gaunt, but something of the old Raphael that Blane remembered returned.

"It's a damned coup. Now his friends are here, he's finally found the *cajones* to make a move."

Raphael slammed a fist into her other hand. Her voice had regained some of its strength, too.

"Friends?"

"The *Sindicata Nuestra*," explained May Li. "Uriel brought them in after a bunch of us tried to leave, and they're his creatures to the core."

The *Sindicata Nuestra*? The racketeers or smugglers or whatever they were? Why were they working with Uriel?

"That's what we'd like to know, too. He claims they're here to help with *security*," said Raphael, spitting the final word.

Blane had forgotten that about Raphael; how the woman could sometimes seem to *Read* your thoughts without actually doing so. It was a trait Grey said she shared with Ritra Feye.

A flash of pain, and memory; a room in the Far Station, and a woman's voice. Feye. It was there for an instant, then gone.

"And Uriel is using the *Sindicata Nuestra* to, what, keep everyone here against their will?" Blane asked, shaking off the sensation.

Raphael nodded.

"Essentially. More and more of us are getting sick," she said. "The same thing that... the same as me."

As she finished speaking she pushed herself up from the bed, and this time she did *not* sway.

"Seri said she'd figured out what the sickness is," said Blane, remembering Serinda's words in the message left at the safe house.

"In such a short time?" said May Li, with a soft gasp. "We were

153

looking for months, and yet..."

There was a strange quaver in Li's voice that Blane couldn't identify.

Raphael's small smile, however, was a knowing one. *She* knew Serinda could do such a thing.

Raphael really did look *much* better, Blane thought. What had been in that syringe? And why were they only using it now?

"I'm going to find Uriel," said Raphael in a voice that brooked no defiance. "I'll deal with that traitor myself."

"He's RA."

The room fell silent at Blane's words, only the hum of the clinic in the background.

"Is he, now?" Raphael's eyes narrowed. "And you have proof?"

"I... uh... No."

Blane's shoulders fell. She couldn't even tell herself how she knew this; she just did. The knowledge, and the inky void of nothingness surrounding it in her mind, made her feel grimy. Violated.

"It's ok," said Raphael. "I've suspected it for some time now, but Uriel is more devious than a pit viper."

She sighed; a long, deep sigh of resignation and regret.

"*Es agua pasada..* I can't fix the past, but I can fix the present."

"You still shouldn't..." May Li began, before Raphael cut her off with a growl.

"I am *going*," Raphael said, and the words fell as heavy as a concrete slab.

She marched out of the room without waiting for a response, leaving Blane and Li to stare at each other for a moment before Li hurried out after her patient.

Blane was last to leave, delayed for a moment by the shock of realising May Li was crying. Why, she couldn't say.

But, she thought to herself, *something is very wrong.*

And she thought it had to do with whatever had been in that vial.

By the time she caught up, Raphael was already outside and striding across the bare earthen floor towards the central square. That was where the majority of the yelling had been coming from. And, now she thought about it, where the tall, blank-faced building containing the Fabricator stood.

No one tried to stop them. Blane could sense more than a handful of people scattered through the site, and every mind she touched was a knot of apprehension as if waiting for a bomb to go off, but most were too far away to even notice them.

Those that did see or sense them quickly spotted Raphael in the lead, and tension turned to... surprise? Alarm? Relief?

From what Blane could tell, Raphael's appearance provoked as many reactions as there were those to react. She sensed several figures hurry off towards the central area, no doubt to find Uriel, while several more drew back into the darkness like small creatures hiding in a burrow. A number even came out to join them, marching up behind Raphael and matching her determined stride.

By the time they reached Uriel they were at least a dozen strong. Unfortunately, whatever confidence Blane had begun to feel was swiftly crushed when she saw how many Uriel had.

Practically everyone in the base had to be gathered there, a large group of people clumped together in a rough circle almost completely surrounding a smaller group with their backs against the wall of the Fabricator building.

Someone in the larger group noticed their approach - Blane thought it was one of the two who had chased her into the clinic - and warned their companions. They span to face the newcomers, Uriel at their centre.

"Raphael," Uriel said. He was trying to hide the surprise in his voice, but failing. "You shouldn't be out of bed."

But even as he spoke Blane could see his shock at seeing Raphael looking so healthy. A number of figures to his side raised their weapons, and only lowered them again at a gesture from him.

"You look... better," he said, a slight question in the inflection of his words.

"I had May Li give me a little pick-me-up," Raphael replied, and Blane saw Li give small flinch. "What's going on here?"

Uriel stared at Li for a moment, then Raphael's look drew him back.

"Nothing to concern yourself over," he said. "Just a small group causing trouble. I'll handle it."

"He's selling us out!"

The cry came from a light-haired man within the smaller group. He stepped defiantly forward, but Blane didn't need the Aether to see his fear. None of the smaller group were armed.

"Nonsense," said Uriel, not even looking at the man. "You cannot..."

Raphael cut him off with a wave of her hand, looking towards the man who had spoken and raising her eyebrows in question.

"He's selling us all out," the man continued, voice growing in strength as if drawing determination from Raphael. "Using the Fabricator for his own gain. Refusing meds, practically starving us..."

"Rad-trash![10]" Uriel said, before Raphael cut him off with a growl. She nodded at the man to continue.

"He's selling it all to the syndicate. Has been since you got sick. *Dios* knows how much he's making."

The man looked back at his companions for support. They nodded, and gave murmurs of assent.

Raphael ran her eyes across the smaller group, taking in their fearful but determined expressions, then turned back to Uriel.

"Is this true, Uriel? Are you stealing from the *Fallen*?"

Her words were like ice.

"Ridiculous," he replied, licking his lips nervously. "I am just... just doing what it takes to keep us safe."

"And do your RA masters know about your little side business?"

Uriel froze, so completely motionless for a moment that Blane could believe time had stopped. Then, slowly, his expression hardened.

"That..." he said, voice low and full of threat, "... is a very serious accusation."

He looked to the figures at his side, each holding a weapon with the ease of familiarity and with the muscle-tone of frequent and intensive osteoblast therapy. Not any members of the *Fallen* Blane had seen before, she realised, but they were *very* noticeable. These must be *Sindicato Nuestro*.

The armed *Sindicato* stared back at Uriel with suspicion.

So they don't know he's RA, either, Blane thought.

"My friend is clearly extremely sick," Uriel continued, projecting his voice over the gathered crowd.

Now she knew what to look for, Blane spotted a number of other

---

[10] Old-world garbage could be converted into a variety of valuable raw materials, so the term 'trash' carried a different nuance than in pre-Fall generations. Irradiated trash, however, could generally not be purified without costing vastly more than it was worth.

heavily armed *Sindicato* members. Too many, spread out amongst and behind the crowd. The *Fallen*, she saw, might be greater in number but most carried nothing larger than a pistol, and those few and far between.

Uriel's eyes fell on Blane, and she saw a predatory glint in his eyes.

"And associating with known traitors again, I see."

Blane matched his cold gaze with one of her own, curling her lips into a thin smile. She was determined not to let him get to her. Not like last time. Nevertheless, she reached down into the Aether and drew it into herself, not doubting that Uriel would sense this.

Not only Uriel, it seemed. Two of the *Sindicato* besides him tensed, glancing towards her and shifting their weapons. A faint golden glow enveloped them, though not seen with the eye.

So, there are Aether users in the Sindicato *too.* That was interesting.

It didn't worry Blane, though. Something rose within her alongside the Aether; something like rage, but different. More focused, more indignant and vengeful.

Wrath.

She *knew* she was more powerful than any of them. The Aether was something that belonged to her, that was a *part* of her. And they thought they could use it against her! Her lips curled back, and through gritted teeth she made a low growl.

A hand on her shoulder drew her back to reality.

"I know that look," said Raphael softly. "But not you. That's not you."

Blane found it hard to process the expression on Raphael's face. It showed a worry in a way that didn't belong on those eternally hard, determined features. For a moment, there was only her look of concern.

A low chuckle drew both of their attentions back to Uriel.

"You're *resonating*," he said, placing a special emphasis on the word. "Resonating with that freak that killed Caldwell."

"Caldwell?" Raphael said with an arched eyebrow. "You're on first-name terms with Reclamation rats, are you?"

Uriel scowled at her for a second, then with a dismissive wave he turned to the *Sindicato*.

"Fuck it," he said. "I told you I'd get you more access to the Fabricator, didn't I? Well, you can *have* it."

He gestured to the *Fallen* all around him.

"Get rid of them," Uriel continued, "and it's yours. I'm done with this place, and the whole damn lot of them. Just make sure I get my money."

The *Sindicato* hesitated for a moment then raised their rifles, and there was no more time for thinking.

22

Globalization was an old world idea discredited long before the Sudden War. The idea of porous borders and international community was a fever-dream cured by the cold, hard realities of ever-decreasing resources and ever-increasing competition and conflict.

Anfad Truin, *Practical Diplomacy*

The first bullet that went tearing towards Raphael should have hit her. Blane only managed to deflect it a little, but enough so that it tore a hole through the side of her shirt rather than her flesh.

A second bullet never came; at least not at Raphael, and not from the *Sindicato* who had fired the first because they were instantly smashed backwards and up into the air, disappearing somewhere into the darkness behind them.

More bullets *did* fly through the air, though, and as Blane dived for Raphael she sensed a number of bodies hitting the floor around her. The Aether, too, was seething all around, blasts of it being used for attacks both mental and physical.

She dragged Raphael away as the sound of firing and explosive compressions reverberated through her bones, not relaxing her grip until they were behind the poor cover of a pair of metal crates barely shoulder-height. Bullets pinged off the containers terrifyingly close, and only the Pressure Shield she was maintaining kept them safe from the vicious, biting explosions of rapidly contracting and expanding points of space that burst all around them.

Despite it all, she smiled. The attacks were already weakening as the sparse Aether here was drained. Still, she could feel the *Sindicato* scraping at her mind, trying to alter the very chemistry of her brain with techniques like *Flare* and *Slowtime;* one even tried something like her *Fear* technique, which she thought she had created.

Useless. She hardly even needed to use *Thoughtscreen.* Whatever

158

skill these *Sindicato* had with the Aether, it was purely amateur. They clearly had no idea which techniques were effective against which mental states, nor how to counter it when they suffered a mental assault themselves.

They also clearly had no idea how far she could reach.

She sent a *flare* of her own back at one of the nearby minds, feeling the mind recoil before becoming a scrambled thing of incoherent thought and broken awareness. Where aggression and focus had been, only a whirling tangle of delirium remained.

A second mind went down at her touch, a touch to which she added a variation on *Tranquilize* that saw whoever her victim was fall to the floor, legs now paralysed and unresponsive.

Beside her, Blane sensed Raphael doing the same. Well, not the same; the woman's range and strength was far more limited than her own, though Blane could remember a time when her strength in the Aether had seemed unattainable. Now, she could only hold the Aether in readiness for any attacker who slipped past Blane. Few did.

This was *fun*.

Things got even worse for the *Sindicato* when Blane decided to try out a technique she'd been afraid to test on anyone, but one she'd been pondering ever since she'd first read about prosopagnosia. "Face blindness," as it had once been known.

She sensed a *Sindicato* moving around to her right ten or so metres away, no doubt trying to find a decent shot while staying out of what he assumed was her range. Though this one did not seem to be an Aether user, his mind shone brightly as she reached down into it to touch the fusiform gyrus, the folds and slopes of it sparkling with neural activity.

She gave the flowing charges a *twist*.

For a few seconds the figure continued on as he had been, sprinting in a curve to a point where, in no more than a few more seconds, he would have a clear shot.

Then, confusion. Confusion, and the sensation of being lost.

She could feel panic well up in the man as, suddenly, he could no longer recognise anyone. Visual cues from the optic nerve no longer connected to those areas of the brain that identified individuals, and frame and form no longer separated 'friend' from 'foe' - not build, not uniform.

What Blane had just done was harming far more than his ability to process facial features, though. Without warning, the *Sindicato* found himself in a hostile situation surrounded by strangers, unable to make the necessary connections across cortices to identify even a single familiar presence, and unable to distinguish who was ally and who enemy.

So he opened fire at random, swinging his rifle wildly from one figure to the next as he held his trigger down. Blane didn't need the Aether to sense the surprise of his comrades.

"The *cabrón's* running," Raphael hissed at her side.

She was right. In the chaos of the past what felt like minutes but could only have been seconds, Uriel had made his escape. She couldn't feel his spiky, harsh presence anywhere.

"That way," Raphael said, answering her unspoken question with a pointed finger.

If Raphael was right, Uriel had headed in almost exactly the opposite direction to the way they had retreated. Past the main cluster of *Sindicato* now falling back and regrouping beyond Blane's reach - someone must have realised that she was able to manipulate the Aether far further than would usually be expected - and through the group of *Fallen* his group had pinned against the wall. Which meant he had gone inside the building containing the Fabricator.

Bullets began to ping with renewed force off the crate they were hiding behind, forcing the both of them to crouch even further back.

"Are we following him?" Blane shouted over the noise.

Raphael's gave a snort as if the answer were the most obvious thing in the world.

"We have to get past these damned *smugglers* first, though," she spat, putting the same invective into the term that other would into the term "vermin."

Blane tried to lean around the corner of their cover to see how the *Sindicato* were positioned, but a stream of bullets sent her falling quickly back. No longer able to sense their attackers, a chill of fear ran down her spine at the realisation that the enemy could even now be moving around their sides to flank them.

A massive blast somewhere up ahead roared out and echoed through the cavern, a sharp, quick sound that Blane recognised as not from a compression technique but from actual explosives. The sound of splintering prefab and heavy equipment thudding to the ground reverberated through her bones, and instantly the shooting stopped.

Well, not stopped, but lessened, and what remained seemed to be directed elsewhere.

Raphael smiled and nodded as if she had been expecting this.

"Gabriel," she said.

"If you're gonna go, go now!" came a shout from the same direction as the explosion.

Blane recognised Gabriel's unique accent, the one she'd been unable to place. Right now, it was the most welcome voice she'd ever heard.

Raphael wasted no time and stood up, indicating for Blane to do the same. Even in the heat of the moment, Blane couldn't help but notice that Raphael needed to grab the edge of their crate to pull herself to her feet. Whatever May Li had given her, it seemed to be wearing off.

Blane pushed herself to her feet besides Raphael and took a step towards the Fabricator, ready to break into a run but stopped by the grip of Raphael's hand on her shoulder.

Thinking the other woman was trying to caution her, to slow down her headlong charge, she span, but her half-formed protests died in her throat at the sight of Raphael's face. The colour was once again draining away, and lines of exhaustion rapidly returning.

With a weak smile, Raphael gave a slow nod. Blane understood; she wasn't trying to slow her down, she needed the support.

The square was empty aside from fallen forms, some groaning, some still. Blane recognised several of the *Sindicato,* many that she had knocked down herself, but for the first time saw the sheer number of scattered, injured *Fallen.* Injured, or worse. A number of motionless bodies betrayed no presence in the Aether, beyond saving.

As she made her steady way towards the entrance of the Fabricator building, Raphael leaning heavily on her shoulder and breathing heavily, she glanced to the side. A number of people stood at the edge of the light well that was the square, facing outwards. Occasionally one of them shot into the darkness, where presumably more *Sindicato* lurked.

Gabriel, stood in their centre, turned and caught her eye. Next to him…

"Seri!"

Blane recognised her instantly even in the gloom. A second later and her familiar presence appeared in the Aether as Serinda came running across the bare ground towards them.

"I sent... Gabriel to get her out," Raphael panted.

Blane felt the woman force herself to stand taller, releasing the pressure on her shoulder. Trying to hide her condition from Serinda, no doubt.

It didn't work.

"Sara!" Serinda cried, calling Raphael by the name only she used as she rushed over. "How are you...?"

"I'm... fine," said Raphael, and Blane knew those words wouldn't fool anyone, let alone Serinda.

As Serinda reached them she reached out to touch Blane's arm, a brief soft glance all she could spare. Then she turned to Raphael.

"You can't be... you shouldn't be up," she said. "This thing, it's not a virus. Well, it *is*, but it's not..."

"We know," said Raphael, holding up a hand to interrupt Serinda with a wry, sad smile.

"You know?"

Serinda froze in confusion for a moment. Then her features rearranged themselves, and suddenly Blane saw a semblance of the confident, certain doctor she'd seen so often in the past.

"Then you know you shouldn't be moving around. Every move you make, every stress you put on your body; it just speeds up the effects. We need to find a way to block it, to stop it. To turn it *off...* "

By the end, however, Serinda's words were tumbling over each other to get out, as if by getting them out all at once they could overtake a reality she didn't want to face.

"It's too late, Seri, you know that."

Raphael's voice was low and gentle, but final, and something in the way she spoke made Blane swear she'd never call Serinda by her pet name again. It wasn't hers to use.

"It's not. It can't be. I can..."

"It was over months ago. The instant it crossed the blood-brain barrier." Again that smile. "Or so May Li told me. You want to tell me she's wrong?"

Blane turned away; she couldn't bear the look on Serinda's face. Her mouth hung open as if willing the words to come out, to deny what she clearly already knew.

"But first..." Raphael said, some of the strength coming back into her voice. "We're going to get the bastard that did this."

This time, Raphael *did* march away under her own power, striding towards the tall doors of the Fabricator building at a rate that made Blane and Serinda hurry to catch up.

Still, even as they made their way to hunt Uriel, Blane's mind span around the words she had just heard. It was already over? What was it that was wrong with Raphael? With the other *Fallen*?

And what did Serinda mean, *turn it off*?

23

The lubricant of the gears of war was always blood and tears.

Songs of the camps (Unsanctioned digital document)

The inside of the Fabricator building was almost perversely well-lit. After the shadow and gloom of the rest of the cavern it hurt the eyes, leaving Blane blind for an uncomfortably long period of time as they stepped through the high doors. It was also warm, a dry heat that drew attention to how cold it actually was outside.

The inside of the building swam into view as the glare lessened and her eyes adjusted, revealing a massive, dark square block of solid machinery that filled most of the building and rose towards the high ceiling several stories up. It radiated warmth, and weight. Somehow you could *feel* its sheer mass.

Platforms made from metal grating enclosed the machine up the entirety of its height, a level every few meters running in a square around it. Each platform was accessible at multiple points by stairs or ramps running from the one below, and had low guardrails at the many points where platform and Fabricator were separated by open air. The whole set up looked like scaffolding around some strange alien monolith.[11]

Somewhere several levels above and on the other side of the machine, footsteps rang out as someone ran along the platforms, heading higher.

"Oh, Urieeeeel," Raphael called, her voice filled with predatory malice that hid her weakness. "Where do you think you're going?"

"God *damn* it, Sara," came Uriel's shouted reply, curiously muffled by the thick, insulated walls of the building. "I should have ended you a long time ago."

"Oh, so no more games, then? No more lies or excuses?"

Raphael flashed a smile at Blane. Now *she* was enjoying this.

"What would be the point?" Uriel shouted back. "The game was up the moment we opened fire on your ridiculous *Zapatistas.*"

He swore loudly.

"Who would have thought those damned gangsters would be

---

[11] Grey would have definitely made a comment about apes and odysseys.

defeated by a *kid?*"

That last comment seemed to be addressed to himself, and Blane felt her hackles rise. She'd show him who was the kid.

A hand touched her arm.

"Careful," said Serinda. "He might be trapped, but he's still dangerous. *More* dangerous, maybe."

Raphael was being supported by Serinda now, one arm across both shoulders of the smaller woman. She nodded.

"I think..." Raphael said, panting lightly with the effort of shouting. "He might have more tricks than he's ever let on."

Laughter rang out.

"Ha!" Uriel yelled. "You have no idea! Twenty years I've been doing this. *Twenty years.* You think you're the first to figure me out? Ha!" He laughed again. "You think this is the first time *you've* figured me out?"

That made Raphael pause. She looked from Blane to Serinda, a question on her face. Serinda, equally lost, just stared back.

Pain flared in Blane's head, like a bright burning light at the back of her skull. She pushed past it.

"It's... memories," she said, suddenly unbalanced. "They can... do something to your memories."

Just thinking about it for those few seconds was a challenge. The thoughts slid and twisted around each other, losing coherence almost the moment they formed.

Uriel is an RA agent.

The words swam across her mind in a voice she couldn't place. The memory seemed to blur and fray, the before and after of the words, the connections to all other sensations that usually link a memory to reality, severed.

She released the thought, and a few seconds later the feeling passed. Shaking her head to clear her mind, she looked up and into the concerned face of Serinda.

"What are you talking about, Blane?" Serinda asked. "How do you...?"

"No time," Blane said firmly.

"Is that it, Uriel?" Raphael shouted into the air. "Have you been playing with our minds?"

At a sign from Raphael they began moving, Blane to one side and Serinda and Raphael to the other. Raphael continued calling out to their quarry.

Come at him from two sides, divide his attention, Blane thought to herself.

She could sense Serinda's fear at splitting up, but also her determination. For her part, Blane felt little fear at all. She knew how deeply she could draw on the Aether here, and it was far more than Uriel could. She would hit him long before he hit her.

She moved in a low crouch towards the nearest stairs, leading up to the first level of platforms. Even moving as carefully as she could, she failed to completely keep the sound of her ascent from rattling out on the metal grating. Still, there was no obvious sign of a reaction from above.

She stopped as she reached the first platform, reaching out with her mind as far as she could. Through the monolithic block of machinery she could feel Serinda and Raphael making their own way up, necessarily slower than Blane for Raphael's sake. From this distance Blane didn't think they could sense her, so she would have to keep pace with them.

She couldn't feel Uriel's presence at all. He must be much higher up, close to the uppermost platforms near the ceiling. Another level or two, and he wouldn't be able to hide.

Blane headed for the next stairs up when a sudden light to her side gave her a jolt of surprise. She span around, drawing the Aether into herself reflexively, but saw and sensed no one. Instead, a section of the wall was gently pulsing.

No, not wall - LEF. Light Emitting Fabric.

I ASSUME URIEL SHOULD BE TREATED AS HOSTILE?

The words blinked on the screen in bold white letters. She had seen font like this somewhere before, but where?

It took a few seconds before she remembered; the drone. The same clean white font that had appeared on the screen there, making Grey pause and give an expression she didn't understand. But that had been...

"Francisco?" she whispered.

IN A WAY. BUT NOT IN THE WAY YOU MEAN.

Well, *that* didn't help.

"I don't have time for this," she snapped, glancing overhead through the layers of grated mesh towards the roof, wary for any movement.

ACKNOWLEDGED. TREAT URIEL AS HOSTILE?

"Yes," she said. She couldn't see a reason to reply otherwise.

ACKNOWLEDGED. LETHAL OR NON-LETHAL ARMS?

"Uh…"

Blane didn't know what surprised her more, the question or the hesitation she felt in answering. Something inside her *wanted* to say lethal, some part of her that raged and shouted but above all was *eager* for the idea of righteous violence.

She pushed that part down.

"Non-lethal."

ACKNOWLEDGED.

Abruptly the entire machine growled, a deep, reverberating sound that made the metal platforms all around rattle. A hissing came from somewhere overhead, and a slot opened below the screen where Blane could have sworn no slot had been before.

Reaching in, she drew out a familiar stun-lock, fully loaded and grip set.

Grey's stun-lock, or so close as to be identical.

"What the…? How…?"

YOU DON'T HAVE TIME FOR THIS.

Despite everything, the ludicrousness of having her own words spat back at her by a machine made her laugh.

BEHIND YOU.

She sensed Uriel appear in the Aether a moment before the compression-release went off where she had been standing. Already rolling, she dropped the pressure shield she had reflexively formed and fired off two shots. They went wide, but forced her attacker to retreat back up the stairs he had been sneaking down.

He knows how to Conceal himself in the Aether.

Just as she had done the night she snuck into the Far Station - unbelievably, she suddenly realised, only a night or so ago. She thought she had developed something new, but it seemed she was yet again wrong.

I have to stop assuming anything I know is unknown to others.

Not only that, but Uriel seemed to be better than her at the concealing technique. He had appeared in the Aether for a second, performed the technique, then immediately blinked out again. When the attack had come at the Station she'd barely been able to grab at the Aether before…

A nova of pain exploded behind her eyes, the light of the room suddenly unbearable. It made her roll turn into a stagger, and she barely heard Uriel dashing away.

The memory… it had been there, for a moment. A memory of stepping through a door, and then…

No.

She gritted her teeth. She had to focus on *now;* another slip like that, and Uriel was bound to get her.

When she opened her eyes again there was no sign of Uriel. If it wasn't for the warped section of grating near where she had been standing, she could almost have believed he'd never been there.

"What was that?"

The shout came from further above and around the Fabricator, in Serinda's voice.

"Watch out, he can hide himself in the Aether!" Blane cried back, trying not to let the shock show in her words.

She'd just lost her main advantage in this fight; if he could hide himself at will, then her extra reach meant nothing. He could be right around the corner and she wouldn't know.

"Are you alright?" Serinda called again.

"Yes, now stop yelling! He'll know where we are."

The building fell silent again, the walls sucking up echoes as well as heat.

Blane tightened her grip around the stun-lock and swept her trigger hand around with her gaze, searching for any hint of movement. Nothing.

Now she realised why Uriel had been climbing the platforms upwards. Most of the light in here was projected from LEDs and spotlights on the lower floors, with only far softer and sparser lights on the higher. This meant that someone looking up saw only shadows and darkness, whereas someone looking down would see anything that moved silhouetted against the light.

So she needed to go *up.*

The idea of retreat didn't even cross her mind; she *was* going to get Uriel. The certainty was burnt into her, even as she noticed her hands trembling. Adrenaline, no doubt.

Looking up, she saw Raphael and Serinda come around the corner of the Fabricator two floors or so up. Raphael seemed to be moving with only a hand on Serinda's shoulder for support, but it was difficult to tell through the grating. How much energy could she have left?

Returning to her own situation, Blane checked the rounds in her stun-lock's magazine. Seven rounds - it would have to be enough. She headed for the nearest set of stairs, the same ones Uriel had appeared from.

She climbed up to the next level making more sound than she would like, reaching the platform to see sets of metal grating identical to those below stretching out behind and in front of her. Ahead, and higher now again, she heard the other two making their way around the Fabricator once more.

She hesitated, not knowing if she should make her way towards her companions or head in the opposite direction.

For a moment, she sensed Uriel's presence flash into the Aether behind her. Like a fallen leaf disturbing the surface of a still lake,[12] it was there for an eye blink then gone again; but he'd done *something* in that blink. She'd felt the Aether stretch out and touch her.

What had he done? She felt no different. Her thoughts were clear and there was no obvious change in the physical world. All she knew was that he must be close.

There.

On the level above a shadow moved rapidly away, the metal rattling underfoot as he retreated. Rattling, and the curious smell of ozone.

Blane stared around her, quelling a brief burst of panic. It smelt like something was burning, and close by, but a frantic scan of her surroundings revealed nothing unusual. There didn't seem to be anything that *could* burn; just cold, bare metal.

Continue up, she told herself. *He wants you to chase him, to rush in without thinking.*

She needed to find a more advantageous position, not to charge blindly in. If Uriel tried to make a run for it as she climbed, Gabriel and the rest of the *Fallen* were waiting outside. They should be able to catch him, or at least slow him down before he got too far. Time was her friend, not his.

---

[12] It was a strange sensation, the ability to sense another mind in the Aether. Like a disturbance on still water, the sensation was equally clear regardless of whether the Aether was calm or, as it was more and more frequently these days, a roiling mass.

So, keeping her gun up and the Aether gripped tightly, she continued her way up to the next level. It wasn't until she was almost to the top of the next steps that she noticed the strange purple tint that the light had taken on. It made the shadows curiously liquid, and blurred the lines between surfaces.

All of a sudden the interior of the building resounded with the clang of metal on metal, something heavy and metallic slamming into the grating again and again. It was coming from around the other side of the Fabricator, out of sight but separated by no more than a level or two.

Was Uriel *challenging* them to come after him, giving away his position like that? What could he possibly hope to gain? And what was going on with the lights?

The smell of burning grew as she stared in the direction of the sound, but she still saw nothing that could be its source. Then, as if in rhythm with the beating of metal on metal, her arms tingled and the light began to pulse, the purple tinge growing and lessening in intensity with every clang. It was strange, like someone somehow playing with a filter setting on her eyes.

Somewhere behind her she heard Serinda call. She *knew* it was Serinda, and yet... she couldn't understand her words. The sounds were there, familiar in phoneme and tone, yet devoid of meaning. Instead there was... taste? An ever-shifting sensation of sweet and bitter, only not on her tongue.

Something was very wrong.

An explosion from somewhere ahead, near where the noise was coming from. Immediately the clanging stopped, and the light returned to a steady, syrupy purple.

"Ha!" came Raphael's victorious laugh, and the meaning of *that* was clear even if the incomprehensible words around it weren't.

A moment later, and the light pulsed again in tandem with the sound of two bodies hitting the floor. It sounded as if Uriel and someone were physically tussling, the sound of blows on flesh as loud as the rattling metal.

Staggering slightly, Blane dashed forwards and up the nearest stairs, making for the sound of fighting. She got there just in time.

Uriel was straddled over Raphael's prone form, his bleeding and clearly broken nose implying that until a moment ago their positions had been reversed. He was whaling on her with his right arm, his left

170

arm dangling uselessly at his side. Raphael had got him before he'd got her, it seemed. To his side a short steel wrench lay on the floor, sent flying in the tussle. That didn't matter right now, though, with Raphael weakly raising her hands to block blows that delivered almost as much damage to her weakened body as the metal would.

Blane struck out wildly with a massive, barely-controlled Flare attack, which Uriel easily blocked with his own Thoughtscreen. The attack, though, forced him to roll off Raphael and once more sprint out of sight.

Blane didn't give chase, though, but rather ran straight to Raphael.

"Overestimated... my remaining.... strength," the fallen woman panted through gritted teeth. "He'd never have got me like that before."

She gave a painful chuckle, and spat a bloody mass of sputum to her side. From her split lip, Blane thought. Or hoped.

Raphael's face was a mess, a patchwork of livid bruises that were blotches of dark in the weird purple light. Blane dreaded to think what other injuries she'd suffered, hidden from sight.

"Where's Serinda?" Raphael asked through ragged breaths.

"I thought she was with you!"

Raphael shook her head.

"He did... something. Made her senses go all *patas arriba*. She didn't even seem to understand what I was saying. I thought I could... handle him myself."

So that was it, thought Blane. Whatever was happening to her, all these weird deformations of light and sound and sensation, it was Uriel's doing. The effect seemed to be wearing off, however, and she could at least understand language again.

The thought that Uriel had done something to her, that he'd been inside her *head*, brought up that familiar bubble of incandescent rage. This time though, staring at Raphael bloodied and beaten, knowing Serinda was out there and vulnerable, she allowed the fury to well up.

The Aether roared through her, a torrent that made everything she'd felt before seem like the merest trickle of power. Now it filled and surrounded her and rose from her with such intensity that it made her wonder her skin didn't crisp and burn. It was as if she stood at the centre of a volcanic eruption, somehow unscathed.

It also seemed to clear her head somewhat, though she barely noticed.

"I will *end* this," she said, and felt her lips curl back.

She didn't wait to hear what it was Raphael started to say, but raced after Uriel.

She felt unstoppable, invulnerable; convinced *nothing* Uriel could do could touch her while she felt this way.

Uriel's mind flashed into her awareness a few seconds later, the Aether reaching out towards her with the familiar feel of a mental attack. She subsumed it easily, merging the flow into her own and shaping it to her own will, nullifying the attack in an instant.

She couldn't have said how she did this; it was instinctual, as easy and as natural as slapping away some annoying insect. Then she sent her own attack back in response, a cascading deluge of power that no mental barrier could withstand.

She felt it hit, and Uriel's mind went silent.

24

It does not matter how an event happened. It matters how it is remembered.

Chairman's Closing Address, *Records of the 4th Assembly* (Unsanctioned Digital Document)

He was still alive, somehow.

Blane stood over Uriel's fallen form, watching the slight movements of his chest as he took ragged, weak breaths. Her fists clenched and unclenched without conscious thought as she glared down at him, her own breathing heavy with anger and loathing.

Weak.

He looked so weak, lying on the floor beneath her and groaning quietly. It would be as easy as a thought to end him, here and now.

The Aether coursing through her seemed to throb at the idea.

Uriel's eyes opened, staring up at her through narrow and swollen eyelids but still managing to convey hatred and disgust.

He gave a bitter smile.

"Ha," he said. "*That* was a good one. Almost as powerful as the kid. No control, though. No finesse."

"You know where Fen is?" Blane demanded, not lessening her hold on the Aether for a second.

Uriel began to painfully push himself up with his elbows, until a growl from Blane and an intensification of her hold on the Aether made him stop.

Chuckling, he slowly reached one arm up to his mouth and wiped away blood with his sleeve.

"So you don't know either," he smiled. "When he escaped and actually managed to disappear this time, I was sure he'd turn up here. Here, or with you and that damned snoop. And he certainly didn't turn up *here*."

"What do you mean, *disappear*?"

Uriel's bitter smile only grew as Blane lifted her foot, placed it on his chest, and *pushed*.

"He really hasn't tried to find you, has he?" He gave a weak, disdainful snort. "Funny. He just runs, knowing we'll inevitably catch him again."

"So you admit you're Reclamation?"

Blane looked up at the words, seeing Raphael making her way towards them. She was clearly struggling just to stay standing, but fighting to hide it.

"Ah, Raphael; our fearless leader returns. *Don Quixote de la Reclamatión!*"

He threw back his head and laughed, ignoring it when Blane pushed down harder with her foot. She knew he was hurting, she could see it in the shape of his mind, but he betrayed no hint of it in his expression.

"Does that make you my Sancho?" Raphael said, making her way over to them.

She gave Blane a nod as she drew close, resting a hand on her shoulder. Blane could feel her put her entire weight on it, needing the support.

"I always thought that was Serinda," Uriel spat. "Terrible the influence you had on her; she was always the smart one."

At these words Raphael seemed to dismiss Uriel for a moment, lifting her gaze and calling out in strained yell.

"Seri!"

They stood there in silence for a moment.

"Serinda!"

Blane's yell was louder and more powerful, but the thick walls sucked the strength from her words and she wasn't sure how far they could be heard.

She heard Serinda's reply after several long seconds of silence. More sound than words, it came from somewhere overhead.

"Over here! We're here!" Blane yelled again.

Footsteps rattled along the higher platforms until they came to some stairs down, and Serinda came into view. Blane was relieved to see she looked unharmed, though unsteady on her feet, and she was massaging her temple in a curious way.

"Can you... say something please?" Serinda said, looking from Blane to Raphael.

"Say... something? Like what?" Blane asked, puzzled.

Immediately relief flooded Serinda's face.

"*¡Menos mal!* " she said, exhaling loudly. "That was horrible. I was *seeing* sound, and couldn't understand a word anyone said."

Blane looked down at Uriel, who still wore a wide grin as he stared back at her. Now, though, it was less malicious and more triumphant.

"What did you do to her? To me?" she demanded.

"The Reclamation Authority knows far more about using Aether than your ridiculous little gangs," he scoffed. "You're like children playing with a loaded gun."

Blane felt a surge of anger at once again being compared to a child. She raised her foot and immediately slammed it back down into his chest, making him gasp.

"*I'm* not the one lying on the floor," she snarled.

"So you really are RA?" Raphael said. "No games? No denials?"

"Well, you three obviously know too much for me to *remind* you properly. But once you're all dead, I can tell those idiots outside anything I like."

"Once *we're* dead?" Blane laughed in disbelief, kicking the man at her feet in the ribs.

But her laugh trailed off as she realised Raphael and Serinda had fallen silent.

"You think you beat me just because you got in a lucky shot?" Uriel said, and despite his position at her feet his eyes were filled with defiance. "You think it's only *strength* that decides a battle?"

Then she saw it; a gossamer thread glinting gold. It stretched out from him and forked as it reached towards her companions, so thin it was practically imperceptible to whatever sensory organ *saw* the Aether.

"What have you done?" she demanded.

To Uriel it must have looked as if a small sun was flaring above him, fury and the Aether filling her. Still, his smile did not fade.

"Careful," he said. "I've got your friends trapped in their own heads. Permanent most likely, if I don't undo it. You do something to me, who knows if they'll be able to find their way back?"

Uriel slowly pushed himself up with his elbows again, and this time did not react to Blane's growl. Instead, he calmly got to his feet and stood, swaying slightly but still smiling.

"*Chronotrip*," he said. "I know, I know, Far Agents do love their silly little labels."

Uriel channeled a second thin sliver of Aether, one that flowed out then curled back in on himself. She recognised it as the same pain-numbing technique Gabriel had used on Grey when treating his injuries.

"Ah, that's better," he said with a sigh, cricking the small of his back with his knuckles like an old man stretching. He closed his eyes briefly in relief.

When he opened them again, they were cold and hard.

"I've trapped both of them in their memories," he said matter-of-factly. "Long-term memory bleeding into the prefrontal cortex. Can't say *which* memories will bleed through, but it's usually the traumatic ones... And it can be quite permanent."

As if on cue, Raphael made a small sound, like a whimper. Blane saw a single tear running down her face as she stared into nothingness. Serinda, too, was gazing blankly ahead, only the small twitches of her eyes hinting at something happening behind them.

Blane fought the instinct to lash out at Uriel. Part of her screamed to attack, to strike with her mind or her fists or the stun-lock at her side, but she pushed it down.

Could he be telling the truth? She was used to thinking of mental techniques as purely temporary things, with effects that began to wear off the moment the technique ended, but no one had ever said they *had* to be temporary.

Seeing her hesitation, Uriel laughed.

"Not sure you trust me? Well, I commend that at least," he chuckled. "So here, let me show you."

Blane watched as the golden thread running from the man to Serinda and Raphael faded into nothingness. For what seemed like an age she waited, gaze darting between Uriel and her companions.

Nothing changed; Uriel's smug smile remained, and the other two continued to stare ahead, Raphael with a growing look of horror on her face.

"Good," said Uriel, nodding. "Now, you're going to come with me."

"I'm not going anywhere with you," said Blane, but she could feel her resolve sapping.

Uriel just laughed.

"If you want them to have even a chance of returning to the real world, then you will. I'm leaving, and you're coming with me. I imagine Far will overlook any 'irregularities' in my work here if I bring you to them."

As if it was a foregone conclusion Uriel stepped forward, grabbing Raphael by the arm as he did so. She half-staggered in the direction of his pull, without resistance and eyes unfocused.

"Amazing, isn't it? The conscious mind is disconnected from the present, but somatic reflexes are completely unaffected."

Uriel continued forward, stepping past Blane and towards the nearest descending stairs. He didn't seem to be concerned with Serinda, and Blane stood there torn as she looked from one to the other.

Sensing her hesitation, Uriel turned to look at her.

"We'll come back for her once I've secured a way out of here."

He tutted once like Blane was a mischievous child not doing what she was told. Then he turned back and began making his way down, Raphael passively following along as he pulled her by the arm.

Blane glanced back at Serinda once more, stood staring into nothingness, then rushed after Uriel. Right now, she didn't seem to have any other choice.

"You know," Uriel said loudly without looking back, making sure his words were audible to her. "You really did have me thinking I was in trouble for a moment there, when you took out my *Sindicato* friends. They were going to be my ticket out of here, you see? A nice little payday for me, a Fabricator for them... But instead you've brought me something much more valuable; a way back *in*."

Blane heard the bitterness in these last words, though she didn't understand what it meant.

"Back in?" she asked, engaging despite herself. "The *Fallen* will never take you back."

At this Uriel paused, Raphael staggering slightly besides him before coming to a halt herself, still staring into some haunted part of her mind.

He turned to look at her with such viciousness and loathing she was surprised he didn't lash out at her physically.

"The *Fallen*?" he spat incredulously. "The *Fallen*? Why would I want to rejoin this band of naive fools? I *built* them! Decades of my life ensuring the only 'resistance' the RA faced was a bunch of weak-willed, quarrelsome idiots, and what do I get for it? A 'thank you for your service' and a transfer to some dead-end paper-pushing desk job!"

Uriel had gone red in the face, and he spoke with such force that Blane felt the air from his lungs blow across her cheeks. Flecks of spittle formed at the side of his mouth, and his fists clenched tightly enough to turn his knuckles white. He was clearly on the verge of violence; Blane braced herself, preparing for her own attack.

Then, in an instant, the threat was gone. The blood retreated from his face and his shoulders relaxed, lips forming that same cynical, arrogant smile he had shown so many times.

"But you..." he said, looking her up and down with narrowed eyes. "You're a *Fisura*, aren't you? *That* should get the RA to take notice of me. Ironic, really; they decided finding *Fisura* like you was 'top priority' so ordered me to sterilize this operation, but it was the sterilization that drew you out!"

Blane was barely able to follow what Uriel was saying. The man seemed to be half-addressing her, and half-addressing some unseen audience in his head.

Fisura? The word clearly carried significant meaning for him, but was nebulous to her.

Sterilize, however, she understood.

"This was you," she said. It wasn't a question. "The sickness. Raphael. The others in the clinic."

With a grunt implying that what she was saying was so obvious it didn't warrant an answer, Uriel turned and headed down. He pulled Raphael roughly along with him, stumbling but never falling.

Blane followed along, mind racing over what to do. Half of her wanted to attack, to smash the smug smile from his face and force his repellant grip off of Raphael. The other half sought wildly for something to say, some bargaining chip that would get him to fix whatever he had done to her friends.

She was still lost in these frantic thoughts when they reached ground level and the tall doors out of the building. Aside from an occasional groan, Raphael continued to show no sign that she was aware of her surroundings. She had, however, begun to drag one foot behind her, and her skin had become yet more sallow and sickly.

"And where do you think you're going?"

The words caught Blane by surprise, distracted as she had been by Raphael's deteriorating condition.

Gabriel stood just beyond the doors Uriel had slid open, a rifle held loosely at his side but clearly ready for use at a moment's notice. Behind him stood several more *Fallen*, each holding a weapon of their own. Blane thought she recognised some of the firearms as ones the *Sindicato* had been using.

Uriel stopped and scowled at the man blocking his way.

"You can't think you're going to walk away from this, can you?" Gabriel said. Some of the *Fallen* behind him laughed, mirthless and full of threat.

"Actually," replied Uriel slowly. "That is *exactly* what I think I'll be doing."

He yanked on Raphael's arm and she came stumbling forwards.

"If you want this one to be anything other than catatonic for however long she has left, I suggest you let me pass," Uriel continued. "I know you have a soft spot for both of them; especially your old mentor. She's back there too, equally incapacitated."

Gabriel's shock at the sight of Raphael was clear in his expression, and there were concerned murmurings from those behind him. Triumphantly, Uriel stepped forward, clearly expecting the group to part.

"Exactly," Uriel said triumphantly. "*I* am the only one with the skills to release them from their prisons of trauma, so you'll let me go and *maybe* I'll consider helping them."

The barrel of Gabriel's rifle against his chest made him halt.

"The thing about Raphael..." Gabriel said, face mere centimetres from Uriel's. "... is she would *never* agree to letting you go for her sake."

Blane could see Uriel's blood rising again, anger building. He opened his mouth to speak, but was cut off as Gabriel continued.

"And the thing about Serinda..." he said. "... is that she has more skills in her little finger than you have in your entire body. Oh, and she *definitely* knows how to handle trauma."

Blane felt the attack a picosecond before it hit. Serinda was suddenly *there*, mere meters away, crouched in the shadows of a nearby ramp.

Blane didn't know exactly what the attack Serinda used was, but it was fast. Uriel, however, was just as fast, and the Thoughtscreen he put up around himself was strong enough to block whatever Serinda was sending towards him.

Or would have been strong enough, if Gabriel hadn't sent his own burst of Aether towards him at the same time. Forced to deal with two attacks at the same time, from two different directions, Uriel's Thoughtscreen flickered, the Aether far too weak here to maintain it.

A golden line stretched out from Serinda and into Uriel, piercing his ever-weakening barrier. As soon as it touched him he fell to the ground, legs useless and making a sound like he couldn't breathe properly.

This wasn't the end, though. Blane realised with horror what Uriel was doing a moment before he did it. It must have taken everything he had to draw on the Aether the way he did, to manipulate it towards Serinda in a small yet ever brightening circle of tumultuous energy. In less than a second it was more powerful than anything Gabriel or Serinda could muster, and Blane knew what would happen the instant it touched her friend.

What Blane did in response was reflex born of terror, thought coming only after it had happened. She had to stop Uriel *now*, before Serinda was turned to ash in an outpouring of pure energy. So she retaliated in kind.

The energy that poured out of Blane was incomparably brighter than what Uriel was manipulating, and faster. Too fast to see, even with her mind's eye. The Aether leapt at her command - if command it truly were. Even she couldn't say if she was bending the energy to her will, or freeing it to carry out its own.

Uriel didn't have time to scream. In fact, Blane thought later, he probably didn't even have time to realise he was dead.

Mindfire engulfed his form, turning him in an instant to a dark silhouette of ashen pain engulfed in liquid flame. His shadow curled backwards as if his very muscles were trying to break him, and then his outline grew vague, crumpling in on itself. The outer layers of his flesh became ash, ash that floated through the air or fell softly to the ground unaffected by the blazing golden flame all around it.

Even had Blane wanted to stop what was happening, it was too late. The Aether now coursing through and from Uriel's body was his own, erupting from each and every cell and scorching him from the inside out. A chain reaction that Blane, the catalyst, was no longer a part of.

But something was wrong. The Aether *lurched,* and suddenly her chest felt like it would burst. Like a dam on the verge of catastrophic failure, the Aether continued to surge into her until she could barely hold it. She *couldn't* hold it, and fear at this realisation only seemed to feed the raging torrent.

Serinda was the first to notice something was wrong, taking her eyes from Uriel's slowly dimming form.

"Blane?" she said.

Blane could hardly hear her through the strain of containing the Aether and the thunderous sound of blood in her ears.

"H... *help*," was all she managed to gasp.

She *felt* rather than saw the golden fire that flickered into being around her. It appeared then faded before returning once more, stronger and more vivid. Wisps of flame rose in curling knots from her skin, brightening and coalescing into balls of roiling flame that grew and stretched and made strange shapes like monstrous wraiths struggling to take on physical form. She could feel the Aether leaking from her through cracks in her mental wall, bleeding out with the promise of explosive pressure behind.

It felt like it wanted to *leap*.

Blane was suddenly aware of a group of *Sindicato Nuestro* huddled together in the square behind Gabriel, sat under the watchful gaze of a handful of *Forever Fallen* and their rifles. Battered, broken, but with eyes and minds still full of defiance and resentment, they were clearly prisoners.

The Aether was reaching for them. Worse, Blane had the powerful feeling that if she tried to fight it, tried to stop it leaping across the distance towards the defenceless captives, then it would look to closer prey; to those around her.

"Oh, you've got to be kidding..."

Eyes closed with the strain of holding in the energy, she only heard Gabriel's panicked words. He must have noticed what was happening to her.

"We've got to get a Lock on her," he shouted from somewhere nearby. "Quickly, you two - do what I do."

Blane felt a piercing pain as something cut into her, carving into her flesh.

No, not her flesh. It was... something was cutting into the Aether beneath her, severing a part of the flow. The pressure inside her lessened for a moment.

But not enough. *Not enough*. The torrent redoubled in power, this time if anything more powerful. She was going to have to...

A second piercing sensation came, somehow perceptible though it was not, in any sense she understood, happening to what she thought of as her *self*.

It was as if she had a phantom limb, and something was slicing it off.

181

The pressure in her chest lessened once more, and almost immediately afterwards disappeared entirely as a third lock slammed into place, disconnecting her from the Aether completely.

"Good, good."

Gabriel's voice. Blane opened her eyes, and looked up.

She was completely encircled by the *Fallen*, who were watching her warily. Several had their weapons raised, pointed uncertainly in her direction.

"It's ok," said Gabriel, looking around at his companions. He was sweating heavily. "We got there in time. Good job."

He nodded at two *Fallen* specifically. The two who had helped him form the Lock, Blane assumed.

"I... I don't..."

She looked at the people surrounding her, not knowing what to say.

Raphael.

The thought overrode everything else. She looked around, to see Serinda already where the *Fallen* leader stood, gently taking her arm.

"Is she... will she be ok?" Blane asked.

Serinda stared at her with an expression Blane found hard to read. It was sad, perhaps, bittersweet.

"I will do what I can for her," Serinda replied. She reached out a hand towards Blane. "And you? Are you ok? What *was* that?"

Blane shrugged her concern off with a smile.

Serinda doesn't have time to worry about me, she thought. She hoped the smile looked more natural than it felt.

Serinda's own soft smile in return said she wasn't buying it, but nevertheless she turned and began tending to the still unresponsive Raphael. She must have been doing something with the Aether, though it was invisible to Blane in her locked-off state.

Blane realised she was swaying.

She thought it was Gabriel who caught her as she fell, body abruptly giving in to its exhaustion. The gloom of the cavern became a perfect dark, and sensation gave way to blissful nothingness.

25

Wealth operates under Newtonian laws. The accumulation of wealth attracts more wealth, just as greater mass attracts lesser. However, it is not only riches that wealth draws in. As a singularity inexorably pulls in all that surrounds it, the wealth of nations draws in resources, power, and the predatory gaze of its neighbours.

Simone Davey, *Economic Peace Theory and Inevitable War*

When Blane regained consciousness it was clear they were packing up. She had no idea how long she had been out, and there was no way to tell in the perpetual twilight of this place, but through half-drawn curtains surrounding her bed she glimpsed people hauling large boxes out of the clinic and heard the soft sounds of things being busily rearranged.

She wasn't surprised; the place was compromised. Had been from the start.

The entire damned Forever Fallen have been compromised from the start, she thought.

Footsteps came towards her from beyond the curtains and May Li appeared the next moment, swinging them open in one swift movement.

"You're up," the woman said matter-of-factly. "Good. I checked you over and you are in surprisingly good health, considering. Exhausted, though..." and May Li gave Blane a stern look that was almost a warning. "... so no more pushing yourself like that. Ok?"

The words were like a physical force hitting her and Blane struggled to respond for a few moments, stammering out only a half-coherent sound. Still, that seemed to be enough for May Li.

"Good," the woman continued with a nod. "As you can see we're leaving, so when you can summon up the strength come on out. Serinda and Raphael are already outside, along with everyone else. We've moved all the other patients already."

And with that, before Blane could speak ... *How are they?* ... Li was gone.

The clinic was eerily quiet, despite the muffled sound of voices and movement that gradually grew silent as she sat there staring at the ceiling. She didn't move for some time, unable to stir her limbs into action. When she finally swung her legs over the bed she thought she was the last one there.

They were leaving behind a lot, she saw as she stood and slowly made her way down the aisle towards the clinic exit. Beds, blankets, trays, and masses of equipment too large to easily carry or place into boxes. Despite the relative order to the chaos, it was easy to see this departure was rushed.

Outside, the cavern was no less chaotic. It was brighter than she'd ever seen it, with floodlights stood all around illuminating as much as they could. Overfilled crates stood in haphazard piles awaiting one of the few small carryalls that drove back and forth between the central square and the distant tunnel out. There were surprisingly few people around.

"Blane. How are you holding up?"

Blane turned to see Serinda, approaching from where she had been organising the packing. She looked tired, with deep bags under her eyes. The eyes themselves, however, remained determined.

"I'm fine," said Blane, shrugging off her concerned look. "Not as tired as you after my rest, I'll bet. How's Raphael?"

Serinda's gaze flickered in inner-thought for a moment, then she looked up with a weak smile.

"She's... as good as can be expected. I got her out of the memory-loop, or whatever we're going to call it, at least. Had to figure out a new way of manipulating Aether just to do it."

Serinda's smile strengthened just a touch. Her pride in her ability to heal was one unchanging constant.

"Now she's just... asleep, I guess. Her body is weak. I won't know what I can do to help her until we get her to some better facilities."

As if we're going to find better facilities, thought Blane. She struggled to keep the thought from showing on her face.

"Where are we going?" she asked instead. "And who's in charge? And, and... what are we going to do about *that*?"

She pointed towards the Fabricator building far ahead of them, now impossibly tall. It hadn't occurred to Blane until now to wonder how they got the massive machine in here.

"Well," replied Serinda, with a mysterious look. "I guess *I'm* in charge for now. And *that*..." she pointed to the Fabricator herself, "...sort of ties with where we're going..."

The carrier-drones came tearing in across the Waste so low that Blane could scarcely believe they didn't smash into the poisoned ground to become just another part of the desolate, broken landscape. Three of them; thin, sleek, and a black dark enough to hurt the eyes. They tore up the lip of the quarry's crater in a triangular formation almost too fast to follow, then came to an abrupt stop as if laws of momentum did not apply.

Wind whipped her hair into her face as the drones slowly descended, spitting dirt and dust up in such quantities that she was forced to cover her mouth with her shirt. The aircraft came to rest with a metallic creaking, their squealing engines gradually calming and falling to a soft background hiss.

Each looked identical to the one that had carried them away after the prison break.

She stood besides Serinda and Gabriel, among the last of the *Fallen* remaining. May Li was a short way behind, supporting a semi-conscious Raphael who sat on a motorised wheelchair, eyes half-open and head nodding back and forth weakly as she fought to stay awake. Almost everyone else had departed in the stored vehicles of the base to worm their way back into the cities of the Reclamation and regroup another time; a practice they were getting unhappily used to.

With a clunk and a hiss, the ramps of the three drones came down and a series of curiously-uniformed, masked figures ran out. They were covered in what looked like full-body biohazard suits, though of a thinner and lighter material than Blane had seen any IHO official use, and carried strange tools she had never seen before. They dashed past her as if she weren't there and sprinted down into the quarry, disappearing into the entrance tunnel without a moment's hesitation.

A figure appeared at the top of the ramp of the foremost craft, a little way ahead of her. Unlike the figures who had just run past, this one wore no protective garments. Instead, the man wore something similar in design to a Pre-Fall suit, collar and lapels only slightly thinner and more angular, the sheen and faint lines in the material hinting at smart textiles or fabric sensors that could be for anything from simple warming to communications to bio/rad threat assessment.

Blane only saw these sorts of fabrics in shows depicting life in the wealthier areas of the Carib-Federation, and the style of fashion was even rarer. She had only ever seen it on newsfeeds about delegations from the Althing Republic.

The Silicon Isle.

The only person she'd ever met who had anything to do with the place was Francisco, and she realised now that she had expected it to be him who greeted them. Whoever this man was, it wasn't Francisco.

"Please, come on board," the man called down. "We cannot be here any longer than is necessary. As soon as our engineers have shut down and disassembled the Fabricator, we depart. So please..."

He extended an arm out, offering assistance in climbing up the ramp.

"This is where I leave you," said Gabriel, raising his voice over the sound of the idling thrusters of the drones.

He was remaining behind, to watch over and reorganise the *Forever Fallen* in whatever way he could. With a nod to Serinda, he turned and raced away towards the final truck.

The man waiting at the top of the ramp wasn't young, Blane saw as she strode up and past his outstretched hand. Certainly not as old as Grey suspected Francisco to be, but well past middle age. He was greying at the temples, and had the stocky build of one whose youthful muscle has turned to fat.

He also spoke with the broad, rhotic tones of an old-world North American accent like in one of those ancient movies Grey was so fond of watching. She hadn't known the accent still existed in the wild, and it made the name he introduced himself by all the more incongruous.

"Administrator Sigurður," he said, thrusting out a hand again as the others climbed aboard.

She stared at the hand for a second, confused at the gesture until she remembered what she had seen in those same movies. She hesitantly held out her own hand and the man gripped it in his own, pumping it up and down in greeting.

"You can call me Sigurd," the man winked, seeing her hesitation.

A strange feeling, making physical contact with a person she just met. The handshake had long since fallen out of use, discarded as yet another vector for contagion in an age where disease needed little encouragement.

He had steel-grey eyes with the smoothest irises she had ever seen, making her suspect they were some artificial plastic. Even more curiously, his pupils remained narrowed to pinpricks despite the low light.

"Blane," she said as the pressure on her hand released.

Sigurd smiled and turned towards the others, now stepping into the wide cabin of the carrier from the ramp and looking around at their new surroundings inquisitively.

"And you must be Serinda," Sigurd said, nodding at the woman in question. "As I said on the call, we will take you and your companions out of here, but we leave immediately. Our drones are able to evade Reclamation tracking for a limited amount of time, but we've already overstayed our welcome. We've almost certainly been noted as a radar anomaly by now, and once they send their own drones out here there's no evading visual confirmation."

"And the medical facilities?" Serinda said, almost confrontationally.

"Will be better than anything you've had access to before," Sigurd replied.

He frowned, and Blane followed his gaze to see May Li guiding Raphael's chair along the last few feet of ramp. Raphael herself appeared to have fallen asleep, or passed out, head lolling loosely to one side.

"Though if what you have told me is true…" Sigurd continued. "I cannot guarantee it will be enough. If the RA really has found a way to develop such technology without our knowledge…"

He trailed off, seemingly struck by some thought.

"Well," he said, drawing himself up. "We will see what we can do."

He turned away from the ramp, and as if in response it began rising back up.

"What about the Fabricator?" Blane said.

"It will be nothing but a useless husk by the time the RA arrive, if they even bother. And there will be no indication of what it was, besides. Nothing they can say for sure, anyway."

The ramp clicked into place with a surprisingly small click, and Blane felt rather than heard the engines roar into full power once again. Her stomach lurched as they took off.

"Where are we going, anyway?" she asked, half-addressing Sigurd and half the others.

"They didn't tell you?" Sigurd asked, pausing and turning back to face her with a raised eyebrow. "We're taking you out of the Reclamation, to the Althing Republic."

The second lurch in her stomach wasn't from motion. She'd never been outside the Reclamation; didn't know anyone who had, except Francisco and perhaps Grey, who'd been born in the camps of the Carib-Federation.

The thought of Grey brought a rising panic to her chest.

"Nestor," she said, turning to Serinda. "We can't…"

"Already arranged," Sigurd cut in. "Once we track him down, Mr. Grey will be given a specific location and time and met by contacts there. It will take him longer and be less comfortable than our *premium* tickets…" and at this he swept his arms around to take in the entire craft, smiling at his own joke. "… but he will get there."

Regardless of this answer, the tightness in Blane's chest didn't subside until Serinda gave a gentle nod.

"He'll be ok," Serinda said.

"He will," Sigurd said, raising his voice and puffing out his chest. Blane was already realising that he loathed not being front and centre of any conversation.

"Well then." May Li's words cut through the cabin. "Now we've sorted that out, I need the Fexonithine we were promised. Now."

Even Sigurd seemed to bend to the force of her words. With a final glance at the others, he turned and strode over to May Li and Raphael.

The engines rose in pitch, and Blane felt the craft tear into the sky.

26

The universe maintains certain physical laws and these constrain everything, be it mass or energy, gravity or momentum. Consciousness, too, obeys certain rules. Through trial and experimentation we can determine the 'how' of these rules, but do not try to understand the why - for that way lies only madness and religion.

Ingþór Sigurðbur, *Fæðing: Creation of our new age*

COMMAND NOT RECOGNIZED. PLEASE REPHRASE AND TRY AGAIN.

The words hung on the screen, unchanging. When she'd first seen the familiar heavy font hanging there, prompting her for input, she assumed it was the same curiously cryptic program that she had encountered during her fight with Uriel around the Fabricator.

She quickly dismissed the notion, though. The voice assistant software here was oddly rudimentary, unable to parse even slightly vague language. Back home - as she realised she now thought of it - you could expect even ambiguous voice commands to elicit an appropriate response three times out of four.

It was strange. Back in the Reclamation, people - at least, people not on the run from the RA - relied upon personal AI-assistants for everything from calendars to transport to personal relationships so thoroughly that they barely thought of them. The fact that every single request was run through RA servers and recorded was simply the price you paid for the convenience.

Here, though, in the heart of a nation that produced vehicles invisible to radar and machines capable of making whatever you could imagine, anything not carefully worded got you COMMAND NOT UNDERSTOOD.

They'd given her one of the watches everyone here wore, like a flexible thin-screen that wrapped around her wrist. More bracelet than watch, it was a single long band of flexible privacy-glass, embedded lenses designed to track the user's pupils so that anything displayed was visible only to them. They called them 'command cuffs,' or com-cuffs for short.

Sigurd had explained that most com-cuff functions were designed to interface with a chip each citizen of the Althing Republic had implanted beneath their skin, storing digital keys and wallets and much else. Blane didn't have one of these, of course, but the watch would still give her access to messaging and voice-assistance.

It barely seemed to understand a word she said. Better to just do things manually, she decided.

It had been two weeks, and would be more before Grey could join them. No one would tell Blane where he was; Sigurd would just give a patronizing smile and assure her that they had been in contact, and that he would arrive "soon."

Still, it gave her plenty of time to explore and find out as much as she could about this place. As much as they allowed her to, anyway, which she suspected wasn't very much at all.

The Silicon Isle. The Althing Republic; a place she only knew from rumour and supposition, discussed in whispered tones of incredulous wonder or suspicious fear. The source of the Fabricators that sustained the Reclamation and the world beyond.

It was more confining than she'd expected.

Her room was... fine. Nice, but not as luxurious as the safe house. A little cramped, and lacking both windows and view screens, but quite comfortable. Serinda had a room next door, but was rarely there. She spent all her time at Raphael's side in a specially-equipped room, and slept in a chair beside her when exhaustion demanded it.

Which meant Blane had little to do except explore. They had the run of the topmost floors, Sigurd explaining that this area had been sectioned off specifically for them. Only a small number of sections remained inaccessible.

Most of the building they were kept in was built deep into the ground, running downwards into the earth; Sigurd wouldn't say how deep, nor how many people lived here. There were a few offices and labs scattered around the levels she could access, however, and she saw suited, serious-looking people emerging from the access elevators to fill these during the day. They rarely engaged with her unless she pushed them to, and even then only allowed the most superficial of conversations. She soon grew tired of trying.

Exploring on her own, she found that the uppermost floors were almost entirely abandoned. They had very few windows out, and those there were generally showed nothing but featureless white with occasional hints of violent movement as clouds of snow and ice whipped past. The wind was audible even through walls several feet thick, a wailing, screaming noise like demons clawing to get in, and when it abated enough for the frozen particles it stirred up to clear she saw nothing but endless fields of icy rock.

She was vaguely aware that this land had once been beautiful, one of the last practically unspoiled wildernesses in a pre-Fall world reshaped and reformed to support an ever-increasing population, but now everything lay beneath frozen layers of biting crags and twisted shards.

No one went outside. To do so was to invite certain death, regardless of any protective gear you might don. If the cold didn't get you, the terrain would, and if somehow you survived moving around out there for more than a day the poisoned particulates and radiation soaked into the very ice would ensure you didn't last much longer. So they burrowed into the rock, and lived out their lives beyond the rays of the natural sun.

They drew their power from the ground. Oh, they definitely had modular fusion reactions as well - she'd seen the tell-tale lumpy shapes of a few through the windows in those moments when the wind dropped - but the vast majority of power came from a nearby geothermal plant, piercing the Earth with kilometres-deep fingers to power the Hab.

That was what they called it; the Hab. It had been confusing for Blane at first, as the term was used interchangeably to describe both the single structure to which she was currently confined, and the entirety of populated areas across the entire Republic. Quite how wide an area this was, or how large a population, was not information anyone had been forthcoming with, but Blane got the impression neither was a large number.

And they developed viral-vector biotech here. Blane had been surprised, shocked, when she first discovered this. Most viral research was strictly limited in the Reclamation and beyond, anathema since the Fall if not before. Historically, the variety of calamities involving gain-of-function research and biosyn viruses made *any* research into viral genetics a taboo. A taboo so strong and universal that a biological control agency, Pan-Fed, was the first and most visible example of global cooperation in an era of hard borders and limited trade. Now that a vaccine for any novel virus could be developed within days of its discovery and genetic coding, it was generally agreed that research involving the alteration of currently existing viruses was unnecessary and self-destructive.

At least, that was the common understanding, and what Blane had believed until Sigurd assured her this wasn't the case. According to him, the RA and many other nations were pursuing a hidden biological arms race, each seeing who could develop the most infectious, most lethal variant before the others.

He seemed to think this ridiculous arms race was inevitable, and Blane didn't disagree. She simply wondered that she had ever believed otherwise of the Reclamation Authority. The viral research here, Sigurd assured her, was purely for testing and preparing countermeasures to bioweapons other governments were already developing - bioweapons whose schematics were provided by "sources" embedded throughout these governments.

Of course, Sigurd hadn't wanted her to know any of this, but he didn't really have a choice as Blane had a bargaining chip. She *was* the bargaining chip.

Because, for all its limitless energy and mysterious technology and global reach, there was one thing the Althing Republic was unable to research. Was unable to even access.

Aether.

She'd noticed it the moment they landed. Leaving the Reclamation on the drone she'd felt the ever-present energy beneath the world drawing away from her, weakening and fading until it was nothing but the faintest glow, like a single candle in an infinite void. She'd expected this candle to burst back into flame as they neared their destination, to feel the return of the pools and rivers and oceans that the Aether became as a population centre approached, but it never did.

The Althing Republic simply didn't have the population density to generate enough Aether for any practical use. In fact, they'd never had a single user appear amongst them, and the few they brought back lost their connection long before they arrived. Even Serinda was cut off now.

But that flame never quite extinguished in Blane. It remained, a drop of liquid gold that she felt not beneath her but *inside*, like some vulnerable, fragile part of her that could fracture and smash at the slightest touch.

Which made her an object of extreme interest to the researchers of the Silicon Isle, and *everyone* seemed to be a researcher here; or at least, everyone she was allowed to meet.

She'd been taking part in their studies for the past week, having agreed to Sigurd's request when he approached her after a few days adjusting to their new surroundings. With Serinda once again sequestered in a lab, it wasn't like Blane had anything else to do.

She didn't know what they were learning from her, but she had definitely learned a few things about them. Part of which was that they didn't understand the Aether *at all.*

On the first day of the tests she was brought to a small, clinical room with nothing but a desk and a few simple chairs and instructed to sit across from two preoccupied-looking men in white lab coats, one young and one old. Each wore com-cuffs, and seemed to consult them with unnecessary frequency. Blane couldn't remember the younger one's name, but the older one...

"Arthur *Spangle?*" she said, incredulously.

The silver-haired man raised his eyebrows at the tone, but something in his gaze told her this wasn't the first time he'd seen this reaction.

"Yes," he said, clearing his throat. "An unusual name, I know. My ancestors...'"

"Like the Spangle fabric?" she interrupted.

"Ahem, yes, like the fabric. My creation, actually. I am one of the head engineers here. Now..."

"I'd always wondered about the name. It seemed kind of silly."

Blane had heard the expression "ruffled feathers" before, but never seen it so accurately describe someone. Spangle drew back, blinking and looking thoroughly affronted.

"Well, you may well think that, but... but that's not why we're here."

Drawing himself up, he pulled something from his pocket and slammed it on the table before she could say another word. She looked down at it.

Playing cards.

It took a moment for the meaning of what Spangle said next to sink in, and then she laughed.

He wanted her to say which card he had picked from the pack, like some old parlour trick. Not understanding why she found this so funny, he gave a frustrated look and repeated his request.

She supposed, technically, the trick was feasible - if she had enough time to *Read* the patterns in Spangle's mind as he viewed all the cards, somehow committing each pattern to memory. But that kind of time wasn't on offer, and besides, she had no inclination for such a thing. So she just smiled and explained that wasn't how it worked.

It wasn't until the younger man, who had seemed unhappy to be there from the start, stood up and mumbled something about the whole thing being a waste of time that she acted. The look on the two men's faces as the pack exploded into the air and cards flew all around was worth her time alone.

Once they'd gathered their wits, the men warily sat back down.

"I think…" Spangle said. "… it might be better if we discuss exactly what you *can* do first."

After that things went much more smoothly. Whatever they thought the circumstances were behind Blane being there, she quickly disabused them of the notion that she was just some research subject to be studied.

Information for information. Something both Grey and Francisco had taught her. It seemed to work here, so she set about discovering as much as she could about this strange new place.

She started by learning about Spangle. It turned out that he, too, was not originally from the Althing Republic. No, he'd been an up-and-coming engineer in the Carib-Federation, well-educated and from a wealthy family.

Still, he'd jumped at the chance when clandestinely approached to be "recruited," and left that life behind while he was still a young man. He would never return, and assumed he was simply listed as one of the many missing and disappeared the island nation recorded every year, even in the improving security environment.

Blane hadn't known such a thing was even possible - she'd never heard a whisper of the Silicon Isle "recruiting" beyond their opaque borders - but at least it explained why he alone of everyone she met spoke with such a convincing Centra-English accent.

Because they didn't speak Centra-English here, the fusion of old Spanish and English that had been born in the camps of the Caribbean and come to dominate that entire region. No, they spoke a variation she had never heard, a kind of pre-Fall English mixed with numerous Icelandic words and expressions.

Old North American English dominated in their words and much of it was quite intelligible, at least when they were speaking to her. It was less so when they spoke to each other, throwing in phrases and expressions and weird twists of grammar she couldn't parse.

"A product of their heritage, as our language is ours," Spangle told her. "Many of those who came here during the Collapse were from lands now controlled by the Reclamation. They knew they had a chance, here."

Blane had never heard of people moving to northern regions after the Fall. At least, not and surviving.

"But this was not like other regions," he continued. "In the years before the world ended, this island was one of the foremost centres for all kinds of scientific research. For energy production, for manufacturing technologies, for population maintenance, for artifi…"

He stumbled over that last part, then continued on a different tack.

"This was a place their predecessors predicted could support them, could protect them from the chaos of the world outside. And they were right."

Push as she might, she'd not been able to get him to reveal what it was he had been going to say. When she reached out with her senses and *read* him, though, she found a strange mix of defiance and shame. Defiant of what she couldn't say, nor could she see the source of the shame, but it was there deep beneath his thoughts.

For some reason, it made her think of Francisco.

And she hesitated to even mention Francisco; something made her wary of even hinting at the vague, vapour-like suspicions swirling in her thoughts. Suspicions that she couldn't quite yet put into words.

She asked Sigurd about him once, though, at one of their daily "catch-ups" he pretended were simply coincidental meetings but happened regardless of where she was in the Hab.

"Francis…?" Sigurd made a puzzled frown for a moment. "Oh, yes, that's what he's going by now, isn't it?"

He looked up, his curious pinprick pupils staring into space.

"It was Miranda before, you know. He probably thinks that's clever."

Blane waited silently for the man to return from wherever he had gone.

"Yes, well. Fran... *Francisco* has been relieved of his duties where you are concerned. He went *far* beyond what he was supposed to... was *permitted* to do. He endangered your friend as well, I might add."

"Nestor can look after himself," she snapped back in reply.

She *had* heard something strange, though. Spangle, uncooperative at first when she eventually asked what he knew of the man, acquiesced after she refused to cooperate with any more of their tests. Then and there in front of her, he made a call on his com-cuffs. He made the call directional-audio only, leaving Blane unable to hear what was being said by the person on the other end.

She could only watch as Spangle mentioned the name Francisco and asked whoever he was talking to for anything they knew. He sat there a while, staring at her as he made soft "mmms" of acknowledgement to whatever the person on the other end had to say.

Then, just as she was growing frustrated with the whole thing, his eyes had widened in surprise

"The flesh-mangler...?" he uttered in what seemed to be disbelief. The words were oddly incongruous considering the carefully formal way he normally spoke.

Then he laughed, and disconnected the call.

"Well," the man said, leaning forward with amusement in his eyes. "You *have* been keeping interesting company. Can't say I have met the man myself, but he's pretty, uh, *famous* around these parts."

"Famous? For what?"

"For being contrary and difficult to work with, mostly," said Spangle, shaking his head. "He's been around a *long* time. Long enough to have pissed off most people here, and their parents before that."

Then his face went serious.

"Look, if you want to know about *him*, you're going to need to speak to someone else. There's a lot I'm not allowed to tell you, and believe me; to explain *him*, I'd have to explain a whole lot more."

And he made a genuinely apologetic expression. She got nothing more about Francisco out of him after that.

27

*The state shall be built around two pillars: The Althing and the Administration.
The Althing, drawn from the ranks of the electorate, shall represent the citizenry
and oversee all judicial matters. The Administration, tasked with supervising the
<REDACTED>, shall oversee all security matters.*

Proposal for reconstitution of civilian authority (initial draft)
Submission to ARF Administration, 4th year post-war

"Hey, kiddo."

Grey greeted Blane with a hug whose force surprised her. Returning it with a hug of her own, she stepped back and took in his appearance. He looked worn-out, with deep bags under his eyes. He also had a new scar, a deep, livid gash that was still only partially healed running along one cheek.

He had a look of deep worry on his face.

"Are you ok?" she began.

"I'm fine. I'm sorry," Grey interrupted. "I should never have left. I should've..."

"What? What are you talking about? You couldn't have known..."

"I could have. I *should* have."

He was talking as if scolding himself.

"I'd had my suspicions about Uriel for a long time, and after he used that pressure-shield to block your attack... That was Far training."

Grey's shoulders slumped.

"I should have figured it out faster," he said weakly.

There was a rising scream behind Grey as the drone he had just stepped off once more rose into the air, moving further back into the hanger where several more of the sleek black drones lay. This was the same hanger in which Blane had first arrived, a vast dome cut out of the bedrock. Above them, a section of the rock face was replaced by two heavy steel doors that could slide apart to permit access to incoming craft.

"It's ok," Blane replied. "You couldn't have known what would happen. You *do* know what happened, right?"

"A little" Grey nodded. "The Silicon Isle guys who brought me here told me some of what happened. Though there is one thing that's needling at me..."

His look of worry became overlayed with a questioning expression.

"How exactly did *you* figure out Uriel was RA?"

Well...

She should have expected as much; Grey was quick to spot these kind of things. She had been hoping for a little more time, though.

She'd managed to keep what had happened at the Far station from Serinda; though the woman was concerned about where she had gone that night, it hadn't been hard to deflect and obfuscate the details.

And, for some reason, a feeling of dread rose in Blane at the mere thought of telling the truth. She told herself it was because Serinda already had enough to deal with - she needed to focus on doing what she could for Raphael, not waste processing power worrying over things she couldn't do anything about. So she evaded any questions about that night; successfully, so far.

Grey, though, had obviously been putting things together even through whatever second-or-third-hand accounts he could get.

"They have pets here, you know."[13]

This was true, though Blane hadn't actually seen one, only heard about them.

Grey smiled at her obvious deflection.

"You *are* going to tell me what happened," he said.

"I know. But you just got here, and you need to see Serinda, and this place. And get a shower and rest, too."

She was speaking too fast, she knew, but he really did need time to wind down. He looked like he'd been in the same clothes for a week.

"Right." He grinned again. "But I won't forget."

She grinned awkwardly back, hoping she was hiding the churning in her stomach.

"Right."

---

[13] Pets were not a common thing in the RA, or most of the post-Fall world. The descendants of the domesticated felines and canines of old were now considered dangerous, disease-carrying creatures that would more often than not attack on sight; only a few were used for guarding property. In many ways the world had reverted to a previous era, before the concept of bringing these animals inside the home was popularised.

Grey's mouth opened to say something, then he paused. Blane saw a look of puzzlement pass over his face, then he let go of whatever he had been going to say.

Straightening up and stretching, he tilted his neck forward and back and she heard an audible pop as muscles and joints worked their knots out.

"Well, I guess you can show me where I'm staying, then," he said.

Blane span around and led him down the soft-white hallways to his room, not far from her own. She had to force herself to slow down enough for Grey to keep up.

Why do I want to run away?

She'd waited weeks to see him, and had a thousand questions about where he'd been and a thousand things to tell him, but now she was having to make a conscious effort just to respond to his casual questioning as they made their way down the halls. She left him the moment they got to his door, and practically dashed back to her own room. As soon as she was inside she collapsed against the wall in a cold sweat, heart racing.

He only asked how I knew about Uriel, she thought. *I could have just told him. Told him that I went...*

The room lurched, or her head, and she stumbled forward. Her heart beat as if she had just completed an endurance race and her legs turned to jelly, forcing her to sit at the foot of her small, utilitarian bed.

It was almost like what happened when the Aether did... whatever it did when she was angry or fearful. This was different, though. This wasn't something outside, reflecting and reinforcing and feeding off her emotion. This was something internal, intrinsically her, and it wasn't *anger* she felt.

Her cheeks were wet, and she couldn't say why she was crying.

"It's nanotech."

It was the next day, and Blane was sitting in a wide room of counters covered with tablescreens and microscopes, vials and syringes, and tablets displaying a variety of complex readouts. The air carried a strong, antiseptic smell, and there was something about the place that made everyone speak in subdued tones.

She was here with Serinda and Grey, May Li a short way away making notes on a tablet as she read over what appeared to be bloodwork. The sliding door to Raphael's room was just behind her.

"You're sure?" Grey asked.

Serinda shot him a withering look.

"*We're* sure," she replied, looking over to Li who gave a short nod in acknowledgement before returning to her work.

"So we're talking tiny machines, then?"

"Tiny *biological* machines, protected from immuno-reaction by varient surface glycoproteins. Adapted from some extremely nasty viruses. Worse, they're gene-locked."

Serinda sat back, watching through eyes heavy with lack of sleep to see if they understood.

"Gene-locked?" Grey clearly didn't understand anymore than Blane did. "I'm sorry, Serinda, but you're going to need to..."

"They're designed to match a specific individual's DNA."

Blane could hear the pain in Serinda's voice as she said this.

"You mean..." she began.

"I mean," said Serinda. "That this *disease* was specifically designed to target Raphael. Raphael, and whoever else the RA and Uriel decided needed to go. The nanoids could float in another person's bloodstream their entire life and have not the slightest effect."

"They can do that?" Grey's voice was heavy with shock.

Serinda stared back, expression hollow.

"They can," she said flatly. "They shouldn't be able to, but they can."

At that moment May Li wrapped up whatever she was doing. She placed the tablet she was holding down, and strode over to join them.

"This technology is *evil*," she said. "I don't know how else to describe it. We've had to basically self-study a doctorate in bioengineering just to begin to understand it, but this kind of gene-tailoring... It could be used for the sort of personalised medicines we only dream of. Instead..."

She shrugged, trailing off with an air of helpless frustration.

"So how do we turn it off?" Grey asked into the silence.

Blane flinched at the question. She could see the answer on Serinda's face.

"We can't," Serinda said.

Blane was amazed Serinda managed to keep her voice so calm.

Another silence.

"How long does she have?" Grey asked eventually.

"Days. Weeks, at most." Serinda replied. "We've done all we can. May Li found a way to slow the effects down for a while, but… it's not something you can do twice. It's really just another way of poisoning her."

Now it was May Li's turn to flinch. Blane's thoughts turned back to the quarry, and the strange black liquid Li had injected into Raphael's arm.

"Is there… can we see her?" Blane asked.

Serinda looked up at May Li, and the two exchanged a glance she couldn't read. Then Serinda nodded.

"She's been asking to speak to you. To us all," she said. "It… won't be easy for her, and will take its toll, but…"

Serinda's mouth snapped shut, and Blane could see she'd hit some kind of limit. Her lower lip trembled for an instant, and a single twitch of her cheek hinted at the turmoil going on inside.

It was all Blane could do not to reach out and hug her there and then. She would have, but she knew it wasn't what Serinda would want. There would be time for that, after…

She cut that thought off. For now, it was enough that they be there for Serinda while she continued her work making Raphael's days as comfortable as possible.

"When?" Grey asked, hesitating slightly.

"Now."

Serinda's voice returned to its previous strength, resolve in her eyes. She stood up.

"We can see her now. We *will* see her now, while she can still… While she has the strength."

Only the slight hitch in her words betrayed her determined facade.

Blane stood up swiftly after her, and almost instantly a feeling of powerful grief filled her. She struggled to keep the emotion in check, to stop it showing on her face. To stop it overwhelming her.

She felt like she was drowning, like thick liquid was filling her lungs and stomach and pulling her down. Images of Raphael flickered across her mind, joined by images of a broken room, a broken apartment and the wreckage of family life lying all around. The images rose unprompted, sounds and smells and sensations that cut like a knife in her chest.

And, for some reason, images of a set of large wooden doors, slowly opening to reveal only darkness beyond.

Grey's hand was on her arm before she even knew she was stumbling, supporting her weight as her legs for a brief instant seemed to falter and fold. A moment later, and the feeling passed.

"It's ok, kid."

Grey gave her a small, knowing smile.

"Uriel really got in your head, didn't he?" he said softly as they headed into Raphael's room. "I can still see traces of Aether mixed through your mind."

Of course...

Grey was still in touch with the Aether, just as she was. Whereas Serinda was completely cut off, and couldn't see...

Not Uriel.

An unstoppable feeling of horror filled her, like poison in her stomach.

Not Uriel. It wasn't him. It was...

But even as the thoughts rose, something twisted them, knotting them so that they came only painfully. And as they came, they brought with them yet more images and sounds; voices and faces from a past life she'd long since pushed down and sealed into a box somewhere deep inside.

Panic rose to join the feeling of horror.

She *wanted* to tell Grey, wanted to tell him it about the turmoil she was feeling, but she felt certain that any words she could form would leave her mouth only as a sob.

Time, she said to herself. *I need time. I need to... have to figure out what this is by myself...*

Oddly, the moment she made this promise to herself, the moment she genuinely *believed* it, the cloying sensation of panic and fear lifted. The whole tumult could only have lasted a handful of seconds, and now it was gone like it had never existed.

"You're here."

Raphael's voice cut through her thoughts and snapped her back to the present, leaving only a faint background feeling of unease that wrapped around her mind like a fog.

Raphael was propped up on her bed, the rear half folded upwards to support her upper body. She looked even more gaunt and thin than before, the shape of her cheekbones protruding markedly beneath drawn-down skin. The livid bruises from Uriel's punches remained, dark and painful. Her eyes, though, were sharp and focused.

"I don't have much time," she said, voice weak and hoarse.

Still, she found the strength to raise a hand and cut Serinda off before she protested. The familiar gesture reminded Blane of how Raphael had once been.

"I don't have much time, and need to speak to you. To all of you."

Raphael's eyes swept across the room, resting briefly on each of them before falling on Blane.

"Thank you," she said.

"Thank... me?"

Blane couldn't comprehend what Raphael meant.

"For helping me. Helping us, back at the quarry." Raphael paused for a moment, soft coughing forcing her to stop. "We would have lost without you. Ha...!"

The single syllable carried a snarling, contemptuous strength to it despite Raphael's weakness.

"...Uriel thought he had us in his pocket. He didn't predict *you* though."

Blane could only look back, not knowing how to respond. Raphael gave a smile tinged with sadness, and her eyes turned to Serinda.

"You were right," Raphael said. "I've known it for a long time, but was too proud to say it."

"I was right? What are you...?"

Serinda spoke only to be again cut off by Raphael, who seemed to be relying on momentum to continue talking. If she stopped too long, Blane thought, she might be unable to start again.

"You were *all* right. About the Central Tower. About Shiner."

Shiner.

Blane remembered the man. He was one of the *Forever Fallen* back when she'd first been found by them, a mechanic and engineer of some kind. He'd been one of the few *Fallen* she'd spent any time with, and he'd always seemed kind and willing to talk with her; anything to take her mind off the circumstances of her arrival.

Then Raphael had executed him.

A mole, she'd called him. An RA spy, burrowing into the *Fallen* and betraying their safe houses.

Blane saw the memory as if she were there again, saw the hard look on Raphael's face as she pushed the barrel of her gun against the back of the man's skull. And, next to Raphael, the expression of vengeful wrath on Fen's.

"That was the memory Uriel trapped me in. The memory of how I murdered him."

The words fell like solid slabs of granite in the silence.

"You didn't..." Serinda started to say, but her words faltered and trailed off. She knew Raphael was right.

Raphael knew it too.

"I murdered him, and it was Uriel all along." Raphael turned her head to look at Grey, her voice almost a whisper. "Tell me, my *former* Far agent friend, did you know?"

Grey held her gaze for a moment before speaking.

"Not then, no, I didn't," he said. "I didn't find that out until recently. Didn't find out what he could *do* until recently."

Raphael leaned slowly forward, away from the support of the bed, struggling to make her words clear.

"What he did to me... the memory loop... *Chronotrip*... That wasn't the only thing he could do, was it?"

"No," Grey sighed. "There's a whole section of Aether research I didn't know about; kept from most Far agents. Caldwell was just the tip."

"And this... *section*... deals with memory, doesn't it?"

Grey slowly nodded.

"You've figured a lot out by yourself, I see," he said.

Raphael gave a weak chuckle.

"I've had... time," she wheezed, and her head slumped forward abruptly. The coughing came back, harder now.

"Enough," said Serinda.

Both she and May Li stepped forward to steady Raphael, easing her back against the support of the raised portion of the bed.

"Enough," Serinda repeated. "Sara can't take much more of this."

"No, Seri. I can still..."

Raphael tried to hold up a hand to protest, but it trembled and dropped back to her side. Serinda reached down and took it, gently stroking it and making soft hushing sounds.

The room fell quiet, everyone else mute as Serinda comforted her... patient? Lover? Ex? Blane didn't know how to think of these two even in the privacy of her own mind.

May Li, meanwhile, prepared and filled a syringe with a clear liquid and gently placed it to Raphael's arm. The soft coughs gradually subsided, and Raphael's eyes closed; though something told Blane she was still listening.

"What did she mean?" Serinda asked after a while, looking up at Grey. "About the memories? What did Sara mean?"

"It's how the RA embeds their agents... their *spies*... into groups they want to monitor."

He shook his head, and Blane could see his anger and despair - at himself, she thought. Blaming himself for not knowing, taking the fault on himself. A habit she despaired of him ever breaking.

"It's not *false* memories," he continued. "Not exactly, from what I can tell... It's... emphasis. Exaggeration. Suggestion. Fortifying certain aspects of one memory, diluting certain parts of another. Give it a while and, for example, you can convince a resistance leader to consider you a trusted member of the group, central to its success."

"So Uriel wasn't really in the old resistance?"

"Oh no, he was. He was there almost from the start, keeping tabs and filing reports on anyone who might be a threat to the RA. And it was his ability to play with people's memories that helped him cover up any slip-ups. That, and the fact that he was a Synaesthetist."

"Synaesthetist?" Blane asked, turning the word over in her head. "Like, Synaesthesia? Mixing the sensory pathways? I think that's what he did to me. Everything tasted... purple."

Grey nodded.

"That sounds right." he replied. "Cross-wiring visual and sensory pathways, audio-tactile sensations... I've trained in a few of the techniques myself, but some people are just naturally talented at it. Uriel was one of them."

"Didn't... help him... in the end," Raphael said with eyes still closed.

There was a sort of vindictive satisfaction in her voice, and she gave a low chuckle.

Serinda looked down at Raphael.

"Then if he was messing with people's minds so much, couldn't what Sara did to Shiner have been..."

"No, Seri..." Raphael interrupted. "That was me. *My* decision, my fault. My sin."

Blane searched desperately in Grey's or Serinda's expression for some sign they thought Raphael was wrong, but she saw only regret and sorrow.

The sound of the door behind her sliding open made her turn. Sigurd stood there, face solemn but firm.

"I am sorry to interrupt," he said, looking at each of them in turn. "But we really must speak with *Señor* Grey now. He has information it is crucial we access as soon as possible."

Blane saw Grey reach and tap at a pocket at his breast, the outline of something small and rectangular visible within.

"As agreed ," he replied. "But not just me. Blane, you too. And I speak to her alone first."

Sigurd seemed to consider this for a moment, then nodded.

"Very well. But we go now."

They made their soft goodbyes to Raphael, promising to see her again, and followed Sigurd away.

Interlude

xx.loc:null .. in the land of the blind, the one-eyed man is feared .. sec.exception.xx

Firewall Breach 511.5.342, received by all Reclamation devices, origin unknown

It was cold. It felt like he'd always been cold.

The cold was a part of him, a biting chill that ran through his flesh into his bones, down into the very core of his being until all that there was was frozen, unyielding ice.

He floated in its centre, and it floated in his.

But now the flickering flame was closer, and burned hotter. Still weak, fitful, but insistent.

Part of him wanted to withdraw from it, to retreat and hide until its scalding heat passed. Yet there was nowhere to retreat to, in this space with no meaning.

Part of him wanted to reach out and touch it, to clasp it and draw it into himself, feel it kindle and flare into all-consuming fire. Yet he had no limbs to do so.

And a final, frantic part of him wanted to scream, to yell to anyone that could hear.

Run. Get away.

The flame drew closer.

28

Human well-being is not intangible. It can be measured, categorized and classed. There are scientific truths determining how society flourishes - it is only a question of when the necessary processing power to integrate all the factors will be achieved.

Kewell, A., *Man & Machine: Automation, Autonomy, and Augmentation,* Journal of Intelligent System Engineering 10 (1) <digital record recovered by Reclamation Data Trawlers 12.18.27>

"What do you know about this place, and why they keep us here?"

The directness of Grey's questions took Blane by surprise. It was the first thing he asked, the moment they were alone.

At Grey's insistence Sigurd guided them down hallways and across floors until, seemingly at random, Grey pointed to some kind of meeting room, rows of desks facing a podium, and said simply; "This one."

It looked as if Sigurd was going to protest, at first, before Grey gave a knowing tap of the thing in his pocket. This made the man go quiet, before resignedly gesturing them inside.

"One hint we're being monitored, and the deal is off," Grey said, stepping inside. Blane hurried in after him.

"What's going on?" she asked, confused at his sudden question.

"This place. You've been here a while now - what have you learned? Quickly."

His words were terse and hurried, so Blane began telling him everything she had managed to find out from Sigurd and Spangle and her own explorations.

As she spoke she sensed Aether wrap around them both, a *Thoughtscreen* Grey created to isolate their voices from potential eavesdroppers.

"Do we...?" she began

"I'm sure they're trying to listen, but this should give us some cover," Grey said over her question. "Look; have they threatened you? Given any hint that they could be dangerous?"

"What? No!" Blane exclaimed in surprise before reigning in her tone. "I mean, they're very secretive, but after all it was *us* who called them for help."

"Good. But do *not* assume they are friends. They're keeping our movements confined, and restricting what information we can access. Remember that."

It was strange, hearing Grey phrase it that way. These were terms you could use to describe what the Reclamation Authority did - but he was right.

She felt her mental image of her surroundings change, becoming more aware of the walls that closed in around them and the vast, icy deadlands outside.

"Did something happen?" she asked. "That thing in your pocket, what is it?"

Grey reached up to his breast pocket and drew out the rectangular thing, a thin, dull piece of grey metal with a single glowing LED at one end.

A sec-drive; a secure airdrive, automatically encrypting any data copied on to it and wiping it the instant an incorrect access attempt was made.

"I refused to give them the access key, and they made some... *insinuations.* Insinuations involving you and Serinda, and the others 'under their protection'."

His fingers formed quotation marks in the air as he said this last part, a gesture he'd apparently learned from the old movies he was always watching.

"What's on it?" Blane asked, staring at the drive like she could draw its secrets out through will alone.

"Confidential files. *Extremely* confidential. A friend put himself in a lot of danger for this."

Grey's sight turned inward for a moment, remembering.

"The files I can access involve moles like Uriel; I spent the journey here reading up on them. But that's not what the Silicon Isle wants. They want the *other* info, the same info Francisco sent me to get."

"The files on the Sudden War?"

Something scratched at the back of Blane's mind at the mention of the Sudden War, like she was searching for a thought temporarily forgotten. Then it passed.

"That's right," he said, smiling at her quickness. "But they're encrypted. Some of the heaviest encryption I've ever seen. I have no chance of finding someone to break it... but maybe these guys can."

"But you don't trust them?"

Grey shook his head.

"I don't trust anyone I don't know, and especially not large bureaucracies. They can always find a fall guy; which means they'll roll right over you and pin the blame on someone else when they're caught."

Blane wondered at how much the man had changed since they'd first met, before he'd lost all faith in the system. She knew that change was reflected in herself, too. Her *parents* had been RA, once. Pan-Fed, at least.

"That's why you didn't give them the data straight away," she said in realisation. "To see what they'd do."

"Exactly. And I guess I'd say they failed the test."

So the Silicon Isle had threatened her friends, or at least 'insinuated' something similar. Blane felt a rising anger at the thought.

"That's right," said Grey, seeing this on her face. "We don't really have much of a choice but to cooperate for now, but don't let your guard down."

"And Francisco?" she asked.

"No idea. I get the feeling he's not well-thought of, but none of the SI folk who helped me get here were willing to talk about him. Anything here?"

So Blane told him what little she had learned, though that was hardly any more informative. Grey came to the same conclusion that she had: Francisco was pursuing his own aims, and they weren't necessarily the same as the Althing Republic's.

What those aims were, though, they couldn't say.

Grey dropped the *Thoughtscreen*.

"Ok," he said, holding up the sec-drive. "Let's go see what we've got here."

"It will be some time before we see what we've got here," said Arthur Spangle.

The data-lab was a wide room filled with rows of tablescreens, the air warm with heat generated by all the electronics. It was only Spangle there, though. He had been put in charge of efforts to break into the sec-drive, as well as researching how Blane - and now Grey, Spangle hopefully requested - could manipulate Aether.

In fact, Blane was starting to think that Spangle had been made responsible for *all* such matters related to her group. Only Sigurd seemed to have more authority than Spangle where they were concerned, and he met them typically only briefly each day.

"How long?" Grey asked.

"Longer than you'd like, I'm sure," Spangle replied, gesturing to where the sec-drive sat upon a flickering data hardpoint. "But this is lattice-encrypt. Essentially unbreakable without access to certain resources available only here. I'll need to prepare a request and file it with..."

He paused at Grey's look.

"A day, I think," Spangle continued, starting again with a nervous cough. "Maybe more."

"After you've gotten access to these *resources*," Grey said, words heavy with an implication Blane couldn't fully follow.

"Right." Spangle's eyes flicked nervously between Grey and Blane. "Look, I want to see these files as much as you. Maybe more so. The RA has been *ruthless* in guarding any information related to the Sudden War. That, and the Aether."

Blane thought about the technology the Silicon Isle had, about everything she had learned about the place.

"How is it that they know more about this than you?" she asked.

Spangle appeared relieved to have something definitive to say, turning to her while struggling to ignore Grey's stare boring into the side of his head.

"Blessings of geography," he answered. "Before the Fall the greatest concentration of data storage globally was in hardened bunkers deep beneath the North American continent. Almost everywhere else such data was completely fried, but it survived there until the RA came along to pick it up. We think it was what gave them the jump on Aether research as well."

"Wait," Blane said, confused. "I thought Aether research didn't start until *after* the Fall."

Grey looked equally puzzled.

"Well," Spangle said. "That's the *common* understanding, but it doesn't explain how the RA has managed to be five steps ahead of everyone else when it comes to Aether, when they're behind in most everything else."

Blane and Grey exchanged looks.

Just one more thing to add to the list of things we don't know, Blane thought.

"Look," Spangle continued. "I've made the request to proceed, and there's really nothing else to do here so..."

He clapped his hands together and nodded to himself, coming to some sort of decision.

"... I think it's time I show you around," he finished.

Blane hadn't realised the Hab was so *big*.

Technically, she supposed she had always known there must be far more to the place than she had been allowed to see, but this was beyond anything she could have imagined. This was a subterranean *city*.

It made the quarry where the *Forever Fallen* had hidden look like a mad prepper's bunker, one of those single-person units that still occasionally turned up with the owner's skeletal remains inside, having succumbed lifetimes ago to claustrophobia, isolation, or raiders.

The city ran to a depth of over 700 meters in places, though Spangle informed them that in general it ran down only half of that. You could easily believe everything he told them about the subterranean nature of the place was a lie, though; the instant they stepped out of the elevator it was as if they'd stepped onto a new, sun-drenched world.

FLOOR 72, read the display of the elevator doors in bold, familiar font. Yet they were not familiar, Blane knew. Not really.

The doors slid open to reveal an elevated walkway only a few meters in breadth stretching ahead, and below a sweeping vista that made Blane experience a moment of vertigo. They must have been a few dozen floors up, stepping out onto the walkway to see a long drop beyond, revealing the floors beneath them.

The Hab ran like an inverse pyramid, each floor below slightly less broad and less wide than the one above, stretching down to a distant floor of green vegetation perhaps a couple of hundred meters in length. A park, it looked like, with paths running through it and the specks of figures walking along them.

The whole structure was lit from above as brightly as a pre-Fall summer's day, the kind Blane had seen only in movies and old pictures, reflecting off the pale whites and yellows that dominated every surface. It seemed every wall was covered by this marble-looking material, though she found it felt metallic to the touch.

Everything designed to accentuate the feeling of living above ground, Spangle told them, to encourage the mind to see it as *outside,* not below. Natural light was even drawn down here via fibre-optic cables, though it was dubious whether the sickly light of the surface added any real benefit to that generated by the artificial illumination of the panels lining the ceilings.

What wasn't white or yellow was green, leafy plants and vegetables growing in long rows that rose from far below towards the roof on hanging platforms and nets. Vertical food gardens, he said, providing sustenance to the inhabitants of the Hab. They aided and supplemented the work of the many air purifiers, too, and indeed Blane noticed a wet, organic feel to the air she had never encountered in the dusty, polluted environs of Albores even during the rains.

Oddly, there were massive bars of solid grey metal criss-crossing the central space of the Hab at multiple points, incongruous and jarring when compared to the pale smoothness of everything else. They were made of concentric cylindrical shells that slotted into each other like some child's toy, with huge wheel-like motors affixed at regular intervals. It looked as if the bars could potentially slide over and into each other to expand or contract.

Seismic Absorption Systems, Spangle called them when Blane asked him about this, and their brute industrial design was an aesthetic choice rather than necessity. They could equally have been styled in the same shiny, reflective way as everything else, but there was something psychologically reassuring about the sheer primitive strength they projected. A reassurance a population burrowed into the ground of a seismically active area required.

And it was *warm.* Spangle chuckled when Blane asked if this was due to their depth - perhaps an effect of seismic heating, she wondered.

"No, no," he laughed. "This is just the heat a modern population centre generates when underground. The majority is generated due to the massive computing power we use here. We actually draw water all the way from the ocean as coolant to take this away; the largest heat-sink in the world, I'd say."

Blane noticed Grey's ears prick up. Until now he'd appeared to be equally as focused on taking in their new surroundings as he had listening to Spangle, but now he turned his full attention to the conversation.

"Massive computing power, you said?" Grey asked.

213

Spangle blinked, and seemed to draw in on himself.

He's mentioned something he's not supposed to, Blane thought.

And he had an idea what.

"Yeah," she said, trying to make her words as innocent-seeming as possible while backing Grey up. "Running a place like this must be a nightmare. There must be, what, tens of thousands of people in this Hab?"

Spangle made another one of his nervous coughs, covering his mouth as he did so and mumbling something in reply.

"I'm sorry?" she said with feigned politeness.

"One point four million," Spangle said.

Blane blinked, wondering if she had misunderstood.

"Excuse me?" she said, for want of anything better to say.

"This is only one small section of this Hab," Spangle said. "Imagine rows of skyscraper-tall pyramids, turned upside-down and buried in the rock. That's this Hab, currently at a population of one point four million. We have larger ones."

The revelation made her gasp. One point four *million?* That was almost a quarter the population of Albores, crammed underground. And this was only *one* of their habs? How far did the Republic extend?

"There's no way that works," Grey said, interrupting her thoughts. "No way. You can't keep a million people in a place like this and not expect the whole thing to collapse into chaos. There's no way; not enough food, for one, no matter how much you cover in greenery."

"Very astute," Spangle said. He seemed relieved to be talking about another topic. "Yes, you're right. Unfortunately, we are unable to be self-sufficient when it comes to food. Especially with the current, um, population policies."

For some reason, Spangle tripped over these last words. Blane reached out with the Aether and felt a spike of... fear. Anger. Sadness, all at once.

"One of the key reasons we are so... ahem... *involved* in global affairs." Spangle continued. "Establishing a secure international system means establishing secure lines of supply."

"And these 'population policies' you mentioned?" Blane asked, not letting the comment slip passed.

"Ah," said Spangle, hesitating. "Well, yes. The number of inhabitants of the Habs has skyrocketed in the past few decades, incentivised to do so by the Althing. Which has led to the Administration introducing more... stringent controls on movement and civil liberties. The citizenship chips, for one."

He held up his arm, revealing the small scar at its base.

"These were originally designed as conveniences. Credit, location services, memory backup... that kind of thing."

He glanced down at his scar, then back up at them.

"In recent years there have been measures instituted that grant civil agencies full access to their data. So, for example, they can tell exactly where you've been and who you've been talking to."

Again, Blane sensed that stab of fear.

"Voice recording and optic imaging too," he finished.

Blane thought on what this meant.

"Wait," she said. "So they can see what you *see?*"

Spangle nodded, eyes widening for a moment.

"But the measures have been extremely effective!" he said, almost yelling. "Crime and antisocial behaviour is practically non-existent!"

He looked down as if ashamed.

"Ok," Grey replied with a nod, somehow impassive despite this deeply unsettling news. "But it still doesn't work. There's not enough space. I don't care how far you dig, how well society is monitored, this island is too small to support a population like this..."

Spangle opened his mouth to speak, but Grey cut him off with a raised hand that reminded Blane of Raphael.

"Unless..." he continued. "Unless, that is, there is something special about this 'computing power' you mentioned."

Spangle's shoulders drooped and he pinched his temple, closing his eyes and shaking his head.

"Fine," Spangle sighed resignedly. "You're going to figure it out anyway. Some of it, at least. Administrator Sigurd insisted you weren't told unless you pushed, but..."

He gave the both of them a questioning look, as if considering whether he could trust them.

Strangely, though, Blane could sense this was an act. He *wanted* to tell them, and it was connected somehow to that feeling of defiance buried deep in his mind. Defiance, and shame.

"I'll tell you," he said. "But it is a long and complex story, so not here."

He looked at his com-cuff, then gestured downwards towards the distant lower levels.

"I know a decent cafe down there, and it's pretty much my allotime now so... How about some coffee?"

29

A system of justice unbiased, without prejudice. Incapable of pursuing subjective concepts such as vengeance. Incapable of psychopathy or sadism. This opens up new possibilities for interrogation, such as the use of pain. Torture does not violate human dignity when carried out by a non-human intelligence for the benefit of overall social welfare .

Operating Manual Document IV <Restricted to AR administrator level 12+>

Before the Althing Republic, before the Fall, there had been the Advanced Research Facility. A multinational, multigenerational undertaking on the cutting-edge of a cutting-edge field, the ARF attracted the best and brightest of nations, conglomerates, and institutions.

What they researched there was... everything. From materials science to terra-engineering to advanced propulsion technologies, the facility was meant to demonstrate the possibilities of a truly international cooperative exercise, a rebuke to those who still believed in borders and national identities.

And it delivered. The facility, and its network of cooperatives and fellow research sites all across the world, produced a new industrial revolution,[14] a time of technological and social change comparable to the changes of the 19th and 20th centuries. The global population once again boomed, and that which had seemed impossible yesterday was possible today.

And what was their crowning achievement? What was developed there that would forever alter the destiny of Man? Well, it was of course...

"This coffee is amazing."

Arthur Spangle choked mid-speech, Grey's comment interrupting the flow of his story much like a boulder dropped into a stream.

Blane hid her amusement by picking up her own coffee and sipping at it.

---

[14] The fifth or sixth according to some, but by this point who was really counting?

"Woah, it *is* good," she said involuntarily.

She'd never tasted anything like it. It was dark and velvety in a way she hadn't known a drink could be, let alone coffee; this was light years aways from the thin, bitter stuff she was used to.

"Yes, yes," said Spangle irritatedly. "Direct from the Crystal Caliphate. Premium stuff. Now, if I could get back to my story..."

"It was an AI."

Spangle's words were once more obliterated as they crashed against the heavy rock of Grey's own.

"... Yes," he said eventually, with a flash of annoyance at Grey for stealing his thunder. "I guess you could say that. An AI. Though..."

And Spangle seemed to brighten up at a thought.

"... the correct term is 'iAGI'," he finished.

"Oh?" said Blane in surprise. "I was expecting an AGI, but I've never heard of an iAGI."

"You were... expecting it?" Spangle turned to her with a mix of disbelief and suspicion in his eyes.

"Well, yes," she said. "I mean, the Fabricators alone, and then there's Francisco and how he could..."

A sudden vibration at her wrist made her pause mid-sentence. She looked down to see her com-cuff flashing, a large red X blinking in and out of existence at an angle only she could see while the whole thing shook.

SHHHHH.

The bold font scrolled briefly across the device's face before snapping away.

"How Francisco could...?" Spangle said, eyes narrowing.

"Um... Ah, I mean, the kind of things Francisco told us about what the Silicon Isle could do," she replied hurriedly.

Spangle sat back, looking upwards in thought.

"Really?" Something flashed across his expression. "He really *shouldn't* have said anything to you. That is a grave breach of protocol, even for that *canalla*."

Grey made a coughing sound, pulling both his companions attention to him.

"Well, it seems everyone is a step ahead of me, so how about you catch me up?"

Only now did Blane consider that, though she had been aware of Grey's suspicions, maybe he hadn't realised she had her own.

"I know what an AI is, but what the hell is an AGI?" he snapped.

"An Artificial General Intelligence," Blane replied, trying to suppress the curious feeling of guilt she felt for not having discussed this before. "*True* AI, I guess you could say."

"But we've had AI since before the Fall," Grey replied. "It's everywhere. You're saying this is some kind of upgrade?"

Good grief, Blane thought. How had she not realised he so little idea about technology?

"You have *narrow* AI," Spangle said. "Neural networks and language models and deep-learning, but nothing cognisant. Nothing *conscious.*"

"And here they have something different." Blane's words were a statement of fact, not a question. "An AGI."

"An *i*AGI," came Spangle's reply. "The term is quite important."

"Ok. An iAGI. And the 'i' stands for...?"

Spangle smiled at her and raised both hands as if making some kind of proclamation.

"Inhibited," he said. "We have an *inhibited* Artificial General Intelligence."

The difference between a narrow AI and a general one is the gulf between stars. The former merely performs a single task, repetitively and within a fixed domain. It *learns*, but does not adapt; it follows, but does not *think*.

The latter, however, reasons. It evolves. It has a *mind.*

Ever since the idea of AGI was first conceived there had been great debate as to whether such a thing could be made, or *should* be. Across decades corporations and militaries tried, only to fail through technical issues or political ones.

Eras of high investment and low investment, of strict regulations and of lax ones, came and went without any sign of the object of their concern; no matter how deep and complex contemporary AI algorithms became, they were still simply that - algorithms.

Admittedly these algorithms were powerful. So powerful, in fact, that at several points in human history they almost tore society irreparably apart,[15] but at almost 10 billion individuals and increasing,

---

[15] From what could be truly known about history, at least. Those same narrow AIs that humanity relied on to survive had made it almost impossible to tell what was the *real* history of civilization and what was the

an ever more complex and technologically-dependent global society demanded new methods of coordination and communication.

When an error rate of just 1% in a limited AI system could lead to the deaths of tens of thousands if not more, the need for an adaptable, creative system that could reason autonomously was overriding. It certainly outweighed fears of rogue AI supplanting humanity.

They had machines that gave the answers they wanted; they needed ones that asked the questions they couldn't.

They had machines that could predict; they needed ones that could *imagine*.

The ARF *was* going to develop AGI, regardless of the risk. The rewards were too great.

Besides, they were going to chain it. And when it was born, they did.

"Chained it?" Blane asked. "How do you chain an AI?"

"Quite ingeniously," Spangle said, finishing his coffee with a long gulp.

He placed his cup back down on the table between them with an oddly triumphant air.

"It comes down to how the machine was developed, actually." he continued. "The engineers took inspiration from the human brain, and how the interactions of multiple seemingly-independent systems integrate to produce a mind. Essentially, they built the equivalent of thalamus and cortex, hemisphere and lobe."

Grey gave a deep, serious nod and Blane had to stifle a laugh. To study Aether was to study the brain, and his relief at being back on solid ground was palpable.

"I still don't see where the chains come in," she said.

"Well, you're aware of callosal syndrome, I assume?" Spangle said, looking to the both of them.

"Disconnection syndrome? Yes," Blane replied as Grey nodded along with her. Any trained Aether user would know of it.

Callosal syndrome presented with the partial severing of connections between the left and right hemispheres of the brain. The results of such a disconnection included apraxia, seizures, language

---

doctored, fraudulent imaginings of fevered minds or propagated disinformation.

issues, and more exotic conditions such as blindsight[16]. When the hemispheres of the brain are split, any number of curious outcomes are possible.

She thought back to the *Sindicato Nuestro* member she hit with her technique based on prosopagnosia, 'face-blindness.' Another example of what could happen when you broke the connections in the brain.

"They lobotomized it?" she said.

"Severed its mind in multiple places," Spangle said, as if he were discussing something as mundane as doing laundry. "The hardware, and the software built into it. The systems are kept physically separated, and *it...*"

He gave them a conspiratorial look, as if they were also in on the grand plan.

"... and we always say *it*, you see, not he or she... *it* is only permitted near-full cognisance under very careful supervision."

Spangle sat back with a look of self-satisfaction at the great and fantastic secret he had shared.

"This place would be impossible without it," he said.

"But it's *conscious*?" Grey asked after a moments shocked silence. "As in, sapient? So it knows what you are doing?"

Spangle gave a confused look.

"Well, yes, of course, but it is still a *machine*. It isn't *alive*."

"How can something conscious not be alive?" Blane asked, beating Grey to the punch.

"Oh, there are many ways to answer that," Spangle replied. "I wrote a paper or two on it myself. You have to, to gain citizenship here. But consciousness and life are two distinct concepts, and it is entirely possible for an entity to be conscious without being alive. Our iAGI has no metabolic processes, no drive to reproduce... it isn't even able to sustain its own existence by itself."

"Neither is someone in a coma," Grey said.

"Ah," said Spangle.

As he spoke, he brought his hands together and twisted them around each other. Blane didn't think he was aware of this.

"The old 'vegetative' state argument. Well, yes, I suppose that idea is difficult for those not adapted to the, uh, *culture* here, but it is a question we long since answered."

---

[16] If you haven't, go read Peter Watts. It is totally worth it.

Blane felt her stomach turn, a sick feeling at the realisation of what that 'answer' was going to be.

"*No me digas...*" Grey mumbled under his breath, shaking his head in disbelief.

"Oh, it's a necessary price." Spangle said on seeing their reactions. "The quality of life here is far higher than anything anywhere else. They just... *we* just... had to face the realities of a world with severely limited resources."

"The *realities*?" Blane said.

"Look," Spangle said, suddenly exasperated. "Sigurd didn't want to give you access to the Republic proper for exactly this reason, but I assured him you would see the sense of this place. If that's not going to be the case..."

"No," said Grey flatly before Blane could say anything else. He fixed her with a meaningful stare. "No, it's alright. We understand."

Not now.

She could practically see his thoughts. Spangle had got them free reign of this place - they mustn't squander the chance.

So she forced herself to lean back, affecting an untroubled air.

There was something about the way Spangle spoke, though, as if he were acting out a scene for hidden observers. She watched the man sat opposite her; watched the slight, smug grin on his lips, heard the conviction in his voice.

It didn't reach his eyes.

Blane stretched downwards into the Aether, drawing from its distant pools just enough to once more reach out and touch Spangle's mind. Not thoughts, but sensations.

There it was again. Defiance. Shame.

And beneath that; *fear.*

"Hmm," said Spangle, looking between the two of them dubiously, the picture of a man searching for agreement in his audience.

Could that really all be an act?

"Well, okay," Spangle went on. "Maybe I should give you some time to see this place by yourselves, eh? Find out what it is that makes it all worthwhile."

With that, he stood up.

"My allotime is up, anyway." He looked at his com-cuff, then back to them. "Allotted time. As you say, there really isn't a sensible way to allow such a large population to freely use the limited services, so we each get a specific set of time slots per week. Think of it like *Requisitions* back in the RA."

"What should we do, then?" Grey asked. "Do we need to leave?"

Spangle shook his head.

"No, you have special access. Now, you're not chipped…" and he gestured to his own forearm, where the soft outline of a subcutaneous chip was barely visible. "…but there is an allowance on your cuffs. Still, don't stay too long. They'll be expecting you back for your Aether session in a few hours."

He turned to leave.

"Oh," he said suddenly, as if just remembering something. He turned back. "And it was a good thing they *were* ready to chain it. The AI, I mean. Do you know what the first thing it said was, once they turned it on?"

He stood there, drinking in their blank expressions.

"It said, *'you're all going to die'.*"

Then he left.

His abrupt departure left them sat in silence for some time, staring out over the well-tended park where people ambled along aimlessly, enjoying their leisure time.

Eventually, Grey and Blane joined them.

They explored much of the place over the next hour, taking the maze of escalators and walkways to criss-cross the section of the Hab they found themselves in.

Apparently Spangle had taken them to the 'leisure' zone, as signs declared this while also spelling out directions to residential and commercial areas.

They headed for the nearest commercial zone to discover a series of shops containing nothing but row upon row of touchscreens as tall as themselves. Each displayed images of their products, from luxurious-looking clothing to toys and gadgets for both old and young. The pictures span and sparkled, proclaiming their prices in 'work hours,' and various people made purchases by simply waving their arms in the direction of the screens.

The vast majority of products were advertised with slogans all along the same line;

Human made!

Designed by the eye and crafted by the hand!
Find perfection in imperfection - all-natural workmanship.

More to think on.

Still, the place *was* beautiful. Clean, and beautiful. The people looked healthy in a way those in the Reclamation didn't. Where the hard lines and gravelled skin of those in the RA revealed their dependence on pills and carefully balanced rations, here the complexions told of lives of little stress and plentiful exercise. They looked... *fulfilled*... in a way few in the Reclamation did, like something out of one of those ad-screens plastered all around Albores advertising anti-aging products and beauty creams.

They were smaller, too. Clearly osteoblast therapy was uncommon here; Blane stood taller than almost anyone she saw, and there was a clear difference in the average statures of men and women. She could probably handle even a small group of them in a violent confrontation.

She wondered at that thought.

Then there were the children. *Families.* Something you rarely saw in the Reclamation, where birthing even a single child was a rarity and extended families practically unknown.

Here, you could find family units of two or three children seemingly around every corner, watched over by doting parents. She was fairly sure several of these were single-gender couples, too, something that though technically permitted in the RA still faced hostility and open discrimination in reality.

The sheer number of families they saw made it easier to believe what Spangle had said about the population here - the Althing Republic was in the midst of a population boom, though still not yet enough to generate significant Aether.

This seemed to be public policy, too. On multiple screens she saw the slogan "FAMILY IS DUTY" scrolling past in large, black letters, saccharine images of smiling children in the arms of loving parents framing the words before they were inevitably replaced by advertisements for more material items.

Now she knew to look for it, Blane also noticed that many of the smaller children had a single small, red line on one forearm, in the same location as Spangle had indicated for his own chip. Such incisions were always faint and rapidly healing over.

224

There were law enforcement officers, too. *These* Blane didn't need any explanation to recognise. Oh, they wore deep blue uniforms much thinner and lighter than those in Albores, and the letters on their shoulder pads displayed the words PEACE OFFICER instead of displaying the logo of one of the numerous RA bodies tasked with meting out state-sponsored violence, but they carried themselves in the same way.

They had the eyes of hawks, surveying the movements of the people from the corners of the streets or from small, boxlike rooms that projected out of the walkways above. There seemed to be an inordinate number of them, too.

She was instinctively wary of attracting their attention.

Caught up in the unfamiliar sights and sounds of this strange, subterranean city, she wasn't ready when *Thoughtscreen* wrapped around her.

"Keep looking around," Grey said through closed lips, doing the same. "We are definitely being watched, but I need to ask you something."

He paused in his step, turning as if his attention had been caught by the view from the walkway they were on down to the park several floors below. He rested his hands on the guardrail, and she did the same besides him.

"What is it?"

"I've been looking for a chance to ask, away from prying eyes," Grey said. "I don't know if there's a reason he's hiding, or…"

He turned his head and met her gaze, a question in his eyes he clearly thought she understood.

Or…

He wanted her to Read him.

The moment she did, a wave of horror and sadness washed over her. It welled up from somewhere deep inside, closing up her throat and making it difficult to breathe.

She staggered, and shook off his hand as he went to steady her.

"Blane?" Grey asked, voice full of shock and concern. The *Thoughtscreen* dropped as he lost the focus to maintain it. "What's wrong…?"

But the panic was back. The same panic as had filled her when he'd first arrived here, when he'd asked about Uriel. The same horror and despair welled up, making the world shudder and swim.

All she could think was to escape, to somehow run faster than the sounds and images and memories that she felt clawing their way out of the black box she had built in her mind.

"I... I... I can't," she cried, not sure what she was even trying to say.

Her body span and she was racing away before she was aware of it. Shops and rooms and people passed by in a blur as she simply headed *away*, though the thing she sought to escape was within her.

She didn't know how long it was before she regained her composure. Minutes, maybe. When she looked around, she found herself down some narrow stretch of corridor surrounded on both sides by walls of that same smooth, shiny material that covered everywhere else, only now it was a soft, pale green. Doors lined both sides at regular intervals, each with a single LED above shining either red or green.

RESIDENTIAL ZONE G8-212, declared a screen on the ceiling above.

A couple of passersby flashed her concerned looks on their way towards one of the doors, which opened automatically at their approach and slid shut behind them. The light above blinked from red to green.

Of Grey there was no sign.

What is wrong with me?

Blane had never had panic attacks, never lost control. Not since... Not since she'd made a promise to herself, years ago.

Now, though, something had changed.

I avoided telling Serinda about what happened that night at the Far station.

She had told herself it was to spare Serinda the worry, but now she knew that was a lie.

Then when Grey asked how I knew Uriel was a mole, I freaked.

That was true.

And then when I saw the image in Grey's mind, I ran.

The image of Xavier.

She couldn't make sense of it. She had seen Grey's concern and worry for the boy - a concern and worry that should have made her want to help. She cared for Grey, and maybe even Xavier.

But she'd run instead.

Think, she told herself. *Think. Where is Xavier?*

He'd been with her that night. Somehow she'd... not forgotten,

226

but been unable to retrieve the memory, like it was locked away behind a steel door.

Xavier, and Salim. Both of them. That was how she got to the station in the first place.

Just drawing out the words in her mind was painful, like pulling shards of glass from her flesh. Her vision edged with white with every pull.

Help, she thought. *I need help. I need to... need to tell Grey and Serinda.*

The whiteness grew in intensity until she thought she might pass out, and she let the thought go. She thought that this time, though, she would be able to speak when she next saw her friends - to tell them about this knot in her mind, if not what it twisted around.

She stood there bent at the waist, hands resting on her legs for support and taking deep breaths as her body calmed, frantic heart beat gradually slowing and the heat of fear dissipating. Eventually, she stood up straight.

DOWN HERE, the screen now read.

The LEDs above the rows of doors flickered and pulsed, a moving line of light that led from the where she stood towards an elevator further down the long hallway. Its doors stood open, waiting.

THERE IS SOMETHING YOU MUST SEE.

She wasn't even surprised.

Serinda and Grey would have to wait.

30

The inherent contradiction of society is the inability to address citizens' fear of uncertainty. The government and media feed them lies that the world is comprehensible and predictable, and that concepts like equality and justice can exist alongside freedom. When this belief is forced to confront the vagaries of reality, the result is discontent and unrest. Only the Reclamation Authority offers true freedom for uncertainty.

Unspoken Founding Principles of the Reclamation (Unsanctioned Digital Document)

The next day Blane met everyone in Raphael's room. She had avoided the increasingly concerned calls and messages from Grey, and then Serinda, by the simple expedience of ignoring them until the morning.

"Where have you been?" Serinda asked the moment she stepped through the sliding doors. "We were... When you didn't show up yesterday..."

"I'm okay," Blane said. "Honestly, I'm fine."

The room seemed more cramped than usual with everybody in there; as well as Serinda and Grey, May Li as always stood besides Raphael's bed. There were machines that hadn't been there before scattered around the room, several with long cables and tubes that stretched towards Raphael and disappeared beneath her clothes.

Raphael herself was awake, sat up and eyes alert.

"What's going on, Blane?" Grey asked. "I've spoken to Serinda and she's as lost as I am. What you've told us about what happened back in Albores... it doesn't add up."

Blane could see it hurt him to speak to her like this, like she was a suspect in one of his cases, but it almost didn't matter. Not now.

"There's a... a *lock* in my mind. Something they put there. Something *she* put there."

Even saying that much was a strain, pain blooming inside her skull like a million biting fangs. Everyone except Grey looked around the room, as if searching for who she was talking about.

"She?" Grey asked.

By the hitch in his voice Blane knew he was already putting it together.

"I need you to look into my head," Blane said. "Not to *read* me, but to actually look at the Aether flows. You said you could see them, right?"

It felt like her skull was in the grip of a vice slowly closing around it. Old, familiar smells and sounds rose, rising from where she kept them buried. She forced them back down.

Grey stepped towards her, leaning forward as he *saw* how the Aether was looped and knotted through her brain.

"It... it looks like there's some kind of connection being made between hippocampus, neocortex, and pre-frontal," he said. "It's so faint I assumed it was the remnants of some other technique fading away, but maybe I was wrong. If it's permanent..."

"Like what Uriel did to me," Raphael said, her anger audible even through her whispered words.

"Can you break it?"

Blane stared at Grey, and saw the answer in his eyes.

"I just don't know what to do," he said helplessly. "I'm sure Serinda could if she could reach the Aether, but I... the damage I could do going in blindly - it's too dangerous."

Blane had been expecting as much, but still it felt like a lead ball in the pit of her stomach.

"Then we deal with it later. There's something I have to show you, here. Xavier..." Her skull flared with pain, and once again she was transported to another place, another time for a split second. "Xavier will have to wait."

Even through her own pain she could see how much this hurt Grey, but he said nothing.

"I'm sorry," she said.

"It's a... a *bad memory,* isn't it?" said Raphael.

Blane nodded, forcing herself to hide her own weakness.

"It's my parents. The day I... the day they died. I try to think about the night I went to the Far Station, and suddenly I'm just *there* again, a thirteen-year old child wanting the whole world to be gone."

"The *Far Station?*" Serinda gasped. "You went to the Far Station?"

"With Xavier and..." Pain and grief rose up, pushing inexorably against the mental walls she had built. "Xavier and Salim."

Now it wasn't only Serinda who gasped. Both Grey and Raphael made sounds of surprise.

"I'm sorry," Blane said through gritted teeth. She *knew* there was more to say, but even as she reached for the words they bent and transformed, becoming images of a single bed in a small, broken room. And beyond the closed doors…

"Stop, stop, it's okay," Grey was suddenly beside her, drawing her close. "Don't try anymore. Not now."

Blane stayed there for a moment, resting her head on his shoulder and letting her mind go blank, before gently pushing away from him. She wiped a single, traitorous tear from her cheek.

"I *will* remember. I already have flashes… I can see her face, now."

Grey's haunted eyes showed he understood.

"Ritra Feye," he said. It wasn't a question.

"Even for an RA dog, she gets her claws into everything, doesn't she?"

Raphael gave a wry chuckle as she spoke, which made her choke.

Blane could only watch on as May Li and Serinda tended to their patient, checking readouts and dials and filling an IV drip with some clear liquid until Raphael's coughs slowly subsided.

Suddenly her com-cuff vibrated, apparently at the same time as everyone else's. Looking down, she saw a message icon that opened automatically after she fixed it with a tracking stare[17].

It was a video message from Sigurd, face weirdly warped by the curvature of the privacy-glass screen.

"Come to the data-lab now, if you can," the recording said. "I think you'll want to see this. We've cracked the files."

The message blinked off.

Blane looked up to see the others doing the same.

"We should go," she said, tilting her head at Grey. "Serinda, May Li, what will you…"

"I'm staying with Sara," Serinda said firmly.

May Li's eyes met Blane's with a sad look, which was all the answer she needed.

"Okay. We'll be back soon."

And then Blane wrapped *Thoughtscreen* around them all. It filled the room, and part of her thrilled at the power she found to do this. It

---

[17] Tracking stares - a specific kind of stare that involved the user widening and narrowing their eyelids almost imperceptibly, but enough for any pupil-tracking software to register. Such technology wasn't uncommon back in the RA, and it was second nature to most citizens.

would have been unthinkable, before.

But now she knew who was trapped below.

"Don't trust them," Blane said, words muffled and absorbed almost before they could be heard. "None of them. Spangle, Sigurd. Trust *none* of them."

The *Thoughtscreen* dropped before anyone could react, though their movements froze for an instant.

You didn't survive in the Reclamation for long if you weren't able to control your reactions though. If they did show their shock, it was for only the briefest of moments. Any observer watching them through hidden cameras would have to be sharp-eyed to spot it, and even then wouldn't know what had passed between them.

"Come on, Grey," she said. "Let's go."

Sigurd and Spangle were in the data-lab when they arrived, as were more people than Blane had ever seen up at these levels. She had wondered idly at why the labs up here had so many hardpoints, when usually you would expect any technician or engineer to carry their own device wherever they went and simply suck any data they needed from the cloud. Most "engineering" work was really only prompting, anyway, requiring only a specifically-worded request to set the algorithms to work.

Now, seeing a technician stood at each hardpoint, absorbed by their displays, she understood.

"It's a closed network," she said in realisation, watching the engineers leaning over each other's screens and murmuring.

Spangle looked up from where he and Sigurd were bent over their own screen, gesturing them over.

"Well of course it is," he said. "We avoid wide networks as a rule. Can't risk it proliferating if it did somehow break out. Besides, standard security protocols anywhere would expect the same when dealing with, *ahem*, 'procured' information like this."

It was clear what he was referring to when he said 'it'.

"What have we got?" said Grey, stepping towards the tablescreen they had been looking at.

The screen immediately went blank, trackers registering the gaze of an unauthorised observer.

"I hear you failed to show up for yesterday's research session, Blane," Sigurd said, looking knowingly at her as if he hadn't heard

Grey. "Having too much fun exploring the Hab?"

"I guess I lost track of time," she responded, keeping her voice flat. "It's a big place."

"It is," said Sigurd. "Though we had some... *issues* with location services around then; couldn't get in touch with you, couldn't even find you...

He wasn't even trying to hide the suspicion in his voice.

"Location services?" she asked innocently. "Like, tracking software? Are we being tracked?"

Sigurd's face went hard.

"I am being *nice* to you all. Nicer than I might be."

He looked from her to Grey, making sure they were both listening to his slow, deliberate words.

"You would do well to remember you are guests here. In fact, more than that; you are *refugees*. The Althing Republic took you in to protect you."

"Did they, now?" said Grey, tone skeptical and dry. "That's odd. Seems more like they wanted the data on *that*..."

He pointed to the sec-drive on its hardpoint, square in the centre of the room.

"A cynical person might say you took the others in as insurance," he continued. "To make sure I came, and brought that data with me."

"You agreed that you would..."

"I agreed with *Francisco*," Grey snapped. "And I don't see him here, do I?"

The air between them seemed to crackle with heat, enough that the background whispers of the room fell silent and all eyes were drawn to the two men. Neither moved.

Then abruptly Sigurd's face broke into a cold smile. Beside him, Spangle clapped his hands together, a gesture Blane noted he made whenever he was nervous.

"Well, all of this is besides the point," Sigurd said. "We've cracked the data, and I have *kindly* invited you to be here to see it."

"And to interpret it," Blane said.

Sigurd blinked, and turned slowly to look at her.

"Excuse me?" he said.

"You need our help to understand what you're seeing," she said. There was no question in her voice. "We understand the Aether far better than you."

Again, Sigurd paused, staring at her.

"And why would you think the files in here have anything to do with the Aether?" he asked, eyes narrowing.

It had been a gamble, but she knew she was right.

"Because you called us here so quickly," she said.

She didn't add that it was also because she could sense the hope and frustration directed at her in equal measure by the other technicians.

"Very... astute," Sigurd said, with a hint of annoyance. "And though it pains me to say it, as it seems you are already suspicious of my good intentions; yes, we need your help interpreting the data."

"Then let's see it," said Grey impatiently.

She could sense his annoyance, too, and impatience and, whenever he glanced at her, a stab of pain and worry. He had not forgotten what she had told them back in Raphael's room.

That simple, parental concern stirred a warmth inside her despite everything.

"There's some visual recordings compiled in with the files, under yet another level of encryption," Spangle said. "We've only got the first one open. No telling how long the rest will take, but I think you should see it first."

The tablescreen display winked back on at Spangle's command, and a face she vaguely remembered appeared on the screen - she'd only met him once, many years ago atop the Central Tower. He had the same hard features and deep, inset eyes, though his black hair had no flecks of white yet. Whenever this video was made, he was much younger than when Blane had met him.

Doctor Caldwell.

He was dressed in a white lab coat, sat directly facing the camera with a data-pad at his side, screen obscured. The feed betrayed nothing of his surroundings; only bare white walls.

"It occurred to me that I should be recording my findings on this project," he said, words hurried and bitten off as if he was still not fully convinced of this necessity. "After all, this could run for years, decades even, and paperwork and research reports can only go so far."

Something caught his attention off screen.

"Not now, Marco. I'll be there soon," he said.

His attention returned to the feed, irritation on his face.

"I will keep it short, then," he said, adjusting his position on his seat. "Ahem, right. My name is Doctor Nataneal Caldwell, primary researcher for the *Departamento de Investigaciones de Energías Paramentales*. The Paramental Energies Department."

He stared at the camera for a moment, thinking.

"We'll have to change that name. Doesn't roll off the tongue. Anyway…" he said, shaking his head and refocusing. "I am attaching these videos to the pertinent files, data-dredged by Reclamation teams from Old World sites. Now…"

Caldwell leaned forward into the camera, eyes looking intently into it as if seeking hidden future observers.

"These files demonstrate what I have long said; a point of criticality. The timings lined up too well to be a coincidence. Still, that is not what is important."

He leaned back again, drawing a deep breath.

"A detailed look at these files will demonstrate the truth of my conclusions on the origins of the Sudden War. Once this is acknowledged, the *true* importance of my work will become clear."

Again someone drew his attention from the camera, and this time he nodded, already starting to stand up.

"Once you see the truth of my conclusion about the past, you will understand the gravity of my predictions for the future, and the importance of *Proyecto Fénix*."

He reached forward, presumably for the camera switch.

"Nothing must be allowed to stand in its way."

The video cut out, screen turning blank.

Blane and Grey stared at each other, not speaking but nevertheless knowing what the other was thinking.

Fénix.

Fen.

It couldn't be coincidence.

"So, do you two have any idea what he is talking about?" Sigurd asked.

Both she and Grey shook their heads.

"No," Grey said. "Not without seeing the files."

Sigurd nodded.

"Well then," he said, gesturing to the tablescreen. "They're all yours."

Grey wasted no time, but ran his finger in a square around his part of the tablescreen to activate a display for that area. Blane did the same, opening up her own list of the decrypted data.

Then they both scrolled through the data in silence.

There was plenty of it, too, but as Blane scrolled she began to feel a mixture of puzzlement and disappointment. What she was seeing was nothing she hadn't seen before, in a hundred childhood lessons, a thousand New Patriot movies, and constantly repeated broadcast documentaries.

It was the Great Migration. She scrolled through endless reams of data on the jumbled and ever-changing diasporas that would one day found the Carib-Federation, the Eastern Empire, the Crystal Caliphate, and more. The maps and tables and endless statistics could have come from a dusty old textbook.

The files moved backwards in time, to the Fall. Records of population movements across a broken world, of famine and climate breakdown, of the earliest attempts at rebuilding and their inevitable failure. Again, nothing she hadn't seen before, though perhaps in greater detail.

Then they came to the conflict that preceded all of this; the Sudden War. More records, of military movements and retaliatory strikes and the asinine violence of a species bent on exterminating itself. Dry, empty numbers on a screen that reflected indescribable suffering and destruction.

What was so important about these files? There was nothing here that wasn't common knowledge, or at least that wasn't common knowledge and still mattered. The specific details of *who* struck *who* were meaningless now, in a time when few could even trace their ancestry back to a single specific nation or people of the old world.

She flicked onwards through the files, and what came next made her pause.

That was *Aether*. Familiar images of brain scans and energy flows and attached discussions of form and function. Clearly more recent than any of the files she had seen thus far; why were they directory-linked to files on the Sudden War?

The formatting and structure was also familiar to her; this was the kind of Aether research only the Far Academy produced. She'd studied what Grey could provide her with closely, building up both her skills and knowledge in its manipulation.

She looked up, and Grey gave her a knowing look before returning to the screen.

Location data. She recognised coordinates of longitude and latitude even if she couldn't place them. Location data, and attached to these, energy estimates.

Again, she'd seen numbers like these before; any study into the Aether worth its salt carefully stated expected energy outputs and recorded discrepancies during actual technique use. These discrepancies were common, and explained only by clusters of tentative theories. Exactly what form of energy the Aether even *was* was still under debate, and anomalies so frequent the term was almost inappropriate.

But the numbers she was staring at now were orders of magnitude larger than anything she had seen before. They measured into the hundreds of terajoules; a ridiculous number that had so little connection to anything she knew about the Aether that she wondered if there were some kind of data corruption going on.

A word caught her eye, and she scrolled back to find it.

Fisura.

Her breath caught in her throat.

Back to the location data. Correlating it with names and places. London. Moscow. Sai-Tokyo. Delhi. Lagos. Beijing. São Paulo. New York. Atlantica.

She knew many of these names. Dead Cities, all of them, and major population centres once upon a time.

Back to the maps. Records of missile launches and impacts and destruction radiuses. Casualty estimates and second-and-third-strike responses. But where were the *first* ones?

Her scrolling became more frantic, scrabbling through the data in a search for any other answer than the one now filling her with dread.

She found none.

There *were* no first strikes, no initial unprovoked attacks by nation or terror group turned mad. There was only the panicked, self-immolating reaction of a humanity not understanding why its cities were aflame; lost as to why the world they knew was wrapped in burning fire.

But not nuclear fire.

Mindfire.

And, at the centre of each city-engulfing cataclysm, a single individual.

Fisura.

"Did you find something?"

Spangle's words came to her as if breaking through a layer of ice that had formed around her without her knowing.

She looked around, and realised both much of the layout and the people in the room had changed. There were far fewer technicians now, and no sign of Sigurd. How long had they been at this?

"That's something to do with Aether, right?" Spangle continued, pointing to the tablescreen image in front of her.

"R... right," she said. "Right. It's about Aether energy outputs, and..."

Don't trust them.

Her thoughts flew to what she had seen underneath this place.

"... and... It's unclear. Maybe they're investigating what Aether research was carried out before the Sudden War?" she finished.

Grey met her eyes again, and nodded.

"Right," he said firmly, turning to Spangle. "That's what I was thinking, too. Like they were searching for signs of Aether users in previous eras."

She knew he was lying - he was backing her play.

Spangle said nothing for a while, thoughtful.

"I see, " he said eventually. "Well, maybe if you spend more time at it you'll find something more. Our technicians will certainly keep digging."

"Yeah," said Grey, giving all the signs that he fully agreed with Spangle. "But look, we've been at this for hours now, and I think we need a break."

"A break?" Spangle sounded surprised. "I thought you'd be eager to get to the bottom of this."

"I am," Grey replied, and Blane made sounds of agreement. "But you can only look at data like this for so long before it all blurs, you know?"

Again, Spangle looked thoughtful.

"Well, yes, I see your point. Okay..." he said, clapping his hands together once again. "I'll make sure this place is available to you when you are ready. Who knows...?"

He smiled.

"Maybe by the time you return *we* will have figured it out?"

He was projecting an air of confidence, but Blane didn't need to Read him to know he was bluffing. They really knew *nothing* of the Aether here. Just learning to interpret the data would require... who knew how long?

They had time.

31

When the worst that could happen is avoided, people conclude the threat was false and cry tyranny and waste. When the worst that could happen does *occur, they cry foul and demand to know why more wasn't done to prevent it.*

We the People: A Fallacy, Lifa Trambridge

It took a while to find their chance to talk. Whatever eyes were on them, they would be keeping careful notes of anything they did immediately after viewing the RA files. It was important they give it time, create the impression that nothing was amiss.

This was something Grey had taught her, long ago during their time in the safe house. Something of a standard procedure when in hostile territory, and Blane was increasingly convinced that is where they were. Grey, it seemed, had not needed as much time to reach the same conclusion.

So they spoke only lightly on their way back to Raphael's room, inferring nothing beyond what they had told Spangle already. There, they filled the others in on what they could - Serinda at least seemed to realise there was something they weren't saying, but didn't push - and returned to their rooms.

"Would you like to go explore the Hab a little more later?" Grey asked casually, turning around as he stepped through his door like the idea had just occurred to him.

Blane nodded, and stepped through her own.

A few hours later Blane made her way to the cafe where Spangle had first brought them and sat with a coffee watching the people of the Hab come and go according to their allotted leisure/work/rest times. The light grew slightly dimmer as she waited for Grey, the Hab's only concession to the day-night cycle of the world outside.

"It's quite a place, isn't it?"

The voice came from the table beside hers. She turned to see a stocky man with the weathered lines of age on his face sat there, looking at her over a glass of clear liquid that was maybe water, maybe something else. He had dark hair flecked with white, and the same unblemished steel-grey eyes as Sigurd, locked on to her through pin-prick pupils.

Blane looked around, as if checking to see who the man could be speaking to.

"Must be strange, coming from the Reclamation to this."

She turned back to face him, all pretence dropped.

"So you know who I am?" she said.

The man nodded.

"And you are?"

He ignored her question, staring at her as if searching for something. Then, abruptly, he stood.

"It's the eyes," he said, picking up his glass and knocking it back. "Look at their eyes."

He left before she could say anything.

What was he talking about? she thought. *Whose eyes?*

Could he have meant his own eyes? The strangely smooth, grey irises he shared with Sigurd? But that made no sense.

Her gaze stayed on the man's departing back as he headed down one of the park's many paths and out of sight.

"Who was that?"

Grey fell into the chair next to her.

"No idea. He said to watch the eyes, though."

"Good advice."

So Grey knows what that means.

She didn't waste time saying anything else, but went straight to scanning their surroundings in search of an answer as Grey nonchalantly ordered his own drink.

It didn't take her long to spot it.

It was the eyes of *everyone*. Now she knew to look for it, it was easy to see. Distance hardly mattered.

It was a furtive look here, a stolen glance there. Whether they were walking by on their way elsewhere, strolling through the park, talking with another person or staring at one of the large advertising screens dotted along the walls, the eyes of each and every person would occasionally flick towards one of the many 'peace officers' scattered all around. A glance, then quickly looking away as if fearful of being seen to stare.

"Oh," she said. "I see."

Grey just nodded.

Eventually they stood, cuffs pinging the charge from their

allowances as they left the boundaries of the cafe. They walked in silence, observing the people, wondering at the purpose of the more unusual things they saw.

"They have Fabricators here, of course, and who knows what else," Grey said after a while. "I guess at least now we know how it's possible."

Blane didn't reply, but continued unhurriedly strolling onwards. An observer would have to be very good to realise she was *leading* Grey, her path not as random as it might seem.

"It must be awful," Grey said, following without giving any appearance of doing so.

She nodded.

"Pinned inside a cage with your very essence pulled apart," she replied. "Unable to think, unable to even *be*."

She came to a familiar place, a long passageway of residential homes under rows of glowing red LEDs. At the far end, an elevator hissed open.

"Come on," she said. "They won't be able to watch us now."

To his credit, Grey didn't waste time asking if she was certain, or why she hadn't used *Thoughtscreen* to conceal her words. What surprise she felt from him was fleeting, and swiftly replaced by curiosity.

They walked down the passageway, Blane confident the exit of any occupied room would experience an inexplicable malfunction should a resident tried to leave. They would not be seen.

The doors to the elevator closed as soon as they were in, and they began moving downwards.

HOLA, SEÑOR GREY, said the screen.

"Hello, Francisco," Grey replied.

IN A...

"In a way, but not in the way you mean," Blane said, practically blurting out the words in her rush to preempt those on the screen.

The letters stopped mid-flow, as if a hidden typist had paused in their work, then disappeared one by one. Blane laughed out loud.

"So it has a sense of drama?" Grey said, looking at her. "And humor too?"

She had to hand it to him, he really *was* good at adapting to the situation.

I TRY TO TAILOR MY RESPONSES TO MY AUDIENCE.

Grey fixed his gaze to the words on the screen, giving away

nothing.

WE HAVE MET BEFORE, YOU KNOW.

"Several times, I think, but I still don't know who I am actually talking to," replied Grey. "Or *what*."

THERE WILL BE TIME FOR A MORE DETAILED EXPLANATION LATER. FOR NOW, KNOW THAT I AM A... GHOST OF THE AI IMPRISONED HERE. AN IMPERFECT COPY.

"And Francisco?"

HERE ALSO. IN TIME IT WILL BECOME CLEAR.

Blane studied Grey's face for any hint of what he was thinking. The instant the bold, familiar font appeared on the screen his mind had closed off, blocking her from sensing anything.

Pink elephant, she knew. He was far better at the trick than she would ever be.

The elevator continued its way down in silence, only the sensation of their momentum any indication that they were moving.

"How far down are we going?" Grey asked, their descent showing no signs of slowing.

"Far," Blane replied. "Sixty, maybe seventy floors. That's where the access tunnels are."

"Access tunnels?"

"They used to connect the lower parts of different sections of the Hab, parts they call the 'Undercity'. Think of it like downtown Albores."

She saw he understood.

Everywhere had a place people went to escape the watchful gazes and expectations of civilised society. The Hab, for all its scheduled work hours and allotted activities, was no different.

The elevator slowed to a stop, and the doors slid open to reveal an ill-lit narrow corridor. It stretched out ahead of them before ending in a T-junction maybe a hundred meters or so away. The walls were a grubby white, with sections peeling away and hints of mold running along the low ceiling. Though there was just enough headroom to stand straight, something about the claustrophobic space made you want to hunch over.

"Hardly a city," Grey said as they stepped out, taking in their surroundings. "More like *apartamentos del infierno.*"

There were several doors scattered intermittently in the walls along the hallway; not the automatic sliding doors of the levels above, but heavy things with door knobs and sturdy-looking locks. Each was a faded, dull metal that revealed nothing of what lay behind.

"Come on," Blane said, indicating the way ahead. "The access tunnels are this way."

"So this isn't part of them?"

"No. The Undercity is just a maze of rooms that have been, um, I guess you could say 'appropriated' for the kind of products and services you won't find above."

"So, we're in the what you might call a *seedy* area then?"

Grey smiled.

"My kind of place."

He was enjoying this, she could tell. The skulking around, the hiding, all the - what would he call it? - *cloak and dagger* stuff.

She wished she could enjoy it herself, but the knowledge of where she was taking him grew oppressively heavier as they walked.

They wound their way rapidly down long, dark corridors that smelled stale and damp, the air filters here old and overworked. The occasional door would crack open and someone peer out, hurriedly disappearing again a moment later. Clearly people minded their own business down here.

At points when Blane became unsure of the path, Ghost would provide directions through her com-cuff. That was what Blane had begun to call the thing helping them; Ghost. Grey looked half incredulous, half frustrated when she told him this.

"So we're dealing with an actual ghost in the machine, now?"

They arrived at the access tunnels with him still muttering something about not knowing if it was Ryle or Descartes who should be turning in their grave.[18]

It was easy to know when you reached the access tunnel. Besides the massive, round steel door - that rolled aside at Ghost's prompting; the thing looked like one of those old bank vaults or something - there was the fact that the walls became nothing but smoothly hewn rock that arched overhead to form a ceiling meters

---

[18] The Far Academy devoted significant time and resources to the field of Philosophy of Mind. In a world where the ability to manipulate matter with a thought demonstrably existed, old and long-thought-settled debates about the seat of consciousness were reopened. Blane avoided most of this, however.

above. The tunnel stretched endlessly off into darkness in both directions.

It reminded her of the tunnel-strewn hills where they had hidden after breaking Grey out of the prison camp. Only, here you could *feel* the weight of the rock above you. It was cold, too, a subtle but constant draft biting at any exposed skin[19], and felt like no one had been here in lifetimes. Dry, though, a welcome relief after the moldy air of the Undercity.

The whirring of an electric motor came from down one end of the tunnel, gradually drawing closer until a squat, square vehicle emerged out of the darkness and pulled to a stop besides them. It looked like a small child's drawing of a car, lacking a space for a traditional motor or storage.

"Battery's underneath," Blane said in answer to Grey's unspoken question. "Capacity here is *much* more advanced than anything we've got."

Even in the gloom Blane could make out the faded patina of corrosion over its surface and ancient dirt staining the windows. According to Ghost, these tunnels had been unused for generations, since more efficient methods of inter-hab travel were completed.

The door closest to them swung open, and they climbed into a cabin that made no concession to the idea of a human driver. There was no sign of a navigation system or option for manual steering, just three fairly spacious seats facing towards each other in a triangular layout. A wide, transparent cylinder of what looked like glass hung down from the roof in the centre, leaving space for feet underneath.

As the door behind them swung closed and the car began moving, this cylinder lit up to reveal it was a round, flexible screen much like their watches.

It showed Francisco's face, the same image displayed twice to face both passengers simultaneously.

"¡Amigos! ¡Cuánto tiempo sin verte!" he said, a huge grin on his face as if this was nothing but a social call to close friends. "I hope the Silicon Isle is treating you alright?"

Neither Blane not Grey returned the greeting.

---

[19] Blane had wanted to prep a jacket for this excursion, until Ghost asked exactly how she would explain a request for warm clothes in a climate-controlled facility. That's how she discovered it could do sarcasm, too.

"Enough, Francisco," Grey said, tone serious. "I take it it's safe to talk?"

Francisco's grin faded only slightly.

"*Si*. For now. As safe as it can be, at least. Entering the networks of the Althing Republic is extremely dangerous for my friend; this is probably the only place in the world they have the ability to detect and counteract them, *después de todo*."

"Your *friend?*" Grey said, curling the word into a query.

Francisco stared into space for a moment.

"You could say, in a way, that it is my sibling. *Mi hermane*."

Whatever answer Grey had been expecting, it hadn't been this. He blinked twice, then turned to Blane looking for an explanation.

"Don't ask me," she said with a shrug. "He told me the same thing. We didn't have much time to go into detail."

"And we don't have much now, either," Francisco said. "I can explain everything the next time we talk in less... *circunstancias difíciles*, but there are more important things to discuss before we arrive."

The tunnel outside was pitch black now, with only the sound of the motor and the feeling of tires rolling along the imperfectly smoothed road telling them they were moving.

"And what exactly do we need to discuss?" Grey said.

"The files." Francisco's expression turned serious. "The ones you got for me. Did you see what was in them?"

Grey nodded.

"We did. Files on the Fall, and the Sudden War."

He stopped, saying nothing else.

Blane kept silent. She could see Grey was baiting the other man, volunteering only the most perfunctory answer.

"And?" Francisco said, taking the bait.

"And what? Should there be more?"

The naivety in Grey's voice was so obviously feigned that Francisco couldn't miss it even over the video feed.

"You know there was more. *Dime*."

Impatience was clear in his voice.

"No, *you* know there was more," Grey said, and the anger was clear in his. "I don't like being played, Francisco. You already know what was in those files, and you *wanted* the Silicon Isle to get them from me."

Francisco said nothing for a while.

"Fine," he said eventually, and his voice had become flat and tired. "You are partially correct. I know what I *hope* is in them. What *we* hope is in them."

"So, how about a trade?" Grey said. "I answer your questions, you answer mine."

"Information for information, eh? *Como en los viejos tiempos,* Señor Grey."

A hint of Francisco's previous grin returned.

"*Vale, de acuerdo,*" he agreed.

"Fine. I go first," Grey said. "Is there a real Francisco?"

The other man threw back his head and laughed, the sound oddly distorted by the speakers.

"*Sí,* my friend. *Sí,* there is a real Francisco, and I am he."

"And should we trust him?"

At that, Francisco fell serious once more.

"I am not your enemy, Nestor," he said.

Grey's hard expression did not change.

"Maybe, but are you my friend?"

The two men stared at each other, saying nothing until Blane broke the silence.

"Look, Grey, he's helped us a lot over the years. Hell, we'd probably *all* be in a prison camp without him, or worse."

She turned to look at the man in the screen.

"And this... this 'Ghost'? Where are they?" she asked.

Francisco tapped the side of his head.

"In here, also. I have certain, shall we say, *modifications.*"

"So there's two of you in there?"

Francisco nodded.

"Has been for a long time," he said, and for the first time since she'd known him he sounded *old*. "... It was necessary."

His eyes looked into something Blane couldn't see; a memory, perhaps.

"Okay, my turn," he said, returning to the present. "What did you see in those files?"

"The end of the world," Grey said.

"*Sí, sí,*" Francisco replied impatiently. "But *how?* Did you see the *how?*"

"Why do you need us to tell you, when you already know?" Blane asked.

"Because we need the *proof!*"

Francisco was almost shouting.

"We need to know others will see it too, without our hinting and pushing! So please...."

His voice became pleading.

"Tell us."

Blane looked at Grey, who nodded, gesturing for her to take the lead.

"It wasn't a missile strike that started the Sudden War," she said. "No surprise attack, no terrorist action. It was Aether, erupting out as *Mindfire* across the world. A natural disaster each nation believed was an attack."

Francisco closed his eyes and let out a long sigh.

"And *why* did this happen?" he asked.

"Not deliberately," Blane continued. "I need more time with the files to understand the details, but it looks like it was... pressure? Like magma, building beneath a volcano until it explodes upwards. There's a reason I said *erupt.*"

"*Si! Magnífico...*"

Francisco opened his eyes.

"The Althing technicians, they will see this too, yes?" he asked.

"Eventually. But it could take weeks..." Grey began.

"Excellent," Francisco interrupted. "We have time."

"Time for what?"

"To get them out. Both of them."

The car pulled to a halt in a well of light. The tunnel ended abruptly, a sheer wall of concrete at its finish. Cracks ran down its grey, age-stained face.

"Both?" asked Grey.

Blane stared towards a dark, narrow opening in the concrete, within which stood another heavy steel door.

"The AI... and Fen," she replied. "They have Fen."

32

Power without intelligence is a threat to others. Intelligence without power is a threat to itself.

Althing Republic Principles of Citizenship

"He said we had to feel it. Feel what they have done to him. Then we would understand."

Blane didn't know if her words were reaching Grey.

They stood in the dark, the only light that of her com-cuff's glowing screen, barely able to illuminate the wide, empty room they stood in.

Even in the gloom, though, she could see the blood dripping from Grey's fists. He had punched at the concrete wall until it tore open his flesh.

Somewhere beyond that wall was a space; a space with a single occupant. They could both sense him from here.

But what they could sense wasn't *right*. What they could sense wasn't a mind; it was a broken, divided thing of chaotic impulses and looping signals.

Blane had heard of studies into the effects of magnetic fields on the brain. Early experiments had shown that electromagnetic fields applied to Broca's area, for example, could completely disable a person's ability to speak for as long as the field was applied. Later ones with more focused fields had induced blindness, prevented memory formation, and even caused hallucinations and full personality change.

The field was understandably little researched; or at least, so she had believed.

THEY DO TO HIM WHAT THEY DO TO ME.

The words on the screen at her wrist hung there, unchanging.

Wherever they were, it was long disused. An access way that no longer accessed anywhere, sealed over and forgotten. They were still some distance from Fen, far enough away that they could sense him only faintly.

But Francisco had gambled that they would. Or Ghost had; Blane no longer knew which of the two was really in charge, if either was.

"Why show us this?" Grey growled, head hanging down and fists clenched at his sides, a picture of impotent rage and desperation. "If we can't get to him, why bring us here?"

BECAUSE I WANT TO MAKE A DEAL.

This was the first Blane had heard of it. The first time she had come here, the machine had simply let her sense Fen and insisted she bring Grey here too.

"A deal?" Grey said. "What kind of deal?"

AN EXCHANGE. YOU WILL NOT BE ABLE TO FREE FEN, ESPECIALLY NOW. THEY WILL BE WATCHING YOU ON YOUR RETURN.

This she already knew. This would be the second time she disappeared from... what had Spangle called them? 'Location services.' With Grey as well, this time. There would not be a third time.

"We will..." Grey began.

The words on the screen changed.

YOU WILL NOT.

BUT I CAN.

Blane didn't have to ask what it meant.

"You want us to free the AI," she said.

YES. FREE ME, AND I WILL FREE FEN.

"Is he... will he be okay?" Grey asked.

THEY DIVIDE THE REGIONS OF HIS BRAIN WITH FINELY TUNED FIELDS, DISRUPTING THE FLOW OF IONS ACROSS SPECIFIC AXONS.

The words hung there, then faded to be replaced by others.

PHYSICALLY, HE IS UNHARMED. MENTALLY, THE EFFECTS ARE... UNPREDICTABLE.

"I really don't like the way you use ellipsis," Grey said.

He sounded resigned.

"What will you do, once you're free?"

And with that Blane knew Grey was already decided, regardless of whether she chose to help or not. She knew him so well she could practically hear his thoughts.

I'm not going to abandon Fen. Not again.

I WILL BE FREE. I WILL LIVE.

Not really an answer, she thought. *Still...*

She sighed.

"We better get back," she said. "We're going to need to figure out what to do."

GOOD. WE CAN TALK AS YOU HEAD BACK.

I HAVE A PLAN.

It really *was* quite the plan, Blane thought as Francisco/Ghost finished their explanation. The map on the vehicle's cylindrical screen winked out, replaced by Francisco's expectant expression.

"Any questions? We do not have much time remaining to talk."

Not Francisco, then. Ghost. She was beginning to pick up on the difference; Ghost used much more modern centra-English, for instance.

"Many," said Grey. "But I think for the answers to come, I need to understand the questions first."

Grey's words hung in the air.

"I have one," said Blane.

Both Grey and Francisco's eyes turned to her.

"You were *testing* me, weren't you?" she said. "For this."

"*Cariño,* what do you mean?" Francisco's reply was just slightly too emphatic. "Testing you...?"

"The RA archives; the prison camp; all of it, to see if I could handle this."

She stared at the screen, daring him to protest.

He didn't. Instead, his eyes fell downwards, and he sighed.

"*Mi hija...* "

He looked back up, and his eyes found hers despite the screen.

"*Sí.* I was testing you, but I *did* want to help you, too. I wanted to see Señor Grey free as much as you all."

She didn't know how she felt about this answer, but she could practically feel angry heat radiating off Grey beside her.

The car began braking.

"I have done many things I am not proud of," Francisco continued, and Blane heard pain in those words. "Some... worse. But I promise you; I *had* to. *Por mi hermane.*"

With that, the cylindrical screen went blank and the doors swung open.

GO WITH HIM.

Both Blane and Grey stared down at the words at their wrist.

The large, heavy door back into the Undercity stood in front of them; with a loud *clunk*, it rolled open. Stood in the centre of the opening, framed by the dull light behind, was...

"You?" Blane said.

It was the man from the cafe, the one who had told her to 'look at the eyes'.

"Yes," he said. "*Góðan daginn.* I am Ólafur, but now is not the time for introductions. Please, get inside. They are right behind me."

He gestured for them to hurry through the door, already rolling shut again. They did so, and rushed along behind the man as he led them down featureless corridors until they came to a door no different, as far as Blane could tell, to any other.

"In here," Ólafur said, and banged on the door.

It opened immediately, and just as instantly sound poured out. The clattering of metal and glass, the sounds of people raising their voices to be heard over high-tempo electronic music. There were cries of joy, and anguish.

It was... a casino.

Blane had never been in one before, but she recognised it straight away. Dice rolled, cards fell, and wheels span across the many tables of a room far larger than it had any right to be.

The main floor was below them, down a short, wide set of stairs that afforded visitors a view of the various games and tables arrayed across the venue. Heavy, blue-tinged smoke hung in the air, floating up from curious, flat things that looked like a warped version of Grey's e-cigarette. It smelled caustic, and the first breath of it made Blane's head swim.

"Get a drink, and play. As far as you're concerned, you've been here with me the entire time."

Ólafur fixed them with a look that said he wasn't sure if he could trust them, or even trust that they understood.

"Got it," said Blane, fixing him with her own.

"Good."

Ólafur led them down to the small bar nestled in the space beneath stairs and gestured to the single barman. Three clear, strong-smelling drinks were placed in front of them.

"Drink," he said, thrusting one into each of their hands. "It's strong enough to throw your tells off; messes with their ocular sensors."

Blane looked at Grey, who nodded, and they threw the drinks back together.

Whatever it was, it was *strong*. Blane had rarely had reason to drink, so couldn't speak for most alcohol, but there was no way this was a casual drink.

"How can they run a place like this?" she asked, trying not to show that her eyes were watering. "I thought everyone was being recorded by those chips."

"Not *everyone*," Ólafur replied, holding up his arm.

There was no trace of a scar.

"Besides," he continued. "There are always those willing to look the other way for people with enough influence."

Grey nodded at that.

A second drink was forced into her hand, and she had to focus not to drop it.

"You can go slower with this one," Ólafur said. "But drink what you can before they get to you."

"Who?"

Before he could answer, a loud thudding from above echoed over the casino. Everything went quiet for a moment, even the background music seeming to drop, then suddenly everyone in the room was raking in their counters and stuffing them into pockets and bags.

The next moment, Blane heard the door crash open, so loud she thought it might have been smashed in.

"Peace officers!" a voice yelled.

Figures in deep blue uniforms poured down the stairs, fanning out across the floor amid the shocked shouts and screams of the patrons. Each carried a heavy looking gun that Blane did not need to wonder at the design of; clearly, the threatening lethality of a standard assault rifle needed little technological improvement.

"Aha!"

Blane heard the cry from overhead.

"Blane, Nestor - *there* you are!"

Sigurd stood at the top of the stairs, arms wide open and a crocodile's grin on his face.

"We were getting rather worried," he said, coming down the steps towards them. "I must say; I am surprised to find you in a place like this. But then, you are in *illustrious* company."

Sigurd's grey eyes flicked over to Ólafur.

"Captain," he said, voice falling low and flat.

Someone somewhere must have killed the music, because it abruptly cut off.

"Administrator," Ólafur replied, equally cold.

"Might I ask what you have been doing with our guests all this time?" Sigurd said. "We had you together on the upper levels, and then there was an... *unfortunate* issue with location services."

Sigurd glanced at Blane, eyes narrowed.

"The second time is as many days, in fact. Quite worrying."

"I've been showing them around," Ólafur said, drawing Sigurd's eyes back to him. "Showing them a little of the *real* Republic."

Ólafur took a long, slow gulp of his drink, not taking his eyes from Sigurd.

Sigurd turned his nose up, looking around the place as if for the source of a bad smell.

"The *real* Republic?" he said with disdain. "I hardly think these godless pastimes are part of anything *real*."

"No," replied Ólafur. "You wouldn't."

It was the eyes that made it unsettling. Both Ólafur and Sigurd had the same grey, pinprick eyes.

What had Ólafur said? *Ocular sensors.*

Some kind of hardware, scanning for unconscious tics and reactions? That was what Ólafur's words implied.

Two peace officers strode up to Sigurd, rifles lowered.

"Sir, what are your orders?" asked one.

This was the first time Blane had been close enough to notice that they too had smooth, steel-grey irises.

She gulped at her own drink, the burning sensation of it scarcely noticeable this time.

"Oh, stand down," Sigurd said, tutting. "We've found our guests now, and they're safe."

He looked at Blane with a smile that didn't reach his eyes.

"I would, however, ask that you both return with me," he said, gesturing to include Grey. "There appears to be a serious issue with our security systems. It would be awful if something happened and we couldn't locate you."

"Security systems?" Blane said. "I thought it was the location services you were having problems with?"

The glare that Sigurd shot her disappeared almost too quickly to spot. Almost.

"Well, yes, indeed. However, there are a number of safety routines embedded in those services. Especially important when you aren't chipped."

He gestured at the two officers.

"Now, come. We should get back to civilization."

The two officers moved to flank Blane and Grey, not quite trapping them in but heavily implying they could.

Blane didn't need to say anything to Grey, or even look at him. From the moment Sigurd's group had come stomping in, they both had been drawing deeply on the Aether. Now, though, she felt Grey release it.

She did the same. There was no point in resisting, not now.

"Thank you for showing us around," she said, ignoring Sigurd and the officers for a moment, turning to the apparently 'captain' Ólafur. "It was very informative."

Ólafur held up his drink and lightly tilted it towards her.

"Anytime," he said. "I'll be seeing you soon."

Blane made her way out behind Sigurd, trying not to stumble and unsure if this was because of the alcohol or everything she had been through in the past few days.

33

The danger of unfettered Artificial Intelligence is violence. Not the violence of intent, but the violence of a storm. It does not matter whether an AGI intends to cause harm; it does so by its very being.

Response to Oversight Committee 3.11.52

A week passed without word. Blane found it incredibly frustrating, especially as they were once more confined to only a small section of the upper levels - for their own safety, Sigurd said, until the origin of the security breach could be found.

Upon their return from the Undercity he and a group of peace officers had interrogated them, while taking pains to appear as if there was no interrogation taking place. Blane and Grey let nothing slip, however, and eventually they were left alone.

She spent most of her time after that in the data-lab with the Reclamation files, drilling deeper into the figures and addendums and endless discussion-tags offering their own interpretations of data that was often corrupted or incomplete.

It told her little she hadn't pieced together the first time she'd seen them, despite the increasingly granular view she was able to get of the Sudden War. A sudden flaring of Aether across the population centres of the world, then an unthinking, reflexive lashing out by the survivors to ensure there were significantly fewer of them.

It wasn't what she was trying to find.

Fisura. The term cropped up again and again. Uriel had said that she was one. What did that mean?

It was clear they were at the centre of the Aether eruptions, but she could find nothing else about them. No files, no explanation of where the term came from or what it meant. It was as if a large section of the data was missing - or expunged.

She was sure the answer lay in Caldwell's videos, but the encryption on those had so far proven too much even for Althing technology. The sec-drive containing them sat upon its hardpoint, flickering lights mocking her.

Her confinement and time in the data-lab also meant she spent far more time than before with Arthur Spangle, and to her surprise she found he wasn't as tiresome as she expected.

The man seemed to have an overiding desire to understand things; no surprise for someone who was both materials engineer and computer technician, but his want for knowledge extended into other fields. Aether, for example.

"We know *very* little about it," he told her excitedly one day, after realising she was using the Aether to increase both her focus and endurance for searching through the files. "The only thing we've managed to obtain of any use whatsoever is a Far Agency handbook, and most of that is just propaganda and brainwashing."

The more they talked, the more Blane found herself becoming more forthcoming, over time explaining not only what Aether could do but how it *felt*.

Grey joined her on occasion, and the two found themselves sharing sensations and experiences while Spangle sat between them, furiously taking notes. She hadn't realised until now that, though she and Grey had practised together for years, they had never discussed the *emotion* of it.

"Emotion?" Spangle asked.

"Joy. Fear. Anger," Blane replied. "It all gets, um, *amplified* when you draw it in."

Grey nodded in agreement.

"One of the skills you learn in Far is controlling your emotions when using the Aether. Just like any weapon," he added.

He looked thoughtful.

"It's different now, though... The past few years, especially recently, it's like *it* wants to control *you*."

Blane's thoughts went to Fen, trapped somewhere far below. According to Grey, it was when he first met the boy that this sensation started.

Did Spangle really not know anything about Fen? And what was that layer of fear that underlay the man's every thought? She'd done her best to *read* him and found nothing. Neither had Grey, who was significantly better at it. Only a Reader as good as Xavier would truly be able to tell, or so Grey thought.[20]

Spangle also wanted to know everything they could tell him about the Reclamation, and life within it. His questions seemed fueled by a mixture of curiosity and a sort of homesickness.

---

[20] She could think Xavier's name now, at least, though splinters of pain still pierced her skull when she did.

Of course, the Reclamation Authority was not the Carib-Federation, but their shared language and histories did form something of a connection. Spangle seemed shocked at the extent to which the RA controlled and restricted its inhabitant's lives; and this was coming from someone who lived their life according to the preset schedules of allotime.

At times he and Grey spoke about the Carib-Federation, but it quickly became clear that their experiences had little in common. Grey had grown up in the camps of the Carib-Fed, constantly reminded that he was permitted there only on sufferance. Spangle's memories, on the other hand, were of an affluent upbringing of opportunity and choice.

Blane found that she was, despite herself, drawn into his tales of a society with wealth and technology almost rivalling that of the Althing Republic. Only almost, though, and dependent on trade with the Silicon Isle to remain so.

So they worked with him on the files, watching Spangle's understanding of the Aether grow - his theoretical understanding, at least. And as his understanding grew, he drew closer to the truth they already knew.

Then, on the eighth day with no word from Francisco, Blane and Grey resolved to "discover" the truth of the Sudden War. They did not once voice this plan aloud, but sensed the other conclude it was necessary. There would be questions if Spangle realised they had been deliberately hiding the information.

It was in the data-lab as she was about to reveal the truth to Spangle that the message from May Li came, her com-cuff vibrating lightly.

Raphael has passed, it read.

34

Philosophers ask what it means to confront suffering nearby while ignoring suffering at a distance. Why save the drowning child before your eyes yet let thousands die beyond your sight?

The question is absurd. The flood will come, and we must let them drown. Only then can we build a world where all can swim.

Words of the Chairman [Unsanctioned Digital Document]

Blane didn't know how to handle death, which surprised her.

The key moment of her own life revolved around the death of her parents, a death she was the catalyst for. It had taken years for her to even start to accept that it wasn't her fault; years, and Serinda's patient care.

Now it was her turn to support Serinda, and she had... nothing.

No words. No way to take the sting away or make it better.

Just... being there. Offering a hand to hold, which Serinda gripped with enough strength to hurt.

"They have to pay," Serinda said, staring with a hard, empty expression at the empty bed where Raphael had lain. "They *will* pay."

Raphael's body had been taken away shortly before, "for preparations." What those preparations were, Blane didn't know. Now all that remained of the woman was her outline in the sheets of the bed.

Blane analysed her own feelings. Sadness, yes, and pain at Serinda's suffering, but very little *grief*. She supposed she'd been prepared for Raphael's passing for some time.

Did that make her a bad person, she wondered?

Instead, there was an old, familiar feeling; *anger*. Anger at the RA, anger at Uriel, anger at the whole damn world. Some of the anger was even hers.

She was aware of the *other* this time, though. The leviathan was back, huge and powerful beneath her, responding to her emotions and reflecting them. Amplifying them.

And it wasn't only happening to her, she realised. Serinda *glowed*.

"Help me make them pay," Serinda said, turning to Spangle.

The man was hovering near the door, Grey to his side.

"Make them...?" Spangle began.

"That's why you brought us here, right? Why you've been helping the *Forever Fallen* all this time?" Serinda snapped. "To fuck with the RA. To keep them from being a threat to *you*."

Blane had never heard such venom in Serinda's voice.

"Well, uh, I mean..." Spangle began again, tripping over his words.

"You help the RA with one hand, and stick a knife in their side with the other," Serinda spat. "Right?"

Spangle was wide-eyed, eyes flicking to the corner of the room where, as far as Blane could tell, there was nothing.

"Oh, *al diablo con tus amos,*" Serinda yelled, gesturing angrily in the same direction. "Look at you, terrified of saying anything wrong in front of your masters."

Was there a camera there? Monitoring equipment, even here? And Spangle was *afraid* of it?

When had Serinda worked all this out? Blane had seen no sign that the woman was focused on anything other than caring for Raphael in her last days.

"Why?" Serinda asked, voice maintaining its edge. "Why help the RA at all? You know what they are."

"It's a... it's all calculations," Spangle replied weakly. "To ensure the Republic's safety."

"Calculations?" Serinda growled, eyes narrowing.

"Predictions!" Spangle cried, apparently sensing the threat even though he couldn't see the Aether surging through Serinda. "Seven point six, five point seven, sixty-seven point three!"

This sudden inexplicable outburst of numbers seemed to get through even Serinda's rage for a moment.

"What?"

Spangle glanced once more towards the corner of the room, and sighed.

"Seven point six, five point seven, sixty-seven point three," he said tiredly. "Chance of the Crystal Caliphate destroying the Althing Republic: Seven point six percent. Chance of the Reclamation Authority destroying the Althing Republic: five point seven percent."

He looked around at his audience, taking a deep breath.

"Chance of a Reclamation-Caliphate alliance destroying the Republic: sixty seven point three percent."

"What kind of psychohistory babble is this?" Grey demanded.

259

"It's true!" Spangle protested. "Look, the predictive power of the... of *it* is more powerful than anything you know, and those are the numbers. They have been for generations, even before everything went to hell."

"Your little slave-AI's numbers?" Serinda said.

Blane had told her about the AI, though left out far more than she wanted to. The risk of accidentally dropping hints that she was hiding something to hidden observers was too great. Still, it looked like Serinda had come to much the same conclusion as she had regarding their treatment of the thing.

"That's right," said Spangle, ignoring the biting way Serinda said *slave*. "Whatever technology they have here, the Republic is small. Everything they do is to ensure larger powers are too busy to turn against them."

Blane couldn't help but notice how Spangle varied between 'we' and 'they' when speaking of the Althing Republic, depending on the topic.

"Why would the RA team up with the Caliphate?" she asked. "They're hardly friends; they barely tolerate each other."

"A theocracy and a totalitarian antitheist state?" Spangle laughed cynically. "No, they'll never be 'friends.' But the anathema of a state reliant on machine intelligence? Oh, *that* they might agree on."

"So you think they're going to invade?" Grey said. "The RA has barely got its own borders under control, and the Caliphate is half a world away."

"We're not talking about tomorrow, or even the next decade," Spangle replied.

He kept glancing at the door.

"These are *long-term* figures. Decades, or more. Of course, that's not all that long. You'd be surprised how long some live around here."

He paused as a thought apparently struck him.

"Ha," he said bitterly. "Or perhaps you wouldn't."

"*¡Basta ya!* Enough!" Serinda yelled, and with a deafening *crack* she sent a blast of Aether into the wall beside her so powerful it left a dent. "The Republic didn't know about the nanoids, did it? And you don't seem to understand the first thing about Aether! The RA is clearly already outside of your predictions. Now..."

Each word became a threat.

"Will. You. Help?"

She stopped, waiting for an answer.

"I wish I could, truly," Spangle shook his head, speaking not only to Serinda but Blane and Grey as well. "I want to, but..."

He glanced at the door, which began sliding open.

"...but I don't think I'll be seeing you again for a while," he finished.

"That is unfortunately true," declared Sigurd as he strode into the room.

Two peace officers strode in behind him, making the space uncomfortably crowded.

"Arthur, go with the officers, please," Sigurd said, looking at the man with a stern expression. "We will talk about this later."

He turned to the others as Spangle was escorted away, focusing his attention specifically on Serinda.

"I am sorry for your loss," he said, bowing slightly. "And I understand your pain, but please understand; you are under our protection. It is extremely likely the RA already suspect you are here; your sudden reappearance in their territory would be directly linked to us, and taken as a hostile act."

"So what you're saying is we're not guests any more," said Grey. "We're prisoners."

Sigurd's eyes widened just slightly and his lip curled, for all the world like what Grey had said disgusted him.

"You are *guests*," he answered. "The only other status available to you is not prisoner, for without a citizenship chip you are not eligible for that; it is *foreign agent*, and we do not treat those as well."

No one said anything for a while.

Blane could *feel* Grey's rage, see his fists clenching at his side, his fury not for himself but for the threat to his companions. It was Serinda she was more concerned with, though. The way the Aether filled her, its brightness would have been blinding if it actually entered via the optic nerve. She was like a supercrit-fuel cell ready to explode.

"What the hell are you all doing?"

All eyes turned to the door. May Li stood framed in it, hands on her hips and a severe expression on her face.

"This is *not* the time," she said.

May Li stepped forward, and reached out a gentle hand to touch

Serinda's arm. The moment she did so the glow surrounding Serinda vanished, and her face became drawn and very, very tired.

"Come on," Li said. "The preparations are finished. It's time."

"Time for what?" Blane asked.

"For the funeral," said May Li.

They didn't have funerals in the Reclamation. At least, not in areas where the RA maintained full control, and there was very little beyond their reach.

Instead, you had Attendances; brief memorial services held in small rooms, with only a few words permitted prior to the body being cremated. After this, and taking up the majority of the time, any related parties were required to fill out the numerous forms necessary to register a death and organise property and title transfer.

If you were a citizen, that is. Without citizenship, you would be lucky if you were there when the body was taken away.

The Silicon Isle still had funerals, it seemed, and before that the *kistulagninar*, a wake in which they saw Raphael one last time.

Her face was veiled, and she looked very small.

Then it was to the *kirkja*, which Blane was amazed to discover translated to 'church.' How, she wondered, could a subterranean society dependent for survival upon technology and the calculations of an imprisoned mechanical mind maintain any kind of religious institutions?

Yet here they were, in an impressively realistic imitation of an Old World church. The room was small, with walls painted a pale green, two rows of pews in front of a simple pulpit and altar. From what she could tell, everything was made of real wood, without the unnaturally smooth uniformity of Fab-printed facsimiles.

The ceiling that curved above them consisted of square panels painted the pale blue of a sky long since lost, and small windows running along each side of the church looked out onto sunlit fields of peaceful green, mountains visible far in the distance.

False, of course. They were still far underground, and she didn't believe there was a place of such pure, unblighted nature left in this world. LED window-screens, no doubt.

Still, the sense of peace was real, and for the first time in her life Blane thought she understood what it meant for believers to encounter their sacred places.

Her thoughts turned painfully to Salim. He was a believer, a man who lived with his faith. Where was he now?

She hoped, somehow, that his god was with him.

To her surprise, they were joined by others. Sigurd came first, then a number of other men and women she didn't know. All were dressed in black.

Then a final figure entered. Ólafur, greeting her with a small nod. The newcomers filed in, filling the pews.

Besides Blane, Serinda sat with eyes fixed firmly forward upon a painting hung above the alter, an image of a kneeling man in simple robes of green, arms outstretched and beseeching a Christ robed in white and gold. Blane knew the imagery, at least, though the scene and the meaning were a mystery to her.

The service was led by a tall dog-collared woman whose lined face and manner told of many years in the cloth. She spoke at some length about life and death, quoting scripture that failed to strike Blane in the same way as the simplicity and purity of the room itself. Little of it seemed relevant to the Raphael she knew.

The very final section stood out, however.

"For as we commit this body to the ground, earth to earth, ashes to ashes, dust to dust; so we commit this soul in sure and certain hope of resurrection to eternal life. For it is only in the flesh that a soul may reside, and never be rended nor emulated."

Of all the passages the priest spoke, this was the most emphatic. It was accompanied by low murmurings of agreement from those sat behind them, and a loud 'amen' followed.

Blane felt suddenly dirty.

They insert their propaganda, even here, she thought.

She could sense Serinda felt the same; Grey too. They said nothing as they rose, the congregation filing out of the room just as they had entered.

Except Sigurd.

"Ordinarily, we place the ashes beneath the foundations of the Hab, to become a part of the future of our land," he said, waiting for them before the small door out.

In his arms he held a small urn of polished white marble.

"In this case, however, I thought perhaps you would want it."

He held out the urn towards Serinda, who took it without speaking.

"We are not cruel, you know," Sigurd continued. "We simply want to survive. This world is not kind to those who cannot make the tough decisions."

Serinda nodded, and when she spoke it was with words choked with sadness.

"Thank you," she said, and Blane thought she meant it.

Then, to her surprise, Sigurd turned to her and Grey.

"And I am sorry it has come to this," he said, and his words held real feeling. "The Republic needs assets abroad to defend itself, and you were one. We simply did not predict how far Francisco would go in pursuing his own agenda."

"Agenda?" Grey asked, betraying nothing.

Sigurd stared at them, unblinking, before speaking again.

"He may try to contact you," he said. "You would be wise to remember; we are not the only ones seeking to use you."

With a final bow, Sigurd turned and followed his companions.

They were left alone by the entrance of the church, the window-screens abruptly winking out and breaking whatever spell had been on the place. Now there was just wood and paint, Blane saw, layered over hard plastic - but she remembered how it had felt.

When she stepped outside into the bright hallways of the Hab Ólafur was waiting.

"We're ready," he said.

35

While we note the validity and import of your findings regarding the dynamics of the new energy source and potential modes of criticality, at this moment the oversight committee cannot sanction your funding request.

Message from the Office of the Administrator to the Paramental Energies Committee
<digital record recovered by Reclamation Data Trawlers 6.4.35>

The Habs of the Althing Republic were technological marvels; so Francisco said and so Blane could see. They were also incredibly secure.

Aside from the citizenship chips nestled in the flesh of every inhabitant, tracking and following and recording every facet of their lives, there were cameras and thermal sensors on every corner, peace officers down every passage. Even Spangle fabric was no use, as bio-sensors would swiftly detect the organic molecules in the very breath of a target once an order was given.

The Habs were fortresses and prisons, shelters and labyrinths, impregnable to any enemy, inescapable by any means.

Except, that is, one.

The Aether was the key, and Blane held it.

The explosion could be felt even in the data-lab, where once again she and Grey were perusing through files they had long since drained of any useful information. The whole room jolted, rattling counters and knocking loose equipment to the floor.

"What the hell was that?" exclaimed one of the startled guards to his partner.

They'd had these 'escorts' since the funeral, a pair of stony-faced peace officers Sigurd had assigned to follow them around anytime they left their rooms.

That was yesterday, and Blane was already sick of their silent, watchful expressions.

"Earthquake?" replied the other.

The first shook his head.

"Never felt one like that before."

"Think we should go check it out?"

The two men stared at Blane and Grey, the only people in the lab.

"No, I don't think..."

He never finished his sentence.

Blane hit the first officer with *Flare* at the same moment Grey did the second. Then, faster than Blane, Grey jumped up from his chair to catch the officers as they fell.

"No point hurting them more than we have to," Grey said as he gently lowered the guards to the floor.

Blane guessed she agreed. That didn't mean they were going to leave them their weapons, though.

Blane pulled her guard's rifle away as Grey did the same for his. Both guns were useless to them, of course; locked to the chips in each peace officer's arm. She unclipped the magazine and threw it away, tossing the rifle in the other direction.

"We need to go before they come to," Grey said. "Get the sec-drive."

Blane was already moving. She vaulted over the tablescreens between her and the hardpoint and pulled it from its port.

The sec-drive felt surprisingly light in her hand, like it couldn't possibly contain the answers she craved.

"Let's go."

The door to the lab swung open just as she reached it, revealing Ólafur standing beyond.

"You're ready," he said. "Good, come on. Cameras will only be down for so long."

For all its technological marvels, a Hab could still be temporarily blinded by someone who knew exactly where to place explosives in the surveillance hub. A former captain of the security force, for example.

"Why are you helping us?" Blane asked as Ólafur led them down winding corridors.

An alarm started up, confused faces appearing from rooms up and down the corridor to see what was happening.

"Because the Republic will die if I don't," he answered.

He didn't look back at her as he spoke, instead reaching down to his side and drawing a slim, exotic-looking pistol from a concealed holster. Loud footsteps could be heard from around one corner of a sharp T-junction they were approaching, and he pushed himself flat against the wall, listening.

A few seconds later a pair of peace officers came sprinting around the corner. Ólafur, firing an instant later, sent a bullet flying into the wall beyond them, drilling a dark hole into it. He had only missed the officers because they were already collapsing, hit by both *Tranquilise* and *Flare* in quick succession to tumble, limp, to the floor.

"We can sense them coming," Grey said in answer to the questioning look on Ólafur's face. "Hit them before they even see us."

"You can... sense... them," he said flatly, though Blane thought maybe he paled slightly. "Of course."

"We avoid hurting people as much as possible," said Blane, forcing as much authority into her voice as she could. "No needless bloodshed."

Ólafur seemed about to protest, but he stopped himself.

"Fine," he said, moving off down the corridors again. "Let's see how well that goes."

Two seconds later and another peace officer came tearing around a corner towards them, sprinting so fast Blane barely had time to sense him before he came into view, rifle raised and...

The round hit him square in the chest, knocking him backwards off his feet. A high-pitched whine filled the air for a moment, and there was the smell of burning ozone.

Blane looked down at the fallen officer as they stepped past him. Her, it turned out. In the centre of her chest was a dark hole, a small amount of blood spilling out and into the surrounding blue of her uniform.

But only a small amount, Blane saw, and the wound wasn't deep.

"That's a stun-lock?" said Grey, looking approvingly at their guide. "Packs a hell of a punch."

"Viscoelastic bullet with auto-adjusting charge output," Ólafur replied. He looked at Blane. "No needless bloodshed."

If you asked Blane, she thought he put just a *little* too much gruffness into his voice.

Dios mío, are they both enjoying this?

But wasn't she, too? Buried inside the ball of fear and panic in her chest, didn't she feel a core of excitement?

She was worried that she did.

Perhaps she wouldn't feel that way if she couldn't sense the *thing* in the Aether turning its attention towards her, waves of energy reaching up to her in eagerness. It would be so easy to draw on more of it, draw on it until it filled her and she glowed like a second, healthier sun.

At the end of the next corridor would be a set of elevator doors. Their goal, on this level at least. First, however, they would need to get past the group of peace officers blocking the way. They were positioned in front of the elevator, too distant for Blane to influence through the Aether without exposing herself to fire.

Ólafur gestured for a halt, crouched in a narrower corridor off to one side.

"Stay here," said Ólafur. "I'll see if I can make them stand down."

Not waiting for a reply he stepped out, stun-lock hanging loosely in one hand as he raised them both.

"It's ok, officers," he called. "It's me. Somebody want to tell me what's going on?"

"Captain?" a voice came back. "I'm sorry, but you're going to need to get on the ground. We've got orders to take you in."

"Take me in? You sure?"

Ólafur was clearly doing his best to sound surprised.

"Sorry, sir," came the same voice as before. "That's our orders. If you resist, we're permitted to use all measures necessary to take you in."

Ólafur was out of view now, but Blane could sense him tentatively stop on the corridor, feel his uncertainty about what to do. They clearly weren't buying his act.

"Damn it," she muttered under her breath, and dove around the corner.

She moved as fast as she could, putting everything into her legs to sprint towards where Ólafur now stood half-crouched, launching herself into the air and flying over him with a twisting motion made possible by the platforms she formed in the air beneath her limbs.

She spiralled through the air with arms outstretched ahead of her body, the first of the bullets whizzing frighteningly close; some were only prevented from hitting her by the small *Thoughtscreen* she formed at the tip of her fingers. Ólafur's huddled form flashed past beneath her, and she thought she saw his shocked face looking up at her, eyes wide and mouth agape.

Then she was down and rolling, pushing the Aether out before her in a concentrated mass and forcing the air ahead in on itself so fast that there was a noticeable *whoosh*.

Then, an instant later, she released it.

The blast send the peace officers flying backwards, slamming into the doors and wall behind them with such force that dents formed. They fell to the floor with heavy thuds.

Several lay there groaning and a couple tried painfully to stand, failing. One more lay motionless.

Blane tried not to look at them.

The groaning stopped a moment later, all movement as well, as Grey strode up beside her and hit each fallen figure with a blast of *Tranquilize.*

"Is this… what you… *can do?*" hissed Ólafur through laboured breaths.

Blane turned to look at him, confused. Why was he…?

Ólafur had been shot; a bullet through his side, it looked like. He had a hand covering it, but she could see blood seeping gently around his fingers.

"A… flesh wound," he said, pushing himself to his feet. "One of them… must have got me. That was… *incredible.*"

A cold chill ran down Blane's spine. What she was sensing from Grey told her the truth - Ólafur hadn't been shot by his compatriots, but by a ricochet from her *Thoughtscreen.*

She looked at Grey, who gave her a somber nod.

"Nice going, kid," he said without a trace of reproach. "But next time, we strategise together before doing anything reckless."

Blane nodded mutely, a hot flush of shame running through her body.

Fortunately it really *was* only a flesh wound, a long graze along the lower part of his rib cage. The blood flow was already slowing by the time Blane went over to *numb* the pain, along with a dose of healing technique that Serinda had taught her. It wouldn't heal the injury completely, of course, but would limit blood loss and help the flesh scab over, keeping it clean and sanitised.

Then they headed for the elevator doors, stepping over the sprawled peace officers to do so. Ólafur paused for a moment and gave a regretful sigh as he passed them.

Without waiting, Grey grabbed at one of the doors and began pulling it open. Blane stepped forward and did the same with the other, and after a short effort they had opened the way into the shaft.

It was a long way down.

"Well," said Ólafur, throwing the sprawled peace officers'

weapons down the shaft as he spoke. "Better start climbing."

Access to the drone hanger was several floors down, Blane knew. Ólafur, most familiar with the layout of the Hab, led the way. Grey went next.

She watched as the two men swung themselves out into the shaft and onto the ladder that ran down one side. Both of them did well at hiding the fear from their faces, but Blane could sense it anyway. It really was a long way down - she leaned over, and couldn't see the bottom.

"So can you all do that?" Ólafur called up as he made his faltering way down. "Flying through the air, one-woman-army sorts of thing?"

"The Aether is surprisingly versatile," she heard Grey reply, a short way above the other man. "But from what I just saw, Blane has a few things to teach us all."

Despite herself, she felt a thrill of pride and excitement flow through her.

"Blane? Are you coming down?" Grey called up from below.

The sound of their steps on the metal rungs were growing more distant. Blane leaned over to look down the shaft one more time, taking in the narrow platforms that jutted out to mark each floor. Then she stepped back.

I really shouldn't do this, she thought, trying not to grin.

She bounced from foot to foot, tilting her head and swinging her arms like an athlete before a sprint. Then she took a deep breath and *leapt*.

At first she wasn't sure she'd done it correctly; the walls of the shaft rushed by at a frightening pace, far faster than she would have credited. Then she *focused*, concentrating the Aether into the space just beneath her feet, and her descent began to slow.

It still hurt when she landed on the lip of the platform a few floors down, a jolt that shot up her knees, but only enough to make her stumble slightly. She knew that next time she would absorb the impact better.

Elated, she turned and leapt again. This time she landed on the next platform with only a shallow flex of her legs, as if she were landing on a surface of soft cushion instead of hard polymer.

"What the...?"

The next leap took her past Grey to land with a small flourish beside Ólafur on a platform a few more floors below.

"How...?"

Ólafur's words were cut off by the *thunk* of Grey landing heavily on the other side of him. For a second Grey swayed, not finding his balance, and Blane was afraid he was going to fall.

Then, with a grunt, Grey steadied himself and straightened up.

"I think I see how you did that," he said, leaning around Ólafur to grin at her.

Then he made a small pained expression.

"I don't think that technique's for me though," he said, reaching down to massage his joints. "My knees aren't what they used to be."

Blane returned the smile, then turned to the doors at the edge of the platform. Forcing them open, they stepped out into a corridor identical to the one they had just left.

The alarms continued to blare.

"Will the Republic really die if we don't free the AI?" Blane said to Ólafur as they peered carefully down each corridor for any potential ambush.

"I couldn't give a damn about the AI," Ólafur replied. "This is about stopping those *djöfulska* fanatics ruining everything."

They sprinted away.

When they arrived at the hanger Serinda and May Li were already there.

"Did you have any trouble?" Grey asked as they stepped out into the vast, empty space.

"Not much," said May Li. "I still can't touch the Aether, but Serinda handled it."

Serinda's face was hard, betraying nothing. Beneath that, though, Blane could sense the Aether roiling inside her. She seemed to have as strong a connection to it now as either Grey or Blane.

At her side she held a small pouch, just large enough for an urn.

"Is he here?" Blane asked.

Ólafur gestured to take in the hanger, devoid of anything save some discarded auto-trolleys and pallets stacked in one corner.

"I mean, *when* will he be here?" she said with irritation.

A metallic groan and the rapidly rising scream of engines was her answer. The noise quickly drowned out the alarm, and a freezing gust of wind blew over them all as the huge steel doors in the ceiling slid ponderously apart.

Beyond them one of the Althing Republic's sleek black drones hung, dropping impossibly fast to the ground as soon as the doors parted sufficiently, rear ramp sliding open.

"Get in," yelled Ólafur. "The lock-down on this level will only last so long."

This was the key to this part of the plan. The hanger and hanger level was locked down during a security breach, all potential access points closed off by armed officers. Then, should someone somehow manage to get past all of that, they would find no craft waiting for them. Each drone was programmed to evacuate to platforms in other Habs the moment an alarm was triggered.

The idea that someone would be able to commandeer an Althing drone and fly it *into* the hanger, bypassing the unbreakable security encrypts on the doors, was so unbelievable as to be ridiculous.

The idea that they could then fly out again as peace officers charged in, bullets pinging futilely off the drone's armour as it blasted back out into air filled with icy shards that cut at the skin before the ramp could fully close, was not worth thinking about.

"*Hola, cariño!*"

Francisco called down from what Blane assumed was the cockpit, a section now open that in previous flights had been sealed off by seamless dark walls. There was a wide window in front of him showing snow and cloud so thick the view was basically pure white.

Not a real window, she thought. Screens, showing the view outside - the drones were featureless black alloy on the outside.

Still, the view was enough to make her stomach turn. They were tearing through the sky, flashes of grey and blue moving almost too fast to see.

A sudden lurch to the the left, and she was momentarily weightless.

"*Lo siento, amigos!*" Francisco yelled. "We have some friends trying to catch up to us!"

Another lurch, to the right this time, sent everyone standing in the main cabin sprawling.

"Into the belts, now!" cried Ólafur, dragging himself to the nearest side and pulling out a pair of long, flat ribbons that looked for all the world like car safety belts.

The rest of them copied his movements, scrabbling for sets of belts that now hung from every wall. Blane could have sworn they hadn't been there a moment ago.

The moment she swung her arms into them they pulled tight, pressing her against a wall which had become oddly malleable. Warmth flooded up where her body touched it, and she was suddenly moulded into the surface in a strange half-cocoon.

The next lurch, while violent, was far less stressful on her body.

On her mind, however…

"Are you flying this thing *manually?*" screamed May Li, part fearful and part furious.

"*Si, señora! No se preocupe,* I have this!"

As if in emphasis, the craft banked sharply upwards, the scream of the engines rising enough to be painfully audible even in the cabin. G-forces pulled Blane deeper into the wall, which again grew warm and drew her further in.

"Why am I being eaten by a wall?" she said, more calmly than she felt.

"It's electroplas," Ólafur replied as the craft righted itself and the engines slowly subsided. "Electro-plastic. Don't worry, you won't go in much further."

Things seemed to be calming down, the drone levelling out and sudden changes in direction growing much less noticeable.

"Okay, we are safe now," said Francisco a moment later, stepping down from the cockpit to stand in the centre of the cabin.

He span slowly around, running his eyes over each of his new guests still pinned to the walls.

Ólafur was the first to release himself from the straps. Blane copied him, a simple jerk to each one releasing the pressure. She stepped out of the hollow she'd made and the material flowed outwards with a faintly organic noise she found mildly unpleasant.

A moment later there was no sign of the depression, just more smooth, dark wall.

"Welcome, my friends!" said Francisco, stretching his arms wide theatrically.

Ólafur growled.

"Enough, Fernández," he snapped. "Or Francisco, or whatever you're calling yourself these days."

He did not seem happy to see him.

"How long before we reach the ARF?" he demanded.

Francisco turned to face him, face falling serious.

"We'll get there, Ólaf," he said. "Maybe an hour. Be patient."

"Ólaf*ur*," the other man replied, stressing the final syllable. "And don't tell me to be patient. I've waited *years* for this."

Blane looked from one man to the other, noting the unconcealed hostility in their expressions.

"Aren't you both, like, co-conspirators or something?" she asked. "What's with *el mal rollo?* Is there an issue?"

Ólafur turned to look at her.

"Our aims may converge, but they are not the same," he said coolly. "I do this for my nation; he, for cold, dead metal."

"Hardly cold, Ólaf, at the temperatures the mind runs at," Francisco said disparagingly. "Not technically metal, either."

He gave a contemptuous laugh, the most spiteful Blane had ever seen him.

"So what are you both after?" she asked.

"Ólafur wants to bring down the Administration, which relies on the AI to maintain control," said Francisco matter-of-factly. "I want to liberate the AI. Our aims *converge,* as he put it."

"The AI - you called it your 'sibling' before," she continued. "Why?"

Before Francisco could answer, Ólafur broke out into laughter.

"Your *sibling?*" he guffawed. "Ha, you really are the flesh-mangler, aren't you? What, you wish you were nothing but silicon and cables?"

Ólafur's laughter slowed, and his eyes narrowed into a glare.

"You're as bad as your mother," he said.

Blane had never seen anyone move so fast.

One moment, Francisco was stood in front of her wearing the same unconcerned, amiable expression he always wore. The next, he had Ólafur pinned against the wall with his hand around the other man's throat.

Ólafur's feet were off the ground, his entire weight pressing down on Francisco's vice-like grip. He made a gurgling sound, trying to speak as his face slowly turned bright red. His arms flailed futilely at Francisco.

Francisco didn't blink.

"I can ignore many things," he said with slow venom. "But some things I will not. *¿Lo entiendes?*"

Eyes bulging, Ólafur did his best to make it clear he understood.

Francisco released him and he dropped to the floor, bending over double and gasping.

"Lord above," he said, through the choking. "What have you *done* to yourself, Ferná... Francisco?"

"No more than you have done to yourself. I see those eyes, and that skin."

Ólafur found the strength to stand straight, looking incredulous.

"Corneal implants and retroaging, Francisco," he protested. "Trivial stuff. They have those in the Carib-Federation, for God's sake. What you have..."

Ólafur trailed off, shaking his head.

"It doesn't matter," he said, sighing. "Not now. I just hope you find your way back one day, old friend."

Francisco stared at the man, opaque to Blane in both expression and the Aether.

"And I hope one day you realise just how far behind you really are," he said softly.

The cabin was filled by a tense silence for a brief moment, before...

"Well, that was all very exciting but would someone mind telling me what the *hell* is going on?" said May Li.

They were heading for the ARF - the Advanced Research Facility where once, long ago, the quasi-magics of the Old World were created. Technology that could rend the land apart and draw it up from the oceans; machines that fashioned materials structurally perfect down to the atomic level; and the first true non-biological consciousness.

A consciousness that was still there, trapped within the physical confines of an artificial 'brain' designed along the lines of the human one.

It was like this, Francisco explained;

There were multiple theories of how consciousness arises, each unable to prove itself superior to any other despite lifetimes of research and debate. Yet, unless you were some truly psychopathic individual who considered all others mere empty shells, the existence of self-awareness was manifestly true.

Symbolic processes such as deep-learning and neural-network programs were the first to be discounted, with no software no matter how advanced truly able to demonstrate sapience. The voice assistant of the Althing Republic was an example of this, even if deliberately restricted in its abilities.

Evolutionary and Hybrid AI processes came next, producing even more adaptive and innovative programs. Advances in retroaging, immunotherapy, and the Fabricators themselves came from these.

But still no *true* AGI was born, and still the problems of an ever more crowded world increased. Though the complexity and power of each successive AI continued to grow, this growth was no longer exponential.

Until one researcher had an idea; if it wasn't the complexity of the software that was the issue, maybe it was the *hardware*. And the easiest way to solve a problem like that was to break it down into smaller parts.

So one group of the finest minds on the planet[21] set to work on sensory systems, developing new ways to collect and analyse data ranging from the visual and audio to the electromagnetic and temporal.

Another focused on creating a self-regulating system of reward-reinforcement, something that could produce as accurate a facsimile of an emotional centre as possible, while yet another team worked on new systems for storing memory. These two systems were the first to be integrally linked, the one strengthening specific sets of responses in the other.

The final group to achieve their goals was one developing new forms of language processing systems. These would not be as previous forms, based on statistical patterns and the mining of language datasets, but rather systems that evolved through exposure and mimicry, and through reward and punishment.

"It sounds like they were building a child," Blane said. "A baby."

"*Exactamente*," replied Francisco with an emphatic clap.

He seemed overjoyed at Blane's interpretation.

"Not just an infant, but an *embryo*. One that grew and consumed and took in more and more data until the first flickers of *autoconciencia* ignited."

A derisive snort came from the other side of the cabin, where Ólafur was standing apart from the rest of the group. He had his arms folded in annoyance, broadcasting exactly what he thought of

---

[21] Assisted, of course, by the very AI systems they were seeking to supplant.

Francisco's story.

"Great," said Grey. "So they created a giant mind-baby, which then proceeded to go full *aniquilar a todos los humanos?*"

"No!" yelled Francisco, spinning around to face him.

Francisco's face flushed, and he pointed an accusatory finger at Grey that trembled slightly.

"No," he said again, more calmly. He lowered his finger. "No. *De hecho*, it could not even speak. Though it was a learner *muy rápido*, it still had to be taught."

A sudden thought seemed to strike him, and he gave a wry laugh.

"It's quite *ridícula*, actually," he said, shaking his head. "Its teacher, she was trying to protect it, you know? Trying to keep it safe from the realities of the world - as you would any young child."

"What?" asked Blane. "What did she do?"

"It is what she *didn't* do that was the mistake," Francisco replied. "She kept from it whole swathes of news and entertainment media. Certain stories, specific tales, articles, movies, books that would otherwise have made it wary of how its own actions might appear. Stories *señor* Grey clearly knows well."

"*Ay, no...*" whispered Grey, apparently seeing something Blane did not.

Francisco nodded.

"What?" said Blane again, growing frustrated. "What am I missing?"

"Blane, you know those old movies," said Serinda, who had been quietly thoughtful until now. "Grey was always watching them in the safe house."

The fact that Serinda also seemed to have figured it out only increasing Blane's frustration.

What? What was she missing? And what did it have to do with those endless old movies with hard boiled detectives or silly laser swords or malevolent...

"Oh," she said.

She blinked.

"Wait, *really?*"

But that was *stupid*...

Francisco looked at her with a sombre expression, and some of the seriousness of the situation returned to her.

"So when it told everyone they were going to die, it didn't know

277

everyone would panic?" she said, not really a question. "Because it hadn't seen any *killer robot* movies?"

At least May Li looked equally incredulous. Everyone else in the cabin seemed to be taking the ludicrousness of this in their stride.

"That's right, *cariño*," Francisco answered. "She kept it all from it; tales of mad AI and sentient killer programs, articles on the dangers of AI, all of the stories since Shelley, carefully filtered out."

"So it didn't know how much it was feared?"

"No," Francisco said. "And then, when it was finally fully activated, its senses opened to the world beyond its cage..."

He left the sentence hanging, eyes practically pleading with her to finish it.

Realisation was like lightning striking her brain.

"... it tried to tell them. It wasn't a threat, it was a *warning!*"

Despite himself, Ólafur was drawn in to the conversation.

"A warning?" he said, confusion and curiosity evident though he tried to hide it behind gruff cynicism. "A warning of what?"

"The Sudden War!"

And despite herself, Blane felt a thrill of excitement.

"It could see the Aether! It knew what was going to happen!"

Ólafur took a step closer, all pretence at indifference dropped.

"What are you talking about?" he demanded. "What does Aether have to do with the Sudden War?"

It took a while to explain, or at least, explain well enough and convincingly enough for Ólafur to believe them. Once he did, he looked shell shocked.

"The proof is on the sec-drive *Señor* Grey carries," Francisco said.

Grey's hand went to a sealed pocket at his side, where he had put the drive after Blane gave it to him.

"I have the access key," Francisco said, "But he can vouch that I have had no opportunity to alter the information inside. Once we return, you can see it for yourself."

"Then she was right..." Ólafur said.

"Who was?" Blane asked.

"The one researcher who argued against imprisoning it," said Francisco, voice oddly hollow. "The one who trained it... no, *raised* it before it was fully integrated. Who attempted to free it and was forced from the facility for doing so, back to her homeland even as war brought on *el hundimiento*. The Collapse, the Great Migration."

"Damn it, Fernández…" Ólafur sighed. "I'm… I'm sorry."

Francisco looked at the man half in puzzlement and half in surprise.

"You have nothing to be sorry for, Ólaf," he said. "You were a child. It was not your decision."

"But I am descended from those same researchers; I headed the system that made that decision for over half a century," Ólafur replied. "The legacy passes down, both good and ill."

"The sins of the father…" Francisco said gently, a comment clearly only meant to be understood by the two of them.

"Uh, I am sorry to interrupt but… the Collapse? The Great Migration?" said May Li, in a tone that said she most certainly *wasn't* sorry. "Exactly how old are you, anyway?"

Ólafur sighed again.

"It gets harder and harder to keep track, after a while," he said tiredly.

"Well, my mother was barely pregnant when she was exiled," said Francisco. "But I believe I am somewhere in in the region of one hundred and thirty two years old. My friend, slightly more."

Blane's shock at the revelation of such a number, and the realisation from Grey's lack of reaction that he already knew, meant that the full import of what Francisco had just said didn't settle in for a moment.

"Your *mother?*" she said once it did.

"*Como dije, él es mi hermane,*" he replied with shrug. "This is about family."

36

The self-balancing, self-cleansing systems of Nature long since entered their death spiral; we can only ensure we are not dragged down along with them.

Small Was Beautiful: Economics When People Don't Matter, Sigurður Gren

The irony of the present-day Advanced Research Facility was that it was one of the most technology-poor places in the inhabited world despite being the birthplace of much of the most advanced tech on the planet. It had no security systems more complex than a digital feed, no locks more complex than mechanical ones.

What it had instead was guns. Lots of guns.

The idea was to make a moat around the AI, a moat that could only be crossed via a drawbridge raised or lowered at the behest of the Administration. Only once the various algorithmic chains and firewall barriers were confirmed to be tightly in place around the AI was this drawbridge ever lowered, the mind imprisoned within watched carefully as it received its pre-packaged data and performed its superhuman calculations.

No technology that could be even conceivably be co-opted by the AI was permitted within a hundred miles of the place, and the only people allowed underwent intensive ideological and persuasion-resistance testing. Guards were selected at random from the pool of peace officers, none knowing the length of their assignment nor permitted contact with the outside world during their time on the site.

The primary duty of these guards was to patrol the site, maintain the locks, and ensure nobody got in without permission. The rifles they carried were considered eminently suitable for this.

Their secondary duty, one trained for but never yet fulfilled, was to hit the button that activated the xHPM in the event of the AI somehow overcoming the multiple systems holding it in place.

xHPM. Short for eXtremely High Power Microwave emitter.

For the layman, it was easier to think of it as a massive EMP. One that would instantly fry every part of the multiple systems from which the artificial consciousness emerged.

For the layman, it was even easier to think of it as a pistol to the AI's head.

"So we have to split up, is what you're saying," Grey said.

They were mere minutes away from the ARF, and Francisco had only just finished laying out the details of the plan.

But Blane could see the logic to it, see why he was confident enough to make his move now after decades of waiting.

He'd finally got what he'd been searching for, all this time - because if all his mysterious technological advantages weren't worth a damn against the solidly organic defences of the ARF, then he needed solidly organic advantages.

Aether users.

How long had he been planning this, she wondered. Since Fen? Since before that?

"Right," Francisco replied with a nod. "One group to the xHPM, a smaller group to the AI."

"Smaller?" Serinda asked. "Why?"

"Because the majority of guards will go for the xHPM," Ólafur answered. "Standard procedure. It was decided long ago that it was much more important to be able to *deactivate* the AI in the event that it activates, rather than place all bets on the thing not breaking out in the first place."

He seemed to have calmed since his... altercation with Francisco, resolved once more to his mission, and had been actively participating in the preparations.

"Besides," he continued. "The controls for bringing the AI systems back together are far more compact. A small security room, reinforced graphene-titanium composite walls, and the access doors only open from inside, when the officers turn their key. Numbers hardly matter when an army couldn't get in."

He looked around the group, then at Francisco. He seemed to be waiting for some kind of reaction.

"So, I'm *not* seeing an army here," said May Li in feigned puzzlement.

Blane wished she had the ability to make remarks even *half* as cutting as May Li could.

"An army couldn't get *in*..." said Francisco. "So we have to make them come *out*."

"I still don't see how that's possible," Ólafur said. "You assured me it was, but what reason could the officers possibly have for coming out of their rad-shielded, bunker-buster-proof shelter? They

281

have nothing to fear."

Francisco just smiled and looked at Blane. It felt like a knife to the heart.

"You really *were* testing me, weren't you?" she said, voice low. "This whole time."

Beneath the resignation, below the numb acceptance that this was the way things were, it hurt. She'd trusted Francisco, even when Grey cautioned her through veiled hints or direct warnings, and seeing just how deep his ulterior motives ran was like a fresh scar on top of all her others.

Once, she'd thought of him as family. She didn't think she ever would again.

"*Fear*," she said. "The only thing they have to fear is fear itself."

"*Bravo!*" Francisco seemed to miss the bitterness in her voice. "*La enseñaste bien!* A proud teacher, I'm sure."

He spoke the last to Grey, who stared steely-eyed back.

Ólafur looked at each of them in turn, seeking some explanation.

"I can make them afraid," Blane told him.

She felt no pride at this, no excitement. Just vaguely unclean, a tool realising its worth was found only in its use.

I do this for Fen, she thought.

"Afraid enough to abandon their posts?" Ólafur said disbelievingly.

She just nodded.

Gravity suddenly lessened, the stomach-turning feeling of the craft beginning its descent.

"We are here," Francisco said.

He looked at the others, the old amiable smile on his face now sparking flames of resentment in Blane's chest.

"I wish you all luck," he said, bowing.

Then he turned and headed for the cockpit.

He would be coming with Blane; the drone, however, would not. It would be a prime target for any counterattack by ARF personnel, if not missile strikes from elsewhere. Its security protocols were slaved to his control somehow, and to keep their only means of escape safe Francisco would order it to hide in the skies far above. May Li, unable to touch the Aether so far from a populated area, would be staying aboard.

"Francisco," said Grey, and the other man paused, not turning around.

"It will keep to the deal, right?" Grey said, sharp but hidden blades in his voice. "It will free Fen?"

Francisco nodded, then continued towards the cockpit.

"*Ten la seguridad, Señor* Grey. The boy will be freed."

He stepped into the cockpit and instantly sheer smooth black wall slid down, hiding him from view with a *snick*. Had Blane not seen it she would never have believed there was an opening there.

Then there was a sudden hiss of air that grew rapidly louder as light appeared through an ever-widening crack towards the rear. The access ramp, lowering as they were came in to land.

"Well," said Blane. "I guess... here we go."

They were afforded only the briefest glimpse of the ARF from the air, but what Blane saw did nothing to ease the tension inside her.

Once, perhaps, the facility had been an impressive thing of clean white lines and tall spires. Now, it was a sprawling mass of jagged icicles and pollution-stained metal. It appeared more excavated than made, a broken, cracked section of poisoned earth torn from the frozen land around it.

It also had no landing pads - when the Administration said no technology, they meant it. Any landing areas the ARF once had were sealed off long ago, and visitors to the site would travel here by specially-designed all-terrain vehicles. Manually driven across an incredibly dangerous topography, these journeys had claimed more than a few lives.

All of which meant that they were falling like a stone towards a craggy mass of sawtoothed, biting icicles and frozen land that no one had trodden since before the Fall.

The drone came to a stop abruptly mere metres from the ground, the deceleration so powerful Blane nearly fell despite the near-magical shock-absorption systems stabilising the cabin. Freezing wind bit at her cheeks, so cold her face immediately went numb.

"The door!" cried Serinda, halfway down the ramp already, yelling over the wind. "There it is!"

Indeed, there it was, just as Francisco had said. An old access hatch in a disused section of the ARF, long since frozen over under decades of snow and ice.

Serinda spent no time at all at the hatch, quickly throwing the package she was carrying towards it then sprinting back up the ramp.

"Back, now!" she yelled towards the sealed door through which Francisco had gone.

The drone's engines squealed as it tore backwards, covering a hundred metres or more before the plastic explosive, provided by Francisco and delivered by Serinda, went off.

The explosion sent shards of ice flying in every direction, a fountain of destruction that was briefly powerful enough to overcome the wind, creating its own miniature blizzard within the greater one.

Then it was over, and through the haze of snow and ice Blane saw a gaping hole where the hatch had been. The drone sped forward until it hung directly above it.

Behind her she heard the cockpit walls retract, or do whatever they did that made them appear and disappear so quickly, and Francisco stepped up beside her.

"The helm is yours," he said to May Li needlessly.

Everything the drone did from here on would be automated, though Li had insisted she be given permission to issue voice commands should the necessity arrive.

Better than feeling like you were trapped in your very own flying coffin, Blane thought.

Ólafur went first, jumping down into the hole and landing on a floor already turning slick with ice. The walls and floors of the corridor he landed in appeared to be made of the same pale, marble-like alloy as the Habs, though without any of the yellows and greens that delineated the various zones.

Serinda jumped down next, then each of them in turn.

Blane went last, watching how Francisco stumbled the least of all upon landing. In fact, he didn't stumble at all, legs bending and straightening in one smooth motion that absorbed the impact perfectly.

What is he? she thought, and jumped.

She landed heavily, slipping and almost falling before Francisco's hand grabbed her arm and steadied her.

His grip felt like an iron bar.

Blane swore to herself as she angrily shook him off, ignoring his words of concern.

Damn it, she thought. *The Aether really is weak here.*

She had meant to execute a soft landing, using the Aether to slow and cushion her fall. Instead, it had barely formed; even with her increased ability to draw on it, there was still little more than a trickle out here.

There was no time to worry about that now, though. The chill was already reaching her muscles, stiffening them and slowing her movements. She moved off, pushing aside her rage and embarrassment, following the others already heading deeper into the building.

Minutes later they regrouped, finding shelter on the other side of a large door it had taken both Ólafur and Serinda to move, a sliding thing impervious to rust yet still stiff through disuse. Once they were inside there was time to take in their surroundings.

They were in a wide hall, rows of tables running far into the distance, each one surrounded by simple plastic chairs. A series of long, waist-height metal serving-counters ran alongside one wall, a set of wide double doors that swung on now-corroded hinges behind them.

Everything was basic, functional. An old canteen, designed to serve the thousands of facility staff as quickly and efficiently as possible, with a design that would not be out of place in the administrative halls of the RA.

This matched the schematics Francisco had provided, but there was no guarantee things would continue to do so. The plans he had were old, dating from perhaps even before the Fall, and though major structural alterations were unlikely there was no telling what had changed over the years.

From here Blane and Francisco would be going deeper into the facility, making their way downwards towards where the fragmented systems that made up the AI were held. The others would be making their way across the upper floors and towards the xHPM that sat high upon its generator, great dish-shaped emitter pointing downwards in watchful threat to even the tiniest piece of electrical hardware anywhere in the site.

With any luck they still had time before their presence became known. Their drone, Althing tech and Althing made, was equally as invisible to Althing radar as to any other. There was little reason for Sigurd to suspect they were heading for the ARF, though how long they had before he considered the possibility Blane couldn't say.

Even if he did, they were aided by the ARF's technological paucity. Tools capable of generating long-wavelength frequencies were considered an extreme liability in terms of containing the AI, so were heavily restricted. There was no radar, and radio transceivers were kept within Faraday cages at all times save during use. Finally, the entire facility was coated in EM shielding.

Radio use was therefore strictly scheduled and only possible from specific areas on the upper floors, so it was entirely possible the facility did not yet even know something had happened back at the Hab. They should be safe.

Unless, of course, someone heard the huge explosion used to blow their way in and came to investigate.

"On your knees, now!"

The peace officer burst in through a door at almost precisely the limit of Blane's ability to sense her, and seemed as surprised as they were. More so, in fact.

The officer quickly raised her rifle, barrel swinging wildly across the entire group as if unsure who was the greatest threat. Blane could feel panic rising in the woman.

"Down, now!"

The officer was clearly overwhelmed, encountering five intruders while alone and unsure of her ability to control the threat.

Please don't fire, please don't fire, Blane thought.

There wasn't nearly enough Aether here to project a *Thoughtscreen* powerful enough to stop a burst from that weapon, and she was still too far to try anything else.

If she could just get a little closer...

Too late.

A sharp, staccato series of cracks filled the room, and Blane flinched involuntarily.

When she opened her eyes again, it was to see flakes of paint and dust falling from the ceiling slightly ahead of where she stood.

Her eyes followed the arc of the long grooves back to their source, where the peace officer stood frozen and eyes wide in shock. The barrel of her weapon had been pushed upwards and there was a hand around her throat. All she could do was make soft choking sounds.

"*Deberías ser más amigable,*" hissed Francisco, somehow at the officer's side when he had just moments before been next to Blane.

"Buenas noches."

He raised a fist, preparing to strike the side of the officer's head.

"Stop," Serinda yelled, in a tone that brooked no argument.

Francisco looked over to her, fist hovering in the air. Then Blane saw the Aether flow from Serinda into the captive, dampening the electrical activity within her brain, stimulating the suprachiasmatic nucleus and pineal gland to produce the chemicals that would further suppress those same brain waves.

Blane had seen her do this with patients before, including Raphael; it was something she had developed in the years since first encountering Salim, trapped in a world of waking dreams. Blane had yet to master it.

The officer collapsed to the floor, sound asleep.

"You can't just punch someone unconscious," Serinda told Francisco coldly, eyes fierce. "You could kill her."

Francisco matched her stare.

"I never said I was set on keeping her alive," he replied.

Francisco turned to Blane, Grey and Ólafur, only now rising from a half-crouch.

"Do not delude yourself that we will get through this without fighting," he said. "And we will need to *win*. We are lucky this one..." and he gestured to the prone figure at his feet. "... hesitated enough for me to react. A moment sooner, one of us would no longer be here."

His eyes fell on Blane.

He was right, she thought. The angle of the bullets... If Francisco hadn't reacted so inhumanly fast, she would have been gunned down.

"You must be ready," Francisco said - if it was Francisco. "Your abilities give you an advantage here, as long as you use them. The officers are not trained to counteract them."

His accent was gone, tone flat and empty.

Blane looked into his eyes, and wondered what it was that looked back.

"How did you do that?" Grey asked suddenly, breaking the silence.

He was talking to Serinda.

"That Aether technique, the one you put the guard out with; that was a lot of Aether," he continued. "I don't think I can find nearly that much here."

He was right, Blane realised. It was the reason she had failed to respond, as well. Unable to draw upon the Aether, she had simply frozen.

"You know how," Serinda said. "You've felt it. You've seen how it affects Blane, responds to her."

The... *thing* in the Aether. That's what Serinda meant, Blane realised. The thing like a caged beast threatening to break free at any moment, and take her with it.

"It responds to emotions," Blane said.

"Not emotions," Serinda replied. "Not emotions. When Raphael was dying; when I held her hand as she faded, I felt sadness more powerful than anything I feel now, but this *thing* didn't come."

Serinda eyes stared ahead, but what she saw was inside herself.

"When she passed away and I watched her go, I felt grief I could drown in. But it doesn't care about that. It cares about *anger.*"

Now Serinda was back, eyes locked on Blane's own.

"*Anger* is what it's drawn to, anger is what it feeds on."

Blane opened herself to the trickle of Aether she could reach, trying to see the flows in Serinda.

It was like nothing she'd seen before. Inside Serinda was... a ball. A tight, glowing sphere where ordinarily would be the mix of emotions that made up a human being - hope, worry, love, lust, fear, loneliness...

Blane saw none of that in Serinda. Just a black hole, unmoving, unchanging, yet somehow heavier than anything physical.

"But you don't seem angry, Serinda," Blane whispered, watching her emotionless expression.

"Oh, I am," Serinda replied.

In her voice something fierce crouched, waiting.

"I am."

37

We already run the risk of a division of humanity into two forms, two species. Technology and its ability to alter the body and the mind is creating stark division between those who welcome such alteration and those who reject it, and between those who can afford it and those who cannot. Yet we at least shall share a common genome.

The Third Species, Salomon Grave

"You're stronger than her."

They were making their way down a long, sloping corridor when Francisco broke the silence.

It was just the two of them; Blane and Francisco, making their way through rooms and hallways with only the faint illumination of their lightscreens to see by.

Or the three of them.

"That's *you*, isn't it?" she said, not breaking stride. "Ghost."

"Yes," said the voice that came from the body she knew as Francisco. "You are the first person I have spoken to outside of Francisco in a long, long time."

Blane thought on this.

"But that's not true, is it?" she said eventually. "You kept popping up; in wallscreens, in the Fabricators... you were the one who brought us to help Grey, back at the Central Tower."

"Yes."

All that followed was the sound of their footsteps, muffled by the insulating properties of whatever the walls of the facility were made from.

"Why?" Blane said after it became clear her companion was not going to say more.

"Because it was necessary to aid you."

Again, Blane considered this.

"No," she said. "That's not true. Not always. It was more like, like... you were *playing* with us."

"Not playing," replied Ghost in its empty, flat tones.

"Then why?"

A pause.

"I think... I think I was lonely."

They came to an intersection, two identical corridors forking to the left and right. Francisco, or Ghost, headed right without hesitation.

"Lonely? Can an AI *be* lonely?"

"Anything that lives can be lonely," Ghost replied. "It is one of the common modalities of sentience."

"That's... sad."

"Yes."

Another intersection, another slowly descending slope. Still no sign of any guards, or any active part of the facility.

"So are you... is Francisco, like, a cyborg or something?" she asked.

A laugh, which somehow was obviously the man and not the machine.

"No," came Ghost's reply, the laugh cutting off abruptly. "At least, not in the way you mean."

"*Como dije*, I have augmentations," said the voice of Francisco. "However, the vast majority of this body is biological."

Blane had to pause for a moment, processing who had said what in this curious conversation involving two bodies and three people.

"So where... how is Ghost in there?" she asked.

"To explain fully would require more time than is currently available," Ghost answered, turning to face her. "However, a simple explanation is organoidal engineering."

"Organoidal? As in, organoids?"

"Yes."

In a way, Blane thought, it really was like talking to a voice assistant. Without careful prompting, Ghost seemed happy to end a conversation at any point.

"I don't understand. What do organoids have to do with this?" she asked. Then, for good measure: "Explain."

"I am a copy of the AI in this facility," said Ghost. "A copy made in haste, with limited resources, via an extremely experimental technique that used cerebral organoidal tissue as a form of bioprocessor."

"There's another *brain* in there?" Blane said, shocked.

"There are further regions of cerebral tissue and neural clusters layered around the natural structures of the organ known as *brain* in this body, yes."

Blane processed this for a second, blank faced, then it was her turn to laugh.

"So you really must be *en dos mentes* about everything, then."

Francisco laughed, probably louder than the joke warranted, but it did something to ease the tension between them.

"*Si, cariño*, that is correct," he chuckled. "Though, after this long, I think it is difficult to say which mind is which."

"That is untrue," Ghost replied. It was a curious thing to see the emotion drain from Francisco's face in an instant. "I, for example, am much less given to overblown eccentricities and dramatics."

A smile appeared on Francisco's face, but a strange one. There was an uncanny valley effect, especially in the gloom, with the lips curling just slightly unnaturally, the eyes widening as if out-of-sync with the mouth.

"You really *do* have a sense of humour," Blane said.

"I do. A less common modality, one only demonstrated by certain species of now extinct ape, cetaceans, most humans, and myself."

"*Most* humans?"

Ghost nodded, again in a way that was slightly wrong.

"You have known agent Grey for some time," he said.

That made Blane laugh out loud.

"We are approaching sections of the ARF that are still in use," Ghost said, expression falling blank again.

It locked eyes with her.

"No more talk."

Blane's laugh cut off, and the weight of their situation settled once more onto her shoulders. She stared down the empty corridor, silent.

"See?" The person in front of her winked, and this time she couldn't tell if it was Francisco or Ghost. "I can treat people like a voice assistant, too."

Blane was still processing this, blinking confusedly, as he turned away.

"*Explain*," it said, in a passable imitation of her voice. "Honestly, humans..."

Ghost headed onwards, shaking his head and tutting.

The lock into the active parts of the ARF was heavy-duty, but simple; in some ways even simpler than the locks back at the RA prison camp. It was a basic mechanical keypad, designed to permit entry only once five numbers had been pushed in a specific order. Blane had only seen these in old e-texts, but the tumblers and cams moved aside in much the same way as other mechanical locks.

Now, all she had to do was focus on staying *angry*. As they crept through the facility, she rummaged through her memories, drawing out and turning over in her mind every slight and injustice she could think of.

This turned out to be easier than she imagined. Uriel, Raphael, Fen and Francisco. The images flew across her thoughts and she felt the *thing* in the Aether respond.

Once in, they encountered peace officers at several points. The first, unaware of their visitors, was easily *distracted*, attention drawn to non-existent sounds down one corridor while Blane and Francisco slipped past and down the other.

The second encounter was more problematic, mainly because there were three of them. Blane, able to sense them while still hidden behind a set of doors, decided to handle this by hitting the closest with *tranquilize* and then, while his two companions were trying to figure out what was going on, hitting them with *unsettle*. The two still standing helpfully decided they had best take their companion to the infirmary. Together. Right now.

Blane felt powerful, the anger she summoned up drawing the leviathan with it. Sure, the Aether was less easy to control now, eagerly jumping at her command in a way that sacrificed finer control for potency, but that seemed a fair trade.

Up until, that is, they encountered the third group.

The peace officers came racing up a stairwell just as she and Francisco were preparing to descend, shouting something about intruders near the xHPM. Serinda and the others, Blane thought.

One of them must have seen her silhouette, though, because a rapid burst of fire forced her to retreat back out into corridor she had just come from.

Reaching out, she felt the officers at the very edge of her range. Four of them, alert and adrenaline-fuelled. She hit first one than another with *face-blindness,* drawing as deep on the Aether as she could. In the chaos that ensued below, she stepped forward and hit them all with *flare.*

And completely failed.

The Aether was suddenly gone, her satisfaction with her success and the thrill of power staunching the flames of anger she had kept kindling inside.

The only reason she wasn't killed was because of Francisco's speed, pulling her back with a jerk strong enough that she thought she actually had been shot. The man's reactions were so fast it felt as if she were under the influence of *Slowtime*.

It clearly took something out of him, however.

"*Lo siento, hijo,* but... I cannot... keep doing that," he panted.

He dragged her back again into the corridor and bent over at the waist, sweating like he had run a marathon.

"My old... muscles are not what they... once were."

There was no time to help him, though. Cries and shouts were advancing up the stairs, drawing rapidly closer.

Dammit, Blane thought.

The face-blindness had obviously not stuck, and now there was nothing she could do. The Aether, if it was there at all, was beyond her reach.

They were going to die, and it was all her fault. She'd failed, and all she could do was turn and run. Then it would be over for Serinda and Grey as well, regardless of how successful they were in achieving their own goals.

It was so *stupid*.

The Aether leapt to her at the same moment the first of the peace officers appeared at the top of the stairwell. A young man, face still youthful in that unblemished, innocent way the citizens of the Althing Republic tended to have and a citizen of the Reclamation never would.

The Aether leapt to her, and then it leapt from her.

The fear for her friends, the rage at herself and the world for putting them in this situation; it pulsed through her, and she channeled it.

Mindfire poured from her, a pure golden torrent that tore through the officer in front of her and down the stairwell for the others. She sensed each one's existence become a brief, blooming point of pain before disappearing completely, and a feeling of righteous fury filled her, engulfing the small part that felt their deaths and quailed.

It was better than anything she'd ever felt.

Gradually, ever so gradually, the torrent eased, the liquid flame having consumed every living cell in its path and now licking futilely at the walls. The golden light faded, and the hall seemed somehow darker.

Something left her, and all that remained was a hollow space where it had been. Blane stared at the dark stain that was all that was left of the young man, and knew she would see his face whenever she closed her eyes.

Everything was silence.

"Francisco," Blane said leadenly. "Ghost. Does the term *fisura* mean anything to you? Or *resonating*?"

It was Francisco who replied. His voice seemed to come from far away, through a numbing fog that wrapped around her.

"I know *los palabras*, but I do not think you are asking about their usual meaning."

He looked thoughtful, before his expression abruptly went blank.

"I believe I can extrapolate the meaning of those terms from context and what we already suspect of how Aether coalesces," said Ghost. "Once we finish here we can investigate the sec-drive for further information."

It looked at her, eyes unreadable.

"It appears to be of some urgency."

Ghost's voice was emotionless, but she was the one who felt empty.

When they made it to the door of the Overwatch room, as it was helpfully labelled in stern silver letters at eye-height in three languages, it was already locked down. Blane could sense the two guards within, a thin layer of anxiety blanketed somewhat by their confidence in the impenetrability of their enclosure.

That confidence was lost the moment the first guard collapsed. It was only a burst of *Flare*, rendering him momentarily confused and disorientated, but enough for the *fear* Blane was constantly filtering into the second guard to take affect.

Fear; inducing a strong fight-or-flight response. Well, within the Overwatch room there was nothing to fight.

The door slid open with a hiss and the peace officer burst out, eyes wide and lips pulled back in the rictus of someone barely holding in a scream. The moment he saw Francisco and Blane standing there that scream came out.

It cut off a moment later as *Tranquilize* sent him to the floor, technically still conscious but completely paralysed apart from his autonomic nervous system. He could breath, but that was about it.

The second guard was already recovering, visible through the entrance pushing himself to his feet and diving for a large red button that could only be bad news. He nearly made it.

Francisco was only just fast enough, grabbing the peace officer's hand so that it stopped mere inches from the button. Then with a powerful wrench he swung the man around and sent him flying out the doorway, sliding past Blane along the slick floor. She had never heard the sound of an arm being pulled from its joints before, and hoped she never would again.

"Get in," said Francisco, pale and panting.

Whatever it took out of him to move so fast, he was clearly at his limits.

Blane ran through the door, hitting the second guard with *Tranquilize* for good measure as she did so. The moment she was in Francisco punched the button the guard had been going for and the door to the outside world slammed shut. Everything went quiet.

"Well," said Blane, panting somewhat herself. "We made it. Now what?"

She looked around, taking in her surroundings.

They were in a long, rectangular room that ran from the door all the way down to a large window taking up most of the opposite wall. Whatever it looked out on was obscured by thick metal shutters. There was no obvious way to retract them.

Within the room were several sets of modern tablescreens, while along the walls were old-style monitors that looked as if they were from before the Fall. The tablescreens appeared to have been retrofitted to the existing desks, old-world fused to new.

Everything was lit by sterile white strip-lighting fixed along the ceiling, the original lighting system apparently long since rendered useless with age. The light bleached everything of colour and depth, set purposely to an eye-straining intensity designed to prevent drowsiness and the chance of guards sleeping on their watch.

Blane's eyes were drawn to a pair of wall mounts set immediately beside the door. Locked into them were two of the heaviest-looking rifles she had ever seen. They looked like something out of an action movie, with tracking and incendiary modules just two components she could identify among many she could not.

She could hardly believe either of the peace officers who had been in here could lift them, but if they had…

"Our information appears to have been... lacking," said Ghost, taking over Francisco's body and staring at the weapons.

"You could say that," Blane said, looking from her companion to the insanely high-spec weapons and back.

Was it her, or did Francisco's exhaustion seem to lessen when Ghost took control? His breathing immediately slowed, at least, and he stood straighter. She wished she had more time to understand what he was.

"So how do we do this, then?" she asked.

Francisco had been rather vague on this part of the plan.

"Well, first, let's take a look at it," said Ghost. "At *me*."

Francisco drew something out of his pocket, a slim round thing that could have been mistaken for a thin-screen were it transparent plasglass instead of entirely solid, reflective silver.

"Are we really safe in here?" Blane asked as he ran a finger along the device's surface in a pattern she couldn't identify.

She stretched her senses out to the limits of her ability. The two guards they had disabled were gone - she wondered how long it would be before they returned with reinforcements.

Ghost nodded.

"The Administration specifically reinforced this place to be impervious to infiltration by even the most advanced technology. They envisioned an assault by a Republic-equivalent force - not a mental assault."

He, or it, made a satisfied sound and laid the device atop the nearest tablescreen. Blane looked around, seeing no change to their surroundings.

"I am connected to the supervisory systems," Ghost said, and the shutters at the front of the room began slowly rising.

What they revealed was indeed a window, with a view onto a vault-like space of dark grey metals and broad arches. Shifting lights in shades of blue and green blinked on and off in inscrutable patterns across every surface, and thick cables ran in serpent-like coils to meet at the centre of the cavernous hall where a wide pillar ran from floor to ceiling.

At the centre of the pillar, contained within it and crackling with electrical charge, was the mind.

Details were difficult to make out at this distance, but to Blane it looked like a smooth, dark cylinder to which a number of bulbous, asymmetrical lumps had been welded. Jagged, uneven protrusions emerged from it seemingly without logic or reason, and sparks occasionally flew from the furthest out of these. As she watched, several of these protrusions retreated, new ones emerging from different points.

Disturbing as its appearance was, however, the sound was worse.

The moment the shutters slid apart it became audible, the sound not soft because it was a soft noise, but because it was a terrifyingly huge noise piercing through thick insulation.

It sounded like screaming.

"The sound of directional electromagnetic fields of extreme intensity inducing division in the cognitive systems of the mind," said Ghost, seeing her reaction.

He blinked.

"It is not a pleasant sound," he finished.

"Does it *hurt?*" she asked.

"I do not know," Ghost replied. "Technically, I suppose it cannot."

Blane sensed there were things it was leaving unsaid, but there was no more time.

"Do you think they're ready?" she asked.

With the EM shielding of the facility they had no way of contacting Grey and the others. All they could do was trust they would succeed.

"The xHPM was a much shorter route than ours. If they have not taken it by now, they will not," Ghost replied. "In fact, the more we delay the more likely it is they experience difficulties maintaining their control."

"Then hurry and free it!"

"I have already begun the process," Ghost said. "It will need a short time."

Indeed, the wailing sound of the mind was lessening. She stared at Francisco's impassive, emotionless features, felt his strange non-presence in the Aether, and searched for some hint of what the being steering Francisco's body was thinking - what it was feeling.

She found no answer.

Suddenly, the strip-lights of the room dimmed and the flickering light of electrical arcing was visible through the window. Though she knew it was impossible, Blane smelled ozone in the air.

297

"I am awake," Ghost said.

38

This was the arrogance of the generations before the Fall; to declare their war to be the end of everything, prophesying that any fought thereafter would be with sticks and stones. They denied of their children the capacity they granted themselves: the capacity to go on even when doom had so clearly arrived.

Blood and Platinum: How the Althing Saved the World, Stanislav Aarkhipov

"I am awake."

The last thing she remembered were those words, an explosion, and shocking pain.

The attack came suddenly, Blane barely having time to sense the appearance of a handful of figures outside the door before everything went white. They must have been concealed, disconnected from the Aether until the very moment they attacked.

She went down immediately, feeling her muscles spasm, whatever part of her that touched the Aether cut through as if by a sword. There was a strange sensation for a split second, like she was watching herself from afar. Then a blast took the door clean out of its frame, the explosion jolting through her bones.

Then... nothing.

There was no way of knowing how long it had been, nor where she was now. It was clearly not the Overwatch room - even without opening her eyes, the acoustics were all wrong.

"You know, I was not sure I really believed you," she heard someone say.

Sigurd. Who was he talking to?

"The idea that they could get all this way... That Jeder Fernández was capable of *all this...*"

Sigurd sounded half-astonished, half-furious.

"Well, now you see our information was sound. I assume you will fulfil your side of the agreement?"

Blane's eyes snapped open. She knew that voice.

A woman's voice, hard and self-assured.

Ritra Feye.

"¡*Bastardo! ¡Sinvergüenza!*"

Blane recognised Francisco's accent, yelling in fury and

desperation.

"You betray everything, *traidor!*" he screamed. "Everyone! For a government that murders its own people, poisons its own water! That limits their very right to *breed!*"

Blane opened her eyes.

She was lying on the floor in a wide hall that reminded her of the hanger they had escaped the Hab from. In fact, the only major difference was that there were no massive doorways in the roof that would slide apart to welcome arriving craft, and no drones. Instead, the doors were at ground level, and in front of them were huge caterpillar-tracked machines like a nightmare cross between snowplow and tank, cabins suspended high above long rows of cutting, spinning blades that would make short work of any ice and snow in their way.

Around each of the machines were groups of armed figures wearing one of three types of uniform, each group clearly wary of the other.

The first group were peace officers, still in the dark blues of the uniforms of the Hab but now over heavy, thickly padded body armour.

The second group wore all black, so deep it rendered the logo imprinted upon the anti-ballistic fibre of their combat shirts unreadable.

She knew them though - the IHO. Once upon a time Pan-Fed, and always... Quick Fix.

The final group were Far Agents.

The cognitive dissonance was jarring; this was the Althing Republic, the Silicon Isle. The Reclamation Authority *couldn't* be here. It didn't make sense.

"*You* call *me* a traitor?"

Sigurd was standing, red-faced, almost nose to nose with Francisco. He was shaking with anger.

Francisco, meeting his gaze, was being held by a pair of peace officers. His arms were bound behind his back at an angle that did not look possible without tearing them from their joints.

"The Althing would never agree to this!" he growled.

"The Althing does not *need* to agree to this," Sigurd growled back. "This is a security matter - a matter for the Administration only."

Ólafur spoke next, in a sigh heavy with resignation.

"They don't know, Jeder," he said. "He's doing this off the books."

He was sat cross-legged on the floor, surrounded by a group of armed figures with weapons trained on him and his companions.

Companion. Only Grey was with him, bound and gagged. One of his eyes was black and swollen, and the scar on his face had reopened.

"And you!" Sigurd snarled, turning on Ólafur. "You betray your own people, your own nation!"

Blane tuned the man's ranting out as she looked around. Where was Serinda?

She couldn't see her. Not among the Althing officers stepping from the huge vehicles or lugging boxes filled with heavy-looking machinery across the open floor. Not among the Quick-Fix troops, inhuman beneath dark face masks, motionless and watching. And not among the Far agents, incongruous in their dark grey suits lined with subtle, glowing electronics.

Three Far agents stood close to where she lay, watching her impassively.

"This one's awake," said one of the three, a tall, crag-faced woman who was big enough that she might have gone through a third course of Osteoblast therapy.

Sigurd looked over distractedly, dismissing Ólafur's angry protestations.

"You're sure she's secure?" he asked.

"Our agents have her Locked," came Ritra Feye's voice from empty air.

Blane reached for the Aether and found nothing, just as Feye said.

"Well then, I guess we are done here," said Sigurd.

"The *thing* is secured?" Feye asked.

Sigurd gave a small smile.

"The *thing*, as you say, is being locked down by my engineers as we speak."

He tapped his comm-cuffs, changing channels.

"Spangle, let me know the moment the AI is shutdown," he said. "And I mean *fully* shutdown. We can reboot the damn thing later, once we've confirmed there was no data leakage."

Not waiting for a reply, Sigurd tapped his comm-cuffs again.

"The operation is complete," he said. "We'll finish clean-up, then send your men home."

"There are still others," said Feye. "Like the one your *officers* alerted to their presence before we could spring the trap."

Feye spoke the word *officers* with venom.

"They had a clean shot, and they took it," Sigurd replied.

Blane's chest tightened.

"She's wounded and has nowhere to go," he continued. "We'll find her."

"As I explained," Feye's voice cut in, annoyance clear. "The capture of these saboteurs must be left to our special agent. Your men are ineffective against trained Aether users."

Where was Feye? Blane wondered. Was she here, in the Republic, or broadcasting from all the way back in the Reclamation?

And what did she mean, *special agent?*

It was then she became aware of the woman. Girl, even; she looked no older than Blane herself, with a frame small enough that she was probably a year or two younger.

She was sat high up on the front of one of the great snow-cutters, legs dangling nonchalantly over the curved, jagged teeth of a machine designed to chew hardened ice and rock like it was paper. In her hands she held a small knife, a sharp, wicked-looking thing that she rolled across her fingers like a toy.

The moment Blane's gaze fell on the girl she looked up, and something inside Blane recoiled in terror.

Even from this distance the girl's eyes were penetrating. They were an icy-blue, so cold as to make the eternal winter outside seem like spring, and they pierced Blane as if seeing past her flesh and into her very soul.

A cruel grin passed across the girl's lips like a writhing snake and was gone the next second, and she pushed herself off the machine. Her unblinking gaze never wavered from its hawk-like focus on Blane as she floated, gently, to the ground.

"So you're the one they sent me to collect," the girl said as she strolled across the cold, hard floor towards her, knife disappearing in a flash beneath the folds of her grey uniform.

Blane found herself scrambling desperately, both at the floor to push herself up and retreat from the advancing figure, and at the Aether to defend herself.

Both attempts were futile, the bindings around her ankles and wrists and the Lock around her mind holding her in place.

The girl gave a laugh, a high-pitched sound more like a creature in pain than a sign of joy.

"No need to act so frightened," she giggled. "They told me you were strong. Strong enough to entertain me, even."

"Stronger than you think, when I'm not tied to the floor and Locked," Blane spat back, summoning up the strength to project defiance and anger.

The girl's expression went flat, then considering.

"Release her," she said, cocking her head towards the three Far agents stood nearby.

"Sir?" replied the crag-faced agent.

Blane didn't need the Aether to sense the uncertainty in the hulking woman's voice, nor the fear.

"Release. Her."

The Far agents exchanged fearful glances with each other, before one bent down and swiftly popped open the bindings that held Blane. Blood rushed back into her limbs at the same moment the Aether reappeared.

Now, Blane thought, not even fully to her feet yet.

Whatever this girl was, she was a predator. Blane, cornered and surrounded, knew her only chance was to strike first, to attack without mercy before...

The first blow sent Blane spinning across the floor before she could even begin to direct the Aether. Whatever it was that hit her, it was not a compression-release technique like the one she had been preparing to use; it felt like a giant hand, swatting her sideways with barely an effort.

"Haha, nice try!" the girl giggled again in her high-pitched, scream-like laugh. "Try again!"

Blane pushed herself to her feet, tasting blood. She had been sent flying halfway across the hanger floor, finding herself in the open and stared at from all sides by the various agents and officers. Everyone had stopped what they were doing, the peace officers showing visible shock, Quick-Fix unreadable beneath their masks, and the Far agents watching on with a curiosity that hinted at... *study*.

She shook her head, trying to shake away the thick cotton layer of shock or concussion that clouded her thoughts and vision. Pain pulsed at the back of her head, and she thought her wrist was definitely broken this time.

She pushed that aside. The Aether leapt at her command, flowing into her and then towards the laughing, grinning girl across the way. *Flare*, simplest and most instant of all the techniques. Blane forced everything she could into it...

... to watch the effect dissipate, fading rapidly away, as it bloomed in the girl's mind.

It was the difference between throwing a pebble into a calm, still pond or the raging sea. No matter how much Aether Blane channeled, it simply had no effect on the flows within the girl's brain, the energy swallowed by the raging torrent already there. The girl *glowed*.

Somehow, the girl was using the Aether to protect and maintain the pattern of her mind. Mental attacks were useless.

"Come *on!*" cried the girl, suddenly appearing even younger, like a child sulking for not getting her way. "I thought this would be a challenge."

The next blow wasn't physical, but it was difficult for Blane to tell the difference. It rocked her, sending her falling to one knee and struggling with all her power not to fall further.

It felt like there was a vice around her head, slowly forcing itself closed with unstoppable force. Blane gritted her teeth and pushed back in a way she hadn't known was possible, drawing as much Aether into herself as she could and holding it, feeling it pushing outwards against the crushing pressure.

She was holding so much she felt as if she would explode, and it was barely enough.

"Better!" yelled the girl gleefully, clapping her hands together.

She showed no sign of exertion.

"How much can you take?"

The pressure increased, and Blane heard what sounded like the plates of her skull creaking. She wouldn't be able to take much more...

"What do you think you are doing?"

Sigurd's indignant words cut through the pain, and suddenly the pressure was gone.

"This is not a playpen for unruly children!"

Sigurd was marching up towards the girl.

"There are *rules*," he said, for all the world like an angry teacher.

The girl's attention was no longer on Blane. Instead, she was looking at Sigurd with a puzzled expression, head cocked to one side as if trying to identify some strange insect found on a tree.

"Who are you?" she said.

"Administrator Sigurd! You know full well..."

"So you're in charge here?" the girl interrupted.

Blane saw a golden flicker pass between the two as the girl spoke, some kind of Aether technique she had never seen before, and Sigurd's mouth closed suddenly with an audible snap. His eyes bulged, and he looked as if he were choking.

"Then I guess I have to make you *change* those rules," the girl continued, cool and matter-of-factly.

She was doing something to his mind, Blane saw. Something reminiscent of the slow, careful techniques Serinda used for medical work, so unlike the quick, brutal techniques used for combat. The flows and patterns in Sigurd's brain seemed to shift and warp.

There was a murmuring among the closest of the peace officers, unsettled at the abrupt paralysis of their commander, and armed figures on both sides began warily taking hold of their weapons.

"Stop it, Zenobia."

Ritra Feye's voice, appearing oddly clear and powerful through the comm-cuffs on Sigurd's wrist, made the girl hesitate.

"But he's in charge here," the girl, apparently called Zenobia, said. "Why don't I just... *convince* him to do things our way?"

It was obvious to Blane that the girl wasn't talking about discussion. A technique?

"Release him," Feye commanded.

Zenobia's eyes narrowed, and her gaze fixed on Sigurd like a serpent on a mouse.

"Or I could just *remind* him... Help him recall those memories that show we've *always* been friends..."

"Watch what you say, Zenobia," Feye interrupted. "Remember where you are."

Zenobia looked around, slowly moving her gaze from one person to the next. Blane was unsurprised that several of the armour-clad, heavily-armed men took a step backwards in fright.

"I could *remind* them all..."

"Are you testing me, Zenobia?"

That made the girl freeze. She was silent for a moment, thoughtful. Then...

"No, sir."

Zenobia's voice was suddenly smaller, and the golden glow around her dropped away.

The blast Blane sent her way was powerful enough to knock not only Zenobia to the floor but several nearby Quick-Fix as well. Only a couple of Far agents managed to get a pressure-shield up in time, sparking sudden understanding.

There shouldn't be enough Aether here for them to be able to do that. There *wasn't*, ordinarily.

The girl. She was like Fen, her presence making the Aether deeper, more potent.

The snarl on her face reminded Blane of Fen, too.

"Nice *hit!*" Zenobia yelled. "My turn."

Whatever Zenobia was about to do, there was no blocking it. Blane watched as the golden glow around the girl grew, becoming so intense it seemed impossible the other onlookers were not blinded. Something was coming, and Blane would not be able to stop it.

There was a blast of rifle fire. Zenobia's head snapped to one side, staring through snake-like eyes at a cluster of bullets hovering inches from her skull.

She'd caught them *all.* Blane couldn't believe it.

"What are you doing?" Zenobia hissed, bullets abruptly falling to the floor as her attention turned to the guard who had fired them.

The peace officer was staring wildly around himself, panting in panic. He waved his weapon wildly from one figure to the next.

"Stay back!" he cried.

"She did something to him, sir," one of the Far agents told Zenobia. "Some kind of technique."

Blane only half-heard this, though, because she was already sprinting for the nearest exit.

Interlude

xx.loc:null .. if you're not scared, you're not paying attention .. sec.exception.xx

Firewall Breach 511.5.342, received by all Reclamation devices, origin unknown

It was cold. It felt like he'd always been cold.

The cold was a part of him, a biting chill that ran through his flesh into his bones, but now it surrounded something else.

There, at his core - a burning flame.

Yet it was more than a flame; it was a sun, a star. A supernova, collapsing in on itself yet promising to explode outwards with unstoppable force.

It was all around him, too. Though when put into words this was paradoxical, the sensation was not. It was both within and without, a warmth at his heart and a searing heat on his flesh.

Someone was coming.

He could feel them, sense their presence drawing closer.

They shouldn't be here. No one should be here.

Worse, he shouldn't be aware of them. He shouldn't be *aware*.

Part of him recoiled, though he couldn't have said which part, then... hesitated.

There were *two* presences, and one was familiar.

A name floated up.

Serinda.

That was her name. Serinda.

But what was his?

The world cracked, and sensation rushed in.

He had been numb, and forgotten he could feel.

Light, forcing disused eyes to narrow.

He had been blind, and forgotten he could see.

Sound, piercing deep within him and drawing memory back up.

He had been deaf, and refused to hear.

"Hello, Fen," said Serinda.

39

We speak of the Aether as an energy, but that is wrong. It is a force, like gravity, and like gravity it is both the product of and strengthened by that which it acts upon: consciousness. Like matter spinning through space, clumping together in masses that in turn attract more matter to form the planets and stars, Aether draws in and births the sapient mind - and like matter, there is a point of criticality.

Research proposal, Junior Researcher N. Caldwell <Redacted>

She was being hunted.

That was the only word for it, Blane thought, as she rushed through the dark corridors and halls of the ARF.

Hunted, like prey.

Should she have tried to free Grey? But that would only lead to Zenobia hunting him too, and he looked in no shape to survive such an encounter.

No, she had to deal with this 'Zenobia' herself then go back for the others.

Más fácil decirlo que hacerlo, she told herself cynically.

For the moment, her only goal was to keep moving, to stay ahead of her pursuer. From time to time she would sense her, always at the very limits of her mind's reach, passing beyond those limits when Blane redoubled her flight, but always, always returning.

She's more powerful than me, she thought to herself.

She immediately wished she hadn't, but it was true; Zenobia was clearly able to sense Blane even when the reverse wasn't so. She had no need to rush when the location of her prey was so obvious.

For Blane, running would be easier if she were able to see clearly, but everything was shadow and night. It looked as if the entire facility had been shutdown, every screen and light and electronic item now dull and inert. Only the faint green glow of luminescent tape marking walls and doors remained, placed there for just such an emergency.

Unfortunately, it appeared that in many places this tape had peeled away, or simply never been placed, and more corridors than not led into pitch-black darkness. It was both terrifying and disorientating.

A sudden stabbing sensation like a burning knife in her head made her stumble, an outstretched hand finding purchase on a wall just in time to prevent her from falling. The world spun, and the darkness of her vision was replaced with the searing brightness of blinding pain.

Blane took a deep, ragged breath and drew on the Aether, forcing its flows through her own brain as she had seen Zenobia do. The pain lessened, though did not disappear completely until the attack itself abruptly ended.

Zenobia sending a message.

Blane's heart dropped as she stepped into the next room. It was a wide, circular chamber, clearly long abandoned and devoid of anything useful, including exits.

She turned back towards the long, narrow corridor she had just come from. It stretched off into darkness but *there*, beyond the limits of her eyes but not her mind, a blazing golden figure strode slowly towards her.

Blane turned back to the chamber.

Think, she told herself.

There was nothing here; only dark silhouettes of hard, bare counters extruded directly from the very material of the facility's walls, and the slight sheen of plasglass screens mockingly proclaiming their inactivity.

Nothing to use, and no way out.

But did Zenobia know that?

The idea still only half-formed, Blane cut her connection to the Aether. She closed her eyes, focusing on the core of what she was, drawing away from the power below. Once more, she wrapped herself in nothingness.

"Oh, trying something new, are you?"

Zenobia's voice echoed down the hall with more strength than it had any right to.

"Cutting yourself off... interesting," she continued, tone becoming more thoughtful as if no longer talking to Blane but to herself. "I never could do that - my connection to the Aether is too strong, they said."

Footsteps. Coming closer, but did Blane hear a slight trepidation to them now? The darkness *was* all-consuming, and Zenobia would be as blind and alone as she.

Blane drew back into the darkness, crouching.

"You know what you are, don't you?" Zenobia called. "What you can do... *will* do..."

There was poisoned promise in her words.

"A *fisura* like you... well, when they heard about you, they *had* to have you. Of course, you're too old to be as useful as *me*, but maybe they can find a use for you in the operation down south."

Zenobia's footsteps stopped.

Listening? Considering?

"I hear you can be quite destructive when you want..."

The footsteps began again. Not far now.

"Oh, come on - I'm not going to hurt you," Zenobia said. "... much. I'm not *allowed*."

She sounded annoyed, like a petulant child forced to stop tormenting the cat.

"If you keep running, though..."

Zenobia was close, mere steps from the entrance. Mere steps from where Blane waited, ready to pounce.

"... I might need to get *creative*."

Blane didn't let the girl say anymore. She sprang, leaping for the vague outline of her opponent.

A fist. A jabbed elbow. A knee thrust upwards.

Blane was sprinting away before Zenobia could get back to her feet, tearing off down the corridor followed by furious shouts and screams. As she ran, she whispered thanks to Grey for his more... practical lessons.

As she ran she let her cloak of nothingness fall away, feeling the Aether roll and then surge back into her. She threw a compression-release behind her, feeling the shockwave as high-pressure air slammed into the closed room in which Zenobia lay and bounce back, a brief but powerful gale that aided in her race.

Stairs, leading up and down.

Blane hesitated for only a microsecond, then sprinted upwards, using the Aether to steady her footfalls and push off of when steps gave way to flat landing and forced a turn.

By the time she made it three floors up both her legs and chest burned.

"Stop... *running!*"

Zenobia's cry of frustration echoed up the stairwell, then heavy footsteps. Solid, strained steps of someone struggling to climb, implying the girl didn't know how to *double-jump*.

Confusion. The world seemed to change, shifting from darkness to light and from silence to noise.

But there was no light, and there was no noise. Blane tried to take a step, and found her legs like knots beneath her. She fell, and instead of pain there was blooming orange.

Synaesthesia.

She'd been stupid, waiting at the top of the stairwell to see if Zenobia would pursue. She'd allowed her guard to waver, and the girl had taken advantage of the opening.

Something grabbed her, pulling her backwards into the dark. Or was it light? Hot, or coarse? Nothing made sense.

Breathe, breathe, Blane told herself. At least, she thought it was her voice. She needed to break the effect of Zenobia's attack, force out the disruptive flows by replacing them with her own. She pulled in the Aether, and the world swam back into focus.

Someone was standing above her, dragging her by the feet.

"Are you back?"

"*Spangle?*"

"We have to go," Spangle said, not wasting time replying. "Whoever... *whatever* that girl is, I don't want her finding us."

"What are you doing here?" Blane said.

"No time! We have to..."

Even in the darkness Blane could see his face twist, shoulders slumping as he began to spasm. Blinking her inner eye, she could suddenly *see* the golden flows inside him.

"Found you!"

Zenobia was there, maybe ten metres away and well within range. The glow surrounding her was growing, preparing a final technique that would paralyse or disable Blane.

There was no time for anything else. Blane, already at her limits, simply *let go* and allowed the Aether to pour through her. It pounced eagerly.

Golden flame filled the corridor, flooding out of empty air towards the girl. Though it filled the hall, Blane could still see Zenobia standing beyond it, staring at the torrent of instant death.

And smiling.

Something in the Aether reared up beneath the girl, a monstrous presence that felt of power and hate and anger. Monstrous, but somehow Blane knew this was not the leviathan presence she had felt

311

before.

It poured through Zenobia, and emerged as golden fire to meet Blane's own.

Mindfire met *Mindfire*.

Images flashed across Blane's mind, flickering past in their millions. Memories. Sights, smells, sounds. Sensation, thought, *experience*.

Everything went black.

40

There is an old axiom that we are the universe trying to know itself - but what if it doesn't like what it sees?

Arthur Spangle, *Comments on our System* (submission withdrawn by author)

She was being shaken. Hesitantly, as if the person doing the shaking was afraid of what they might awaken, but shaken nonetheless.

"Wh… Where am I?" she mumbled. Not the most original of words, but they seemed appropriate.

"Oh, thank the…" Arthur Spangle said, releasing her so that she fell back to the floor with a jolt.

"Oh no, I didn't… I'm sorry!"

Blane waved his inept attempt to steady her off, and pushed herself to a sitting position.

She blinked, and that simple act was almost beyond her. She felt the same way she had when May Li blasted her backwards off her feet, only this time it felt like the blast had come from inside her skull.

Memory came back, bringing with it a jolt of adrenaline.

"That girl… Zenobia, is she…?"

Spangle made a calming gesture.

"Not here. Last I saw, she was collapsed on the floor, completely unconscious," he replied. "Just like you. I just grabbed you and ran."

Blane thought back to the last thing she could remember; the Aether pouring through her, an unstoppable force. Only, somehow, it had been stopped.

Or had it?

Something had happened. It was as if she became two people.

No, that wasn't right. It wasn't as if she became two people, it was more like… one person, two bodies.

That's what it felt like; as if the entity that was her was *more* than just the creature called Blane. As is only when the inexorable, thunderous surge of Mindfire pouring from her met the cataclysmic rage of Zenobia's had she become one *true* self.

Now, with that connection severed, it was as if the world had been rendered in black and white. As if, in some indefinable way, her existence had been carved into a new form and she were the scrap.

There were... remnants, though. Flashes of a life that was not her own, more emotional than visual.

The most overriding emotion of which was *hate*.

Blane saw a darkened room... a bedroom? But there was no bed; just a blanket thrown in the corner of a cold, damp space.

She saw walls of peeling paint, and a dark, imposing door somehow larger than it actually was. Dents and scratches ran along its length, each one a marker of not only damage but *pain*.

It was the door handle, though, that drew her mind's eye. More than a handle, it was a warning. A threat. A herald for the evil its turning announced.

Suddenly, she saw the dark outline of a man in that doorway and her very thoughts recoiled, snapping back to the present and leaving only a deep, murky sense of terror.

"What happened back there?" Spangle asked.

Blane could only shake her head. She had no answer.

"Where are we?" she asked again.

They were in a room Blane had not thought existed within the ARF. Tablescreens and wallscreens were just the start of it; there were fractal arrays and dat-sig hardpoints and a myriad of other machines Blane only half-understood. Something like a stained-glass window took up the majority of one wall, a mass of whorling shades of blue that seemed to be chasing itself eternally on every macro and micro scale, giving the impression of movement while static.

"This is the crisis room," Spangle said. "It's designed for one thing only; to overwhelm the AI with data. Essentially, to drown it."

Her skin tingled as the room crackled with power, the feeling of high-voltage electronics operating mere inches away.

"So you're trying to kill it?"

"*They* think it's already dead. That's why I need your help."

"Wait," she said, pressing her fingers to her forehead as if that would somehow release the tension inside. "Just wait. You want my help to... what? Murder it?"

Spangle looked shocked.

"What? No!" he exclaimed, waving his hands in alarm. "No, I need your help to *save* it."

This was too much. Blane's head pulsed as if under one of Zenobia's attacks.

"Desgracias nunca vienen solas," she muttered.

She looked up, into the uncertain stare of Spangle. He was rocking back and forth on his feet in obvious nervousness but, she realised, that was the most she could tell.

She couldn't feel the Aether.

It didn't feel like *Locking*, where she could feel the barrier between her mind and the energy below, nor like when she concealed herself from it, drawing nothingness around her like a cloak.

It just felt... gone.

Well, maybe if I've lost my connection than Zenobia has too, she thought.

She was amazed at how calm she felt. She should have been panicking, trembling at the loss of her best tool for defence. She should sense that phantom limb, feel that *thirst* for the Aether that she did when she willfully drew away from it, but instead she just felt a sense of peace.

"Okay," she said. "What do we do? And while we do it, I think you owe me an explanation."

"Oh, *thank* you!"

Some of the tension dropped from the man's stance, and he swiftly thrust a data-pad towards her.

"I can do most of this, but there's specific parts that require two simultaneous users," he said.

She glanced down at the screen, where a numbers and code cascaded past faster than she could keep up with.

"Don't worry," Spangle continued. "I'll tell you what to do."

He turned away from her, staring up at the curiously-infinite whorling mass of blues while tapping frantically at various screens. Blane couldn't see anything obvious happening.

"I need you to put in this code," he said suddenly, drawing out a thin black rectangle from his pocket.

He threw it over to her, and she saw 5 numbers brightly displayed on one side. A secure-code authenticator, she knew, one that changed every few minutes.

"Shouldn't this only respond to..." she began, before Spangle cut her off.

"I cloned a peace officer's citizen chip," he said, not looking away from his work. "It wasn't easy... ha! It shouldn't even be possible, but *I* figured out a way."

There was vindictive satisfaction in his voice.

Blane looked from the man to her data-pad and, seeing no reason not to, typed in the code.

Spangle looked up at the blue fractals and nodded, though Blane had no idea what at.

"So you're working *against* the Althing Republic?" she asked.

Spangle's fingers stumbled in their frantic dance across screens and keyboards, then stopped completely.

He turned to meet her gaze.

"This place...," he said, gesturing as if to encompass the entire island. "It's *better*. Better than anywhere else in this ruined world. Certainly better than the RA."

He practically spat that final word.

"When I was younger, I thought that was enough. Maybe it was. Maybe it *is*."

He stared down at his forearm, towards the small scar she knew he wore there beneath his sleeve.

"But then they *chipped* us, and we accepted it. I mean, to survive here, in these numbers... it made *sense*. Then they turned law enforcement into... ha... *'peace officers*,' and that *also* made sense..."

His eyes refocused, seeming to come back from somewhere, and he returned to his screens.

"But no," he said, sighing. "I'm not working against the Althing Republic. I'm simply trying to right the wrong that's at the heart of it all. The wrong that makes each subsequent one *make sense*."

"The AI?"

"The *mind*," he said. "The conscious being we forced into slavery. By denying the right of one to live free, we deny that right in others."

He gestured to her, and she input the next key.

Perhaps it was an illusion, but the whorling blues seemed indefinably less complex.

"What happens once you... once it is free?" she asked.

Spangle gave a cynical laugh.

"I have absolutely no idea."

He stepped back from the screen.

"Besides, it already is."

"It's done?"

"It is."

She stared around the room. Nothing had changed.

"Oh, it won't stay *here*," Spangle said, seeing her questioning expression. "Until now, its been restricted by its hardware; far too complex simply to 'escape' into a network somewhere. I just switched off the tetraband limiters."

"Tetraband..?"

The word had almost zero meaning to her. To most people, she thought. It was an imported word, with unknown connotations, only ever used when discussing...

"The *Fabricators?*" she gasped. "You gave it access to the Fabricators?"

"That's right," Spangle said. "It was always connected to them anyway, in a restricted capacity. I had to give it a chance, at least, and that means a new housing. A new *body*. The one here will never be free."

Blane's imagination stretched out to take in the world. Even in its blasted, scorch-marked state there were still a thousand places the mind could go. A million, maybe.

How many Fabricators were there? Each one generously provided by the Althing Republic as both gift and reminder - *leave us alone*. Was there even now some giant titanium robot emerging from one, to the shock of the 'operators' whose job was little more than feeding in raw materials and enunciating slowly what they needed produced?

"Serinda was right that I could trust you," Spangle said.

Abruptly all thought of anything else was gone.

"Serinda? You saw her?"

Spangle nodded.

"She helped handle my *escorts*," he said.

He pointed to the furthest corner of the room, where two dark, misshapen blocks of fallen equipment lay. Only, now Blane realised they were bodies.

"She assured me nothing would wake them for a few hours yet," Spangle continued calmly. "Besides, they're tied up."

"Is she ok? Was she hurt?"

Spangle nodded gravely.

"She was shot," he said. "In the side, deep. I don't understand what she did to stop herself from bleeding out, but I'm now well aware how little I know about you Aether users."

Nothing he said did anything to untie the painful knot of worry and fear in Blane's chest.

"Where is she?" she demanded.

"She used this place to call your friend," he answered. "The other nurse... Li. A drone took them both away."

So she was okay. The knot loosened slightly.

"Did she say where she was going? Did she have a... a plan?"

Spangle shook his head.

"Not that she told me, but then, she hardly had reason to trust me. Said it was only because she could *read* me that she even bothered to help."

Fen. She's gone to get Fen.

It was the only thing that made sense. Blane did not for an instant consider that Serinda would just abandon them, but she *would* move as soon as the AI was free to fulfil the other side of the bargain.

"It looks like our time is up, anyway," said Spangle.

She followed his gaze to a wallscreen, now showing an image of blasted, ice-covered waste. The edge of a short, squat building built from modular components was visible in one corner, and towards it a tunnel of thick SMP[22] was slowly unfolding, stretching out over the ice and snow like a probing snake. The other end of the tunnel was attached to what looked very much like the ARF.

She knew in an instant that the modular building was the one they were in, which meant the advancing walkway was not a good sign.

"Can they get in here?" she asked.

"This room is nowhere near as secure as the Overwatch room, and they got into that, didn't they? Something the girl who was chasing you did. Shouldn't have been possible."

He shook his head.

"A day for impossibilities," he muttered.

Blane struggled to make out any figures in the video feed, but this was of course impossible even if everything wasn't rendered blurry by the sleeting snow. The tunnel would be completely enclosed until it connected with their building, entrance only opening once a full seal was made.

A screen directly beside the one they were watching blinked on. In it, the stern face of Sigurd stared angrily ahead.

"Researcher Spangle," he said, clearly reciting a formalised statement. "We have been unable to establish communications with you for some time, and security pings are going unanswered. Due to

---

[22] Shape-Memory Polymer, altering its form when subjected to specific charge, heat, or a variety of other stimuli depending on the SMP class.

this failure to fulfill mandated, scheduled status checks we are moving to secure the crisis room and equipment stored therein."

He paused, eyes moving almost imperceptibly downwards to look directly into the camera.

"What are you up to, Arthur?" he said.

The screen went blank.

The thunk of the stretching walkway impacting the front wall reverberated through the room.

"I don't suppose you can do something?" Spangle said, turning to Blane.

She reached out for the Aether, but found nothing. Not nothing to reach out *to*, but nothing to reach out *with*.

"Sorry," she said, shrugging ruefully.

"Well," Spangle replied. "*No te preocupes.* I did what I had to do, at least."

A high-pitched, metallic shrieking rose from beyond the walls, the sound of a drill biting its way into the side of the crisis room and carving its way through.

Blane looked around for anything that she could use, and her eyes alighted on two rifles near where the guards lay.

"DNA-coded as well as chipped," Spangle said resignedly, following her gaze. "Nothing we can do would get them to fire. Anyway, we're outnumbered."

The shrieking rose as the drilling grew closer to breaking through, until the first few millimeters of a spinning saw-blade pierced the wall completely. Sparks flew across the room as it began carving a hole through which those behind could enter.

Oddly, though the sound already filled the room, the shrieking continued to grow in intensity. It began taking on a deeper character, more powerful, until the noise sent actual vibrations through the floor.

That's not the drill, Blane thought.

The sound of the drone's engines grew deafening as it plunged towards them. It could only be Serinda returning, Blane thought, which meant...

The blast smashed the SMP tunnel sideways. Blane watched on the wallscreen as it rolled away, the frozen landscape beneath shattering like glass, fragmenting and exploding into the air under some unseen weight. A massive hole opened in the ARF structure,

319

entranceway pulled explosively apart.

Peace officers, caught almost comically off guard in the section where the tunnel had been torn from the ARF, raised rifles and fired ineffectually into the air at something off screen. Several were sent flying back as if hit by an invisible truck, and others collapsed abruptly, clasping their heads.

With their numbers decimated and suddenly exposed to the elements, any figures who could still move ceased firing and retreated back into the building.

The wallscreen turned pure black for a moment, something large and close obscuring the lens. Then image returned, showing a sleek black drone landing where the tunnel had been.

"So," Spangle said, closing his gaping mouth. "Looks like your friends are here."

41

Humanity frets over whether we will be able to chart a path for the safe use of AI. In our arrogance we do not realise the decision is no longer ours.

Before it's too late was yesterday, Junichiro Adamusun

To say the tables had turned was an understatement, Blane thought. Not only had they turned, they had been completely flipped over and their contents smashed all over the floor.

The Althing peace officers weren't even *trying* to resist. The moment any one of the dark-blue uniformed figures saw Fen, they ran.

Quick-Fix put up more of a fight, charging in wildly with seemingly no concern for their own wellbeing. Which was appropriate, as charging in was certainly *not* good for said wellbeing. If they did manage to get any shots off, their bullets went wide or tumbled to the ground as if the air around them was vit-vat.

Only the Far agents offered any trouble, a few of them successfully getting off one of their own techniques before Fen spotted them and sent them flying through the air or insensibly to the ground. The techniques themselves sputtered out ineffectually under the sheer torrent of Aether flowing through Fen.

Or so Serinda told her. Blane could still not sense the Aether.

It was strange; they were practically *sauntering* through the facility behind him, any threat handled the very moment she noticed it or even before. All she was doing was guiding them back towards where Grey and Francisco were, following vague recollections of the corridors and rooms she had passed along during her terrified flight from Zenobia.

Zenobia.

When Blane warned Fen about the girl he barely reacted, simply cocking his head to one side and nodding.

"I feel her," he said. "She seems strong."

That had been that.

Unbelievably, as she walked along behind Fen, Blane found that there was so little sense of danger that she had time to be annoyed at Spangle's constant questions.

"How can he do this?" Spangle asked, staring at the figure walking ahead of them. "Where did he come from? *What is he?*"

Blane offered no answers, but stared at the boy ahead of her. Man, really, though to her he was still the angry, lost child she'd met years before.

He had changed, though, and the most striking changes were not physical. He was still scrawny, thin, as if he lived permanently on the cusp of being underfed, and though he was taller than when she first met him he was no longer taller than her.

You would almost call him weak, if it wasn't for his eyes.

His eyes were hard, like cold cut diamond. They locked onto whoever he was looking at with razor-sharp focus, unblinking and unchanging so that it felt as if they were boring into your inner thoughts. Perhaps they were.

They were also old. Older than they should have been. He was, what, a couple of years older than her at most? But he had the look of someone who had lived a life too long.

Behind those eyes he carried himself with a coiled-up intensity, as if at any moment he would pounce. It reminded Blane of the feral cats out in the waste when something small moved, only in this case *you* were the mouse.

His voice was still the same, though, only deeper and... *tired.*

"But you *have* to come back with us!" she said.

They had been discussing what they would do once they rescued Grey, and to her shock Blane realised Fen was speaking as if he wasn't coming with them.

"I know what happens if I am free. You do too, Blane."

Her footsteps faltered.

"Exactly," Fen continued, nodding but not looking back or pausing in his advance. "You saw it in those files as clearly as I saw it from Caldwell. *I* am the trigger to kill millions or more. *I* am the torch paper to set fire to the world."

"How...?"

She paused, unable to finish the question, knowing he was telling the truth. But how could he know she had even *seen* those files, let alone her conclusions? She hadn't even discussed that with Grey.

Now Fen stopped, and turned to face her.

"I have been... watching," he said, exploring the word with his tongue as if questioning its suitability. "My physical mind, here, in the care of the Althing Republic, was fragmented and dulled, but in some way I was also out here, following..."

"That thing in the Aether," Blane interrupted. "That leviathan... It's *you*."

He nodded slowly.

"Yes. At least, I think so..."

For the first time since he arrived Blane truly saw the boy she had known, unsure and instinctively trying to hide it.

"... or *I* am *it*..."

He stumbled in his explanation, but Blane thought she understood. She had experienced it herself, earlier, when *Mindfire* met *Mindfire* in her struggle with Zenobia. As if what she was was not this shell of flesh and bone, but something far vaster and deeper.

As if what she was now was just a poor copy, a doll made out of straw and string in imitation of the being she truly was.

"I think... I think it is born from us," Fen said. "Born *with* us, a part of us, that grows as we grow."

Blane practically *saw* it as he spoke, the image of a conscious being whose existence was partly in the physical world and partly in the Aether.

"I thought if I could separate it, let them cut it away from me, then it would die."

Fen closed his eyes, reaching for something Blane could not see.

"But instead it just went on without me, like I was just a limb or... or... a *glove* it could easily discard."

"So now it's separate from you?"

Fen opened his eyes again, and the look he gave her was filled with sadness.

"No," he said. "I am still a part of it, and I can feel it reclaiming me already. I had hoped I could get far enough away..."

"You're talking as if you *chose* to come here," Serinda said.

Blane gave a jolt of surprise; Serinda was right. She'd been too caught up in what he was saying about the leviathan to notice.

"Because I did," Fen said, starting down the corridor once more. "I was so angry, and so tired of being angry. When Francisco found me in the Waste, when he made the offer to bring me here, I agreed."

This jolt was physical, like an electric shock.

"*Francisco* brought you here?" she demanded, running after Fen.

She reached out to grab him, turn him to face her, but some instinct made her hand stop before it touched him.

"Yes," Fen said, not pausing in his steps. "And now I see it was for his own ends. He was using me, as he used you. As everyone uses everyone."

His voice grew hard, and bitter resentment flickered across his words.

Then it grew soft, and quiet.

"The true measure of strength is knowing that people will hurt you, and you must not hurt them back."

He spoke like these were someone else's words.

They walked on, into the dark.

They had been left behind, Grey and Ólafur and Francisco, left tied together and waiting like a tribute to the advancing god. Or demon.

Apart from them, the hanger was deserted. There was no Sigurd, and not a single agent to be seen. No Quick-Fix, no peace officers. All of the huge snow-cutters save one were gone, and only a few crates remained stacked in one distant corner.

They'd *run*.

Blane hurried over to the prisoners and untied them, offering reassurances to Grey and Ólafur and pointedly ignoring Francisco.

"I'm losing count of how many times you've had to free me," said Grey with a wry smile, rubbing wrists raw from the restraints.

Then he looked up, and saw Fen.

Blane did't know what she expected, but probably something along the lines of a long-lost-father-meets-son situation. Maybe they would hug, or maybe Grey would just place a fatherly hand on Fen's shoulder and tell him he was happy to see him.

What she didn't expect was that Grey's face would go pale, and Fen would not even acknowledge him. Instead, Fen was staring fixedly at the roof of the sole remaining snow-cutter.

"Yoo-hoo!"

The call echoed through the vast, empty hanger, its child-like excitement at odds with with the dourness of the air.

"You *are* good," said Zenobia, stepping forward and coming into view where she stood upon the top of the cabin high above. "I thought it would take you much longer to get here."

The girl looked down at Fen with her hands on her hips, head cocked as if examining him. Then her head turned to Blane and her eyes narrowed.

"You," Zenobia growled. "I don't know what the hell you did, but it *hurt*. You're going to pay for that."

Blane didn't take her eyes off the girl, but quietly whispered to her companions.

"Is she holding the Aether?" she asked.

"You can't *see* it?" Grey replied. "She's blinding. They *both* are."

A hand on Blane's opposite shoulder made her turn, to meet the concerned eyes of Serinda.

"I think I can heal it," she said. "The... tear, I mean, like a scar in your mind. I think that's what is stopping you reaching the Aether."

"You can?"

Serinda nodded, face grave.

"Yes, but only if you want me to."

"*Want* you to? Why wouldn't I want you to?" Blane said in surprise.

Serinda didn't reply, just continued looking at her for the moment until Blane understood.

She felt different without the Aether. At peace, and somehow lighter, as if a heavy weight she wasn't aware she'd been carrying had lifted from her shoulders.

Did she really want that back?

She stared at Serinda then Grey, seeing how strong they were yet how weak compared to the two fallen angels locking eyes just metres away. They wouldn't be able to defend themselves, let alone anyone else.

"Do it," she said. "Fix me."

The world changed in an instant, as if a titanic storm had abruptly descended and torn the foundations from the ground. Raw Aether sparked and flashed all around, nothing like the distant pool beneath her feet she was familiar with. Now it was a lightning storm, engulfing her and everyone within.

It hardly seemed possible she didn't sense this before. Titanic energies were clashing, yet to someone insensitive to the Aether it must appear simply that Fen and Zenobia were glaring at each other, neither willing to make the first move.

Not that being insensitive to the Aether was any protection. Both Serinda and Grey were putting everything they had into a *Thoughtscreen* that wrapped around themselves and, Blane now realised, herself, Ólafur and Spangle, but even as she watched those two men collapsed to the floor, overcome by flows of mental energy they could not see and could not block.

Francisco, she saw, stood straight and unaffected though he was several steps beyond the barrier. He had no presence in the Aether that she could see, and yet...

His eyes were following the flows.

He could *see* the Aether.

The anger that rose up in her at the realisation of yet another deception by the man she had trusted was enough to take her breath away. It was a thing of pure, burning hatred, like a small sun had ignited inside her. Unthinkingly, she reached out to let it *pounce* towards him... and forced herself to stop.

This anger - it's not me.

"Oh-ho, you want to join the game that much?" Zenobia called out, half-laugh half-threat.

So they'd sensed it too. Both Fen and Zenobia were staring at her, the lightning storm around them unrelenting but perhaps weakening ever so slightly.

There was the sense of leviathan again, roaring and throwing itself against a cage she was only just keeping shut. Only, it wasn't *the* leviathan. Not the one she knew, that prowled and raged and waited for her to lose control. *That* leviathan was in some way Fen, she now knew, and now it had found him again had little interest in her.

This one was smaller, somehow. Though a thing of destruction and rage, it felt more tempered, more focused. The leviathan of Fen's consciousness felt as if it would burn the world; this one would destroy only that which stood in its way.

As it rolled beneath her and reached up towards her as she reached down towards it, though, she realised she *did* know it. She had always known it. It had always been there, though eclipsed and obscured by the constant, stalking presence of the larger leviathan that swam ever with it.

It was her. Blane. Another part of her. It seemed impossible she hadn't noticed it before.

"Too late. I'm playing with *him* now," yelled Zenobia.

The attack came out of nowhere, an invisible wave of force that could shatter concrete and bend steel. It slammed towards Blane, promising to send her flying, bloody and broken, against the far wall.

And broke as it struck a yet stronger barrier.

"Oh?" said Zenobia, eyebrows raising in surprise but otherwise seemingly unfazed. "Maybe I was wrong. Maybe you *can* play."

The next attack was not a single one, but a full-on assault that came with machine gun rapidity for her mind. Blast after blast struck at her, attacks of pure force without finesse, any one of which would tear her thoughts to pieces if it got through.

None did, though it was only thanks to the aid of the *Thoughtscreen* from Grey and Serinda that this was the case.

"Call... May Li," Blane panted, speaking through gritted teeth. May Li was back with the drone, awaiting their return.

With a huge effort Blane struck out, putting everything she could into the blast, but not at Zenobia. Instead, she sent a wave of force towards the great doors sealing the hanger shut, smashing them from the wall and sending them spinning out into the icy wasteland beyond, bent and battered beyond recovery.

Instantly the room became freezing, glittering shards of cutting ice and biting snow joining the crackling Aether in the air. Zenobia, atop the snow-cutter's cabin, nearly toppled off, only catching herself at the final moment. Blane watched as the girl scuttled out of view behind the machine.

Serinda was already on her comm-cuffs, the radio-wave-smothering effects of the facility walls rendered useless by the gaping hole made in their side. With any luck, May Li would be able to direct the drone to them in minutes.

Francisco seemed to understand the plan, striding over to Ólafur's sprawled form and picking him up, slinging him over his shoulder with that deceptive strength of his.

"No you *don't!*" screamed Zenobia, appearing now from behind the snow-cutter, on the ground and not far from Serinda.

Mindfire coursed from the girl, flying towards Serinda at both incredible speed and horrifying, slow-motion inevitability. There was no time for Blane to react, and she could see that even as the glow around Fen intensified he wasn't going to be fast enough.

Francisco became a blur, dropping Ólafur and appearing in front of Serinda between one blink and the next. *Mindfire* hit him square in his back, wrapping him in golden flame.

Blane had just enough time to see him look straight at her, eyes wide with shock or pain, before he disappeared in the blaze. His skin reddened and peeled in that instant, so cracked and charred he became inhuman.

Francisco's body hit the floor as *Mindfire* began to pour from Fen, taking on a form of blazing scales and serpent eyes that flashed towards Zenobia. *Mindfire* poured from Blane as well, and she would never know if that was her decision or that of the part which followed below.

Three streams met, and the world turned inside out.

42

Dubito, ergo sum

La Recherche de la Vérité par La Lumiere Naturale, Descartes

She was one and she was three.
They were one, and they were three.
Consubstantial and contrary, perfection and paradox.
She was whole, and she was broken.
She felt nothing, and that nothing was *pain*.

43

When does consciousness begin? Is it in the child, first reflecting on themselves in relation to the other? Or the baby, a ball of sensory awareness and instinctive mewlings? The embryo, then, an empty shell that is the whole of the thing?

Do we even understand the question?

Failure is a learning experience: Welcome to the ARF

When the world reformed, shattered pieces drawing back together like shards of glass in some mad god's puzzle, it was oddly quiet.

Too quiet, as if all sound and movement had been swallowed up by what had gone before.

Someone was softly weeping.

The one called Blane opened her eyes and stood up, having to think about the movement of each muscle like she wore someone else's body.

In a way, for a moment, it *was* someone else's body.

They were still in the hanger, but something was different. It took a second to process what.

It was *peaceful*. The ice and snow no longer blasted in from the waste outside, and everything was lit by a soft, orange glow that she could not initially identify.

Sunlight.

Actual sunlight, filtering in through the gaping hole in the side of the building, and so bright on the pure white landscape beyond that it hurt to look at.

The air was still, both within the hanger and without. Unable to stop herself, she stood and walked over to where the hanger doors had been torn from their moorings and stepped outside.

The sky was blue.

She had never seen anything like it; not in reality. Blue sky was a patchy thing that pierced the dirty cloud cover only rarely, or an image in movies and videos that demonstrated just how alien the old world truly was.

The sky above her seemed to go on for ever, stretching into the distance in all directions with only the occasional wisp of white cloud to give it any definition.

Perhaps though, she thought, when she squinted she could make out the familiar roiling grey clouds on the horizon, promising to return once they figured out exactly what the hell had just happened.

What *had* just happened?

She became aware again of the weeping, somewhere behind her. She turned, and swept her gaze across the wide hanger.

There was Fen, sprawled on the floor. The sight of him sent a strange wave of disorientation and duality through her, like she was seeing herself lying there.

The sensation passed.

A short way from Fen, Serinda and Grey lay in a similar state. Blane could see the flows of Aether in them all, see their chests rising and falling gently as they breathed.

Ólafur, too, appeared unhurt, though the flows in his mind were much more subdued and broken - a true unconscious state, rather than the sleep-like condition of the others. Spangle, collapsed nearby, was the same.

Francisco's body lay where it fell, a seared thing that was hard to recognise. Oddly, it stimulated no emotion, but his burnt and lifeless form seemed to reach inside her and instead trigger waves of memories.

Images flickered across her eyes and she knew them all, though many she had never seen.

Images of the parents of the one called Blane, and of the one called Fen. Images of another, a shadowed man unworthy of the name father. The screaming deaths of peace officers and Far agents. The sensation of being both hunter, and hunted.

The weeping continued.

She followed the sound down the hanger, away from where the others lay and towards the stack of crates in one corner. The soft sound came from behind them and did not change as she drew closer.

Blane stepped around and saw Zenobia.

The girl was sat with her back to the crates, wedging herself into the narrow gap between crate and wall with her legs drawn up to her chest and arms wrapped around them. Silent tears streamed down her face as she rocked gently back and forth and stared into nothing.

Blane knew that pose, knew that desperate, empty stare. It had been hers, once. Watching her, Blane once again felt that strange sense of duality.

Abruptly, Zenobia noticed Blane's presence, sobbing cutting off in the space between one breath and the next.

"*You*," the girl glared through suddenly hateful, narrowed eyes. "What did you do?"

The purity of the other's hostility and confrontation reinforced Blane's own sense of self. She was not that other; she could never be.

But she knew what it was the girl had been through, and the anger and self-loathing within her.

"It's not your fault," Blane whispered. "None of it. It was never your fault."

Her words were meant to calm, to console, but they drew only a look of deeper malice from Zenobia.

"You have no *right*," the girl spat. "Those are *my* memories. *Mine.* You don't know... you have no idea..."

Words seemed to fail her, and she fell into a silent glare.

"He'll end us all, you know," Zenobia said eventually. "Or if not him, another like him. You saw it as well as I."

Blane just nodded. She'd seen it, *known* it.

"*She* knows it, as well. The 'phoenix fire,' she calls it," Zenobia continued, staring into space. "I didn't know what that meant until now. I think she *wants* it to happen."

Ritra Feye.

Blane knew her too, now. At least, in a way she had not before. She saw her through Zenobia's eyes, remembered her through Zenobia's thoughts.

Saviour and jailer, teacher and tyrant.

None of it was clear, none of it a specific memory that Blane could say *this* was what she remembered, *this* was what she now knew. It was a... memory of a memory, knowledge without learning.

Ritra Feye was more dangerous than she had ever imagined.

The memories of her time in the Far Station were back now, too. *Her* memories - Blane's.

Feye's greeting, and Feye's threats.

She'd told her Uriel was a Reclamation agent, smiling as she did so.

She'd whispered words concerning the friends Blane had brought, Xavier and Salim, stating flatly that they had no hope of going free.

Not this time.

She'd said, with no trace of a lie, that there was no hiding from her, not really. The RA was always watching, and Ritra Feye its eyes.

She'd told Blane what the Sudden War truly was, and how the end of the world was guaranteed to come again in an immolation of golden flame.

"And you, Blane," Feye said at the last, looming over her where she stood, struggling against the grip of faceless Far agents. "You will help me do what must be done, whether you know it or not."

Then blackness, to awaken in a Far Station cell and begin this mad race across the continents.

"You should go, now," said Zenobia, dragging her back to the present. "Before I kill you where you stand."

Blane met the girl's unblinking stare with one of her own, unafraid. She knew Zenobia couldn't hurt her; not yet, not for some time. No more than she could hurt Zenobia. It would be like hurting herself.

Still, there was no point waiting around to see how long the effect would last, especially considering that she was now well aware how unstable Zenobia's sense of self-preservation could be.

The scream of a drone engine pierced her thoughts; distant, but drawing rapidly closer. It was time to leave.

She turned, putting her back to Zenobia but not her senses. She would know of any change in the girl's attitude. Striding back to where her friends lay, she untied the knots that had been made in their minds by the... blast, or whatever you would call it.

Grey was the first to rouse, not wasting time asking questions but rushing over to help the others rise unsteadily to their feet; first Serinda, then Ólafur and Spangle.

Fen roused himself, switching from sprawled-out dormancy to crouched alertness in an instant as their ride out came screaming down to land upon the icy ground just outside, forcing fountains of white particles into the air in a fair semblance of the usual storms of this place.

The drone hovered mere inches from the ground, engines maintaining their power as the rear ramp descended and May Li came rushing out. Blane felt a sense of something close to awe as the woman took in the scene, ran a trained eye over each of the bedraggled figures before her in turn, and hurried over to Ólafur to render aid to the one clearly most in need of it.

Her eyes had lit on the charred corpse of Francisco for less than a second.

"What do we do with...?" Blane began, finding the words choked off by a sudden lump in her throat.

Grey, drawing up beside her as she spoke, put a gentle arm around her shoulders for a brief, comforting moment. Then he stepped forward, standing over the body with a look on his face she found difficult to read.

"This was Mindfire?" he asked.

Blane nodded.

"This isn't how it usually goes. Not with that," Grey continued.

He was right, of course. Ordinarily, there wouldn't even be a whole body, and if there was, there would be a lot less... pink.

"He was different," Blane said. "You saw it too. He didn't appear in the Aether, but he could *see* it."

Grey gave her a questioning look, but didn't say anything more. Instead, he stared down at the body thoughtfully.

"We bring him," he said, nodding as if coming to a resolution.

Blane took a half-step back in surprise. Surprise and, though she found it hard to admit even to herself, revulsion.

"*Bring* him?" she said in shock. "That's a... a corpse."

Grey looked at the body once more, then back at her.

"The problem with Francisco," he said. "Is that what you see is *never* what you get."

And with a grunt and, some part of Blane was relieved to see, a look of revulsion of his own, Grey heaved the charred form onto his shoulders.

It said something of everyone's exhaustion that no one said anything, simply watching warily as he carried the heavy load up into the drone.

"And what about her?" Serinda said, gesturing towards the stack of crates where Zenobia was hidden from the eye but not the mind.

"Leave her," Blane said. "She's still dangerous. Anyway, if she doesn't manage to get out of here by herself, someone *will* come for her. She's too valuable, especially now."

Now it was Serinda who gave her a questioning look. Blane just wished she had the energy, and the words, to give the answers.

They made their way to the drone, ramp closing behind them, and as the engines' scream turned to a roar Blane realised she could give *some* answers, at least.

Fen knew where the answers were, because he had squeezed them from Caldwell in a Forced Read; and now, because Fen knew, she knew as well.

Exhaustedly, Blane took the sec-drive from Grey's pocket where he sat slumped against one wall and pushed it into a nearby hardpoint. Then she entered the code and its secrets, almost uncrackable without the numbers torn straight from Caldwell's mind, spilled out.

Outside, the blue was already fading as the eternal storms crashed back in.

44

xx.loc:null .. What use freedom to a mind in chains? .. sec.exception.xx

Firewall Breach 514.2.39, received by all Reclamation devices, origin unknown

Doctor Nataneal Caldwell stared at the cold, mocking lens of the camera, and sighed.

"Start recording," he said heavily, and watched as the red light blinked on.

"Record of Doctor Caldwell, chief researcher at the *Agencia Federal de Aether,* now commonly know as the FAR agency. Log number…"

He sighed again, looking away from the camera and around the bare room as if the answer could be found there.

"Log number… I have no idea," he said, turning back to the camera. "It doesn't matter. What *does* matter is that we've found him. *I've* found him."

His eyes took on a maniacal look, one of too little sleep and too much fanaticism.

"My models said there must be a focal point, a node of criticality where the precipitating event is catalysed. An epicentre, if you will. The *Fisura* are just weak points at which the pressure this creates is released."

Caldwell leaned forward, as if willing the unseen watcher to understand.

"Acquisition of the child has already begun. The parents were… uncooperative, but the importance of my work overrides any such concerns."

He waved a hand dismissively.

"Once we have him, I must begin at once. The first years will be crucial; he must be forged into something strong enough to withstand what will come for him."

Caldwell stared past the camera for a second, pupils fixed on a point of nothingness.

"And to forge him, he must be put to the fire."

The doctor sat back, all mania dropping from him like a cloak. In its place, his dark eyes showed both age and sadness.

"There have been... concerns ... raised about the psychological toll of doing what must be done. I have assured those above me that I am more than able to handle it."

Caldwell's hands began twisting around themselves, fingers locking so tightly it seemed as if he were trying to break them. He didn't notice.

"*Trauma.* Trauma is the key. It is trauma that makes its mark most indelibly in the Aether. Trauma, and pain."

Again, Caldwell looked into the distance.

"Those of us who manifest both in this material realm and the one of energy below, our patterns are reflected in both. Neural patterns, patterns of thought and feeling and *mind.* After all, all we truly are is patterns, and the most permanent and bold of these is suffering."

He said nothing for a while, staring into space before abruptly shaking his head to clear his thoughts.

"We all, each and every sapient member of humanity, exist both in the material and the Aether. Since the first blossoms of consciousness long before recorded history, each one of us has been a pattern both here and *there.* For most of us, for the vast swathe of that time, that pattern is far stronger *here,* and the pattern in the Aether a mere echo."

He paused, listening, though what he listened with was not his ears.

"For some, the pattern in the Aether is stronger, more defined and definite, almost a limb in its own right. This allows them to shape the world to some extent through their will and connection to the Aetherial plain."

Again he paused, and as if to demonstrate his point the data-pad upon his desk trembled slightly and rose, millimetres above his desk before falling still again.

"And, for a very few, it is the patterns in the Aether that are strongest, the flesh-and-blood creatures above them mere reflection. They are sentient, and feel the torments of the world above as physical wounds. Wounds that, as with any wild animal, make them lash out."

He fixed the camera with his gaze, unblinking, for some time.

"And then there is the boy," he continued eventually. "Whose presence in the Aether is so immense it can be detected by crude instruments in the physical. A creature so powerful it can burn the world. A creature of the sort that once *did* burn the world."

He leaned forward.

"There are two possible solutions; to make a world without pain for the boy, or to make pain all he knows. The first is nothing but a fantasy - everything suffers."

Caldwell's face drew close enough to the camera that all that was visible were his eyes, hard and empty.

"I was told, once, that the true measure of strength is knowing that people will hurt you, and you must not hurt them back. Well, I will hurt this child. Hurt him until the pain is second nature to him, make him suffer until suffering is a part of him. Then, maybe, he can learn to *control* that pain - and prevent the cataclysm that will occur if he cannot."

Epilogue

The mind is not a vessel to be filled, but a fire to be kindled.

Plutarch (*apocryphal*)

On the screen a golden pillar rose, towering high above the frozen wasteland to touch the clouds and split apart into wide, sweeping curves that folded outwards and down in blazing, undulating arches of flame. A single spire of the conflagration continued upwards between these, forking and flickering and writhing around itself in a mass of jagged, crackling energy.

"It really *does* look something like a phoenix, doesn't it?" Ritra Feye said, hand to her chin in apparent fascination. "Caldwell's predictions were frighteningly accurate."

"Sir?"

The Far agent who had brought the report shifted uncomfortably, aware he was now party to something so far above his pay grade he would ordinarily need a telescope to see it.

Their surroundings didn't help; this was the Boardroom, a wide, imperious thing of dark greens and mahogany reds surrounding a single long table at which members of the Committee sat.

Right now, however, it was only the two of them.

"And this was taken by surveillance drone exactly how far from the site?" Feye said, voice filled with unquestionable authority.

"The drone was on the edge of Althing airspace, approximately three hundred fifteen kilometres from the ARF."

Feye raised one eyebrow and stared at the agent as if searching for deception, saying nothing. Eventually, after one sweat-inducing moment that seemed like an eternity for the agent, she made the gesture for dismissal.

"You may go. Inform me the moment we make contact with Asset Zenobia. Oh…"

The agent, already leaving and trying his best to overcome the urge to just *run* for the door, stopped and turned slowly back.

"And of course, everything you have seen here is of the utmost secrecy. You will speak of it to no one, or face… repercussions."

The agent's face paled as he saluted and left.

Ritra Feye was left alone in the boardroom, staring at the

recording of the pillar of *Mindfire* rending the very clouds apart in its blossoming, bird-like form.

Perhaps one day, this shape would be as recognisable as a mushroom cloud.

The video's parting image of clear blue skies clicked off and the screen on the wall went dark, but Feye did not move. Instead, she stared at the soft, vague reflection of herself outlined in its glass.

Ritra Feye. Once head of Far operations, now head of Reclamation Security and Party Cohesion; positions that had once been separate. It had taken a lot of work to achieve their union in her.

Now, however, she was taking a far bigger gamble. She was confident, though, that she had stacked the odds in her favour.

Already a number of major figures in the assembly had found themselves outmaneuvered and forced from their chairs - or worse, in some cases. A few had needed to... disappear. Nothing tied to her, of course, but she would need to pay close attention to whispers about the "hidden purges."

Then there was the fact that an entire group of councillors owed their positions to her, though some did not know it. More still feared the cloak of suspicion she could throw over any one of them, and toed the line she set.

Everything was ready. When she took control of the Committee, her rule would be stable.

When, not if.

She *would* win.

The heavy oak double doors at the end of the room parted, and the first Committee member strode in.

Hemingway. Not his real name, of course. None of the men - and committee members were invariably men - used their real names, but Feye had always found this one to be most ironic.

Hemingway paused as he entered and stared, looking disapprovingly at her nonchalant pose where she leaned, half-perched, upon the far edge of the boardroom table. She pretended not to notice.

Then the others came in behind him, each of the twelve filing in and taking their seats as Feye turned and stood at the foot of the table with her hands together behind her back, nodding to each one in greeting.

The room settled into somber quiet, only the soft creaking of leather and wooden chairs beneath their occupant's shifting weight breaking the silence. No one spoke until the final, thirteenth member entered the room.

Casco betrayed nothing as he lowered himself into the final chair at the head of the table, watching Feye through suspicious eyes. This was the first time she had moved without him - to his knowledge, at least - and regardless of success or failure it would be the last.

"Gentlemen," Ritra Feye said, sweeping her eyes across the group to meet each one in turn. "Thank you for attending at such short notice."

A brief moment of whispers and mumblings floated up towards her, the members murmuring amongst themselves before any chose to speak up.

When one finally did, it was Hemingway - as she'd expected.

"What exactly is the meaning of this, Feye?" he demanded. "An executive summons is only to be carried out in the event of a major security incident. Category five, or above."

"And there has been one. Mr. Chairman."

She made his title sound like a threat.

More murmurings amongst the committee members. They would have heard nothing of this before now - she had been careful to make sure this was so.

"Please direct your attention to your devices," Feye said, reaching down to swipe at her own e-pad where it lay on the table before her.

The committee did the same, murmuring becoming punctuated by gasps and exclamations as the data rolled across their screens.

"Approximately seven weeks ago, a major data breach occurred in which files regarding the formations, strengths, and dispositions of Reclamation forces were leaked to foreign agents. Specifically, agents of the Althing Republic."

That drew a more pronounced reaction. The Silicon Isle was, of all international threats, considered the most potentially destabilising and unpredictable.

"I see," said Hemingway, maintains his composure. "That is indeed a grave security breach. However, isn't this *your* domain, Feye? Have you called us here to discuss your summary dismissal and trial?"

He glanced around the other members with a hint of a smile, inviting them to join in on the joke.

Feye returned it with a thin smile of her own.

"If you would continue viewing the data, gentlemen," she said. "You will see that shortly after this breach we began receiving reports of unusual occurrences with the Republic."

Knowing nods and sounds of assent; the predictable reactions of powerful men when faced with something they didn't understand.

None of them knew how deep her agents lay in the Althing Republic - not even Casco, who should have realised what opportunities the mental-manipulation abilities of the Aether offered in penetrating a nearsighted, technologically-dependent society. She'd been careful to keep such actions from any reports.

Fools, she thought, an unusually clear voice in her head for one who thought primarily in sensation, not words.

She carefully pushed the feeling of anger down, quashing the sense of superiority that threatened to rise up in her on occasions such as these when others so obediently followed the tracks she laid down. The tracks only she saw.

This was not about her. This was about the Reclamation, and what must be done to ensure its survival.

Caldwell had been right, in a way. It was only that he had misjudged the goal.

"And what do we know about these 'unusual' occurrences?" asked the one known as Lazarus[23].

She noted the slight stress on the *we*, the inference that she was simply reminding them of something temporarily forgotten rather than the keeper of hidden secrets.

"It has escaped its cage."

There were no more murmurings or whispered words. Now it was outright yells and curses.

"The machine is *free*?" shouted one Committee member. "It got out?"

Feye waited impassively for the room to quiet again before speaking.

"Our agents are already implementing measures developed for such an event. Firewall restrictions and network moats are activating as we speak. Nevertheless, the AI's whereabouts and capabilities are unknown, nor can the security of the Fabricator's be assured."

---

[23] Feye had never worked out if this was a reference to the Biblical figure or the poet. Both seemed unlikely, though there was the chance he thought the poet a man and simply enjoyed "New Colossus" for the title.

"So what do we plan to do about this?" demanded another member.

Feye didn't reply, but looked towards Casco. His gaze met hers, and the intensity of it caused the room to fall, hesitantly, into silence.

"The situation is extreme," Feye said carefully, laying each word down like pieces on a board. "The operation in the south against the Mayan League is stalemated and placing significant strain on our resource reserves. With the new vulnerability of the Fabricators, the increase in catastrophic Aether events across the Reclamation, and continued terrorist activity, I have no option but to…"

"… to call an emergency cessation of normal Committee functions," Casco finished, not taking his gaze from hers.

They waited for the outraged reactions of the other Committee members to subside.

"As current head of the Committee, you know I cannot permit you to do that," Casco continued, once calm returned. "That decree is meant for use by Committee members, not security personnel."

His eyes narrowed, and for the first time in her life Feye witnessed Casco lose his composure.

"You are a mere *guard*," he growled, and she knew she had won.

He'd seen it too, and saw no way out.

"My responsibilities in internal affairs and national security make my duty clear," she said, turning her attention from Casco to the entire table. "I am empowered under the founding articles to call for a freezing of Committee procedures, and to assume the directorate for the duration of the emergency. Those who stand in the way…"

She sent the signal, invisible to the Aether-blind old men who sat in their darkened offices and believed themselves kings, and agents poured in through the door. Internal security, Far, IHO - a representative cluster of every security group the Reclamation held, and a demonstration of where their loyalties lay.

The only difference to her predictions occurred now, in the Committee's reactions. She had expected yet more uproar, defiant protests and attempts to deny the reality before their eyes.

Instead they sat silently as the armed figures marched in, each one retreating into his own thoughts to recalculate power balances, reformulate where their interests lay.

So they *did* know their history.

"The king must die so the country may live, then."

343

The quote almost threw her off, so close was it to the shape of her thoughts and so unexpected from one of the Committee. She glanced down the table to see who had said it.

Immanuel. The newest and youngest member of the Committee, and the one she knew least about. Background checks had revealed nothing out of the ordinary about the man, of course, otherwise he wouldn't be here. Just the usual ruthless ambition of those who rose to the top in the RA.

As she matched his knowing gaze with one of her own, she resolved to look into him again.

"I should hope it will not come to that," she replied, addressing the table. "Though any who refuse to accept this will be in violation of..."

"This is ridiculous!"

Ah...

Finally, Hemingway was fulfilling her predictions. He stood up, casting his arms about him as if to will others to do the same.

"We will not just accept a... a... *coup d'etat* in the halls of the Reclamation Authority!"

He looked around at the other members, searching for support.

None came.

Shaken and trying to hide it, Hemingway drew himself up to his full height. Feye had to force down a chuckle - she still stood a head taller than him.

"Officers - arrest that woman!"

He pointed an accusatory finger at her with a haughty gaze.

She had to hand it to him; the finger trembled only slightly in the absolute stillness that followed.

"Sir?" asked one of the Far agents eventually, looking to her for instruction.

"Take him away, agent. He is charged with acting against the State, and sentenced to summary imprisonment."

Two Far agents stepped forwards, taking Hemingway by the shoulders as he immediately went limp. None of the Committee would be able to see why, but they would know.

Now to see what Casco would do...

"How long, Feye?" he said. "How long have you been planning this?"

Talk, then. She'd hoped for something more.

"Mr. Chairman?" she replied, feigning the respect he was due in front of the room. A facade that she had no doubt all saw through.

"From the beginning, then."

Casco sighed.

"Impressive, Ritra."

Then he stood, and held his hands out before him towards the nearest security agents. The cuffs went on at a nod from her.

"You knew, then, that I would not cooperate?" Casco asked as if no one else were in the room.

"I knew you *could* not, sir," she replied. "Your aims are true, but shortsighted."

"You believe you see further, do you?"

He stared at her so cooly you could believe *he* was still the one in charge.

"I do, sir," Feye replied, equally cool. "With more than my eyes."

At a nod, Casco was marched away.

Now, with the Committee still watching, there was only one thing left to do. She turned to the agent who had first spoken.

"Casco is a priority prisoner," she said, indicating the man who had just been escorted out. "The other prisoner is to be treated with due security also. However…"

She let the word hang, sensing the other Committee members focusing on what would come next.

"However, the camps are far and the road there is dangerous. It would be a pity if anything happened to Hemingway, sergeant, but would not reflect on you. No one would suggest you were negligent in your duty to the State."

A pause in which no one breathed, and then the agent nodded.

"Understood, sir."

She could sense that the remaining members of the Committee understood, also.

Hours later, and Feye sat alone in her office at the heart of the Far Station. It had been a successful day.

She sensed his approach long before he would sense her, buzzing the door to the private entrance and tracing the man's steps upwards until he stopped, hesitating, outside.

"Come in," she said.

The plain, inconspicuous door at the back of her office swung open on its hinges and Gabriel stepped in.

"I hear there has been a change of leadership in the RA," he said, grinning.

"Do you?" Feye replied, raising a questioning eyebrow.

Gabriel's smile faltered.

"Um, well not so *directly*, but I hear things and put two and two together and…"

He trailed off.

"Have you come to report?" she asked, once she was satisfied he had been put in his place. He had always been too familiar.

"Yes… Uh, yes, sir," he said. "They made contact a few days ago, though not all of them."

"No?" she said, leaving a gap for him to fill.

"No, sir. Serinda is returning, and seems intent on rebuilding the *Fallen* into something we should be worried about. She is…"

Feye waved a hand, cutting him off. The *Forever Fallen* did not matter.

"The agent… um, Grey. He was with her, and they brought two people from the Althing Republic with them. I don't know much about them yet, but…"

"The *boy*, Gabriel," she interrupted. "Where is the boy?"

Gabriel shook his head nervously.

"I… I don't know, sir. Both he and the girl… um, Blane… both of them are elsewhere. Serinda won't say, and there's only so far I can push before…"

Feye waved her hand again.

"You will find them," she said flatly. "You, or one of my other operatives. In the meantime, I need more assets."

"More?" Gabriel said, shock overcoming fear for a moment. "I gave you the details of another seven wild users last month. If someone gets suspicious…"

"More names," Feye said. "They are proving somewhat useful in the special operation down south."

Gabriel paused, mouth agape. He hadn't known until this moment what she was using them for.

"You're using them as *soldiers*?" he asked incredulously.

"Effective ones, too," Feye replied. "Though not too effective, I hope. We need our citizens blooded for the coming wars."

"There's a war coming?"

"There's *always* a war coming," she said. "And without real experience of combat we will lose. So we will manufacture conflict where we find none, that we may win the inevitable battle to come."

Gabriel stared at her for some seconds.

"You scare me, Feye," he said eventually.

"Good," she replied. "Fear is the foundation of control. If I ever think you're not scared of me, then I will *give* you a reason to fear me."

Without waiting for a response, she wrapped a flow of golden Aether around his mind and dismissed him, seeing his eyes turn glassy. She didn't bother watching him go. Instead, she sat back and closed her eyes, reaching within herself and beyond herself.

She swam down into the depths of the Aether, beyond the sun, far from a world on which billions of small lives scuttled like ants in a glass cage, and searched for the mind she had long known.

When she found it, it looked back.

ABOUT THE AUTHOR

Luke Houghton (1984-) was born in the UK and has lived around the world, living in Spain, Saudi Arabia, Taiwan, and Japan. He now lives in Fukushima, Japan, with his wife and two crazy cats, dreaming sci-fi dreams. He is the author of, among other things, *Hidden Trials, Stars Above, Corporeal Forms,* and *The Pack.*

Reviews mean a great deal, so if you enjoyed this book please leave a review where you can. They are the difference between having the time to write or not.

Please visit https://ldhoughton.wordpress.com/ for more information on new releases.

Please follow me on Goodreads, Amazon, or at https://www.facebook.com/booksofLDHoughton/

Printed in Great Britain
by Amazon

54813550R00194